MAKING ENEMIES

MAKING ENEMIES

Francis Bennett

VICTOR GOLLANCZ

LONDON

First published in Great Britain 1998
by Victor Gollancz
An imprint of the Cassell Group
Wellington House, 125 Strand, London WC2R 0BB

© Francis Bennett 1998

The right of Francis Bennett to be identified as author of
this work has been asserted by him in accordance with
the Copyright, Designs and Patents Act, 1988.

A catalogue record for this book is
available from the British Library.

ISBN 0 575 06552 4

Typeset by Rowland Phototypesetting Ltd,
Bury St Edmunds, Suffolk
Printed in Great Britain by
St Edmundsbury Press Ltd, Bury St Edmunds, Suffolk

98 99   5 4 3 2 1

For Tessa

18 February 1947

The first impression is of a strange percussion, of instruments playing different rhythms interrupted by a discordance of human voices. And then the music is all too quickly recognizable: the steel ring of boots clattering on stone stairs, rifle butts hammering on locked doors, shouted orders, cries. Old people, their coats over their nightclothes, are forced out of their apartments at gunpoint, bewildered, sleep-ridden, terrified but strangely obedient as the soldiers drive them down the stairs and out into the night.

Some of the women are crying, clutching at their husbands. One white-haired woman drops her false teeth and screams at a young soldier who is behind her on the stairs. She is brutally beaten, with a rifle butt to the groin. She lies crumpled against the wall, groaning. Two soldiers pick her up and carry her into the hall of the apartment building.

Four lorries wait around the corner, their engines running. The old people, shivering, their light clothing no defence against the extreme cold of the winter night, are lifted into the backs of the lorries. A canvas flap is lowered to conceal the human cargo, the tailgate is bolted into place and the lorries drive away.

The soldiers regroup. One of them, a young man, leans against the wall of the building and vomits before he takes his place. The men are led away. As they go, a sergeant turns to one of his corporals.

'Like Jews,' he says. 'They went like Jews.'

★

The apartment block is deserted. The wind whistles in the stairwell. Lights burn in windows; the building looks like a ship steaming through the night. The noise of percussion has passed, leaving silence.

Suddenly there is an enormous explosion. A sheet of flame bursts out and sweeps up the side of the building. Glass shatters and rains down in a lethal storm, doors are blown in, the earth shakes and moves. Black smoke and dust rise upon the echoes of the blast.

Fire streaks hungrily along the paint on doors and window frames; curtains and fabrics catch alight. The wind blows through broken windows, the doorways of empty apartments, down the stairwell and out into the hall. The flames quickly become an inferno. The building blackens.

★

Despite the night cold there is a feeling of dampness in the air, moisture exuded by the dark overhanging branches of fir trees. In a small clearing in the forest, prisoners dig a long trench, their exertions illuminated by the headlights of lorries manoeuvred into position. The earth has frozen hard in the winter cold; they have to break the surface with mechanical drills and pickaxes before they can clear the lumps of earth with shovels. It is slow, terrible work, exhausting their already weakened bodies.

Their guards drive them on, urging more work, faster, striking at those who show any sign of weakness. The pit must be dug quickly and properly. There are measurements for its width, its length, its depth. All are checked at regular intervals. There is also a deadline for completion.

Shortly after three o'clock it is finished. The prisoners are taken back to the lorry which brought them here, to the middle of nowhere. They are driven away and the pit is left, a gaping hole beneath the swaying trees, waiting to be filled.

The old people arrive soon after. They are lifted off the lorries by the soldiers who are waiting for them and told to line up. Cowed and shivering, their bodies racked with fear, they cling desperately to one another. As a last gesture of cruelty, the men are separated from the women. This is the unmistakable sign of their fate. A wail begins, a scream like the howling wind, echoing among the trees and deep into the night.

The cry goes unheard. The trees bend away from them as if repelled by their entreaty. The forest and the fields are barren of any living thing.

A car is driven fast across the field, its headlights describing its bumpy journey. It disappears behind the plumes of smoke from the exhausts of the lorries, and then pulls to a halt beside them. The door opens and an officer from Military Intelligence runs across the field. He is waving something in his hand, a handkerchief or a scarf. He distracts the commander of the soldiers who turns towards him. The two men engage in animated conversation for a minute or two. The intelligence officer takes hold of the commander's arm, but he shakes the man off and pushes him away. The two men shout at each other, their words lost in the dull roar of the diesel engines. For a moment fists are raised. The commander draws a gun. Then the intelligence officer turns away and walks slowly back to his car.

The old people are pushed at gunpoint to the edge of the pit where they stand, outlined against the lights of the lorries, staring down into the blackness below. On the command, the soldiers raise their rifles. At a signal from the officer in charge, they fire. The old people fall into the cold pit. The smell of cordite lies briefly on the night air. The crying has ceased. The only sound is the wind in the trees.

The soldiers exchange their rifles for spades and the earth is shovelled back. Dead branches are drawn over the grave. It is not a token of last respect to the victims. It is a gesture of concealment, meaningless because there is no one who will search the forest for this grave except the few wild boar that remain.

The colonel from Military Intelligence has turned away from the execution, but he has heard everything, the screams of those about to die and the reports of the rifles. Now all he hears is the silence of the night. His face is young and unlined; his eyes, visible briefly by the light of his torch, are pale. He stops by his car and takes off his rimless tinted glasses. He wipes his eye with a handkerchief.

'You could say,' the captain of the execution squad remarks to the intelligence officer, 'they have died for their country.'

His words are the only memorial to the lives that have been lost, and they are soon forgotten in the cold night air.

PART ONE

1

RUTH

'Begin again,' he says.

'What time is it?' she asks.

'Almost midnight.'

'Midnight already?'

'There's plenty of time.'

How long since they'd arrived? One hour? Two? It seems like a few minutes and so far she has achieved nothing. Broken sentences. Broken thoughts. This is not how she imagined it would be. She wants to cry with frustration and anger.

'Come outside. You'll feel better.'

The sun, yellow-orange behind a veil of night mist, has dropped to its lowest point above the horizon. There it hangs, until in an hour or so it will start to rise again, bringing the new day with it.

'Breathe deeply.'

One short night with no cover of darkness. That is all she has. A few precious hours. And what is she doing? She is wasting them in silence.

'No one knows where we are,' he says. There is no insistence in his voice, only encouragement. 'We can stay here as long as we choose. Tell me as much as you want to.'

She has never talked to anyone about these events, not her son, certainly not her mother, not even Miskin. For so long she has concealed her true self in a secret hiding place where her memories are buried so deeply that any coherent explanation is a struggle.

Now, slowly, the calm of this isolated place works on her as he has known it would. Her mind relaxes, the tensions that made expression so difficult begin to ease, her confusion settles into some kind of logical purpose. She must tell him the truth, as much of it as she knows, and she must do so now. Her life depends upon it.

So she begins again.

★

'I knew something was wrong the moment I turned into Glinka Street. You can see the apartment window from the corner where I cross the road on my way back from the Institute. In the winter, the light is always on as I come home, shining behind green curtains. It reassures me in a way my mother knows nothing about. It is a sign that she has survived another day.'

('When did all this happen?' he asks.

'December last year,' she says. 'Six months ago.')

'That night the window was dark. No light, and the curtains not pulled. I knew she wouldn't sit there like that, nor could she leave the flat on her own. I was very frightened. I remember thinking, Is it my turn now? Are they there in the dark, waiting for me? What has happened to my mother? My son? Tears came into my eyes, not for myself but for them, for their lives without my protection. But I never once asked myself if my mother was dead.

'My fear gave way to a sense of violation that someone should dare to force their way into my home. It was strong enough to make me enter the building, but it didn't last. I am not a brave woman.

'The babushka didn't look at me as I walked to the elevator. She may never have smiled at me in the past, but at least she had registered my presence with a glance. Now her eyes avoided me; it was as if I was not there. That was a signal too, like the unlit window.'

(I am learning to speak again, she tells herself. I am using words I have not dared to use for years. The experience is exhilarating. She wonders what impression she is giving. She knows she is not presenting herself as she wants to, but by now it is too late, there is nothing she can do about it.)

'How many times had I worked out exactly what I would do in such a circumstance? Get out of the elevator one floor up and wait. Listen. Creep down the stairs. Look for signs of forced entry, splintered wood on the door frame, scratched metal on the lock. Push the front door. Does it yield? If so, then run. Run as fast and as far as you can.

'But rehearsal is no preparation for reality. I leaned against the wall at the top of the stairs, dizzy with apprehension. I forgot all the

14

rules I had so carefully set myself. It took me some moments to pull myself together. Then I opened my bag, found my keys and crept downstairs. There was no one in the corridor, though it was hard to be sure, it's always dimly lit. I gave the door to our flat a light push and it moved under the pressure of my hand.

'I knew they were there before I saw them. The bitter smell of Russian cheroots always makes my eyes burn. There were two of them, both dressed in overcoats and still wearing their hats.

'I asked where my mother was. They didn't answer. I remember repeating: "What have you done with her? Why have you come?" But they said nothing because all they had were their orders. Explanations are a rare commodity in our society.

'They stood up and said: "You will come with us." Nothing more. No explanation of whose orders they were following, nor where we were going, just a simple instruction. I complied as they knew I would. I followed them obediently out of the apartment and down the stairs.

'Why did I assist in my own arrest?' she says defensively. 'Why didn't I make them drag me out into the street, screaming and shouting?'

The aggression in her voice challenges him to answer. He says nothing. He is smoking and listening to her intently. He will not interrupt her now she has started.

'Resistance demands will. We are a people crushed by the system we helped to create. The currency of our lives is fear, we are afraid of each other, we are afraid of the air we breathe. To find the strength to resist demands a courage that few possess. We submit because we have lost our will. That night I let them lead me away because, with those two men beside me, I, Ruth Marchenko, had become invisible. That was when I began to feel afraid. When you become invisible, you no longer exist.'

I remember thinking as I was bundled into the back of a black Zil: Why had they removed my mother? What possible use could they have for a crippled woman of eighty? As we drove through the city, I was not aware of crying but I remember my cheeks felt wet. But slowly my anger and resentment gave me strength. I had always wondered how I would cope when it happened to me. Now I was learning first-hand.

They drove me to the Lubyanka, where else? The building seemed to stink of fear and corruption, the stench of evil. A smell, no more than that, but nowhere I went in that endless other world was I free of it.

I was taken to a room and told to wait. A man in uniform came in. He sat down at a desk, opened a file (*my* file, how could *my* file be as thick as that?) and began to question me, writing my answers on a form in front of him.

Was I Ruth Marya Marchenko?

When was I born?

Where?

My father's name.

My mother's name.

Where were they born?

'Why are you asking me this? You brought me here. You must know who I am. Where is my mother? What have you done with her? She is an old woman. Where have you taken her?'

'Your mother is safe.' The lenses of his rimless glasses caught the light from his desk lamp as he looked up at me.

'I want to see her.'

'That will be arranged in due course.'

'I want to see her now.'

'There are formalities to be completed first.'

'Why did you take her from our flat?'

He refused to answer the question, so I repeated it again and again, louder each time. Finally, he said: 'I have asked you here to see your husband, Ivan Mihailovitch Marchenko.'

Ivan? He wants me to see Ivan?

'We have been divorced for over ten years.'

'He has asked to see you.'

I had not seen him nor thought of him for years. I had tried to remove all traces of his presence from my life. Why now should this stranger have the right to bring him back into my life?

'I must inform you that Ivan Marchenko has been found guilty of embezzlement against the state.'

'Is he here? In this place?'

'Yes.'

'Is this a place of execution?'

'No.' I knew he was lying. The smell of death permeated the air. That was the poison I was breathing.

'But he will be executed?'

'Yes.'

'When?'

'Soon.'

'How soon?'

'Two days.'

You can never prepare for death. However one may accept it intellectually, its reality is always unexpected, so much more shocking than one imagines. The man whose life I had shared for a time was about to die. Whatever I may have felt, I had never wished him dead.

'I don't want to see him.'

'He has asked to see you. In the circumstances, it is difficult to refuse such a request.'

To my horror I found that I was crying again; tears were pouring down my cheeks, tears for the waste of another human life. My interrogator waited until I had recovered some composure.

I followed him down into a basement, left and right, through steel gates and long passages. I was in a dream, floating among lights and sounds and shapes and smells that made no sense to me. Then a door was unlocked and I was in the arms of a man I had not seen for years. His body was shaking but his cheeks were dry. There were no tears in his eyes. By now he was empty of tears.

'Save me, Ruth,' he was saying. 'You must save me. I cannot die now. I have years to live. You must do something.'

Had this thin, shrivelled creature once been my husband? He was not the man I remembered, he was bent and old and deathly pale. He had withdrawn from the world into the prison of his own mind, and there his life had ended when he gave up hope.

We talked. Not of the past, nor of anything important. What can you say when there is no future to talk about, nothing to hope for? How much of our lives is about our unquestioned belief in tomorrow and the day after! Once he mentioned our son. It was the only time he smiled.

'What will you tell him?' he asked. My son never asked about his father but I could not say that to him.

I tried to smile and said: 'He will never know the truth, or certainly not from me.'

'Thank you.' He touched my hand in gratitude. I remember, it was like ice being laid across me.

What did I feel then? Not love rekindled, nor pity but hopelessness. Emptiness. Powerlessness. Dread and disbelief that this small, crumpled man, his drawn face lined with fear, would in a few hours be led out to his death, that the nerves and muscles in his body, the life-giving patterns of the particles that made him whole and distinct, at someone's command would suddenly and brutally be shattered and then as quickly would begin the reverse process of disintegration and decomposition. In those microseconds between the entry of the bullet into the brain and the destruction of the nervous system, can the mind register what is happening? Do you know that you are being killed? I prayed that in that awful moment of obliteration he would have no awareness and feel no pain.

'It's time I left.'

'One last thing.'

He lit another cigarette from the one he had just finished and drew on it heavily. I have always hated the smell of Red Stars.

'I have not led a good life. I have been a bad husband and a bad father. Perhaps I do not deserve to live. I cannot die without telling you that I have betrayed you. I did it to save myself. I informed my interrogators about Stevens. I told them everything I know. Perhaps more than I know, perhaps I embellished the truth because I thought a bigger lie might buy me my life. I should have known that there are no bargains to be traded in this state. Now I am afraid they will use it against you. I should not have done what I did. I know that now. I do not believe in redemption. But I beg your forgiveness.'

I held his poor cold body in my arms for the last time, I gave him what warmth I could, and left him to his fate.

She has fully re-entered the world of her past. The only reality is her memory, which runs through her with the force of a tide going out, an invisible power that nothing can stop. After years of living in the eternal present of the system, she is taking possession of herself through the rediscovery of her memories.

It is like waking up after years of sleep, a moment of liberation, releasing great energy within her, flooding her body with a warmth which she has not felt since the last days of her innocence so many years ago. Through her words she is discovering who she is. She talks without restraint.

Her interrogator is called Andropov. She imagines he must be an officer in the KGB. He is courteous and correct, never raising his voice, never touching her. She finds his reasonableness frightening because in this house of terror he is all she has to cling to. He is using his guile to make her trust him, even to like him and she has to fight off the temptation. At times it is very hard.

She returns to the interview room. The interrogation begins again.

'During our investigation of his crimes, your former husband gave us certain information about you. I wish to verify the truth of his allegations.'

Did they have to force these secrets out of Ivan? No, he would have volunteered what he knew without being asked. Always an angle to play with Ivan, another line to shoot. Ten years apart and he still thinks that betraying her will save his skin. She realizes how desperate he must have been. For a moment she feels close to forgiving him, but the feeling passes.

'In June 1932, as a member of a Soviet delegation, you attended an international conference on physics in Leiden. Is that correct?'

'Yes.'

'You were a member of a team from the Institute of Physics?'

'Yes.'

'The conference lasted five days.'

'If you say so. I don't remember.'

'While you were there you met a British scientist?'

It is her first conference, her first trip outside Russia in her life. She is twenty-eight, married for one year to the engineer Marchenko, excited by her work, already regretting her marriage. During a coffee break on the second morning she is introduced to Geoffrey Stevens, a physicist from Cambridge, one of the major speakers at the conference. She knows of him by reputation, has read some of his articles in *Nature* and *The Physical Review* and is interested in his theoretical work on atomic energy because it is close to her own. She has come to hear him speak. Meeting him is more than she had hoped for.

They discuss the talking point of the conference, the publication earlier in the year of a paper by the Cambridge scientist, James Chadwick, which reveals the existence of the neutron. This discovery, Stevens tells her, is a turning point in the history of physics. It may lead to the liberation of energy from the atomic nucleus and the subsequent use of atomic energy for industry. She is exhilarated by the fire of his enthusiasm for a world in which a new and inexhaustible source of energy makes possible an undreamed-of era of industrialization. Differences of culture and political belief vanish as they exchange ideas and information. The experience leaves her

19

almost breathless, excited in a way she has never been before, the reasons for which she doesn't yet fully understand.

For the rest of the morning, sitting in the lecture theatre, she hears only his voice in her head, nothing from the platform. At lunch she eats with her colleagues, listening to their complaints, their bitter assessments of their fellow physicists, their criticisms of a way of life of which they are secretly jealous. She says little, her mind is elsewhere. To her surprise Stevens brings his coffee to her table and sits down beside her. He fetches sugar when she asks for it. She registers the disapproval of her colleagues and feels pleased.

At the start of the afternoon session Stevens takes his place on the platform. She watches him put his hands to either side of his head as if to shade his eyes from the light, lean forward on his elbows and then slowly, very slowly, survey the auditorium until he can see where she is sitting. He drops his hands at once, sits back in his chair and stares at her.

She asks herself: what is happening? Why am I like this? Why is he like this? She thinks back over what has happened between them. There is no concealment in his expression, no dissimulation. She is unused to this directness and she finds it disturbing. In her society men and women are practised in the art of concealment. The idea of revealing what you think or feel is extraordinary. But when he talks to her, he tells her the truth. That has not happened to her before.

That evening, at a reception, she wonders if he will seek her out again. Surely not. It is too risky. She stations herself near the exit, talking to a dull Polish mathematician and watching over his shoulder as Stevens gathers up a group of colleagues at the other end of the room and then, with handshakes and smiles, slowly makes his way towards the door where she stands. At least she will catch a glimpse of him, perhaps a smile, a wave, the promise of a meeting tomorrow. She admires the casual way he spots her (did she imagine it or had he already seen her standing by the door?) then greets her as if they had known each other for years.

'Ruth.'

He reaches past someone to touch her outstretched hand in greeting. They're going to eat at a restaurant nearby. Why doesn't she join them? He gathers her up into his group, introduces her to people whose names she doesn't catch and sweeps her out into the warm summer evening. She submits to her conquest with abandon.

They eat in the garden of an inn popular with the students, seated on benches around a long wooden table. There are a dozen of them, British, Dutch, German, two Italians; mathematicians and physicists. She is the only Russian. She sits as far away from him as she can. But throughout the evening she feels his eyes on her, even when she has her back to him. Once, or does she imagine it? she sees him raise his beer glass and toast her secretly across the table. She experiences a moment of fear that others might see but nobody does. Or she thinks nobody does. She is grateful that it is dark enough to hide her confusion. She is sure her face is on fire.

It is an extraordinary evening, unlike any other. They talk enthusiastically about their work, these young scientists, 'the sons and daughters of quantum physics', Stevens calls them. They share an excitement in their discoveries, a confidence in the role that science must play in the life of the planet, an eagerness for the new world of quantum mechanics, how they will unravel the deepest secrets of nature to release atomic energy and the uses to which this source of energy will be put. She shares in the sense of brotherhood that Stevens stimulates in them, how they share 'a responsibility to work together for the good of mankind, a confederacy of scientists to whom science and democracy mean more than nationality'.

'We must be leaders,' Stevens tells them. 'Not in a political sense. We must work alongside politicians to achieve the new world we can all sense within our grasp. We must *influence* politics with our understanding of what can now be achieved through the application of science.'

The flames of the candles burning on the table are reflected in their glasses as they raise them to acknowledge Stevens. Did that happen, or was it an illusion? That summer night, did they swear allegiance to one another, did they create a brotherhood that would ignore political loyalties? If only she could remember now.

She responds to their optimism and envies their innocence (there is no innocence left in the Soviet Union, there is only caution).

Later on (is it midnight? Later still? She has lost all track of time by now), they walk in a garden, she and this English professor. (She can't remember where it is or how they got there.) Where the rest of the party is by now she has no idea either; for a time they were with them, drinking and debating, and then they were not. Did he engineer that? She doesn't care how it has happened, she knows they are alone, perhaps they are alone in all the world, and she feels

21

reckless and free and excited. They stand watching the stars in a clear, dark sky. It is very still and warm.

Suddenly, under the branches of a walnut tree he takes her hand in his: she is surprised how hot his hand is. Then he apologizes immediately and releases her hand as if it had burned him. He retreats from her. Perhaps it is embarrassing to her, he is so sorry, he is not good at this sort of thing. But he is glad she was there at dinner. He smiles at her, that open, defenceless smile that touches her heart. The moonlight shines through the leaves and makes a pattern on his face. In that moment she loves him more than she knew it was possible to love anyone.

She remembers standing on tiptoe, reaching up to put her arms around his neck, drawing his face towards her, that dear, open smiling face, and then she is kissing him, was it once or many times? How can she know after so many years, except that she remembers the shyness of his kiss, the tremble of his body in her arms. She puts her hands to his face and kisses his eyes and his lips, and she feels his arms around her, pulling her body closer to his.

How long they stay like that she does not know. With her lips still on his face, she moves in his embrace, very slowly at first, almost carelessly, so that his hand touches her breast. She hopes he will think it is accidental. But she does not remove it, she lets it lie there for a while, and then she covers his hand with hers. She looks up at him and smiles, leans her head against his shoulder and then leads him by the hand through the garden, through the deserted streets of the sleeping town and up the stairs to her room.

'Did sexual intercourse take place?' Andropov asks.

Why are men always interested in sex? Those days had not been about sex or not only about sex, but about something more fundamental even than that. How can she explain that to this man?

They stand facing each other in the darkness of her room. She whispers 'Wait,' and goes into the bathroom. There she takes off her shoes, her dress and her underclothes. She likes her dress, it does not disgrace her, though she sees how unfashionable it is by comparison to the dresses she has seen in the streets of Leiden. But she is ashamed of her underclothes, worn grey through use and darned. She washes her hands and face and between her legs, cleans her teeth and combs her hair. She wears no jewellery apart from her wedding ring and she does not bother to remove that. Then she turns out the light and goes back into her bedroom. For a moment, before she is used to the dark, she sees nothing and she thinks he has gone. Then she notices his clothes tossed carelessly over the back of a chair. He is in bed, lying under a single sheet.

She gets in beside him, her heart beating so loudly she is sure he will hear it. They lie beside each other for a while, not touching. Then she reaches for his hand and turns her body towards his, her head down as if she is afraid to look at him. He takes her chin in his hand and raises her face so he can see her in the moonlight that streams in through the open window. Then slowly and softly he begins to kiss her.

Afterwards, while he sleeps, she holds him in her arms and feels a sense of completion she has never known before. She tries to define the emotion. Is it love? She has only experienced what she imagines is love once before, and it was with Marchenko in the first months. It was nothing like this. There was no tenderness in what he did to her, no meeting of equals, only a man with his desire and she with her ability to satisfy it. She recognizes now what she has always known but refused to admit. She does not love Marchenko, has never done and will never do so.

She lies against Stevens, and knows that in this room and on this night in this strange foreign town, her being and that of this man whom she hardly knows, fused for one moment. She was not obliterated by this act (as she has been before), she was enhanced by it, liberated: perfected, that is the word she chooses. In giving herself to this man she has been brought to an undreamed-of perfection. She is now more herself than she has ever been. She exults in the emotions of tenderness that flow through her. She is lost to one world but she has found herself in quite another.

They are lovers until the end of the week. Everyone knows about their relationship at once (at conferences everyone always knows who is sleeping with whom) because she is constantly by his side. He insists they eat together though she thinks this is unwise, but he will hear nothing of her objections. When she is with him, she cannot resist smiling at him. She takes time off with him from the conference to buy some lipstick, skin cream, scent, some special soap for the bath and new underclothes. She goes to the hairdresser. Stevens wants to buy her a dress but she refuses to let him do this.

She expects her colleagues to criticize her behaviour (she even fears she may be sent back early to Moscow) but they don't, though they express their disapproval (or jealousy) through their silence. She is not sure why they don't criticize her. Perhaps they realize that these events may be stored away for future use. Patience is one of the arts of living under communism. You hoard the indiscretions of your colleagues and neighbours against the day when the evidence can be used to your advantage.

Isn't that what Ivan had done? Isn't that why she is in this room now, answering Andropov's questions? The day of reckoning always comes (it is one of the few certainties of life in Soviet Russia), but for these few days in Leiden she chooses to forget so many of the lessons she has learned in her adult life. She knows she has made enemies, but she consoles herself with the thought that everyone has enemies, so what does it matter? Recklessly, she gives no thought to the future because she sees none beyond the end of the week.

'You don't deny it? I am surprised,' Andropov says.

'What is there to deny? It all happened so long ago. It was not important then. How can it be now?'

At the end of the week, Marchenko returns to Moscow, Stevens to Cambridge. They part knowing it is unlikely they will meet again, though they say to each other that they will move heaven and earth to make such a meeting possible. In the emotion of their parting, promises are made. There are other conferences and Stevens has his red university diary with him. He skims through the pages and recites the names of cities she has heard of but never seen.

Milan. Basle. Oslo.

She says she will try, but the decision is not in her power; she thinks it will be difficult if not impossible to persuade the Institute's authorities to let her go.

Moscow, then, Stevens says. He will come to Moscow in January. He will give a paper to the Academy of Sciences. Only a few months to wait, then they will be together again.

For a moment they dream of a few days in the city in which she has spent all her life. But in their hearts they know how enormous are the obstacles they must overcome and that makes their parting so difficult. Now, all these years later, she knows that what they dared not say to each other that day has come true. They were not to meet again, and now there is no likelihood that they will ever do so.

'Perhaps there are people who would not share your view that your affair with Stevens was unimportant.'

She hears the threat in Andropov's voice, but she cannot stop herself defying him.

'They would have to explain their reasons,' she says.

Enemies, she thinks, have long memories. She never expected the enemy to be the man with whom she briefly shared her life.

'Stevens was married. So were you.'

'Adultery is not a crime.'

'We are dealing with deviant not criminal behaviour.'

'I cannot see why a brief encounter with an English physicist so many years ago is of the slightest concern to anyone. It was a trivial event.'

Andropov considers her answer. She does not know whether it is important in his eyes, since he has chosen to resurrect the event after so much time, or whether it is just an excuse to arrest her.

'Let us wind the clock forward sixteen years. What has happened to Stevens? He is still at Cambridge, he is one of the most important scientists in the British nuclear programme, he is a Nobel prize-winner. He has an international reputation,' Andropov is saying, but she is hardly listening to him: a flood of memories is enveloping her. It is a joyful process, remembering those days with Stevens.

'He was always going to succeed. It was obvious even then.'

She says it carelessly, without thinking. It is her only mistake but it is enough. Andropov has been waiting for such a moment. He has caught her off guard. In those few words, she has betrayed herself and possibly Stevens too, and though she stops herself from saying anything more, it is too late. She has revealed her secret to Andropov, and he knows that Stevens is not dead for her, that some memory lives on deep within her, nourished secretly all these years. That is what he came to find and he has not been disappointed. He has learned her weakness, and now he has the power to exploit her. She knows he will do so mercilessly.

Andropov leans back into his chair, confident and relaxed. She shivers even though she is not cold.

2

DANNY

'If we believe all they tell us,' Toby Milner said at the end of a grim day of listening to men and women denying a past that was undeniable, 'there weren't enough Nazis in this country to fill a paper bag, let alone form an army. So how did Hitler manage to survive for so long? That's what I'd like to know.'

The snow was falling again and had started to settle in drifts. It had been snowing on and off all day, and the bitter wind had returned. The city was silent.

'God, I hate this place. Why can't we go home and leave them to it? They got themselves into this mess in the first place.'

Many of us in Berlin thought like that. We saw ourselves working for the people we had defeated. We saw the efforts that were being made to rebuild their country and obliterate the evidence of the recent past, and we wondered how much was being done to restore our own shattered homes. From what we heard and read in the newspapers, not enough.

'Here we are, babysitting the people who yesterday we tried to kill. And what does our vanquished enemy do? He tries to make us believe that he was really on our side all the time. Always someone else's doing. Him or her but never me. Pitiful.'

'Can you blame them for turning against each other if that's how they think they'll survive?' I asked.

'I blame them for everything,' Milner said bitterly. 'In particular, I blame them for keeping us here, in this godforsaken hole.'

I'd been in Berlin for eight months by then, working for the Allied Control Commission. Our task was to interview the locals living in the British zone of occupation to find suitable people to take part in the new civilian administration the Allies were setting up. We were expected to exclude former Nazis and communists from our selection. It was a thankless exercise, without certainties and with little reward.

Each morning we were greeted by the same lengthy queues of hopeful Germans; each day we asked the same questions and we listened to the same stories, so often pathetic inventions to hide a truth we all knew. We inspected papers, some genuine, some forged, some stolen, the currency of hope on which to build a new life out of the ruins of the old. Each day we made our decisions, a tick or a cross, a simple mark on which so much depended. That is the true expression of victory, the exercise of absolute power.

'Don't you worry about the ones you let through?' I asked. 'Putting the guilty back into their old positions of power?'

I found it increasingly difficult to know if my judgements were right. I was haunted by the thought that I might be reinstating the old guard of unreformed Nazis or a new guard of communist activists.

'Nobody gets it right every time,' Toby said. 'We're bound to make mistakes. It's a question of degree. Are we more right than wrong? That's how I look at it. You've got to come away at the end of each day thinking you've got money in the bank.'

'I wish I could see it like that.'

'You know where you go wrong? You treat them as people.'

'They are people.'

'Wrong. They're problems. Nothing more.'

'I can't hate them enough for that.'

'I don't hate them and I don't despise them. The truth is, I don't care about them any more.' There was more than a hint of exhaustion in his voice. 'They sit there in front of me, I listen to their self-pity, their petty acts of betrayal, their self-righteousness and what do I hear? The litany of guilt. They were all in it, every man jack of them, and we're fooling ourselves if we think otherwise.'

A dog howled from somewhere inside a ruined house on the other side of the street. The desolate sound seemed to sum up the mood of the city.

'That's when I want to put a cross against all their names. But I suppose there comes a moment when you have to stop settling scores and look to the future. Then they become names on a sheet of paper, decisions to be made, right or wrong, yes or no. That's all. No emotion. No involvement.'

I hated the hopeful faces that looked across my desk each day. But I was prepared to do it because I was ordered to do it. Like countless others, I had been under orders for years. Obedience was a way of life. I was still too frozen by the experience of war to feel even the slightest pull of rebellion.

Toby Milner touched my arm in a gesture of parting. 'We're supposed to be building a new world,' he said. 'The trouble is, we're using the bricks of the old.'

With a wave he turned the corner and disappeared.

★

I never told anyone about Miriam, which means I am ashamed of this short episode in my life. The facts are these. During my months in that ruined city, I shared the bed of a woman called Miriam. I gave her food, sometimes clothes and cosmetics, she gave me herself, or at any rate, her body.

That she was, or had been, technically the enemy was something that never entered my mind. She was simply a lonely woman trying, like so many others, to bring herself back to life. She saw no wrong in the exchange of her body for the material things she lacked, and at that time neither did I. The relationship was one of convenience, and I justify what I did by saying that we both knew it. My presence in her life encouraged her to hope for more. Hoping was a symptom of coming back to life. She knew I would go away, that nothing was permanent. She had only to look at the ruins of the city she had grown up in to know that.

Memory is the enemy of all that cold rationality. When she cried herself to sleep I knew she was remembering how life had once been so different. She had been a schoolgirl when the war began, with ambitions to become a research chemist. She had lived with her parents and her sister in a suburb of Berlin. Home, parents, sister, all her dreams, had been obliterated in the smoke of war. Her thoughts would turn to the past, and she would cry.

'One more day,' she said as I let myself into her room. 'One more day and then I shall be all alone.'

'Not for long.'

I was hanging my greatcoat behind the door, watching the melting flakes of snow slide slowly down the sleeves to form a pool on the floor.

'Even one day is too long.'

It was an unspoken convention that there were no endearments between us, no words that might lay claim to an emotional territory

28

that was out of bounds. But the expression in her voice told me that tonight she wanted the rules to be broken.

'I'm coming back.' I hoped I didn't sound as weary as I felt.

'My father was in Cambridge years ago. He was a student there. He went to learn English and write a thesis.'

'What did he read?'

'He was a philosopher. He said Cambridge was the home of philosophy. He admired G. E. Moore. He admired the English.' She looked at me over her cup. 'We have more in common than you know. My father was a teacher too.'

'I've brought you these.'

I opened my briefcase. In it were some tins, meat and condensed milk, a packet of biscuits and some lipstick.

'Cigarettes?' she asked. They were cheap for us, but on the black market cigarettes had become a currency of their own. By selling what I gave her, Miriam could supplement what she earned working in the kitchens of our headquarters.

'Of course,' I said, putting a carton of two hundred on her table. She never told me that she sold them but we both knew she did.

'Look at this.' She had found the lipstick. She tried it at once. 'It is wonderful. Wonderful.'

She stood in front of the mirror, anointing her lips.

'Do you like me?'

She turned, smiling.

'You look lovely.'

'I look frightful, a mess. Look at me. Look at my hair.' She laughed. 'This awful skirt, woollen stockings, mittens, and now lipstick. Absurd.'

But there was a note of excitement in her voice I had not heard before, and she was laughing. She came as close then as she ever did to touching my heart.

'I have something for you.' She gave me a small parcel, wrapped in used brown paper, tied with string. 'Open it later. When you are in Cambridge.'

'You won't be there.'

'You can think of me when you open it.' She took the parcel from me and put it in my briefcase. 'We will be together then, if only for a moment.'

I should have been able to read the code. That night she gave me all the clues I needed. If I had wanted to, I am sure I would

29

have. But I did not have a mind for code-breaking in that city. Her messages remained undeciphered and unanswered.

I spent the night there, even though I had told myself I wouldn't. The snow was falling too heavily by then and I was tired. I have a memory, not of that night in particular, but of any night in that small, cold room, how we would cling to each other in the dark, and after a time I got used to sleeping without turning over. The need for warmth was as great as that for sleep, and there is no warmth like that of another human body held close.

★

I travelled with an American on my journey home. We nodded at each other as he entered the compartment, the salute of one uniform to another, but we said nothing. I huddled in my corner and looked out of the window as the train set off.

In a world of bullets and bombs you expect destruction. As an inevitable consequence of my makeshift life as a soldier, I had become used to the sight of the torn skeletons of buildings. They looked as if they had been ravaged by a disease whose scars were a bitter reminder of what once had been the homes of people like myself. But I was not prepared for the impossibility of living among the ruins of what I and so many others like me had done to our enemies. I wanted to remove the image, like turning a page in a magazine to look at something else. But at that time in Berlin there was nowhere to turn to.

I looked at the countryside with relief. If the signs of war were there, they were invisible from my compartment window. It was the towns I hated. Each time we passed through a station I tried to close my eyes and forget where I was. But the images of the shattered buildings and the endless piles of rubble were imprinted on my mind. I wanted nothing more than to leave Germany and never come back.

Holland was different. You cannot spend your early life on the edge of the East Anglian fenland and remain indifferent to flat marshy country. I loved the fens then as I do now, and I feel the same attraction in Holland. Endless dark fields passed by that day, the earth hardened by the winter and lined with frozen irrigation canals shining silver in the cold light. Always the same flat line of horizon, wherever you looked, its limits marked by the silhouettes of trees or, occasionally, a windmill.

If Germany was a country living with the unburied corpse of its past, Holland was springing back to life. What you could see of the faces between scarves and hats had purpose. There was none of the dazed, lost look with which I was so familiar. As we pulled into Utrecht, I saw skaters, bodies bent forward, hands held gracefully behind their backs as they leaned into the wind, their movements expressing a pleasure I had not seen for months. My spirits lifted.

'Care for some coffee?'

My American companion had taken a thermos flask from his haversack and was pouring the hot, black liquid into a cup. I took it gratefully, letting the steam warm my face.

'Going far?' he asked.

The train, not unsurprisingly, was prone to unscheduled stops in the middle of nowhere. We were already some hours late.

'London. If we ever get there.'

'Me too. My wife's English. I've got a little boy I've never seen.'

The carriage door opened, letting in a blast of cold air. Two Dutch women sat down beside us. One of them dropped a package as she settled herself in her seat. The American retrieved it. The woman smiled and said something in Dutch. The American said, 'You're welcome.' The train jerked its way slowly out of the station.

'You married?'

'No.'

I smiled but said nothing more, and my companion settled back into the silence of his own thoughts. The Dutch women shared some food, talked quietly to one another, and I slept fitfully as the countryside moved agonizingly slowly past us.

I awoke to someone shaking my arm.

'Amsterdam,' the American said. 'We get out here.'

I took my haversack down from the rack and followed him on to the platform. Dusk was falling and lights were coming on. But the growing darkness could not hide the sharp outlines of damage, even after seven years. Now we had the unenviable task of putting it all back together again. What demons might we be storing up to ruin another generation's future?

'Care for a drink? We've missed one connection. We've got to wait a couple of hours for the next one.'

We found a bar not far from the station and a warm corner. I shed my coat for the first time that day.

'You stationed in Berlin?' he asked.

'Yes.'

'Me too. God, I hate that city.'

'Too many ghosts?'

'Times past? No. All that's buried. Done with.' He thought for a moment. 'It's the Soviets. I hate the way they think they won the war on their own and that victory allows them to dictate the peace. Look at the way the bastards make trouble just for the hell of it. Whatever you give them, it's never enough. They want more. Sometimes, when you sit across a table with them, you want to grab them by the lapels of their uniforms and knock their stupid heads against the wall. You know,' he said, finishing his beer, 'I thought war was bad enough but politics is worse.'

'Their kind of politics.'

'Right. Everything is about advantage. Win, win, win, every time, on every little thing.'

Someone had turned on a radio and I could hear dance music, then a woman's voice singing. The bar was filling up as the working day came to an end. The warmth and the people gave an air of festivity to the place.

'How about you? What keeps you in Berlin?'

'I vet the locals. See if they've repented.'

'Have they?'

'None of them was guilty in the first place, or so they tell me. They were all secretly on our side but they never had an opportunity to do anything about it.'

'Are they suitable citizens to run their own country? Right?'

'We can't defeat the Nazis one day and install them back in power the next.'

'Why not? Anything's better than the Reds.'

It was an astonishing statement. For a moment I wanted to challenge him, then I thought better of it.

'And let the guilty get away with it? The people we've been at war with for six years?'

'So what? That war's over and done with. We've got to build up their country as fast as we can. Who cares if they were Nazis once? They're Germans now and they're on our side. The world's moved on. New times, new enemies.'

'Reds?'

'Right. Bastards. Real godforsaken, motherfucking communist

bastards. They're the enemy now. Berlin's the front line and we're the guys getting shot at.'

I had met a few Russians in the course of my duties in Berlin and their behaviour had been impossible, unreasonable to a degree I'd never experienced before. My companion sensed agreement in my silence.

'I'll tell you something else. This is the way the world's headed from now on. Us against the Reds, eyeball to eyeball, wherever you turn. Try telling that to a politician. Your people. Mine. Who gives a shit? The war to end wars is over, they say. War talk is talking dirty. We all love the Russians because Stalin was on our side when it counted, so he's a great guy. Nobody wants to know what he's doing to us now. That's what scares me. I tell you, there's a new war starting, right here, right now, and it's going to get a lot worse before it gets better, especially when they get their own nuclear bomb.'

He took my empty glass from me and stood up.

'The Russians snatch people off the streets every day in Berlin, but who cares about Berlin? If it were London or Washington we'd be on the brink of World War Three. By the time our politicians come to their senses, it *will* be London or Washington. What will the fuckers do then? Call in the military to save their skins once more. Nothing new in that, is there? That's what men in uniform have been doing since time began. Saving skins that don't deserve to be saved. If the guys back home would listen to us, none of this need ever happen.'

He laughed and broke the mood.

'Let's have another drink.'

He returned from the bar with two other Americans and they spent the next two hours telling stories about their wars. It was the companionship of uniform, fine as long as it lasted but soon enough forgotten.

Our journey began again shortly after midnight. I tried to sleep but the cold crept into my bones and I sat for most of the night staring out into the darkness, seeing nothing but the occasional light reflected on the snow. We could have been going anywhere. I hoped we were going to Calais.

3

RUTH

Andropov is questioning her once more. How long is it since her first interview? She can no longer remember.

Her mother has been released unharmed. She continues to live in her apartment, her son has not suffered at school, her neighbours are not whispering about her or avoiding her, the babushka in the front hall recognizes her when she leaves the building or returns home (though she never smiles), she continues her work at the Institute. On the surface it is as if the interrogation had never taken place. But she knows that her own freedom is now a technical matter.

'If I were to ask you what is the most valuable piece of information the West has given us about their nuclear programme, what would you answer?'

She shifts uncomfortably in her chair and says nothing. To her relief he is not waiting for her to reply.

'Sixteen months ago, when they dropped their bombs on Hiroshima and Nagasaki, they told us that a nuclear device can be exploded. That moment shifted the balance of power decisively in their favour. The West has done what we have so far found impossible to do. That puts our own nuclear programme under very considerable pressure.'

What is the phrase she has heard Yuri Miskin use? Problem Number One, for which a State Committee has been created. (Every problem in need of a solution has a State Committee.) The pressures of Problem Number One are obvious even to her, and generally she has little contact with the political staff. Work harder, work faster, achieve more, they tell the Institute from their protected position on the sidelines. Be patriotic, think only of the state. How little politicians and their apparatchiks understand about the scientific process.

'I have given you our best industrial and technical resources,

34

scientists, technicians. We have sown our people like seeds in the American laboratories and those seeds have ripened. Our spies have brought us secrets from the West, samples of uranium 235, drawings, calculations. But still there is no bomb, no explosion.'

Andropov is pacing around the room. She does not follow his movements. She looks down at her hands (she clasps them tightly together in her lap) or straight ahead at his empty chair. Andropov reaches past her to put out one cigarette and light another.

'The words of Comrade Stalin.'

Comrade Stalin? Does he have any idea of the enormous technical problems they have to resolve, of the vast industrial resources such an ambitious project will absorb, of the months and years of intense, painstaking work that must be dedicated to their task?

'The Soviet Union must defend itself against its enemies by exceeding the nuclear successes of the West. At this moment, we have no more important task, but we are not moving fast enough.'

Beria has been appointed Chairman of the Special Committee on Atomic Energy, he tells her, and discussions have taken place recently on how the Soviet nuclear programme can be speeded up. Without a nuclear capability, Soviet foreign policy is at risk. She already knows that because Miskin sits on the Committee representing the Director of the Institute and, though he tells her little, he has described how intense is the pressure on the Institute. Miskin has never mentioned Andropov to her but that is not surprising. Probably Andropov would only attend by special invitation, and Miskin has no head for people. Any issue that Andropov might raise would not catch his interest. Miskin has mastered the art of being present while his mind is far away.

She lets her own mind wander as Andropov talks. She imagines the room. High windows, dim lights, a wide table strewn with papers, too many people. There are always too many people at meetings in the Soviet Union: the watchers watch each other. There is too much smoke. And endless talk.

She hears the discussion. Like all committee discussions, it is circular, political, ragged with bad temper, posturing and self-justification (she has attended too many meetings herself not to know that, whatever their purpose, the attitudes are always the same, only the papers are different). The impatience of the Central Committee and the presence of Beria produce an unusual nervousness.

'We must steal more secrets from the West,' the administrators on the Committee will have said (that is what they always say), as if by voicing their thoughts the act is done. 'We must copy the American design. Then we will have our Soviet bomb.'

Because the design is American, they are saying without using the words, it is automatically superior, more practical, more liable to work than any Russian design.

But how? How are they to steal more American secrets? Here the representatives of Military Intelligence who have been seconded to Department S will have interrupted, to remind the meeting that contacts with secret Soviet sources in America have been shut down since Gouzenko's defection because of fears that the FBI is close to uncovering their agents. America and its nuclear research is presently out of bounds and it will be some time before either can be reactivated. The plain fact the Committee must face is that the supply of stolen nuclear secrets has dried up because the American project is now heavily guarded.

(Will anyone have the courage to inform Comrade Stalin? Foolish question).

She is secretly pleased that American secrets are closed to them because it may at last allow the Institute a chance to prove it can match anything the Americans may do, but she is wise enough to keep such ideas to herself.

'Then we must explore other avenues,' the chairman will have said; that is the kind of remark he was appointed to make.

'We should approach Western scientists who are known to be open to the idea of sharing atomic secrets,' the political administrators will have suggested. 'What we cannot take secretly, let us ask for openly.'

At moments like these, the same names are wheeled out, Oppenheimer, Nils Bohr, Fermi, Szilard; the same accounts of secret meetings are rehearsed, the same conclusions are drawn. There exists in the West (so the argument goes) a group of pioneer researchers who are believed to be willing to give away their nuclear secrets in support of their ethical belief that no nation should possess a monopoly of nuclear knowledge. Now it is their turn to be the saviours of the Soviet nuclear programme, stepping in valiantly to rescue Stalin's political programme. That this idea is once more being floated is, she knows, a sign of the Committee's desperation in its search for a solution. This group may exist: she has her doubts, but she has never heard that it has ever given away a single secret.

But, she also knows, the West is alert to this tactic too. The representatives of Military Intelligence will have made it clear at this meeting, and probably at many others too, that all the avenues for gathering secret information from these sources are being closed off. The West has woken up to the risks. These scientists are quarantined in security, their secrets increasingly unreachable.

Where is Andropov in all this? Is he the thin, pale-faced figure, silently awaiting his moment in the company of his bull-necked, square-headed superiors whose backsides have warmed the chairs they sit in for too long, men who will agree to any course of action in order to secure the privileges they can no longer live without: their large apartments, sable coats for their wives, official cars, holiday villas on the Black Sea?

But the reality of Andropov's voice interrupts her imagined meeting, and she is brought back to full attention. She warns herself that she must concentrate on what he is saying. She has already paid the price of letting her mind wander once. She must not let that happen again.

'An intelligence officer from the Second Bureau makes a contribution to the discussion at this point.'

(Why can't he tell her that *he* made the suggestion?)

'If we are denied all access to Western secrets,' he says, 'perhaps we should look for other ways of getting their scientists to work for us.'

She looks at him and fear flutters in her heart.

'The immediate response to this suggestion is laughter,' Andropov tells her.

'The British and Americans are hardly likely to accept an invitation to come to Moscow,' a senior Politburo member says.

She imagines Andropov sitting at the table, lips drawn tight, hands clenched, waiting for the mirth to subside, his cold demeanour slowly commanding attention. The laughter dies away and the room falls silent.

'Perhaps if the approach were different, they might be persuaded to help us,' she hears him saying.

The meeting waits in anticipation.

'You have a proposal, Comrade Andropov?'

'We know,' he says, 'that there is a fundamental disagreement in the West about the development of the atom bomb. Some of their most influential scientists believe that the military use of nuclear power should be banned, no single state should have a military

37

advantage over another, that nuclear secrets should be shared, the nuclear industry managed under the control of the international scientific community.'

Here he pauses and looks around the table at the faces watching him, waiting for the denouement that will get them all off the hook on which at this moment their future is dangling.

'It would be interesting to see what effect our support for such a campaign might have on the progress of the West's nuclear programme.'

There is now complete silence around the committee table. They know that this is not all his plan but as much as he will choose to reveal now.

If you cannot buy secrets, buy time, he says. It is a risky idea, but they are desperate men. Sow doubt and confusion in the suggestible minds of the West; create a sufficient interruption in their development programme by manipulating the weakness of democracy, its use of debate in the search for consensus, to allow Soviet scientists time to complete their work.

At first Andropov is not understood. Why should there be any debate in the West? Why should this plan affect the development of their research?

Andropov smiles briefly. He introduces to the Committee the idea of free speech. There is general puzzlement. How can a society work where anyone may voice his opinion? It is a recipe for chaos and unhappiness.

Andropov argues that by infiltrating the Western mind in this way, by encouraging its powerful leaders to express their doubts, he will provoke a furious and fevered debate on the morality of nuclear energy, slowing progress on their bomb. The outcome will be a paralysing internecine war of words, unresolved and unresolvable, on which the West will choke itself, allowing the innate superiority of the Soviet system to prove itself and passing nuclear leadership to the Soviet Union.

A small bald-headed man gets to his feet. He has the chest of a miner, with short powerful arms. He bangs the table with the flat of his hand.

'We will spread a poison of self-doubt into the West,' he shouts. 'We will confuse our enemies, lead them astray, we will watch them destroy themselves in the agonies of useless debate. Only then will the victory of Marxist-Leninism be complete.'

There have been whispered comments behind his back, while he is speaking, between the chairman and the secretary of the Committee. Now the chairman thanks him for his useful contribution, reminding all present that the purpose of all their actions, especially those under discussion today, is the ultimate defeat of their enemies in the West who threaten the Soviet Union.

'I would like the permission of this meeting to present a plan for consideration in seven days.' That is Andropov's request.

Ruth imagines the glances exchanged, the whispered murmurings, head bent to head, the nods, the hierarchical process of agreement where underlings wait for their seniors to declare their opinion before nodding furiously themselves.

'Four days, Comrade Andropov. The Committee will hear your plan at a special meeting in four days' time.'

Four days later, Andropov will have submitted his plan and the same absurd process of evaluation and discussion will have occupied another day in the glorious history of the Soviet Union, at the end of which the chairman will have turned to Andropov and nodded his assent.

And because of that nod she is sitting here now in this room in the Lubyanka, listening to Andropov resurrect her affair with Stevens all those years ago.

Sixteen years. They have waited sixteen years and now she will be made to pay for this single indiscretion of her life.

Andropov waits for a sign that she has understood fully what he is telling her.

'I am your target,' she says.

'No, Comrade Marchenko. You are my instrument. Professor Stevens is my target.'

4

MONTY

Corless takes his seat in the only armchair in the room. Cups of tea are hastily drained and pushed into the centre of the table. Crumbs from Rich Tea biscuits are surreptitiously swept on to the floor. We stop talking.

'All present and correct, Arthur?'

'All present and correct, Rupert. Yes.'

Arthur Gurney looks round the table to double-check. The weekly ritual has begun.

'Shall we take the minutes then?'

The minutes of the last meeting are solemnly read in silence to ensure they are a true record of a meeting none of us can be bothered to remember. Arthur Gurney hands the top copy to Corless who asks, 'May I sign?' To which none of us ever answers, so Corless signs, Arthur dates and then blots ostentatiously as if his life depended upon it.

'Any matters arising not covered?'

No one says anything as Corless knows they won't, and so on we go to what Corless cheerfully describes as 'the work of the morning'. He glances down at the agenda that he has set himself and feigns surprise. 'Three items, I see.'

None of us is ever taken in by this element in the ritual. The agenda seldom changes. It would be a shock if it did.

'Sweet, but not, I suspect, short.'

That is the signal for the business to begin.

Colin Maitland hands Corless the Peter file. There has been a bitter scrap over this, Arthur Gurney demanding the right of first access to what he insists on calling 'source Peter' but Maitland, an old hand at departmental politics, has got to Corless first and put Gurney's nose seriously out of joint. Maitland is the guardian of the

Peter file. Dislike seethes between them like electric static between two poles.

'The decrypt of the latest message from Peter was only completed at six this morning,' he informs us ('A problem with the teleprinter from Moscow,' we are told), so none of us has seen it yet.

Whatever attitude we may adopt, each of us is secretly excited by every new piece of intelligence from Peter. There is nothing like an association with a major secret to give you an enhanced sense of your own importance.

'You'll receive your copies in the usual way after the meeting. Will you summarize its contents, Colin?'

This request underlines Maitland's role as Rupert's deputy. He, alone of all of us, has already seen the decrypt, a privilege that separates him from his rivals in the room. He opens the folder slowly and surveys the papers, making the most of the moment.

'We are the target of renewed subversive activity by the Soviets,' Maitland says. ('So what's new?' Adrian Gardner whispers in my ear.) 'Peter tells us that Soviet connections in this country have identified a leading British nuclear scientist in Cambridge from whom they are confident (Peter's words) that they will receive secret information.'

There is a stunned silence around the table.

'If Peter is correct, gentlemen, and we must assume he is until proven otherwise, then there is only one possible interpretation. Within our academic community we harbour a man or woman who either is already working with the Soviets or intends very soon to do so. Put more simply, it would seem that we have a traitor in our midst.'

★

Rupert Corless's relationship with Peter the Great was one of intimacy though the two had never met. We all knew the importance of each to the other. Without Peter, Corless's career would never have risen above the mundane level he had achieved before Martineau's gift fell into his lap. To be fair, he understood Peter's importance and his good fortune the moment it arrived. Without Corless's persistence against the shameful doubts and rejection of the early Peter intelligence by his superiors, the information we had from inside the Soviet Union might never have attained its present level of importance.

Corless's second coming was due to an extraordinary piece of luck. Intelligence about Soviet intentions, always light on the ground, was at a premium in the last months of the war when some of us began to fear the consequences if the Soviets increased their sphere of influence in the post-war world at the expense of their allies. If getting our own people to understand this possibility was difficult, getting the Americans to change their view of how this last campaign should be conducted was impossible. The Soviets were our allies, Zhukov a trusted comrade; we would all meet up soon in Germany, wouldn't we?

The difficulty was, we had no hard evidence to support our fears that Zhukov was working against us, only deductions, opinion, surmise. It is hard to believe how little we knew about the Soviet Union in the last months of the war. The Soviets put the lid on everything and screwed it down tight. Hard fact, naturally, was what the Americans wanted before they'd listen to our concerns, in the certain knowledge that we couldn't lay our hands on any Soviet intelligence worth twopence.

Then, one morning in February 1945, Corless got a coded message from Bobby Martineau, an SIS man in Moscow. He had been approached by, and was now running (bona fides, such as they are in our business, having been established), a major source of Soviet intelligence, code-named Peter the Great. Its importance was such that he wanted (in Bobby's version he 'demanded', but opinion is divided as to the veracity of a number of points in Bobby's account) Peter intelligence to be given the highest level of secrecy, and that in Moscow he alone was to run Peter.

A morning's work on the samples he sent us was enough to convince even the cynics in Horseferry Road (by this time Adrian Gardner was already well established as faction leader) that Peter was an impeccable source within the military planning section of Soviet High Command. We were now able to read Zhukov's mind. It was an astonishing reversal. We knew what the Russians were going to do because Peter told us their plans, and what we learned confirmed our deepest fears. The Russians planned to get to Berlin before the Americans and the British, and to use their arrival for their own political ends. We took the evidence to our military, only to have it rebuffed.

'Won't wash, old boy. Boris and Ivan are good eggs, they're sticking it to Jerry like nobody's business, and we've all got a date under the Brandenberg Gate before long. What a night we'll have then, what a party!'

That was when Corless's hard training in adversity, his ability to absorb knocks and carry on fighting, came into its own. He refused to be brushed aside, refused, as he put it, to break faith with Peter's courage.

'If Peter risks his life for what he believes is right,' he said, 'then we have to fight his corner with him.'

What Peter told us of the Red Army's plans proved startlingly accurate. By the time Corless's advocacy of the Peter intelligence was taken seriously the Russians were in the outskirts of Berlin. It was then too late to make use of what we'd learned, but Corless had won his own personal battle. The final score sheet showed a walkover for Corless and a whitewash for his and Peter's detractors, from which we doubted they would ever recover. Corless's star was in the ascendant. From then on it was a brave man who challenged Peter's authority, and after VE Day no one sought the accolade.

Then, within a few weeks of the end of the war, there came the fallow period of 'Peter's silence', the immediate post-war months when no intelligence came out of Moscow and Corless's reputation as wunderkind began to suffer. 'Source' Peter dried up. A number of theories were swapped in the corridors and committee rooms of Horseferry Road. Peter had been betrayed and shot; he had been seriously injured in the race to Berlin; he was languishing in prison. All guesswork, because none of us, Corless included, had any idea who Peter the Great actually was and Martineau couldn't or wouldn't help. All we had was the past evidence of his secret messages and the proof of their accuracy, just as we now had his silence.

'Keep faith,' Martineau wired from Moscow. 'Peter not dead. Will rise again.' It all sounded barmy, typical Martineau.

During those uncomfortable weeks, the Peter cynics, nursing their wounds after Corless's rise, regained lost ground.

'Peter's lost his tongue,' Adrian Gardner said with malicious pleasure. 'And Rupert's lost his balls.'

An anti-Corless whisper campaign spread like a bush fire. A number of us were sure Adrian Gardner was behind it. If he was, he concealed his involvement skilfully. Corless's people advised a show of force. Corless had to fight his corner again and he showed great determination to do so. Over the years, steel had entered his soul and now he was a match for anyone.

Whatever the reason for Peter's loss of voice, he said, he had no doubt the ailment was temporary, patience would prompt his recovery and before long Peter would be returned to us.

Corless was gambling his career on Peter's return. We thought it was madness. All he had to go on was Martineau's dotty telegram, and none of us would have staked sixpence on that. But Rupert was adamant. Peter was missing, not lost. He would return. It was just a matter of time.

His courage and obduracy stemmed the tide. Rupert must know something no one else did, the whisperers said. How else could he make such a stand? Miraculously, in the face of such apparent certainty, the tide of hostility receded.

A week later, without warning or explanation, Peter suddenly reappeared and once more the intelligence flowed. Somehow the lid on the Soviet Union had been prised open again and we could look in. The light was bad and we couldn't see far, but Peter's silence had shown us that without his connection we were totally in the dark. We had lived on a diet of surmise and prediction, which are never good for the decision-making process.

'Peter risen,' Martineau wired, 'halleluja.'

Once more the cynics retreated, Adrian Gardner among them. Corless's star was on the move again but not quite with the heady speed he had experienced previously. The damage may have been limited by Peter's Lazarus-like return, but damage there was. Seeds of doubt about the credibility of Peter the Great had been sown. The period of silence would not go away. Why had Peter vanished? What had happened? Was Peter still kosher? Explanations were asked for but none was forthcoming. Corless ignored the questions and got on with the business in hand.

'Peter has come back to us', he said. 'We should rejoice.'

That was his way of closing the door on an unhappy episode that he wanted to forget. The only test, he said, was the quality of Peter's intelligence. If the early reports were anything to go by, it was proving to be better than ever. We had an inside view of the rapid expansion of the Soviet sphere of interest as communism engulfed Poland, Czechoslovakia, Romania, Bulgaria, the Baltic states, Yugoslavia and Albania. It was a progress we could do nothing to halt.

Corless held centre stage once more, but there were assassins waiting in the wings, and Adrian Gardner was one of them. Corless had only to slip up once and his enemies on his own side would get him. He delighted in this new circumstance. That he was now a major player in departmental politics and a target of so much jealousy proved he had arrived where he wanted to be.

By his own terms, Corless had made it.

★

The Soviet Intelligence Group, or SOVINT, was an ad hoc collection of working committees made up of intelligence officers, civil servants, seconded military and academics (economists, historians, specialists in politics, Russian speakers) whose task was to interpret any information coming out of the Soviet Union. The aim was to build up a picture of what was going on in Russia by pulling together all the available evidence and submitting it to a critical and high-level analysis.

SOVINT's findings were then passed to the appropriate authority in Whitehall (nuclear issues to the Ministry of Supply, politics to the Foreign Office and so on, with copies of every report to a special Committee of the Cabinet), in the belief that this continuous stream of information would assist the decision-making process in the difficult post-war years when no one was sure which way the Soviets would jump. In the eyes of its progenitors in the Cabinet Office, this loose association of experts was SOVINT's strength. The ability to call in experts when they were needed while otherwise leaving them undisturbed was seen as a time- and money-saving device, and satisfactorily progressive.

'A structure to fit these hard-pressed times,' was Rupert Corless's verdict.

Quite deliberately, and in our view, very properly, the Cabinet Office decreed that the precise nature of our work was to be kept secret. In any civil service, there is nothing like a hint of secrecy to arouse intense speculative interest, not to say suspicion, and SOVINT became the focus of wide attention within days of the creation of our strange, unshapely federation of talents, 'our archipelago of specialists' as Corless once described it to me.

Those of us who were seconded to SOVINT from the Intelligence Service (Corless, Colin Maitland, Adrian Gardner, Arthur Gurney and myself) found it difficult to adjust to the broadness of our role until the arrival of Peter information, when Corless successfully forced through his plan for the Peter Committee. Our definition was now much tighter: we were the guardians of this rare seam of

Soviet information, its richness and the accompanying secrecy being the cause of so much of the jealousy against Corless. In this role our group concentrated solely on Peter, its purpose being to decrypt and interpret Peter intelligence.

We were a small and disparate group, some long-standing players in the intelligence game (Maitland, Gardner, Gurney all ex-SOE and SIS), others like myself with only our wartime experience. We had what Adrian Gardner always described as our two minders, Guy Benton from the Foreign Office ('too effete to sit with foot soldiers like us,' Adrian Gardner used to say) and Gordon Boys-Allen, a serving naval officer now seconded to the Ministry of Defence, whom even the gentle Arthur Gurney dismissed as 'nice but dreadfully dim'.

An unlikely collection with an unusual purpose, yet under Rupert Corless's chairmanship, and with his dogged protection of our sphere of interest, we flourished. Painstakingly we built up a picture of tyranny, its people crushed into servility, its economy remorselessly directed towards the creation of a gigantic war machine on which the success of its political policy rested. Our central concern was the Soviets' progress on their nuclear bomb. How close were they to emulating the Americans' nuclear achievement? One year? Two? More? Any activity that speeded up the process was seen as strengthening the threat posed by the huge Soviet army which already cast its dark shadow westwards, a vast bird of prey. Slowly but inexorably we imagined it coming our way. Greece. Italy. France. Sometimes in my nightmares I heard tanks and the crunch of marching boots.

★

'The question we are faced with,' Corless tells us, 'is which of our two professors is stealing secrets for the Soviets? Professor Geoffrey Stevens, nuclear physicist and Nobel prizewinner, or Professor Edgar Lodz, theoretical physicist? Both are leading lights in our thermonuclear development programme.' Corless's gaze settles on me. 'Cambridge is your parish, Monty. What can you tell us about Stevens and Lodz?'

Unexpectedly I am the centre of attention. I am quite unprepared for this.

'The first thing that anyone connected with the university will tell you is that these two men hate each other's guts. They're bitter rivals.'

I tell the Committee what I know.

Stevens is a professor of nuclear physics whose work in the 'thirties, with a Finn called Laurentzen, earned him a Nobel Prize in the year before war broke out. In his early years in Cambridge Stevens made his reputation working with Rutherford and Kapitza at the Cavendish before setting up his own laboratory with Laurentzen, a partnership that lasted until 1938. During the war, he did not go to America to join the Los Alamos Project, though he made a number of visits to New Mexico and is well known to Oppenheimer and his colleagues there. He is generally recognized as the source of inspiration behind much of British nuclear research. He and his small team are rumoured to be working on the initial design of a 'superweapon', a thermo-nuclear device of prodigious destructive capacity to replace the atomic bomb.

'In your opinion,' Arthur Gurney asks, 'is Professor Stevens a likely candidate to betray secrets to an enemy?'

'I have known Professor Stevens for twenty years,' I reply. 'He is many things I heartily dislike, but I cannot see him giving secrets to the Russians.'

'Selling secrets?' Corless asks. 'He's got a second wife, a young family. Does he have money worries?'

Even after years in the department I am still not used to the way in which, because of the nature of the work we do, any evidence, however intimate, is grist to the intelligence mill. I shrug my shoulders and say nothing. I make a note that Corless will expect me to check Stevens's bank account.

'What about Lodz?'

I tell the Committee that I've never met Lodz. What I know of him I have gathered second-hand from Stevens and my other Cambridge connections.

'Eddie Lodz is Austrian by birth. Brought up in Vienna. Went to university in Germany, studied with Heisenberg in Göttingen, and came to England as a political refugee in the early 'thirties just before things got tough for Jews in Germany. Cambridge snapped him up because of the reputation he had already established. Married an English woman, the daughter of the master of his college. Of the two, he's reckoned to be cleverer than Stevens, but less pushy, less forceful. A kinder man, in every respect.'

'He could be a communist. Vienna was a hotbed of communist activity before the war,' Benton says.

I tell the Committee that there is no evidence whatsoever to link Eddie Lodz in any way with communism. Corless thanks me for my contribution and moves the discussion forward. Full reports on both men, including the state of their private finances, will be presented to the Committee within twenty-four hours. He has already asked Colin Maitland to get the Registry to dig out all files with any reference to either man.

'If we're in the hands of the Registry,' Adrian Gardner whispers to me, 'it will be twenty-four days before they can even spell either name correctly, twenty-four months before we get any reports. By which time all that will be left of the planet will be a huge mushroom cloud hanging in space.'

'On the face of it,' Corless sums up, 'the idea of Professors Lodz or Stevens giving nuclear secrets to the Soviets looks unlikely. But we can't ignore a message from Peter just because we may not like what he tells us.'

I am to go to Cambridge with a small specialist team and find out what I can. We are to work discreetly and thoroughly. Until I report back, Peter's allegation is to be kept strictly within the Committee: it is not to be released to anyone, not even to SOVINT.

'No formal action on Peter's allegation is to be taken until we can confirm the charge.' Corless reminds us that inaction, even if temporary, may be the best way of preserving Peter. For the present, we are to work entirely on our own on this one.

'What about the minutes?' Gurney asks as we push our chairs back into place. 'We have a wide circulation list. Eyes only, of course, but many recipients. What do I do?'

This is serious stuff. We are stopped in our tracks. Gurney looks haunted with anxiety. What *is* to happen to the minutes?

'Bugger the minutes,' Gardner says, and for once the feeling of the room is with him. 'They can wait. Peter's more important.'

Gurney looks very unhappy. 'It's very irregular,' he says. 'I don't think our masters will be happy about this.'

'Stuff our masters,' Maitland says, seizing his chance for ascendancy. 'Lose them for a few days, Arthur. No one will notice.'

'Who reads them anyway?' Gardner whispers to me, with a wink.

Corless nods his agreement. Not a single word about what we are doing is to leak out. Gurney is to sit on the minutes until he receives further instructions.

'Your decision, Rupert, of course,' Gurney says. It is as close as he will ever come publicly to dissent.

★

We spent two weeks in an icy, mist-ridden Cambridge and found no evidence that Stevens had met any known members of the Communist Party, let alone strangely accented men in ill-cut suits; nor that he had corresponded with scientists in Moscow or indeed anywhere else in the Soviet Union, or had any contact with anyone remotely connected with Russia or the Russians. Indeed, no meeting of any kind had taken place that could not be completely and promptly explained as part of Stevens's academic duties or his activities as a scientific adviser to the Government. The truth, however uncomfortable, was inescapable. Professor Stevens was clean.

By the time I got back to London a new message had come through from Peter. This time he named Stevens as the traitor.

5

DANNY

'Danny! Danny!'

I was hardly out of the taxi before Celia had thrown herself into my arms.

'We thought you'd be here on Christmas Eve. The children were so looking forward to it. Come along and bring your things. Everything's ready for you. Your room's made up. I even saved some Christmas pudding.'

My stepmother was much younger than my father. She had been one of his students at a time when the relationship between my parents had hit one of its coldest patches, and I suppose my father had found Celia's warmth impossible to resist. To this day I am sure he engineered the discovery that he had a mistress. He wanted, if nothing else, to surprise my mother, to show her she had misjudged him. In my darker moments, I think he rather enjoyed showing her he had power over women, or one woman at least, and an attractive, young one at that.

There was no explosion after the revelation that my father had been unfaithful, only a deeper and more wounded silence in the house. From the little I saw, there was no attempt at reconciliation, only a slow and painful settling of accounts and then my mother left. She had always hated Cambridge and now there was nothing to keep her. Much later there was a divorce, rather messy as they were in those days, but my father rode the storm and settled into a new life with this woman half his age.

Celia was clearly happy with him. She produced three children in quick succession but cleverly found time, when my father was home, to devote herself to him. She was an uncomplicated woman; my father knew he was the centre of her life and in his own way he loved her for it.

'Geoffrey's in the study.'

In my presence she always referred to my father as Geoffrey. 'Go and say hello. I'm saving the children for later. That's your penance for not seeing them open their stockings.'

'How is he?'

For a moment she hesitated, a look of anxiety suddenly clouding her naturally open expression. If she wanted to tell me something, she changed her mind abruptly.

'He's working too hard but there's nothing surprising in that. Go on in. He's expecting you.'

My father's study was a large, untidy room at the back of the house overlooking fields that marked the outskirts of Cambridge. The relics of a long academic career were scattered like trophies everywhere, books, papers, journals, files, proofs in bundles, covering shelves, chairs, even now invading the carpet. There never had been room to sit. Now you could hardly stand. The disorder in which he lived was in reverse measure to the order of his mind.

I found him as I had left him over a year before, glasses halfway down his nose, working on some papers spread out on an illuminated lectern.

'Daniel. At last. How are you?'

'Hello, Father.'

We shook hands. I knew there would be no mention of my year's absence. To hear my father you would think he had seen me only a week before. In his mind, it probably felt like that.

'Celia was worried. She thought you were lost. I said people in the army don't get lost, they only get mislaid.'

'Then you don't know much about the army.'

'Come and sit down.' He cleared a space for me on the sofa, piling papers and books on the floor. 'Every year I promise myself I'm going to have a spring-clean, make the place habitable, but I never get round to it. Either that or I've got no sense of time. Are you with us for long?'

'A couple of weeks' leave, then back to Berlin.'

'I don't envy you that.'

'I'll give it all up one day soon,' I said without thinking.

'Does that mean you've made up your mind to come back?'

I hadn't expected our quarrel to surface quite so soon, and my defence was unprepared.

'It means I'll leave the army some day.'

'You know my thoughts on that,' my father said. 'You're wasting your life. It's time to get out now.'

The last time we had been in this room together we had argued bitterly and both said things we regretted. I had told my father that I had passed up an opportunity to leave the army, and the sudden virulence of his attack on my decision forced me into a stubborn defence, a refusal to accept any part of his argument. My pig-headedness, as he called it, only helped to redouble his anger. The memory of that unhappy evening was one of the reasons I had stayed away from Cambridge for almost a year. The last thing I wanted was to stir it all up again.

'For the moment it suits me,' I said, more out of weariness than defiance. 'There's nothing else I want to do.'

'Other men are out of uniform. Why not you? The war's over.'

The last time he had said that, his voice had been shrill and the points of his cheeks red with anger. There was no hint of that now, only that familiar coldness that told me his anger had cooled to indifference.

'It doesn't always seem like that in Berlin.'

'That's a poor apology for inaction. Berlin is not a microcosm of the rest of the world. I thank God I can see more clearly than that.'

'We may have defeated one enemy but there's another in his place now. Someone has to guard the gate.'

The thought was not mine but my American companion's. I was surprised at how easily I had accepted his analysis of what was happening.

'The Russians aren't the enemy some people would have us believe. They're weak, economically in chaos, they can't build a war machine without starving their people, and the Russian man in the street has got too much sense to stand for that. Their leaders want us to believe the opposite and their propaganda is very successful. We mustn't allow ourselves to fall for it.'

That was as close as he could get to saying that I was a victim of their propaganda and he was shocked that a son of his could be taken in so easily. I remembered the speed with which we had seen the Russians set up their own puppet administration in the Eastern Zone of Berlin in defiance of the Allied agreement. It had all the hallmarks of a carefully planned operation by a well-prepared appar-atus, and its accomplishment had left us breathless. It was an illegal act under the treaty, and the Russians had calculated that there was little we could do about it. They'd been right. We'd let them get away with it.

'It looks different when you're living next door to them.' I hadn't the energy to put it more strongly than that.

'Leave Berlin, Danny. You've done enough. Come back where you belong. There's unfinished business.'

I had completed my second year at Cambridge when the war broke out and I had joined up at once. My father had opposed me then and he was still, years later, unreconciled to my view that the war had made a return to undergraduate life impossible.

I wanted to tell him that I was never coming back but somehow I couldn't. I hadn't the heart or I hadn't the courage, and I suspect he knew it.

'I'll think about it,' I said, and to my surprise he dropped the subject. A year ago he would not have done that. Was this real evidence of a change in him? Or had he softened in the time I'd been away?

'It's good to see you again,' he said with uncharacteristic warmth.

My father and I never found it easy to spend much time in each other's company. We never developed any intimacy in our relationship. One of the strange legacies of the war was that we had been forced to spend so long apart that in our minds our relationship had grown closer than it really was.

'I will always be thankful that you were spared when so many others were not. Go and say hello to the children. I'll join you when I've finished.'

I played with the children after their bath and wondered how these small individuals could be related to me. They saw me as I saw myself, more as their father than their brother. But their bright faces and their laughter touched me, as Celia knew they would, which is why she left us alone.

We had dinner soon after Celia had put them to bed. My father was full of university gossip: who was going for preferment where and how mistaken they were to imagine they might get it ('Overestimating one's worth has become a new sport here. No doubt they'll award a blue for it soon'); who had written what and what dreadful rubbish it was ('God knows who'll read it'); and how publishers were good for nothing ('the idlest profession in the world'). Twice Celia asked me about my life in Germany but both times my father steered her away from the subject. I couldn't tell if it was deliberate or not.

53

Celia left us alone after dinner and we returned to my father's study with a bottle of whisky.

'Cambridge hasn't changed by the sound of it,' I said. 'Still the same old place.'

'I only wish that were true.' The bitterness in his reply was unexpected. 'I thought the war might expand horizons, bring some breadth of vision to us. Wishful thinking. We're more trivial than ever. More inward-looking. More conscious of ourselves and jealous of each other. The world might as well be in darkness for all the notice we take of what happens outside the gates of this fenland refuge.'

'Can you blame people for escaping here? Cambridge is as good a place to hide as any.'

'Oh, I blame them,' he said with surprising venom. 'I blame them all right.'

Then he stopped. Whatever he had wanted to say, he had changed his mind. Since our last meeting something must have happened to allow doubts to surface. Doubts about what I didn't know; he had covered up too quickly to allow me more than a moment's glimpse. But though he was now doing his best to conceal his concerns from me, the moment was too strong to ignore. My father was in the grip of a deep anxiety.

'Who wants to hear the miserable litany of an old don in his declining years? No one, thank God.' He pulled down the blackout on himself and switched his attention to me. 'Tell me about Berlin.'

He questioned me intently on the work I was doing, when I thought the civilian administration might begin to take over, did I think the good Germans could make democracy stick? I cannot say that my father opened his heart to me that night because he didn't. But we talked with an openness I hadn't experienced before, and we avoided the treacherous subject of our relationship with each other.

'It's getting late. You've had a long day.' My father got to his feet. He was bringing the conversation to an end, not because he was tired but because he was afraid of where it might lead.

'What's all this? What are you working on?'

I was standing by his desk. There were newspaper cuttings on the lectern I had not noticed before.

'Ah, that.'

My father betrayed all the signs of a schoolboy caught smoking behind the bicycle sheds.

'That is what Celia calls my fall from grace.'

I look a cutting from the lectern. I saw his name under the title of an article.

'Good God.' I was genuinely surprised. 'You never told me you were writing for the papers.'

'My weekly sermon to the masses.'

'This paper doesn't reach the masses.'

'To a professor of physics, being read by more than five people is reaching the masses. Being understood by more than five people is more than one can hope for in a lifetime.'

'What made you do this?'

'Why does anyone do what he affects to despise? It pays well and my colleagues hate it. What further justification should one look for?'

'What do you do in these pieces?'

'What I've always done, only now I do it in the public prints as well. Expound. Disturb. Provoke and generally pontificate. A thousand words each week on a topical issue. Political. Social. Economic. Even moral, if I choose it. I am told I am quite successful. There's talk of extending my contract.'

He looked at me, an image of impish delight. 'What gives me most pleasure is the jealousy my journalistic exploits arouse among my colleagues. Two nights ago in hall, the senior tutor leaned towards me before grace and muttered: "How could you stoop so low?"'

'How did you answer that?'

'I said if the University paid better, then professors with young and expensive wives wouldn't have to prostitute themselves to make ends meet.' He laughed at his own remark. 'You're wondering how this began, aren't you? Quite by accident. I did a broadcast for a colleague who was ill and the editor of this rag heard it and rang me up. I was all for turning down the proposal but Celia wouldn't have it. That woman is ruining my life.'

'May I see what you've written?'

'Good heavens, no. You've got far better things to do with your time.'

'I'd like to.'

'Take them to bed with you then. With luck you'll fall asleep before you've read a single word.'

He gave me a folder full of cuttings.

'They edit me. They cut bits out. They rewrite sentences. I find it very unsettling. I've not been edited since I was an undergraduate. What's worse, they do it rather well.'

★

I did not sleep much that night. I read what my father had written not once but again and again. As I did so, I began to sense the cause of his anxiety. There was a struggle going on within him, a conflict between the beliefs that had made him a pioneer in nuclear research and something new, a moral position he had reached, I presumed, in the year since we had last met. What had led him to this point I had no idea. If I had never really known my father before, now I knew him even less.

The West had exploded a nuclear device, his argument went, and the world knew that the Russians were racing to build a similar or better weapon. There was talk now of a 'superweapon', whose destructive powers were many times greater than those of any atomic device. The dangers the world faced if either side were to explode such a device were too grim to contemplate. We had within our power the ability not only to wreak havoc upon our enemies but upon ourselves as well. We could blow up the world through a never-ending chain reaction, cause the end of civilization, create a poisonous desert after a thermonuclear storm in which life in any form would be unsustainable. The earth would be a poisoned grave-yard, hurtling pointlessly through time. Was this to be the legacy of the war to end all wars?

We had harsh choices to make, made harder by the debts we owed to the New World. But choices, however difficult, had to be made if the possibility of a lasting peace, a world for ever freed of conflict, was not to slip out of our grasp. That, surely, was what the sacrifice of the war years had been for.

Throughout all the articles I sensed a pessimism I had not encountered before. This was not the rhetoric of the politician, seeking to persuade. It was the desolate cry of the parent who sees his child running headlong into the path of an oncoming car.

6

RUTH

'Is Valery home?'

Her mother nods. She goes into Valery's room. He is sitting on the bed facing the wall. His school books are open on his table. For a moment she thinks he is crying, but she dismisses the thought. He has not cried for years.

'Valery?'

He says nothing and does not turn to face her.

'What is it? What's happened?'

She sits on the edge of the bed and puts her hand on his shoulder. He does not respond to her touch. It is as if she were not there. Suddenly, she is terrified.

'Valery.'

She pulls him roughly so he has to turn towards her. His face is pale and drawn and his cheeks are wet with tears. He looks at her as if he had never seen her before and says nothing.

'I cannot help you unless you tell me what's happened.'

She holds his stiff body against hers. She wants to cry but there are no tears.

'Tell me,' she says.

He points to the ceiling. 'How do I know they are not listening?'

'We are not important enough for that.'

She doesn't believe it herself but her son is satisfied. He dries his eyes on his sleeve and talks in whispers.

'These men came to see me at school today. They asked me questions.'

They stand in the opened door of his classroom looking in, these two men. Andropov's men. How she hates the power he has to terrify her into submission.

Which one? the teacher's expression asks. Which innocent victim do I deliver today? He can offer no resistance on behalf of his pupils because his will was broken years before in a camp a thousand miles away. They look around the room and point at Valery Marchenko.

A chalk-stained finger beckons him. His heart beating faster with every step, he walks through the ranks of his classmates. There is not a movement, not a murmur: all he can hear is the sound of his own boots on the wooden floor. He submits without resistance to the guardianship of the two strangers.

They walk him down the corridor, one of them holding his arm in case he should try to escape, until they find an empty room. They push him roughly inside, close the door, sit him down in a chair facing them and the questioning begins.

They ask him about his mother because they are using him to frighten her.

When does she leave the apartment in the morning?

When does she return?

What does she talk about?

Who are her friends?

They will have sown ideas in his head, she is sure, because that is how they do these things. The few certainties in his life will have crumbled in their presence. He is too young and they are too skilful and too brutal for him to find any escape.

She sees the depth of her son's confusion. He is terrified, unsure, he has no idea what is happening nor why they are questioning him. She feels the anger well within her, the familiar controls on her emotions threatening to burst under the strain of her fury. How can we live like this? How can we submit our children to interrogation so they are turned against their parents?

Then the mechanics of years of self-discipline move into place. Accept, she reminds herself. Slip away into the shadows. Live where you cannot be noticed, out of sight, on the margin. Where you've always lived.

But she cannot avoid the grief in her son's eyes nor the coldness of his skin against hers. Anger sits in her heart.

'What else did they ask you?'

'Were you a member of the Communist Party?'

'What did you tell them?'

'I said no.'

'You were right.'

'They said my father betrayed the state.'

'They were trying to frighten you.'

'They said the son of a traitor is a traitor himself.'

'Then they are lying.'

'How do I know?'

That was why he had cried. It was a familiar betrayal, lies as evidence to threaten the bond between mother and son. How can she prove her love for her son except by the life she lives? By the touch of her hand, by a kiss on his sleeping cheek, or by her anxieties, her evasions, all the sacrifices she has made and must make to protect him? How can she tell him this? The state knows she can't, which is why they dress their lies in the clear lines of truth, why they present their case to the defenceless child, why they must destroy the one relationship that can still threaten their dominance.

What can she say to him? How can she tell her own child that his ordeal is to remind her that powerful forces still control her existence? She resists the temptation to say anything.

'How do I know?'

That is his question. How can he be sure of anything any more in a world where the few certainties of his young life have been suddenly and brutally challenged?

There is only one honest way to answer his question. She must initiate her son into the double life, describing the secret territory of the heart which lies untouched in a country where emotions, loyalties, even love are dictated by an external authority, not by the truth you feel.

'They will tempt you with their certainties,' she tells her son. 'Their truths will have the appearance of the hardest rock, the toughest steel. They will build their positions out of the impeccable logic of their Marxist-Leninist arguments, which they don't understand – they can only repeat what they have been told to say, the ideology that has outlawed doubt, where every piece fits tightly with its neighbour.'

She sees his white face, the deep, black shadows under his eyes, she sees him growing older before her. She has always known that one day this moment would come when she would have to tell him the truth.

'You cannot fight that,' she says, 'not one person against this edifice of power. Nor should you try. But quietly and secretly within yourself, you must resist it. You must learn, too, how to be patient.'

'Does that mean there are two truths?' he asks.

'No,' she says, 'there is only one truth. But sometimes, often, that truth must be hidden. You must learn to distinguish between the apparent and the real.'

'Then we live with lies,' he says.

'Yes,' she says. 'We live with lies because we accept as truth what we know cannot be true. We betray ourselves with each lie we tell, but knowing that doesn't stop us doing it, day after day.'

'Why do we have to live like that?'

'That is how we survive.'

Tell him the truth, a voice screams within her. Tell him everything you know, everything you have wanted to tell him for years. Surely he is old enough now? Surely he has a right to know? Tell him.

But she can't. She hasn't the strength. She cannot bring herself to tell him what she so desperately wants him to know.

'Why are we made to live like that?' he asks her.

'If I knew the answer to that I would tell you,' she says. 'How can a belief in social justice, in the equality of men, how can all that is good in theory become so perverted in reality? The doctrines which govern our lives ignore that men are weak, that power corrupts. Soviet man has banished weakness, ideology transforms his nature. That is what we are taught. Never that men will always seek power, that they will adopt whatever philosophy they must to achieve power over others. It is the truth we are afraid to acknowledge.'

'Is it hard to live like that?' he asks quietly.

'The double life is a struggle that never ends. It will not prevent you from making compromises, some of which, many of which, perhaps, you will be ashamed of. But it will allow you to live, it will teach you an inner patience while you wait for better days. Always hope, even in moments of greatest despair – especially then. Always believe there can be another kind of life and that one day it will come.'

(Is that what she did? Were there not moments of despair when, in the safety of her imagination, she flew to the side of her secret lover for his protection?)

'Look at this,' he says, showing her an exercise book lying open on the bed.

She sees his familiar blue script, she recognizes the biology from her own youth, she reads what he has written and then the remarks scrawled at the bottom of the page. She knows then that her son was not afraid of the bullies who asked him questions, they did not make him cry. What has broken his heart is the judgement he has received in the classroom.

Misguided and wrong, she reads. *The dictates of Marxist-Leninism disprove your argument. Poor work.*

'The central theory of molecular biology,' he tells her, 'is that genetic information flows from nucleic acid towards protein. If we believe that acquired characteristics can be inherited, then genetic information must flow from protein to nucleic acid. That is not scientifically possible. Yet that is what I am told to believe. How can I?'

How like his father he is, she thinks, in his defence of his own certainties. How dangerous this trait will be. The boy is a good scientist; at times she thinks he could be more than that. He understands instinctively ideas that she has had to learn. He is being asked to believe in a dogma that he knows cannot be true. What can she tell him?

'Madness rages through our lives like a forest fire,' she says. We all turn towards the heat, we warm our hands and our bodies, we see the flames reflected in the eyes of our neighbours. This is the answer, we say. This is how we will stay warm.

'But soon the fire moves on, the ashes grow cold, we shiver, and because we have known great warmth we are now colder than ever. Then we will turn on each other and say, why did you betray us, why did you pretend this was the truth? Why did you not tell us that the fire would move on?

'That is how it is with us now. This political theory we live with is a forest fire that rages and burns, consuming many in its path, but one day it will burn out, leaving a trail of damage and despair, ruin and decay, nothing on which we may build our lives. The question is: how do we survive between now and then? Some bend, some come out fighting. I cannot tell you what you must do. You are old enough to make your own decisions. But never despise those who did not choose your path. We each fight our own battles in our own way.'

She sees the sadness in his eyes. The innocence of his childhood is gone. He realizes, she knows now, that this is how she has spent her life. He is wondering how many sacrifices she has made. What truths she has concealed from him, and why. He must now have an instinctive sense of what she has had to do for him and for his grandmother.

She holds him in her arms, the last time she will ever embrace him as a child. When they leave this room, their relationship will be changed for ever.

'Mother,' he says to her softly, holding her tight. 'Mother, mother.'

To her those words sound like a farewell. She wants to cry again but still no tears come. They cling to each in desperation as he, for the last time in his life, draws his strength from her.

7

DANNY

'Something's wrong, isn't it?'

I cornered Celia in the kitchen the following day as soon as my father had left the house. I'd got the impression that even in the twenty-four hours since my arrival, she had been trying to avoid me because she was reluctant to answer the question she knew I was going to ask.

'Wrong?'

She took the steaming kettle off the stove and sat down at the kitchen table.

'Something's happened since I was last in Cambridge and you don't want to tell me about it.'

She poured water into the teapot and looked thoughtful.

'Geoffrey begged me not to say anything,' she said reluctantly. 'I knew it wouldn't work. You were bound to hear it sooner or later. I had hoped it wouldn't be from me.'

I said nothing. Celia poured tea for us both.

'Promise you won't say I told you?'

'I won't breathe a word.'

'It's Philip Ridout,' she said. 'He's dying.'

'What of?'

'Cancer.'

Ridout was my father's assistant. He had come up in my second year, had got a double first in physics and had been working with my father ever since. 'Best pupil I ever had,' my father had told me once. 'Brilliant mind. Quite outstanding.'

'He's in Addenbrooke's.' Celia's eyes filled with tears. 'It's so awful, Danny. The doctors say there's nothing they can do. That poor boy. Only twenty-four.'

I had never liked Philip Ridout. He was a shy, unprepossessing man, but highly intelligent, whose one interest in life appeared to be theor-

63

etical physics. My father had taken to him at once and as soon as his degree was completed had made him his assistant, his relationship with Laurentzen having ended. A year later, my father had brought his assistant into the house and had set us up as rivals for his affections. I didn't like it but I could accept it because I was used to my father's ways and I had learned to live without his affection and approbation years before. (Ridout, I'm sure, was oblivious to my father's manipulations.) It was when he intimated that Ridout was the son he had always hoped I would become that I drew the line. This, as much as anything, had underlined my quarrel with my father a year before. Ridout was the innocent victim of a situation he was unaware of, but even so I couldn't bring myself to feel any affection for him, either then or now.

'How's Geoffrey taken it?'

'All the time Philip gets thinner and thinner and more and more ill and Geoffrey refuses to accept what's happening. He keeps talking about when Philip recovers and can get back to the laboratory.'

That didn't surprise me. My father had always ignored any obstacles in his path, an attitude that applied as much to people as it did to problems. While it had brought him distinction in science, it had led to poverty in human relationships.

'I'm sorry,' I said. It seemed a feeble response to the awful news, particularly as I knew how fond Celia had become of Ridout over the many months he had lived in the house.

There had been an accident in the lab, she said. Philip was burned, not badly, but they kept him in hospital for a couple of days. A few weeks later he began to complain of stomach pains and wouldn't eat. That's when they diagnosed cancer.

'He's young, so it's galloping through him. The doctors are saying he's only got a matter of weeks.'

I asked her if the cancer and the accident were related. Celia wasn't sure. 'But how does a perfectly healthy young man develop such a raging cancer so quickly?'

'Do you know anything about the accident?'

'I heard that Philip was doing an experiment with plutonium and it went wrong. Geoffrey refuses to talk about it. I'm convinced Philip was irradiated, though Geoffrey's adamant he wasn't and Philip won't take the accident seriously. I think they're both concealing the truth from me.'

Celia appeared more distressed than I expected. I could only imagine it was because there were other things she hadn't told me.

'This isn't just about Philip, is it?'

I could see the conflict between her loyalty to my father and the attraction of a sympathetic listener. She came down in my favour.

'Philip's illness has changed Geoffrey. He talks less, he's restless, more prone to anxiety, as if some kind of conflict was going on inside him. Have you noticed it? I've tried to get him to talk about it but if I bring up the subject he pushes me away. I can't let it go on like this, I've got to do something but I don't know what. Will you help me, Danny?'

I saw that for the first time, Celia did not know how to deal with my father. I wanted to help her but I had no more idea what to do than she did.

★

That evening, I walked with my father along Trinity Street to the Union. He had been invited to speak to one of the University's political societies. We were expected at seven-thirty. I could hear Great St Mary's chiming the half-hour as we entered the building. My father's respect for punctuality had not diminished.

'Good evening, sir. This way, please.'

We were led to a room behind the debating chamber. It was already full of undergraduates. A thin young man with lank, fair hair came forward to meet us.

'Professor Stevens? How good of you to come.'

My father was introduced to a tall, stooping man in his early forties. At first glance there was nothing memorable about him but a few moments in his presence brought an undeniable if grudging respect. If there was little that was obviously likeable about Watson-Jones, there was no doubting the sense of power that clung to him. Where it came from I never knew but it was part of the man, and whatever his political fortunes it never deserted him.

'We've not met. My name's Simon Watson-Jones. I see we're in opposite camps tonight.'

They shook hands. The fair-haired young man looked at his watch and asked if they would accompany him to the platform.

'Ladies and gentlemen. If I may call you to order.' The room fell silent as people took their seats. 'It's my great pleasure to welcome our speakers tonight, Professor Stevens of this University, nuclear physicist and Nobel prizewinner, and Simon Watson-Jones, alumnus of Peterhouse, barrister-at-law and member of His Majesty's loyal opposition.'

The topic to be discussed was, he knew, close to the heart of the

Society. Was a Future Without War a Dream or a Reality? The Society had invited a prominent physicist and politician to put their views. The politician had elected to speak first.

Watson-Jones got to his feet, withdrew his papers from his pocket and faced his audience.

Only in his dreams, he said, could he see a future without war or the threat of war. Society survives not on dreams but on the acceptance of the world as it really is. In 1939, when political activity had failed, war was inevitable. Were we wrong to fight Hitler? To defend our morality, our institutions, our way of life forged over centuries of our proud history? Of course not. Would we decline to fight if these selfsame institutions and values were threatened again? Of course we wouldn't.

He was not advocating war – he abhorred its horrors and its suffering as much as the next man – but he was a realist who accepted that the defence of right called for vigilance and, sometimes, for sacrifice. That call would never go away.

Democracy had triumphed in 1945. Now we faced a threat that challenged the new society we were trying to build out of the ashes of the old. If we had freed ourselves once from the dictator, we must always be prepared to defend our freedom with our lives.

Was it credible that in the Soviet Union human nature would be perfected by the dogmas of Marxist-Leninism, that social justice would reign for ever more, that all men would live in harmony? Or were such propositions lies and propaganda? Wasn't it more likely that the socialist experiment in Russia was cover for an arrogant adventurism that wanted to impose its own anti-human society in as many countries of the world as it could?

He would leave the audience to make up its own mind but he knew where he stood on the issue. Faced with this threat of communism, a system that must take advantage of any weakness in its opponents, could we truly allow ourselves to renounce war? Could we put at risk by such a quixotic gesture our hard-won freedoms? Did we honour those who had sacrificed their lives by saying that their experience was so terrible that it must never be repeated?

'They died in defence of freedom. We must always be prepared to do the same. If that means developing our own nuclear weapons, and in my view it does, then so be it. Such is the price of peace, and I for my part am prepared to pay it.'

He sat down to rapturous applause from a section of his audience.

Others, I noticed, were more restrained in their appreciation of what he had said.

I had not asked what my father was going to say, nor had he told me. I was struck by his caution, both in content and delivery, as if he was testing his audience, learning his new role of social commentator by a set of careful steps. He warned that we should not see the Soviet Union as inevitably hostile, despite its Marxist ideology and its political posturings.

'We must not forget,' he said, 'that the Soviet Union too has been devastated by war. Their economy is shattered, their people exhausted. The production of nuclear weapons demands not simply a high level of scientific skills, which they possess, but also advanced industrial techniques and resources. There is no evidence to suggest that these exist in that country. For these reasons alone, and there are many others, we must not allow ourselves to see the Soviet Union as our inevitable enemy. We have fought one enemy for more than five years. We must have the courage now not to replace him with another, but to try to create a new era without enemies, a time when we can use the great scientific advances of the last few years to provide a better life for all of us. That is the greatest task that faces us. We must use our experience of the last five years to free our society from the stultifying shackles of war.'

When he finished, there was a round of applause. My father and Watson-Jones agreed to take questions.

Was it not the declared ambition of the Soviet Union to establish communism and eliminate capitalism?

Yes, but one should not confuse the rhetoric of the ideologue with the practical necessities of running a modern state. In other words, we shouldn't always believe everything the Soviets said. Soviet policy need not be driven by Soviet ideology.

The question persisted in other forms and it was easy to see where the mind of the audience lay. Wasn't the Soviet state's basic philosophical position one of enmity to Western systems? Wasn't it prudent to work on worst-case scenarios, Russia as the new enemy, rather than find ourselves surprised as we had been in the 'thirties?

Yes, our experiences before the war had taught us always to be vigilant, but we must not fall prey to the enemy's propaganda. That, after all, is what he wanted us to do. Scepticism was as necessary a quality in a democracy as preparedness.

Wasn't the present expansion of communism throughout Eastern

Europe, possibly into Italy and France, even the spread of sympathizers, fellow-travellers, within the United Kingdom, a threat in itself? My father saw it more as a test of the West's democratic institutions, which he believed were strong enough to resist such a threat.

How secure was his forecast that it would be five years before the Russians exploded a nuclear device?

Oh, very secure. The Soviets were miles behind the West. Five years was probably an optimistic assessment of when they might explode their bomb.

'Time for one last question,' the fair-haired man said.

I saw a hand come up at the back of the room. A young woman stood up.

'Professor Stevens, do you not feel guilty at the potential for destruction that you and your colleagues have unleashed upon the world? Have you not made the world a much more dangerous place, where nuclear war is inevitable?'

The room went still. Up to now the questions had been impersonal. This was different. Watson-Jones looked at my father. For the first time my father's fluency appeared to stumble. He hesitated before answering, then said slowly, 'No, I see no reason to feel guilty. Nor do I believe that the discovery and manufacture of nuclear arms necessarily makes the world a more dangerous place. Nor do I believe in the inevitability of anything, nuclear conflict included. Science must progress, that is the scientist's duty. We cannot look down one particular avenue, like that of nuclear physics, and say oh dear, that route might lead to unknown dangers so we had better ignore it and pass by. Such a course of action is irresponsible and cowardly. The scientist is an explorer. His task is to map ground never trodden before. Until he has been down a particular path, he will not know what he might find. No paths can be closed to him. I believe that the modern state must respond with appropriate political mechanisms for the control of these discoveries because in some cases, yes, there are dangers. The idea of a nuclear war is abhorrent. But we cannot banish the possibility of conflict by placing a moral block on scientific progress. What we need is growth in the philosophy and practice of contemporary political systems to allow us to control our lives in a proper and responsible manner, giving more strength to the institutions we believe in.'

There was a moment's silence, followed by a riple of lukewarm applause.

8

RUTH

She is walking in birchwoods with Yuri Miskin, one of the two assistant deputy directors at the Institute. Yuri has suggested they meet. There is nothing unusual in this. They have been colleagues, friends and occasional lovers for more than five years.

Miskin is a shy man with a permanent look of surprised innocence behind his glasses. She fears for him because he appears ill-equipped to deal with the world of which he finds himself so important a part. But he has survived because he is a good scientist (his theoretical work is of a very high order) and he will survive, she tells herself, because his contribution is essential to the success of their research programme. If Ruth could bring herself to trust anyone, it would be Miskin. But however close they might be, they have never truly opened their hearts to each other. That is an intimacy more dangerous than any other.

As they walk through the trees, the remains of twigs, stiff with frost, crack beneath their feet. In the distance, the pale sun struggles to burn through an icy mist. It is very quiet. They are quite alone here, which is why they come to this particular spot. Sometimes, in the summer, they have swum in the river and once made love on the river bank. It was not an experience she enjoyed.

Miskin smiles and puts his arm around her as they emerge from the trees and walk towards the river. Ice is forming at the point where the water meets the land; crystalline slivers, thin and delicate. There is no wind; the surface of the water is undisturbed even by the slow movements of the current. Through the breaks in the mist the sky above them is an arch of the palest blue. Nothing moves. The air is cold.

She has often wondered about her relationship with Miskin. He is neither a good nor a demanding lover, but she feels a sympathy towards him, and yields herself out of a need for companionship more than desire. Her own satisfaction when he makes love to her is small. He leaves her untouched, but sleeping with him is a small price to pay for his continued friendship.

He has not said anything for some time. She is used to his silences. He is a victim of depression, bouts of melancholia that strike with regularity. Now is not the time in his cycle for such an attack, nor has he exhibited any of the familiar signs that he is beginning that slide away from rationality into the dark quarters of his mind where she cannot follow him. He has displayed no dramatic changes of mood recently, he has had no migraines, nor has he shown any sudden feelings of elation. But she senses that he is struggling with some deep anxiety, and she is afraid this may trigger a new attack. She says nothing to break the silence. If their relationship is to survive (it is too precious to her to imagine it *not* surviving, for reasons she suspects Miskin does not understand), then she must obey the protocols they have established. Each has the right to his or her own silence. But he asks suddenly:

'When do allies become enemies?'

'Yuri?'

She hates it when Miskin talks about politics, it always makes her feel unsafe. Politics strains the bargain she has made with herself. What she cannot control or influence in her life she ignores. Miskin would be shocked if he knew.

'When they believe the little they know about each other.' He looks pleased with the solution to his conundrum. 'A few months ago Russia and the West were allies. Together we defeated our common enemy, Nazi Germany. Now our leaders tell us that the West is our enemy. Don't you ever ask yourself what has brought about this extraordinary reversal?'

How can she tell Miskin that she worries about what she can do to relieve the pain her mother suffers, about the progress of her son at school or whether or not she should tell him the greatest secret of her life?

'The danger in this new world order,' he says, 'is that both of us, the Soviet Union and the West, are riding blindfold towards a catastrophe.'

His pessimism is something she has learned to live with, knowing it has its roots in his depression.

'Let us conduct an examination of the patients and see if we can diagnose their malaise.'

This is Miskin as the academic he should have become but didn't. There is nothing he likes better than the rigour of an intellectual autopsy.

'What do we know about the West? Only what our leaders want us to know, and we have no means of challenging what they tell us. We are a nation in quarantine, cut off from any contact with the rest of the world. This, of course, is for our own good.' He smiles to himself at that. 'The West, we understand, is massing troops on our borders throughout Europe and in the East, preparing to use their nuclear bombs against us because communism is the enemy of capitalism and must be destroyed. The West is our enemy. Obediently, we hate the West.

'What does the West know of us? Only what we want them to know. They see our huge armies threatening their borders throughout Europe and to the East, preparing for the last great struggle, the outcome of which is beyond doubt, the ultimate victory of world communism. The Soviet Republic is the enemy of the West.'

He turns towards her, a smile lighting up his face. 'Tell me,' he says. 'Where is the difference?'

She is not sure she has followed his argument. She waits for him to continue.

'If Marxism had not outlawed the practice of scepticism, we would ask ourselves: Can the great Soviet Republic and the capitalist West really be the mirror image of each other? Surely such a coincidence is unlikely? We would ask questions of each other, demand more information of our leaders; we would test, even challenge the conclusions we are fed. But we are no longer a sceptical society, we have lost the habit of asking questions because we have no mechanism through which to ask them. We have lost the ability to speak out. We have become a sullen, silent and unquestioning people. That is where the danger lies.'

He takes out a cigarette and lights it, drawing heavily on it before he speaks again.

'And what does the state do? Having set the hare running, it must give chase. We respond to the dangers we have created. That is why the Red Army has so many men under arms, why we push out our borders: Poland, the Baltic, perhaps Czechoslovakia, Yugoslavia, possibly even Germany, Greece, who knows where it will end? France, Italy, Britain? Why you and I and others like us devote our lives to the creation of this mighty weapon of destruction. We are

71

not acting belligerently, we are told, but in self-defence: we must protect ourselves because our nation is threatened by the warmongers in the West. The justification of our political strategy lies in the potent image of our powerful enemy.

'There is a paradox at work here, but who is aware of it? The more we work to protect ourselves against this new enemy, the more we are in danger of provoking a similar reaction from the West. Why should they not protect themselves against the warmongering Soviets?'

Now she understands where this conversation is leading. Conversation? It is a monologue, and one that she wishes he would end. Nervously she looks round to see that they are still quite alone.

'Neither image is true, yet both are believed. How can that be? Neither side has sources of intelligence to challenge these images on which we base our political and military strategies. We only believe of each other what we are told. We are the victims of each other's propaganda. What we refuse to face is the unpalatable truth that we may already be on the road to a needless and unnecessary war.'

'Yuri, please, no more.'

She does not want him to go on talking like this. She has enough on her mind without worrying about his safety too. But he is unstoppable now, he cannot hear her objections.

'Our leaders know the truths all tyrants know,' he says. 'Control information and you control the world. Starve the people of truth and in their hunger they will accept lies. Our leaders feed us the images of their own propaganda which have little to do with any objective reality. Often, they are demonstrably untrue. Yet we accept what we are told, we obey blindly because our leaders must be right. Out of ignorance, we have become a nation of slaves.'

As they walk beside the river, the only sound is that of their boots crunching on the frosted grass.

'We are being led into a war against an enemy who may not exist. We will both have in our hands weapons of ultimate destruction. We may go to war without reason and in the process destroy the world. You and I are helping to create the means of that destruction. That is a terrifying responsibility. That is what frightens me.'

★

They are standing on the river bank. She puts the toe of her boot in the water and breaks off the ice which she kicks away. She watches the water flow into the gap and slowly congeal.

'What can you see?' Miskin asks.

He is looking across the river at the snow-covered meadow on the other side.

'Nothing except ice and snow,' she says.

'The dead land of winter.' He digs his heel into the frozen earth to no effect. 'Yet we are surrounded by living organisms; so many different kinds of life lie sleeping beneath the frozen earth and under the icy surface of the river, behind the bark of the birch trees. The question we must ask ourselves is: What if this sleeping world did not wake up?'

'Of course it will wake up,' she says.

'What if it were to die in its sleep? No spring. No rebirth.'

'The earth would become a desert. Human life would become extinct.'

'And we cannot allow that to happen?'

She wants to say: Surely we cannot stop nature, surely it is a power far greater than any we possess. You only have to look at how a blade of grass will find its way round almost any obstacle in its urge to find the light and survive.

'It won't happen because we do not have the power to make it happen.'

He shakes his head at that; his whole being is turned inward.

'But we do; we do. I have calculated the levels of destruction of ten, a hundred, a thousand nuclear explosions. Imagine explosion begetting explosion, the air we breathe alight with firestorms that no living organism can survive. Imagine the noise of the world destroying itself. It is a terrible prospect.'

'It won't happen,' she says again. If this is some kind of intellectual game, she has suddenly become impatient with it. 'No nation will go to war in order to destroy itself in the process of defeating the enemy.'

'If we develop nuclear weapons,' he says, 'if the West develops nuclear weapons, how can there be safeguards?'

How can she stop him? How can she prevent his analysis leading him to conclusions that will trigger the depression whose power is enough to destroy him?

'For the first time in history,' he is saying, 'we have the power of life and death over nature. We hold in our hands the ability to save or to destroy this planet. It is an awesome burden.'

He takes off his glove and reaches into the pocket of his overcoat.

He produces a stone. She remembers he found it one afternoon two summers ago. She did not know he had kept it. He shows it to her.

'There is the mark of life in this stone. Look.' She sees the fossil, it looks like a sea horse, pale lines trapped beneath a smooth flint surface. 'Imprisoned for millions of years, but historical evidence of a living organism. That is a symbol of what we have inherited, of our struggles to survive on this planet, of battles between rival empires and ideologies, of all the marks of our civilizations, of the existence of life itself.'

To her surprise he throws the stone on to the icy surface of the river. It skids across and comes to rest under the opposite bank.

'Do we have the right to threaten the continued existence of all this, the earth, the water, the life it contains; exchanging what you see here, the trees, the meadow, the river, for a desert of emptiness, poison and disease, the matter of anti-life, darkness, death? Nothing will remain except the ashes of our folly, the monument no one will be alive to see. Can we be responsible for that? Can we release this ultimate power into the control of our military and political leaders? Do we trust them not to let their ignorance lead to the destruction of life as we know it?'

At that moment she remembers a phrase Stevens used all that time ago to describe the scientists sitting around the table in a restaurant in Leiden so many years before: *The sons and daughters of quantum physics*. That is the perfect description of Miskin. His life has been dedicated to the harnessing of the power he now wants to reject. Over the past weeks she has been so concerned with her own predicament that she has not seen what has been happening to Yuri. Now she knows the depth of his desperation as he struggles to reconcile his conscience with his duty. If he tries to outface the powers of the state, he will be annihilated. If he does nothing, he will destroy himself. It is a dilemma for which she can see no solution.

9

DANNY

It was a desolate evening as I made my way across Parliament Square and up Victoria Street. A bitter wind blew flurries of icy rain into my eyes and made the street lights dance in front of me. By the time I reached the building where Monty lived, my face was frozen and I could hardly speak. I climbed the stairs to the third floor and rang the bell. Monty Lybrand's flat was a pied-à-terre in a dark grey building in a street of dark grey buildings not far from Westminster Cathedral.

'My God, look who it is.'

Monty Lybrand was coming towards me with arms outstretched. I had little choice but to fall into his embrace.

'Let me look at you. Let me see what the bastards have done to you.'

'I'm all right, Monty. I'm fine.'

Monty and I had known each other since we were children in Cambridge. My father had always disapproved of our friendship because he disliked Monty's father, who had arrived in the town about the time I was born, with a young wife and three children to set up what became a highly successful drapery business. More children, much money and civic honours followed. The Irish draper became a popular local figure. Why my father took against Declan Lybrand I never knew, but it must have had deep roots because his hostility never relented.

My friendship with Monty meant I spent much of my time in the Lybrands' large and untidy house that overlooked Jesus Green. If my father saw me setting off on my bicycle he would say, 'Off to the enemy, are you? Aren't there better ways to waste your time?'

My father was a distant figure in my childhood, occasionally glimpsed on his bicycle in King's Parade or Petty Cury. If we met

I was usually the butt of his criticism or ridicule. Small wonder I preferred the chaotic warmth of the Lybrand household to the ordered coldness of my own home. Celia's arrival as my stepmother gave me an unexpected ally. She disapproved of my father's treatment of me and said so, and I shall always be grateful to her for that. But by then I was growing up. School finished, I went to Caius to read history while Monty started in his father's shop. Then the war came. Monty had failed his medical when we both went to join up.

'Wonky back,' he told me. 'Fallen arches, short sight; in fact, wonky bloody everything. I can see my war's going to be spent fighting from behind a desk. I expect to be invalided out within a month suffering from a sore arse.'

Months later he had a desk in Whitehall and the talkative Irishman became curiously evasive when questioned about his contribution to the war effort. I never understood precisely what he did because he never told me, but I knew he was in some branch of the Intelligence Service. I used to tease him about being a spy but he always denied it.

'I'm just another bloody civil servant, as if there weren't enough of us already.' Somehow his denials lacked conviction.

Monty poured me a drink and refilled his own glass. I leaned towards the gas fire, watching the blue and yellow tongues of flame shoot upwards with a roar into the hood.

'God, Danny, Berlin. You're wasting your life in that godforsaken hole. Why don't you call it a day and quit before you lose your sanity?'

'And do what?'

'You were never a soldier. Come on, admit it. There's other things in life than wearing a uniform all day and marching to the beat of a drum.'

'You've been talking to my father.'

'He wants you to go back and finish your degree, doesn't he?' He shook his head. 'Don't listen to him. You do what you want to do.'

I mumbled something about my inability to take any decision about my own life, how drifting was all I felt capable of.

'It's *la guerre*, Danny, it's knocked the stuffing out of you. You're winded, that's all. You'll get your breath back. Everyone does sooner or later. Just give it time. Tell me about Berlin. We hear the Russians are pushing you all the time. Is that true?'

'How much do people know here?'

'They know little and care less.'

'Don't they want to know what's happening elsewhere?'

'You've been away too long, Danny. Nobody wants to know anything any more. That's the trouble with this country. We've overdosed on reality. We're war-weary, fed up with the whole bloody business of belt-tightening, stiffening our upper lips and making do. On top of everything else, the country's bankrupt. The last thing we're looking for is another conflict, so if there are threats out there, the bloody Yanks can deal with them while we piece our lives together. I'm right, aren't I? Even in the short time you've been back, you've felt that, haven't you?'

My own reticence in talking about Berlin had never once been challenged since my return. Such conversations as I had were all about the rights and wrongs of what the socialist government was doing. Monty was the first person to ask me what the Russians were up to in Berlin.

'Some people think the next war's already started,' I said.

'What do you think?' he asked.

'Sometimes I think they're right.'

'What makes you say that?'

I told Monty what it was like in Berlin, about the relentless challenge of the Soviets about every single thing we did. He listened intently, only occasionally interrupting to ask a question. I got the impression that he learned little from me that night he didn't already know, but I was reassured that my conclusions were not simply my own.

'How to wake up a world that's exhausted itself from five years of conflict to the territorial ambitions of those bastards in the Kremlin, Danny, that's the question. The man who knows the answer to that is the man I'd like to meet.'

The telephone rang. Monty bellowed down it as he always did.

'Leo, my dear boy. Where are you? No. Tonight. Tonight.' He looked at his watch. 'Twenty minutes. Half an hour then. No, my party. My shout. Don't be late.'

He put down the telephone. 'My favourite Russian. You'll like him. He's joining us for dinner. We'll eat, we'll talk, we'll try to forget this barren land we're living in, God help us all. We're meeting downstairs in half an hour.'

'Downstairs' was Monty's name for the restaurant that served the residents of the flats. I had been there once or twice before but I had forgotten how austere a room it was, with little decoration and, when we entered, few diners. It reminded me of communal eating at school, which is no doubt why it appealed to Monty. In some ways he had never grown up.

'Mr Krasov is at your table, sir.'

'Leo. My dear friend.'

Monty's voice is never quiet. This greeting was a roar from one side of the dining room to the other. Heads turned and immediately looked away in disapproval. Monty was impervious to the effect he created. His entire being at that moment was concentrated upon a small, dapper man who rose from a table only to disappear from sight in Monty's huge embrace.

If I hadn't known better, I would have identified Monty as the Russian, with his great gusts of laughter, his extravagant gestures, his flamboyant theatrical style and his enormous physique. Krasov's small head, elfin features and diminutive stature suggested anything but a Slavic stereotype, he looked so small and weak.

'My friends, meet each other and be happy. Leonid Krasov. Daniel Stevens.' He took our hands and joined them in his own ceremony of greeting.

Krasov's eyes were black and heavy lidded and much too large for his face. He looked up at me and smiled, holding me in his gaze as he held on to my hand.

'I have known this man for years,' Krasov said to me. 'Why do I not hear of you till now?'

His voice was a luxurious bass impaired by a slight hesitation which broke his sentences into irregular rhythms. It was either a speech impediment or a self-conscious mannerism, born perhaps of an innate caution that allowed him time to choose the right word.

'Some secrets, Leo, I keep even from you.'

Krasov was a journalist, stationed in London, Monty had told me. He worked for Tass, the Soviet news agency. They had met during the war and become friends. If Krasov was a communist, he appeared to have kept his ideology well away from Monty.

'You see,' Krasov explained, 'to Russian, friendship is gift. If we believed in God, we would say it was gift from heaven.'

He held his glass towards us. 'To friendship.'

We toasted each other.

'Tonight,' Krasov said, 'tonight you see before you gloomy Russian.'

'You Russians are always gloomy,' Monty said. 'The more you drink the gloomier you become. You know the story about Igor and Tatiana? Igor and Tatiana want to get married but the war is still on and they are worried about the future. "I may not be alive in a year's time," says Igor. "Oh, Igor" says Tatiana. "You are such an optimist."' Monty roared with laughter at his own joke and once more heads turned towards the table.

'If you were born Russian,' Krasov said, 'you would be gloomy too.'

'The war is over, Leo. We won, remember? There are reasons to be happy.'

'It is peace that frightens me.' Any self-mockery in his voice had vanished. Monty caught the change of mood at once.

'Are they threatening to send you back to Moscow?'

'Maybe. Maybe not. There are new men at embassy. I think they do not like me.'

'Have they said anything to you?' Monty asked. Krasov shook his head. 'Made any move at all?' Another shake of the head. 'Then there's nothing to worry about.'

'They are more subtle than you think, Monty.'

'You people? Subtle?' Monty roared in disbelief. 'You Russians couldn't hide a scone in a tea shop.'

'They follow me. They are outside now, this minute, as a matter of fact. At first I thought it was your people, until I heard them speaking Russian. I am used to them now, in fact we are almost comrades. They do not try concealment. They want me to know they watch me night and day. Something is going on and I do not know what it is.'

'What can I do, Leo?' Monty leaned across the table, his voice conspiratorial.

'You, Monty?' Krasov laughed bitterly. 'You can fill my glass, tell me world is better place, and when I am gone you and Danny can drink to my memory.'

'I'll stop those bastards.' Monty had got to his feet. Krasov put out a restraining arm and smiled at me.

'I love this man. World is black and white to him. He kisses you on cheek or hits you on jaw.'

'Is there nothing you can do?' I asked.

Krasov shrugged his shoulders. The gesture made him look even smaller. 'I have been in London too long. They fear I become soft.

79

This is probably true. They are reminding me that I am Soviet citizen and they are making sure that when order comes to return to Moscow, I will obey.'

'Will you do what they tell you?' I asked.

'What choice do I have? I am Soviet citizen. If I am not wanted here, I cannot stay.'

'Come on, Leo. You can't go back to Moscow,' Monty said. 'Not after the years you've spent here. You wouldn't last a minute.'

'I have had good life here. Why should it not end now?'

'Because it can't.' Monty brought his fist down on the table and the glasses and cutlery danced. 'Because I won't let it happen.'

I had been watching Krasov eat. For a diminutive man, his appetite was astonishing. He reached across with his fork to spear a roast potato on the side of Monty's plate.

'To Russians,' Krasov said, turning to me, 'fate is immutable force. This man does not believe in fate. That is how I know he is not Russian.'

Suddenly Monty turned on Krasov.

'You bastard. They've told you, haven't they? They've recalled you. You know you're going home.'

Krasov was silent.

'All this is play-acting, isn't it? The farewell scene, only I'm not to know. That way you can slip out of my life without saying goodbye. Goddamnit, Leo. That's not fair.'

Krasov shrugged his shoulders. 'What can I say?'

'Bastards.'

Krasov leaned towards me. 'Monty, when he is like this, can be forgetful. Would you tell him that he has not yet ordered pudding? You laugh, but I have weakness for your English custard, poured over jam tart. I would like some now, please.'

'Is there nothing you can do?' I asked.

'Nothing.'

'Of course there is,' Monty said. 'He can stay here.'

'I am not spy,' Krasov said. 'I have no information to sell. I am journalist. You have enough journalists already in West.' He laughed suddenly. 'And I do not believe in capitalism. I believe West is doomed. Socialism will triumph, you will see.'

'For God's sake, Leo. You don't believe that rubbish any more than I do.'

Krasov leaned towards me again. 'I see you are not touching your tart,' he said. 'It would be shame to waste it.' He pushed his empty plate towards me and took mine.

'Your appetite's indecent,' Monty said.

'I only eat when I am unhappy,' Krasov answered.

The evening drew to an inconclusive end, Monty increasingly silent because of his distress, Krasov becoming gloomier the more he drank. It was nearly midnight when we stood in the street.

'Show me the bastards,' Monty said, 'I'll fix them for you.'

Krasov put a restraining hand on his arm. 'Do not give them satisfaction of knowing we have talked about them.'

He smiled up at Monty. 'Au revoir, my friend.' He turned to me. 'Next time we have jollier evening, yes?' We shook hands.

'What next time?' Monty said.

'Maybe we will meet in heaven. If there is one.'

He smiled briefly and bowed. Then he was gone.

10

RUTH

Along the vertical line of the graph are the percentage values of those killed, marked in descending order from a hundred per cent at the top, through eighty, sixty, forty, twenty per cent to nought at the bottom. The horizontal line is marked in kilometres, ranging from nought on the left to five on the right. The description reads: 'Distance from the hypocentre.' The line on the graph joins a series of dots starting in the top left-hand corner and swooping downward in a slow curve, showing that most deaths occur within two kilometres of the explosion, but that a tail of deaths continues between two and a half and four and a half kilometres.

The graph ignores the lingering impact of radiation and the slow deaths that spread outwards. This is a measurement of the impact of a single nuclear bomb on its target.

One bomb.

What are the lessons to be drawn? Survival in an atomic attack depends entirely on distance from the centre of the explosion. The force of a nuclear device covers areas vastly greater than traditional bombs. There can no longer be any distinction between military and civilian dead. What she is looking at is a mathematical representation of the indiscriminate nature of mass slaughter, the work of a man-made machine of death which, when exploded, deals out a greater destructive power than any weapon before it.

She remembers the awesome statistics she has read of the effects of the explosions in both Japanese cities.

Hiroshima. 6 August 1945. 78,000 dead. 13,000 missing. 37,000 wounded. Three-fifths of the city destroyed. Nagasaki. 9 August 1945. 70,000 killed. Nearly half the city destroyed. Vaporized bodies. Melted eyes and skin. Burned-out humanity.

And still the poison spreads, the slow dying continues, the after-shock of the explosion casts its deadly shadow far into the future. Parents to their children, born and unborn, perhaps to their children's children. How long will it go on?

The spread of destruction and death terrifies her. Why should a single graph have a greater impact on her than photographs and newsreels and the graphic accounts of survivors? Because this is her territory: clinical, neutral, the unchallengeable verdict of mathematics.

How long will it go on? Here, on her notepad, are the mathematical implications of a much larger nuclear chain reaction. She has carefully calculated the size of the explosion, its destructive power and the area over which it will work its devastation. These are her precise, accurate marks, black ink on a white page. These are her numbers, innocent in their ordinariness but terrifying in their meaning. Why should the chain reaction ever end? Why should it not go on and on until there is nothing left to destroy? She remembers what Miskin said when they were at the river . . . *the earth would become a desert, human life would become extinct,* and for the first time she understands what they are dealing with. She shivers. There is no one in the lab with her. She is quite alone. She looks at the photograph of her son in a simple wooden frame on her desk, and feels again the flutter of fear in her.

11

DANNY

I found Ridout sitting in a wheelchair beside his bed in an almost deserted ward. It was, unusually, a clear morning as I walked along the polished linoleum floors of the corridors at Addenbrooke's Hospital, pale winter sunlight pouring in through the windows and falling across the line of empty beds waiting for the sick to be delivered.

'Philip?' Ridout's eyes opened and he looked at me, startled. 'Did I wake you?'

'I wasn't expecting anybody this morning, that's all.'

He seemed neither awake nor asleep but lost in some world of his own.

'May I stay for few minutes?'

'There's a chair somewhere. You'll have to fetch it yourself. Despite this contraption, I'm less than mobile. Someone has to push me if I'm to move.'

I hadn't seen Ridout since my last visit to Cambridge, a few months after the end of the war. He had been well then, wholly absorbed in the physics that was his life. Despite his shyness, there was an energy about him, a suppressed force that I had to admire. Now I saw a shrunken, shrivelled figure, all signs of youth gone; grey-faced, skin transparent, his whole frame was brittle with disease. The overwhelming impression was of life retreating into a redoubt from where it would make a last and desperate stand against the cancer, before giving way to the inevitable.

I found a chair and sat beside him. He summoned what little energy remained within him.

'How are you?'

'Dying, slowly but surely.' I was unprepared for the challenge in his voice. 'Have you come to take a look?'

'I've seen enough men die not to need that,' I said.

'The trouble with a fatal illness,' he said apologetically, 'is that watching yourself deteriorate allows you time to become very self-centred. At least if you're hit by a bullet you've little or no chance to think about what's happening to you, whether you want the process to speed up or slow down. It's all over in a flash, isn't it?'

'If you're lucky, yes.'

I could understand his anger. The one thought we took with us into battle was that if it was to happen, pray God it was quick. Ridout had already been in hospital for ten weeks and was quite able to monitor his own progressive physical decline. It was not his mind but his body that was failing him. I could well understand why he was still unreconciled to what had happened.

'If the mind went at the same time as the body, things might be easier,' he said. 'But from experience I can tell you it doesn't. That's where the trouble starts.'

He struggled to change his position in the wheelchair. The blanket fell off his knees. I picked it up and tucked it back for him, feeling the sharpness of his bones as I did so.

'It's good of you to come. Your father told me you were home on leave. I'm sure you have better things to do than sit here with me. How's Berlin?'

I told him about our difficulties with the Russians. To my surprise the subject appeared to interest him. Briefly, something resembling the force of the past was rekindled within him.

'That's where your father and I disagree. He believes in the good sense of the Russian people. I say there's no such thing. He sees it as a political restraint on their gangster leadership. I tell him he's misguided. He's optimistic about the future. He sees the Russians freeing themselves from tyranny and I don't. The leadership is brutal, the people are exhausted. In a society without restraint, there's nothing you can trust. I'm right but he won't see it. Good sense, if it ever existed, vanished the moment Lenin came to power.'

He looked at me and tried to smile, the reddish creases on his dry skin looking as if they were about to crack.

'The Russians respect brute force. Until we can meet them on equal terms they won't listen to us and there'll be precious little chance of a continued peace. I can't die while there are still so many technical problems to be solved. That's what keeps me going. We have to build our own bomb, and the sooner the better.'

He wiped his lips with a handkerchief. 'Would you mind fetching me some water, please? Talking makes me dry.'

I gave him a glass. He drank from it slowly, then handed it back to me.

He said: 'I think your father has developed doubts about the rightness of what we are doing because of my illness. Although he has never said anything, I think he believes that if we had not conducted certain experiments, perhaps I would not be in here now. I think he is using my illness to question the whole idea of the nuclear bomb. That's the biggest mistake we can make. If we slow down now, if we hesitate for any reason, we'll lose the race. Then who can guess the consequences?'

That was the clue Celia was looking for. Philip's illness had deeply disturbed my father. It had upset his confidence and caused him (a new experience) to question the rightness of his work on the atomic bomb and its successor, the superbomb. His moodiness and withdrawal were the external signs of his struggle with the dilemma he faced.

Ridout smiled again at me, showing his teeth and the raw, red gums. 'If you think that the knowledge that you're dying brings with it a sense of acceptance, you should banish such sentimentality at once.'

At that moment the flame flickered and started to go out. Its suddenness was like a curtain going down. The look of exhaustion on his face was total.

'Tell your father to listen to what I'm saying. I haven't got long left now, a few weeks, who knows? But I'm going to hang on till we've completed the next stage. There's work to be done and he's got to help me. We have to make this bomb. Tell him that, will you?'

'Of course.'

He nodded at me in acknowledgement. 'We are at odds, he and I, over this issue. I shouldn't like to die unreconciled.'

*

'We've not met,' the voice on the telephone said, 'but we've friends in common. Simon Watson-Jones. Ring a bell? Good. I was having a bite with Simon today and he was telling me how much he enjoyed chatting to you the other night. He'd like to see more of you. I'm sure you two have lots to talk about.'

I couldn't remember saying more than hello and goodbye to Watson-Jones that evening. I was sure we'd never got into conversation. I was also sure I wasn't being sounded out. I was being instructed.

'Give him a bell at the House, old boy. He'd be so pleased.'

To my surprise Watson-Jones recognized my name at once when I telephoned him.

'You got my message. Good.' Did I have time for a drink one evening? Then home for a spot of dinner. Nothing formal. His wife Meredith might be there if she was up in town, perhaps one or two chums. It would be fun. Wednesday at six? Splendid. Meet at the House.

Two days later I waited in the lobby of the House of Commons while a clerk telephoned his office. I hoped I would see faces I recognized, men and women who had shaped our destiny, but there was no one around I could put a name to. But I felt the invisible engine of power throbbing around me, I could hear it in the busy echo of footsteps on the stone floor as people crossed and recrossed the lobby, formed groups, talked and broke up again; I saw it in the self-absorption on their faces so clearly telling us how important were the issues in which they were involved. How distant seemed the world I came from. Perhaps that is what makes politics so attractive. The thing over which you hold power is out of sight and out of earshot.

'Danny. Good to see you.'

Watson-Jones appeared from nowhere, smiling and holding out his hand. I had forgotten how tall he was.

'Come along.'

He led me to the Members' bar. He ordered drinks and we sat down at a table by the window. The room was almost empty but when he spoke, Watson-Jones's voice was hardly above a whisper.

'A little bird tells me,' he said in a confidential tone, 'that Berlin might be losing its attraction.'

'I hate Berlin,' I said. 'I always have done. It's a scrap heap.'

'Then why stay there?'

'If that's where the army chooses to send me, that's where I go.'

'Yours not to reason why,' he said.

'Something like that.'

'What if,' he said, and paused. He knew how to make the most of an effect, even with an audience of one. 'What if there was an

87

opportunity to leave Berlin and do something that had nothing to do with the army?'

'Return to Civvy Street?'

He peered at me over the tops of his glasses. 'Is that what you'd like to do?'

'My problem,' I said, 'is that I don't know what I'd like to do. One good thing about the army is it takes away the need to think.'

Watson-Jones laughed. 'That's what your father told me you'd say. The difference between your father and me is, I don't believe you.'

He sat back in his chair, pleased with his provocation.

'I believe it,' I said, 'and that, surely, is what counts.'

He had thrown his stone and it had made no ripples. I wondered if that was an unusual experience for him. I could see him moving smoothly to a new position as if nothing had happened. I admired his dexterity.

'Let me tell you what I have in mind,' he said. 'Of course,' he leaned forward as he spoke, 'you understand this is all very hush-hush. Nothing's official yet.'

He looked up to wave absent-mindedly to a colleague who passed our table.

'There's been a move recently,' he continued, leaning forward once more, 'to get me and one or two others to make more of our position in the Party. Form a group. Create a platform. Consolidate what we believe in. That sort of thing. I didn't initiate it but nor have I resisted it. A group, if it is to mean anything – and I'm talking now in political terms – has to have an organization and organizations have to have money. Well, the money is in place. Now we're looking for the organization. The people to do the job.'

He sounded pleased with himself. I sensed the money came from Watson-Jones himself, or someone close to him.

'What are these people going to do?' I asked.

'Influence opinion. Change minds. Steer this country back to safer waters.' He lowered his voice again. 'Help get our people back into power and the country out of the bloody mess it's in.'

The room was filling up around us and there was a buzz of excited chatter. A man came across to our table and said, 'Simon, a word in your ear later, yes?'

'Surely, Johnny.' Watson-Jones smiled at me but made no introduction. 'Where were we?'

'Changing minds,' I said. 'Getting the country back on its feet.'

'Well, what do you say?'

'To what?'

'Joining us.' I must have looked baffled because he laughed and said, 'I should explain. We're going to start a research office. Do a bit of hard thinking. Facts and figures. Write speeches. Publish papers. Propose policy. Put a bit of muscle into our opposition, and God knows it needs it. We thought you might like to help us do it.'

There was no explanation of the 'we' he referred to.

'Shouldn't you look for someone with political ambitions?'

'We don't want anyone with ambition. That wouldn't do at all.'

I waited for him to qualify his remark but there was no sign he knew what he'd said. Evidence of his thick skin, or my thin one.

'We're not looking for a decision right now,' he said. 'But give me a steer. What do you think of the idea?'

'Berlin or London? Where's the choice?'

'Then you'll think about it?'

'Of course.'

'Splendid. What we hoped to hear. Now,' he looked at his watch. Already his attention was on something else. 'Time for dinner. I think we've earned it. What do you say?'

★

Meredith Watson-Jones was American, and it was immediately clear that the money was hers and there was plenty of it. The house in South Street had a richness about it, a certainty in its own taste that comes from the employment of an expensive interior designer. It was somehow too good to be true. The paintings were early American: scenes of the Civil War, Southern landscapes and some family portraits, serious-looking men and women on horseback, sullen Negro slaves and elegant plantation houses in the background. I wondered if they really were family portraits but they gave you the impression that they were, and that was what counted.

'Darling,' Watson-Jones said as we entered, 'we're late. We were having such an interesting talk, weren't we, Danny? Will you forgive us?' He kissed Meredith lightly, brushing her cheek with his lips, and introduced me. 'Now, is everyone here?'

Watson-Jones's idea of a quiet evening was not mine. There were twelve of us at dinner, none of whom I had met before. The Watson-Joneses had a butler and, I presumed, a cook. Where they managed to get their food from I had no idea. I ate things that evening that I had not tasted since before the war.

I sat next to Meredith Watson-Jones. When she spoke, she leaned towards me, occasionally touching my hand for effect. There was nothing flirtatious in her action, it was a natural, even unconscious, mannerism. Her slow speech, with its fading traces of a Southern drawl, and her sweet smile combined to captivate me. I am sure she was used to captivating men, but it was an act without guile. I saw in her none of the subtlety of the good politician's wife. I wondered what her life was like when she wasn't on duty.

'I gather you're stationed in Berlin,' she said. Watson-Jones had evidently briefed her earlier.

'I was telling your husband,' I said, 'how much I hate Berlin.'

'Then we'll talk about something else, Daniel.' She touched my arm and moved at once to the second subject of her briefing. 'Simon and I are great fans of your father's articles. You must be so proud of him.'

We talked about my father; what it was like to be brought up in a university town; why I had not finished my degree and mercifully very little about the war. I learned that she had rejected the chance to return to America in 1939 because her duty was to be at her husband's side. I managed somehow to get her to tell me how she had met her husband.

'Daddy sent me to England for the summer. I didn't want to come at all but Daddy and Mother said it would be good for me. I had this beau they didn't like and this was their plan to separate us. Someone took me to a party at Cambridge and there I met this tall English boy. Do you know, I couldn't understand a thing – *thaing* – he was saying – *saaiying* – he seemed to swallow every word he spoke. But he had deep blue eyes and they followed me wherever I went. So the very next day I decided that if he was going to look at girls like that, I'd rather he looked at me than anyone else. So I got on a train and went back to Cambridge and told him so. Wasn't that awful?'

The sound of her laughter attracted Watson-Jones's attention from the other end of the table.

'Meredith?'

'I'm telling Daniel how we met, honey,' she said guilelessly.

'I'm sure he won't be interested in that, my sweet,' he said, and returned his attention to his guest.

He did not want her to share intimate memories with me because I was eating at their table not out of friendship but out of usefulness, and Meredith was in danger of overstepping the mark. I imagined she had done this before, and wondered if there would be a reckoning to be faced when we had all left.

'Give me a top-up, will you? There's a love.'

Bony fingers dug into my arm and a wine glass was held out to me. Sylvia Carr, I was told by the many people who knew her, was well past her best when I met her. That best had been something to behold, they said, but the years had taken their toll. Early promise had not sustained itself and it showed in the hoarse voice, the raucous laugh, the over-bright lipstick and the tight, parchment-brown skin.

But there was an honesty about Sylvia, and, I discovered later, an ability to square up to misfortune, which I came to admire. She was a realist, and she knew the world.

After dinner, Meredith led the women away and we gathered at Watson-Jones's end of the table. Port appeared, and cigars. I heard someone say, 'Genuine Havana. How does he do it? Good old Simon.' The conversation turned quickly to politics, the atmosphere thick with cigar smoke. Berlin seemed like another planet.

I listened and said nothing. The drift was clear. The Attlee government was heartily disliked. We were in debt to the world, our export trade was half what it had been before the war and government spending was out of control because of Labour's obsession with social experiment.

'All very well to play around with ideas of equality, but only when you can afford it.'

There was general agreement that the country was being weakened at a time when the Soviet Union was banging its rifle butt harder than ever on Europe's cardboard door.

'The Soviets are out to gobble up the world,' someone said. 'We can all see that. France and Italy will be a walkover because they're going communist anyway. Then we'll have the Russians at Calais and this bloody government saying, "Please come in, Comrade Stalin. We're allies in the great cause of socialism."'

Watson-Jones turned to me. 'You're stationed in Berlin, Danny. Are we wrong to see the Russians as a threat?'

'They mean business,' I said. 'They're out for what they can get and they're very hard to stop.'

'Playground bullies, is that it?'

He was playing the straight man, feeding me my lines. I hoped I'd got my part right.

'Playground bullies with toys that explode. What we've seen is the tip of the iceberg. They haven't shown their hand yet. I worry about what happens when they do.'

The room had fallen silent. I wasn't sure if I was on trial or not.

'Can we stop them?' Watson-Jones asked.

'Not if we don't do something soon. Nobody's doing anything at the moment,' I said, 'and that's playing into the Russians' hands. This government, the Americans, everyone turns a blind eye because officially the Russians are still our allies. They're a brutal lot. They read our policy as a sign of weakness. They respect strength. If you say no to them loudly enough and stick a bayonet up their arse, then they might back off. If you try to reason with them, they'll walk all over you. Unless we do something soon, they'll become a permanent threat.'

'Time to wake up the world to the demon at the gates, Simon,' someone called out. 'Now, there's a cause to get your teeth into.'

There was laughter at that and conversation broke out in groups once more. One or two people nodded in my direction and I had the impression that I had passed some kind of test.

Watson-Jones was bending over my chair.

'There's someone here I'd like to introduce you to. You two should have a lot in common.'

One of the great regrets of my life is that I only met Charlie Faulkner when he was dying. None of us knew it then, including Charlie, and when he did find out, there was a long battle between his will and the disease until it finally conquered him. I suspect that he raged against the illness that was slowly ravaging his body, and from time to time he stunned its advance. He certainly took a long time to die, longer than any of us expected and only in the last days were there any real signs that he was failing.

My first impression that evening was one of solidity, a square head topped with thick, untidy tufts of white hair, a square chin below a wide, often smiling mouth. His body was compact rather than large, his strength concentrated, but he gave the impression of a man almost twice his size. Perhaps it was his hands that did this. He had the largest palms I have ever seen, with short, thick, square-ended fingers.

'Simon tells me you might be interested in joining us,' Faulkner said when Watson–Jones had gone. I recognized the last traces of a Mancunian accent.

'The subject's come up, yes.'

'And?'

'Well, I'd like to know more.'

'Ask me.'

'Why me? The universities must be crammed with young men who would jump at a chance like this. Surely you could have your pick?'

Faulkner laughed. 'Simon warned me you wouldn't think too much of yourself. I'm looking for doers, not thinkers. Thinkers are two a penny these days.

'What makes you think I'm a doer?'

'You've been in the war, son. You can organize other people, make things happen. I've seen your record. I'd say you'd be a good man for the job.'

He leaned towards me. 'The wrong mob's in power at the moment and we've got to get them out. We were too busy winning the war to spot how the war was changing the world we were trying to save. It's time for a rethink: new ideas, new faces, get the party moving again. Well, Simon's got ideas, he's got the courage to challenge the shibboleths. What he needs is a bit of organization behind him, help spread the word. That's what we're talking about. Something to believe in again.'

They'd found premises in Pimlico, convenient for the House, and in a week or two the office would be ready. It was an exciting challenge for a young man, to be in at the start of a movement that was going to take the country forward once more. If Charlie had his time over again, he'd jump at the chance. It was clear from everything he said that I was not being looked over, I was being sold to.

'There's more to it than that.' He leaned forward. 'The Soviets are winning the propaganda war hands down at the moment. They say one thing and do the opposite and nobody calls them to account. We're letting them get away with murder. You're in Berlin, you know that better than I do. We're a soft touch because we can't bring ourselves to believe the Russians are as evil as you and I know them to be. So what's happening? They're running rings round us one minute and knocking us down like dominoes the next. Well, some of us think it's time we woke people up before it's too late.'

How he was going to do this he didn't explain.

'Well, what do you think?' He looked at me eagerly.

'Isn't that the question I should ask you?'

'I'm happy if you are.'

There it was, as simple as that. The possibility of escape from Berlin, a new life outside the army. No more doubts about what I should do. It was being decided for me. All I had to do was say yes.

'Darling,' said a voice behind me. 'I'm a teeny bit squiffy and it's way past my bedtime. Would you be an angel and drive me home?' Sylvia Carr was holding out her keys for me. Then she saw who I was talking to.

'Charlie, I'm sorry. Am I taking Danny away from something important? You will forgive me, won't you?' She leaned over and kissed his forehead.

'This young man and I were just getting to know one another,' Charlie said, winking at me. 'But we can carry on some other time. Sleep on it,' he said to me. He was writing a telephone number on a piece of paper. 'Give me a ring. You can reach me here.' He struggled to his feet. 'Now you take care of this young lady, Danny, and see her home safe and sound. She's very precious to some of us.'

'Tell me about Meredith,' I said when we were in the car.

'It's her money,' Sylvia replied, 'and he spends it.' She clearly had no time for Watson-Jones. 'Meredith's a sweetie, far too good for him. Everyone loves Meredith. It's not real money, darling. Very nouveau. Grandpa Devereaux started the business, he was some kind of mechanic, then Daddy Devereaux made a success of it. He makes bits for aeroplanes – they're the bits that matter because everyone wants them. Two generations, that's all it took. No time at all. I suppose that's America for you, isn't it?'

'Where does Charlie Faulkner fit in?' I asked as we turned into the King's Road.

'He was almost an old flame of mine,' she said, 'except that bitch of a wife Muriel kept too close an eye on him.'

'What's his background?'

'Charlie's a shopkeeper, or was; he had grocery shops all over the Midlands. He made a lot of money in the 'thirties and got drafted in to work for the government during the war. That was when he got bitten by politics. He never wanted to be an MP, but he loves the political process, the comings and goings, the atmosphere of power. That's where he puts his energy now, behind political causes like Simon.'

'He thinks a lot of Simon.'

'Simon thinks a lot of Simon too.'

'Other people speak well of him. He seems to be a coming man.'

'Oh, Simon's coming all right. He's been coming since the day he was born.' I was surprised at her bitterness. 'He's always had an eye for the main chance. Shrewd and shifty is how I'd describe him. If you want my advice, stay away from Watson-Jones. The man's ice-cold inside. Cares for no one but himself. Look how he treats Meredith.'

'How does he treat Meredith?'

'He married her for her money. That should tell you everything you need to know.'

We had reached her house in Beaufort Street.

'That was kind of you. I hope I haven't taken you too far out of your way.' I opened the door for her. 'Give me a call sometime. I'm in the book.'

★

I didn't sleep on it. I made up my mind as I walked back from Sylvia's house. I heard the answer as I listened to the water lapping against the Embankment. I sensed it in the eternally thoughtful gaze of Sir Thomas More as he stared across the river. I saw it in the reflected moonlight bouncing across the underside of Albert Bridge. I felt it even in the enquiring glance of the tart standing by a lamp-post near Lambeth Bridge. I heard it in the refrain of my own footsteps on the pavement of the Embankment.

Why not? Why not? Why not?

It seemed a good offer. It had come to me out of the blue. I hadn't had to work for it. It would be good to get away from Berlin, to escape from the war-torn buildings and the war-torn lives. It would be good to get out of khaki too.

'Why not? Why not?' the voice inside my head kept repeating. Why not? was about as positive as I had felt about anything in a long time.

12

RUTH

She is one of the first to arrive. She takes her seat at the back of the auditorium. Her head is pounding.

Do nothing unusual, Andropov has instructed. Behave normally. Don't excite attention until the right moment.

She watches her colleagues drift in to take their seats, leaving the two rows at the front unused. She realizes how everyone sits in the same seats, how no one has ever sat at the front. She wonders if the director will address them. It is rare for him to do so. She is not surprised when Assistant Director Dimitriov leads in Assistant Deputy Directors Miskin and Tomsky and the stout, drab form of Senior Technician Maximov. They are followed by the two political commissars, ever-present observers to ensure the correct political line is held. One by one they take their places at the table. Conversation stops.

Maximov, who seldom speaks, claps her hands and the meeting is called to order. Deputy Director Dimitriov opens the proceedings.

'Comrades. I am sorry to report that our esteemed Comrade Director is unable to be with us today. He sends his apologies.'

She tries to remember an occasion when their esteemed Comrade Director did *not* send his apologies. There is a silence as Dimitriov puts on his spectacles. He leans over his text and begins.

'Report for the month ending 31 December . . .'

The unvarying rhythm of his delivery as he reads his prepared text and the boring content of what he has to say make these exercises in worker participation pointless and exhausting. She looks around without turning her head. In row after row, bodies are sitting in the accustomed manner, long-practised postures, head and shoulders hunched forward over open pads of paper, pen in hand as though in the act of note-taking. But no hand moves. No notes are taken.

The pads, a blotchy grey, remain untouched. Behind the camouflage, eyes are closing. Those on the dais are too high up to notice.

Even the commissars seem bored. Dimitriov recites the month's achievements and the month's failures. He assumes the achievements are routine ('this is the level of performance expected'), so he concentrates as the commissars have instructed him to do on the failures.

'. . . the failure to remove cups from desks, the wastage of pencils, the removal of pads of paper from the stationery office and their reappearance in the toilets . . .'

Beside him Senior Technician Maximov nods furiously as each crime is read out (it was she who spotted the pads in the staff toilets and triumphantly returned them to the stationery cupboard) while the two commissars stare in front of them, their faces blank.

The pounding in her head continues.

In her mind she repeats the instructions that Andropov has given her. ('Stand up slowly. Speak clearly. Use your notes if that helps.') She holds her notes tightly; they are creased now and some of the words have been smudged by her damp hands. She does not want to refer to them if she can avoid it.

- The known statistics about radioactive fallout
- The likely pattern of irradiation
- How radiation from a nuclear explosion is absorbed into the human body
- The probable death rate per hectare
- The predicted death rate per thousand over five and ten years.

Irrefutable facts and figures derived from statistical studies of the nuclear explosions in Japan.

'These are your questions,' Andropov said to her. 'Raise them at the next monthly progress meeting of the Project task force. We hear the director may be there.'

Dimitriov ends his recital, which he has read without once looking up. He looks very white and for one hilarious moment she wonders if he is not boring himself to death. He closes the file and says quietly: 'I submit my report for your approval.'

There are the usual unintelligible murmurs around the room which are taken for assent. Bodies resume the upright position. Eyes open once more. One or two openly stretch, in anticipation of the end of proceedings.

With obvious ceremony, Senior Technician Maximov takes the paper from Dimitriov, signs and dates it. She makes a show of waiting for the ink to dry. As there is no blotting paper (when did they last have blotting paper?) she must wave the page in the air ostentatiously. There is silence while she does this, broken only by the snapping of lighters as cigarettes are lit. Pale clouds of blue smoke unfurl above them, rise to the ceiling and dissolve. She senses the general relief that the meeting is almost over for another month.

'Before I call the meeting to a formal halt, are there any questions from the floor?'

There never have been any questions, it is unheard of that anyone should ask anything, everyone wants to get out as quickly as they can. Already the comrades are gathering up their papers; some are standing up, the seats of their chairs snapping back into the upright position in a syncopated rhythm; others are making their way to the door.

'Comrade Deputy Director.' She is on her feet. 'I have a question.'

The room turns towards the small woman at the back. Deputy Director Dimitriov, halfway out of the auditorium, stops in his tracks.

'Comrade Dr Marchenko?'

'I would like to ask a question about the risks to the scientific staff and the local civilian population of work currently being undertaken in the Laboratory of the Victory of October the Tenth, otherwise known as D4.'

Dimitriov is as taken aback as anyone by her words. He looks for guidance to Senior Technician Maximov, the mistress of procedure. She can do nothing because on the agenda in front of her is typed the final item: Questions.

She leans towards Dimitriov and whispers in his ear. She shows him the agenda. Dimitriov looks at Ruth. He is more authoritative this time, Maximov having prompted him with what he should say.

'The floor is yours, Comrade. What is your question?'

There is silence in the room. No one moves. All are astonished. She knows them well enough to guess what they are thinking but she sees none of them because she is not looking at her audience nor at the dais: she is addressing the lights on the ceiling.

Plutonium, she reminds them, is a highly toxic material and D4 is now engaged in developing techniques for casting plutonium. The danger arises if the metal oxidizes in the atmosphere, forming a fine powder of radioactive particles. Breathing in these particles can cause injury or death. What arrangements, she asks, have been made to protect the technicians in D4 in the event of an accident? Or indeed any civilians living in the nearby apartment blocks?

At once a murmur runs around the room. The audience swivels round to look at Deputy Director Dimitriov. He has been writing as she speaks. Now one of the political commissars passes a note to him and then leans across to whisper something. Dimitriov nods.

'Thank you for your question, Comrade Marchenko.'

She sees Maximov writing furiously. A full minute of her question will be completed soon after the meeting ends and copies forwarded to the director and, of course, the political commissars, just as Andropov has said they would be. Then they will be sent to Moscow Central Intelligence, where they will end up on Andropov's desk. At least, that is what he has told her. She hopes he is right.

'Soviet technicians are not subject to any danger at all,' he says. 'Our advanced casting techniques allow our technicians to handle radioactive materials without danger to themselves or indeed anyone else. There is no possibility of such an accident. Therefore there is no risk to anyone. Your concerns are without foundation, Comrade Marchenko.'

Dimitriov prepares to leave the room. She is on her feet once again. ('Make an impression,' Andropov has instructed her. 'Push yourself forward.')

'Is the Comrade Deputy Director aware that there have already been two instances of oxidization in D4? Due to the prompt reaction of the scientific personnel, any risks were avoided. Is Comrade Deputy Director not concerned by what has happened?'

Dimitriov looks desperate. 'I am fully aware of the work undertaken in D4, Comrade Marchenko, and I am wholly satisfied with all safety arrangements.'

Inside her head she hears Andropov's voice urging her on. But she has another motive. She is beginning to enjoy the sight of Deputy Director Dimitriov, whom she has never liked, squirming like a fish at the end of a line.

'Would it not be prudent to move the civilian population away from the area while there is some risk during the casting process? Or should we consider transferring this process away from D4 to a more isolated laboratory?'

There is a whispered consultation on the platform.

'I have no further comment to make, Comrade.'

'So we are prepared to risk condemning the civilians in the apartments near D4 to the possibility of a slow and painful death from many forms of radiation–induced cancer because we cannot be bothered either to move them to other, temporary accommodation or to find another site for our testing.'

That is not a question, it is a political statement, and a dangerous one at that. There is more murmuring around the room. Deputy Director Dimitriov looks furious as he gathers up his papers.

'I am only empowered to take questions, Comrade. The meeting is now closed,' he says and sweeps out of the room.

13

DANNY

'I am in Cambridge,' the voice said. 'You must help me.'

I found Krasov sheltering inside a telephone box on the Barton Road. His black overcoat, briefcase and hat made him sharply visible through the glass of the kiosk.

'My dear friend,' he said. He took off his glove to shake my hand. 'Forgive me for dragging you out on such a day.'

He tried to smile but his face was stiff with cold. I was shocked at his appearance. He had not shaved for a day or two, and his eyes had sunk even further into his skull. He seemed smaller and more fragile than ever.

'For now I have escaped,' he said. 'It was not difficult. As matter of fact, those cretins they send to follow me would not see me if they were standing on other side of road right now.'

But there was a hollowness to the bravura. This was not the man I had met only a few days before. The stuffing had been knocked out of him. Krasov hunched against the cold and pulled his overcoat tighter around him.

'I am rather cold,' he said. 'Foolishly, I did not come prepared for English winter. If we might go together quickly to your house.'

We set off through the snow, Krasov with his head down to avoid detection and his arm through mine. I carried his briefcase.

'You're safe enough here,' I said. 'No one will recognize you.'

'Me? I am not even safe in my dreams.'

Celia was waiting for us in the hall and she greeted Krasov with all the authority of a nurse at a casualty station. 'Take your shoes off at once, Mr Krasov, and your socks. They're soaked through. Poor man, you're frozen. Come into the kitchen and warm up.'

Krasov followed her obediently and she sat him at the kitchen table with his back to the stove and gave him a cup of tea. The children crept into the room, attracted by the sound of a strange voice, and stared at him from the safety of the door. Krasov stared back and said nothing. Children, I suspected, had no place in his life.

Celia and I had a whispered conversation in the hall.

'What does he want?' she asked. 'Has he said?'

'Not a dicky bird.'

'Is he expecting to stay?'

'He won't ask. He'll wait for us to offer.'

'And if we don't?'

'He'll go away again.'

'We can't possibly let him go in this state.'

'What about Geoffrey?'

'Leave Geoffrey to me. We've got to help this poor man first.'

She went back into the kitchen, sending the children away as she did so. Krasov looked relieved.

'Mr Krasov.'

'Dear lady.'

'What do you want us to do with you?'

'What do I want to do with myself? That is question.' He shrugged. 'If I knew answer, I would be someone else.'

'Are you in danger? Are you running away?'

He smiled forlornly. 'I have been running away all my life, from myself and other enemies.'

'Danny has told me everything.' Celia was in no mood for equivocation. 'What are we to do with you, Mr Krasov?'

'I throw myself on your mercy, dear lady. Perhaps a day or two. If you could give me that. I will be no trouble.'

'Somewhere to hide? Is that it?'

'Staying in cupboard all day? Creeping out at night? No, I do not want to hide.'

'Then what kind of arrangement are we talking about?'

'An arrangement, dear lady, where I am transparent.'

He stared at her unblinking, black eyes shining out of the shrunken saucer of his face.

'We'll put you in the spare room,' Celia said decisively. 'I'll make up the bed in a moment. Did you bring anything with you?'

'I am what you see. No clothes, no papers. In my country, you can go anywhere without clothes, but without papers you are naked.'

'First you must warm up. I'll run you a bath. Danny, put a kettle on for a hot-water bottle. You will spend the afternoon in bed, Mr Krasov. Then I shall bring you some soup. Later on we will decide what to do with you.'

Krasov followed her upstairs, meek as a child.

★

'He can't possibly stay here,' had been my father's immediate reaction when, on his arrival home, Celia had told him that a Soviet journalist was asleep upstairs. I was surprised at his hostility.

'Why not?'

'I don't want an escaping Russian in my house.'

'Nonsense, Geoffrey. He's a poor frightened man who needs somewhere to rest.'

'We know nothing about him.'

'He's Danny's friend.'

'That may not be a recommendation.'

'If you could have seen him, Geoffrey,' Celia said. 'His awful worn coat. Paper shoes. In this weather, too. The dear man was nearly dead with cold.'

My father gave ground, acknowledging Celia's decision with a shrug and a muttered: 'I'm not at all happy about it.'

'You'll meet him at supper, Geoffrey,' Celia said. 'Provided he's well enough to get up. I shall be the judge of that.'

Krasov was well enough. In fact, he was much restored by his sleep, he assured us as he thanked Celia for her kindness to the 'lonely Russian who had arrived so unexpected on your doorstep', and he was very ready to accept my father's offer of a glass of whisky in his study.

'Will you join us, Daniel?'

I refused. Looking back, how I wished I hadn't. Then the study door closed and I went back into the kitchen.

During the time Krasov and my father were alone together something happened to upset my father deeply. When I opened the door half an hour later to say that supper was ready, Krasov was sitting at my father's lectern looking like a bird of prey poised to swoop and strike. Circling around him in the restricted space of the study, hands thrust deep in his pockets, chin resting on his chest, my father had the appearance of a caged animal. However hard he struggled he could not get free.

Again and again in the days that followed I replayed my impressions of those few seconds. I saw Krasov, sharp, attentive, his huge eyes facing me warily and with suspicion. My father had his back to me. He turned at the sound of my voice and his expression was dazed. Krasor moved quickly away from the lectern to distract my attention from my father, giving him time to recover.

'Time to eat, Professor,' he said, smiling at me. He took my father's arm and led him firmly to the door. The unexpected gesture roused my father, and in the few yards between the study and the kitchen I watched the enormous effort of will he made to conceal his distress from Celia. He was not very successful.

At dinner, he appeared flushed and excitable, his words coming out in a rush as his thoughts tumbled over each other. He was clearly very tense. He hardly touched his food, while Krasov's appetite remained undiminished. I saw concern on Celia's face but she said nothing. But the image of my father coming out of his study, Krasov holding his arm, eyes wide as if he had been badly frightened, did not go away easily.

Krasov's bitter humour entertained us while we ate. He was a fatalist, and that gave him the ability to live for the moment. For the immediate present he was safe, and that allowed him to relax.

Why didn't we question him about his sudden appearance in Cambridge? Why did we let him invade our lives without asking what had driven him to seek refuge with us on the strength of one meeting? The truth is, we saw a man in need and we responded. We took him in because we trusted him and feared for his safety. I shall never understand how we could have been so naive.

14

RUTH

One moment she is caught up in her narrative, the next her mental energy drains away and she hears the sound of her own voice. She is no longer inside the story she is telling, she is drifting apart from it, the events becoming more and more distant as they turn into shapeless clouds and evaporate in her mind. A sense of desperation rises within her that she can hardly control. She stops in mid-sentence, unable to go on, at least for the moment. She looks at Stevens despairingly.

(How much longer do we have? Is it dawn yet? How can I cram everything into a single night?)

He has already got to his feet (she remembers that he is never still when he talks, he is lecturing to his pupils, up and down the narrow dais from which he addresses them) and she knows he is going to give her time to get her breath back. Once again she is aware of how he responds instinctively to her needs.

'The day Krasov came to my house was particularly cold,' he says. 'I arrived home about three o'clock after a Governing Body meeting to be greeted with the news that a strange Russian was asleep in the spare room upstairs, and would I make as little noise as possible. He appeared before dinner and joined me in my study for a drink. An extraordinary, birdlike man: huge head, thin arms, enormous eyes that seemed to trap you in their gaze.'

Little Krasov, she thinks. Geoffrey has met Little Krasov. How strange that their lives should be connected in this way. She listens carefully while he tells her how Little Krasov brought her back into the life of her English professor.

★

'My son Daniel tells me you're running away,' Stevens said. 'Cambridge is an odd place to hide.'

'That is story I give Daniel,' Krasov said. 'Like most Russian stories, it is part truth, part invention.'

'You're not running away?'

'As matter of fact I come to Cambridge to see you.'

'I didn't imagine you were aware of my existence until today.'

'Yes, we know of Professor Stevens in Soviet Union.' Krasov grinned. 'Not widely, you understand, but where it matters.'

'I'm flattered. But that doesn't explain your presence here.'

'I am messenger. I bring greetings from old Russian friend.'

'Do I have any old Russian friends?'

'Ruth Marchenko,' he said. 'Isn't she your friend?'

Stevens was stunned. 'Is she alive?'

'I am told she was few days ago. Of course, in Soviet Union, in few days, much can change.' Again the grin.

Ruth Marchenko.

How can he describe that moment? It was like a huge rush of water bursting through a door that had remained tightly shut for years. The past rushed out at him, throwing him off balance with its roaring flood of memories.

'So, you remember her?' Krasov asked.

'Of course I do.'

'She will be pleased. She was afraid you forget her.'

'How is she?'

'Quite well, I think.'

'How have you come across her?'

Krasov smiled. 'Marchenko is my friend also. We grow up together. We are neighbours. Our parents are friends. She is good woman, always good to me. Clever too. She is nuclear physicist but you know that already.'

'Tell me about her.'

'What do you want to know?'

'We have not seen each other for sixteen years.'

'She lives in Moscow with her mother and son.'

'She has a son?'

'Sure. Her husband was engineer, like me. I was trained as engineer, you know. Husband is dead. She works on secret project at the Institute of Nuclear Research. She has good reputation in Soviet Union.'

'She is well?'

'I think, yes. We have shortages, worse than here. Marchenko is lucky, she is scientist, she has privileged life.'

'Yet something is not well,' Stevens said, 'and you are here to tell me about it. Am I right?'

Krasov looked at him over the rim of his glass. 'I am happy you understand,' he said. 'Yes, Marchenko has problem.'

'What kind of problem?'

'Her life is in danger.'

'In danger from what?'

'I will need a little more whisky before I can tell you that,' Krasov said, handing his glass to Stevens.

'What did he tell you about me?' she asks.

He describes how she stood up at the monthly progress meeting to ask her questions; how a group under her leadership presented a list of demands to the Institute's directorate; how she and her colleagues matched the directorate's failure to reply with a progressive slowing down of the work on the Soviet nuclear bomb, until nothing was done.

'He told me that, almost single-handed, you brought the Soviet nuclear programme to a halt,' Stevens replies. 'Is that true?'

'More or less,' she answers.

'You must have been very brave.'

She is not listening to him. Wait, she wants to say. This is the story I came to Helsinki to tell you but what Krasov told you is not my story. *Wait.* It is like her story but it is *not* what happened. Krasov gave Stevens the version he was instructed to tell. How is he connected to the Institute? Who is telling him what is going on? Why? What is happening?

Who told Krasov to go to Cambridge to speak to Stevens? Krasov is taking instructions from someone, that is obvious. Someone unknown who knows about her. She doubts it is Andropov but if not Andropov, who? Maybe there is some other purpose at work now, a secret agenda she does not understand but which frightens her. Maybe Krasov is working against her. That is what distresses her. Her oldest friend, Little Krasov, whom she has always trusted, is betraying her, and, hanging over everything, who are they after: her or Stevens?

She wants to stop Stevens telling her anything more, she wants to say to him, don't believe any of this, it is an invention, a trap, all lies. There is no truth any more, it is lost, obliterated, forgotten. Krasov lied to you. I was acting on instructions. Nothing is what it seems.

Listen, the voice inside her says. Listen to what he tells you. Let him finish. You may learn something. If Stevens is in danger, then you must help him. If you are in danger, then you may help yourself. Remember those who depend on you.

'Krasov told me,' Stevens said, 'that you and your colleagues feared the continuing silence of the political authorities to your opposition. With each day that passed you became more sure that when they did react to your refusal to work, they would do so repressively. They would arrest you, try you secretly and execute you. That was the message you had asked Krasov to come to Cambridge to give me. I was your last resort. Am I right?'

Before she can answer his question there is something she must know first.

'When did Little Krasov come to Cambridge?' she asks. 'What month?'

'January.'

January?

'Can you remember the exact date?'

He takes out his red leather university diary that she remembers so well.

'It was the day of the Governing Body. January the ninth.'

'*The ninth*?'

'What does that tell you?' he asks.

That was at least a week *before* she had asked her question at the monthly progress meeting. Ten days before the secret committee was formed. How did Krasov know everything before it had happened?

'I asked my question at the monthly progress meeting on January the eighteenth. The events that Little Krasov described to you had not yet happened on the day that he told you about them.'

'Good God.' Stevens stares at her.

'He was lying to you. What his purpose was, I don't know.'

'Did what he described happen?'

'More or less.'

'But later.'

'Days later, yes.'

'Krasov said he was your friend.'

'Until I heard what you told me, he was my friend.'

'Tell me what happened at the Institute. You and your colleagues refused to work on your nuclear bomb programme. Is that true?'

'Yes.'

'On what grounds did you refuse?'

108

How can she answer that? She refused because she was instructed to do so by Andropov. She feared the consequences if she did not obey. Only later (how much later?) did she come to believe the arguments that he gave her; only then did the cause whose script he had written become her own. How can she explain that conversion to Stevens?

'A number of us who were working on the bomb had become aware of the possible consequences of what we were doing,' she says. 'It was a slow process, it didn't happen all at once. We studied the effects of the American bombs on Hiroshima and Nagasaki. We created models predicting the effects of explosions of different sizes of nuclear bomb. We came to understand the implications of the work we were involved in.'

'So you acted on your beliefs,' he says.

What choice did I have? she wants to say. At that time she had no beliefs – they came later.

'Yes,' she says, not sure if she's telling the truth.

'Krasov said your life was in danger. Was that true?'

'Probably.'

'You aren't certain?'

'It was a strange time. Nothing happened as we expected it to. We made our protest and there was no reaction. Only silence.'

'Krasov made a good case. He convinced me.'

'I had no knowledge that Krasov was coming to Cambridge to see you, nor that he knew anything about what was happening at the Institute.'

'Then why did he tell me that he was speaking on your behalf?'

Someone must have told him about Leiden, she wants to say. Why can't Stevens see this? Have the years taught him nothing about the ways of the world?

'If I knew I would tell you. He is the agent of someone – who that someone is, I do not know. What they want I do not know. Krasov and his masters were using me without my knowledge. I am sorry that you believed him.'

'If I hadn't been convinced, I wouldn't be here now. At least we have that to thank him for. He has brought us together again.'

'You are wrong,' she said. 'We did not choose to meet like this.'

'She is a brave woman,' Krasov said. 'But you know that already.'

'Will she survive?' Stevens asked.

'How do I know?' There was an unexpected coldness in his voice which disturbed Stevens.

'I suspect you know a great deal more than you are telling me,' Stevens said.

'Maybe yes, maybe no.'

'That's not an answer.'

'You want me to say yes, but how do I know if such an answer is right? What if I say yes and I am wrong?'

'Tell me what you think.'

'Without your help, no, I doubt she will live much longer.'

'What kind of help?'

'You must make it impossible for the authorities to execute her.'

'How would you suggest I do that?'

'You must defend her.'

'I'm a scientist, Krasov, not a lawyer.'

'You write in newspaper. So, write about Marchenko. Tell the world what she and the others are doing. How brave they are to risk their lives to bring peace. You have contacts in Government. Remind them not all Russians have lost their conscience. You know scientists from other Western countries who agree with these views. Tell them about Marchenko and her crusade. Get them to join their voices to yours. Raise your voices loud enough, all of you, and our leaders may hear. Whisper and they never will. Do you understand what I am asking? Is important message.'

'And if I don't?'

'Will happen as I say. Her life is in your hands. Ah, here is your son calling us to eat.'

15

DANNY

It was much later when the singing began. We had eaten by then and were in the sitting room, sprawled before a blazing fire, the remains of a bottle of claret within reach. We had exhausted politics; whether or not the country would run out of coal before this bitter winter ended; how best to supplement a ration-book diet; and a philosophical discussion on the state of the post-war world. My father's unexplained excitement had cooled.

Perhaps it was the presence of the piano that drew Krasov back into memories of his past. He stood by it for a long time before he played a note or two. No one said anything. Then he sat down, stretched his fingers and played a chord. Then another. He bent low over the keyboard, his eyes tightly shut, and started to sing to himself.

It was a truly Russian song, he explained, full of boldness and pathos, happiness and grief. Something precious, youthful love at its most extreme, was found and then lost. As we listened, the darkness around us was filled with the events of the song. We saw reapers in the field, among them a young peasant boy, tall and blond, and beside him a girl. All day long he works beside her, inspired by her beauty. At sunset, as the reapers drift away from the field, he declares his love. But as she looks up to take his kiss, a gypsy rides by, his black hair flowing in the wind, his gold earrings glinting in the dying sun. One call of her name and she has slipped from the boy's arms and is gone, lost in the night. The young farmhand's heart lies broken like the stalks of corn he holds in his hands.

It was an extraordinary performance, dramatic and powerful, and we clapped him when he had finished. For a moment, in the half-light, I saw my father's face strangely contorted as he listened to this song of love that might have been. Krasov bowed and thanked us, claiming his singing was without merit. He refused to sing any more, saying that songs about his mother country filled him with memories that only made him sad.

It was my father who suggested Rogers and Hart. He had an unexpected passion for popular music, and no voice at all. But Celia could sing and my father asked her to do so now, if Krasov would play. Celia hummed the tune, Krasov picked up the chords. She smiled at him and broke into a song.

Krasov took up the melody and played a soft accompaniment to her quiet alto, catching her phrasing, echoing it, leading her carefully through the music. He had only to hear the melodic line once to be able to improvise with chords and occasional trills, to catch the bitter-sweet mood of the songs.

Celia's voice was not strong but Krasov's presence, his sympathetic accompaniment, his musicality, gave her a confidence I had not seen before. She seemed to be singing for my father, and the sound of her voice was slowly drawing from him the anxiety whose symptoms he had displayed so strongly earlier in the evening.

For a time I thought there was more to it than that, a deeper and more personal message. I sensed Celia was singing for my father alone; Krasov and I were forgotten or ignored. It was like listening unobserved to an intimate conversation. With each line she was declaring her love, as if instinctively she knew she had to win my father back, letting the words of the song say what she could find no other way to say. Only later, when I asked myself why she felt she had needed to do this, did my reason prevail and I rejected my memory as fanciful and wrong. Celia and my father were happy. There was no reason to suggest any threat to their marriage.

We stayed like that until the logs in the fireplace had become glowing ash. Krasov closed the piano, smiled and thanked Celia for her kindness to him. He bowed to my father, kissed Celia's hand and went up to bed.

By the following morning he had got it into his head that his pursuers were on his track and knew where he was. He insisted he had to leave at once. Cambridge was no longer safe. He would return to London where Monty would know what to do with him. He must leave now, this minute, he was sorry, please, we should try to understand.

Bewildered, we watched him go, a small dark figure outlined sharply against the snow.

PART TWO

1

MONTY

Krasov's appearance shocked me; he was pale and nervous. My confident drinking companion had vanished. In his place I saw a man frightened and bemused, no longer sporting the bravado which had been for so long his trademark.

Things were bad and worse threatened, he told me, desperately clinging on to my arm. He could not go back to Moscow because he now knew they would kill him. When I asked him why, all he would say was that there were reasons. He refused to elaborate. I tried to persuade him not to be so melodramatic but he wouldn't listen. I was his friend, he said. We had good times together. I must protect him. He needed somewhere to hide. Now. At once. Before it was too late.

The tightening pressure on my arm banished any hope of arguing him out of his position. We couldn't stand at the cab rank all day. Whether I believed him or not (I wasn't sure but on balance I didn't), what mattered was that to Krasov his fear was real. If I was his friend (and I was) I had to help him.

'All right,' I said. 'I'll make sure you're safe for the present. Then we'll decide what to do about you.'

Looking at the neurotic figure beside me in the taxi (he crouched on the floor for the entire journey), I knew I had taken a huge risk in choosing loyalty to a friend over loyalty to the Department. I justified my action by telling myself it was only a matter of time before Krasov in this mood (unlike anything I'd experienced before) asked for political asylum. I was sure Krasov's defection would deal a significant blow to Soviet self-esteem and be a feather in SOVINT'S cap. A sense of elation overcame my foreboding.

The flat in Lowndes Square wasn't an official safe house but somewhere to be used in emergencies. Krasov's first act on entering was to pull the curtains. I opened them again and gave him his instructions. He was not to keep the curtains undrawn after dark, nor to draw them before it was dark. (It was now midday.) If he played the wireless, then it was to be played quietly. Not to answer the telephone, except at times agreed with me: I made him memorize the hours when I would call him and the procedure I would use. He was not to answer the door unless he heard the signal first. We agreed the times I would come in to check he was all right. On no account was he to go out for any reason at all. Secretly I decided to put a twenty-four-hour watch on the building.

'How shall I eat?' he asked.

'There's enough food here for a week,' I said, 'even for someone with your outrageous appetite.'

'Thank you, my friend,' Krasov said solemnly, as I finished the tour of the apartment. 'You are saving my life.'

'I'm giving you a breathing space,' I said. 'Nobody knows where you are. For now you're safe.'

'Maybe I am too much trouble,' he said gloomily. 'Maybe I change my mind and give myself up.'

To whom? The Russians? Why was he running away from them? Why on earth had he gone to Cambridge? What had he done that put his life in danger? There were any number of questions to which I wanted answers but for the moment Krasov was in no mood to provide them.

'You've got thirty-six hours to think about that,' I said firmly. 'For the moment, you're safe. Be grateful for that.'

'Safety,' he said. 'That is concept hard to imagine.'

I left him trying to do just that.

★

Krasov had arrived in London as Hitler began his ill-starred invasion of Russia. At stake was the route through the Urals and the Caucasus to the rich oilfields of the Middle East. Stalingrad was the gate through which the Germans had to pass if they were to gain this prize. We saw our fate in the hands of the Russians, and over the succeeding weeks, as we followed the fortunes of this extraordinary battle, our alliance with the Soviet Union was at its strongest. From the sidelines we prayed the German advance would be stopped but feared it wouldn't. Then in February, the battle finally over, we cheered the victory and toasted every Russian we knew.

Among them was Leonid Krasov. He worked as a journalist for Tass and within weeks of his arrival he had established contacts in Fleet Street, government departments, political parties and the trades unions. With his fluency in English and his undoubted charm (how unlike our image of a communist he was), he rapidly became a popular figure in London.

In those first months of his posting we kept a persistent eye on him. He paid routine visits to the Russian embassy but we would have been surprised if he hadn't. He did not appear to spend much time there (a good sign); he certainly wasn't friendly with any of the staff, diplomatic or KGB (even better). The evidence suggested that we had to take him for what he said he was, a working journalist posted to London.

I met the diminutive Russian at a party a year after Stalingrad. We had a drink together one evening a week or two later and found we got on. He was the first Russian I had ever got to know and I enjoyed his company. His lugubrious view of the world amused me. I declared this relationship to Corless, who saw it as a possible investment in the future.

'Cultivate him,' he said. 'You never know when a friendly Soviet may come in useful, nor what you might learn from him. But don't forget, he's not only Russian, he's Soviet, whatever he may say to the contrary.'

I was left to work out the difference for myself.

In the months after the Yalta Conference, a group within SOVINT produced a report that showed how the Soviet Union could well become our enemy once the present hostilities ceased. This upset the Russian desk at the Foreign Office, who sat on the report and successfully prevented its official circulation. (Guy Benton denied a hand in this but few of us believed him.) A number of carbon copies did the rounds and unofficially the report had its converts. Corless was one of them.

'We're keeping an eye on the Soviets in London,' he warned. 'Even if they appear friendly, they probably aren't. That includes Krasov.'

I argued that it was hard to see Krasov working against us, but Corless showed me how the inveterate party-goer, friend of politicians, journalists and the military, the atypical communist, could pick up gossip in the normal course of his journalistic activities which, when shipped back to Moscow for analysis, might yield unexpected clues to the whereabouts of senior military personnel or to the direction of political thinking within the Government. That, in turn, might reveal information about British military intentions or our national political temper. Both had a value to a potential enemy.

I kept a close eye on Krasov but remained unconvinced. We ate our way through the best London restaurants (I was continually astonished at his extraordinary appetite), we met at parties where, usually late in the evening, Krasov could be persuaded to play American popular songs on the piano. His great love was Fats Waller, of whom he did a hilarious and much requested imitation.

Women adored him. At parties he would be surrounded by them; when we met for dinner, he would often have to make a telephone call before dessert to confirm the assignation he had set up for when our dinner ended, though he never talked about his conquests.

One night a month or two after the war ended, Krasov arrived uninvited at my flat in Victoria. He was already well oiled and he got drunker as the evening progressed. He insisted I drink with him, which I did with great reluctance. He rambled on about his disillusion with the Soviet Union, his fears for the future, how communism was taking the wrong path, how the idealism of his youth had no place any more. How could he return to a Russia that had betrayed its own revolutionary ideals? What was to become of him? For one awful moment I thought he might be going to cry.

Suffering from a terrible hangover, I reported this conversation to Corless and gave it my own gloss. Was this a sign that Krasov was out of sorts with his own side? Was he warming us up because he wanted to work for us? Corless dismissed my optimism.

'He's Russian,' he said. 'The Russians are unstable. He's acting in the national character, not out of it.' The drunkenness, he maintained, was as much an illusion as his disillusion was a disguise. The hammering in my head made it all feel horribly real to me, though I couldn't tell Corless that.

'Our relations with the Soviets are cooling,' Corless said. 'Krasov knows that. He's unhappy about it. He's letting his feelings show. Don't be taken in. Keep him in your sights. Stay friendly with him. He may tell us something yet.'

A week or two later, in an unusual moment of intimacy prompted by a large glass of my best malt, Krasov opened his heart and poured out his troubles to me. The difference was that this time he was more or less sober.

He was, he explained, 'old London hand'. The new regime of

hardline purists at the embassy feared the dangers of contamination from too close an association with decadent bourgeois. Everyone who had been stationed in London longer than six months, and that included the ambassador and the head of the news agency, was under surveillance. The world was not moving in a direction Krasov liked or understood. How he yearned for the old days and the camaraderie of the war years. Life had been so much simpler then. It was a lament I was getting used to.

'Remember those years in war? Remember parties after Stalingrad? There was strong friendship between our countries then. Now we are being forced to be enemies. It is not what I like.'

How politics ruins the lives of ordinary people, we agreed. If only the politicians could leave us all alone, how much better a place the world would be.

'If this is what peace brings us,' he added gloomily, 'I prefer certainties of war.'

I was his friend, he said. His good English friend. In many ways he felt we were alike. Surely I must understand what he meant? The Soviet Union he had left to come to London was being replaced by a Soviet Union he did not recognize, a world in which he believed he had no part, where he was 'fish out of water'. The purity of the Soviet ideal had been buried in the murky politics of survival and ambition. The revolutionaries had gone, the bureaucrats had won. He was an old revolutionary with nothing to fight for, his ideals had been stolen by those who had inherited the world he had helped to make. It was the long and bitter lament of a displaced man.

When he talked like this, was Krasov putting on an act, or was he genuine? After he'd gone, I wrote down what he had said and analysed it. Krasov was giving me a coded message, I quickly concluded, whose cipher needed no decrypt. He was afraid to return home. He wanted to stay in London. I was to help him achieve this because I was his friend.

Weeks passed. The Department was deeply involved in the processing of Peter information. I saw Krasov for irregular but punishing drinking sessions, often in the company of his English friends. It all seemed harmless enough in its way (except for the morning after when I would always swear 'never again'), and I hardly bothered to tell Corless about my meetings with him.

Then, on the evening I introduced him to Danny Stevens, he told us that the London interlude was finally over, and that he had

119

been recalled to Moscow. He was being watched, he said, to make sure he didn't weaken in the last few days and try to stay.

'So ridiculous. What would I stay for?'

He put a brave face on his by now very uncertain future but I sensed his heart wasn't in it. He came for a drink in my flat the following night and I tried to argue him out of returning. I genuinely feared for his safety when he got back and told him so. He wouldn't listen. He was 'great survivor', he said. Moscow was where he belonged. The old rebel had vanished. In his place I saw a compromising Krasov whom I didn't like because it didn't fit what I knew.

His friends organized a series of farewell parties. I saw him repeatedly but never to talk to alone. It was as if he was deliberately staying out of reach.

'Don't worry, my friend,' he said. 'We will meet soon. We will talk one last time, I promise.'

He didn't keep his promise because he disappeared. For three days I heard nothing. Then Danny telephoned me from Cambridge to say Krasov was with him (what the hell was he doing in Cambridge of all places?) and he was on the run from his own people. He'd put Krasov up for the night but now the little Russian had got it into his head that the vultures were circling the Fens and if he stayed any longer, he'd be carrion.

'I told him vultures have never been spotted in the Fens,' Danny said. 'But I don't think I convinced him.'

Why did he imagine London was safer than Cambridge? I asked. Danny couldn't say. He was putting Krasov on the King's Cross train and begged me to be there to meet him.

The code was easy and I made the translation I was sure that Krasov wanted me to make. He had decided not to return to Moscow and now he wanted protection from his own side as a prelude to coming over. That was why he wanted me to meet him. It was an opportunity not to be missed. I arrived at King's Cross twenty minutes early, and spent the time prowling around on the lookout for obvious Russians. If there were any there, I didn't spot them.

★

Krasov answered all the Saturday contacts, one visit and two telephone calls. On Sunday morning he said he had slept well and was listening to a concert of Russian music on the wireless. I could hear it in the background as we talked, a martial chorus from Borodin's

120

Prince Igor. He was in reasonable spirits when I went to the flat before lunch. By the afternoon, his mood had changed, and he was once more full of doubts about himself and his future.

'If you're afraid to go back to Moscow,' I said, taking the plunge, 'why not stay put? You've got friends. We could help you make a new life here. You'd be safe.'

'Why would you British want me?' he said. 'I have nothing to offer. No secrets, no expertise. I am journalist, not diplomat.'

I tried to argue him out of this position. I was sure, I said, that he had information we would find of value.

'I am Russian,' he said. 'Is not easy choice for me to stay here. How can I live for rest of my life outside my country? I have seen White Russians here, they are pathetic, dreaming of world that never existed, living without money, full of illusions, telling themselves that soon communist world will fall to pieces and then they will return to former lives in glory. I am not delusional. I cannot live in dreamland. Clock cannot be put back. I am not one of these lost people.'

'Then what are you?' I asked, trying to wrench him back to the point.

'What indeed, my friend? What indeed? That is what I ask myself all days of my life.'

The argument was circular. He did not want to return to Russia because he was afraid he would be killed, though he refused to say why. He did not want to stay in England because he could not face a life of exile, and anyway he had nothing to offer the British. Then the fatalism surfaced again.

'It is pointless, this pretending. There is no escape. They will find me, they will kill me. That much is certain. It was bad mistake to go to Cambridge. I will telephone Russian embassy now. I will give myself up.'

I tried vainly to argue with him. He wouldn't listen. No need to telephone, he said. His people were probably waiting outside now in the square. All he had to do was open the door. What did it matter? His life was over. I should leave him to his fate.

I lost my temper.

'For God's sake, Leo. What's keeping you? You're free to walk out of here whenever you like. No one's stopping you. So why not do it? Why not give your people the pleasure of taking you back to Moscow and putting a bullet through your head?'

He looked at me, hurt and disappointed.

'That is first time you shout at me, Monty.'

I felt guilty at once. I was angry at his indecision and impatient of his justifiable reasons for it.

'You're driving me to it, Leo. I can't interpret your wishes. I don't know what you want me to do. If you don't want me to help you stay here, say so and I'll go. All you've got to do is make up your mind.'

We looked at each other in silence. Then he held my arm.

'I am sorry, my friend,' he said. 'I am frightened. That is it. I am frightened of what they do to me when they find me. Forgive me.'

'Keep your head down here and they won't find you. I'll see to that,' I said rashly.

'I wish I could believe that. They have eyes everywhere,' Krasov said.

I wanted to hit him. 'For God's sake, Leo.'

'You are good man, Monty. But you will never understand what is like to be Russian.'

I left him to his own devices soon after that, relieved to get away. I couldn't imagine what it was like to be Russian and I didn't want to. I was angry with him, and angry with myself for not trusting him.

I replayed the conversation in my head, sensing there was more to this whole business than I had allowed for. I had made an offer to help Krasov stay in the West and he had refused without actually refusing. He had never said no but I had got the message. Did that mean he had changed his mind? Or had he never had any intention of defecting, and Corless was right after all? If so, what was the 'escape' to Cambridge about? What was he doing there? I thought of Peter's warning about Stevens. Was Krasov's visit connected with that? Did the change of mind that led to his return to London mean he had completed some task for his Soviet masters in Cambridge? What was he doing hiding in Lowndes Square now if he wasn't on the run from his own people? As I failed to find satisfactory answers, I saw myself being manipulated and the man I had treated as a friend slowly turning into . . . what? A stranger? Or an enemy?

I was out of my depth. The moment I got home I telephoned the duty officer in Horseferry Road who reluctantly gave me a number for Corless. I tried it but there was no answer. I rang Corless every thirty minutes but there was no one home.

Two hours later I went back to Lowndes Square as we had agreed. The flat was empty. Krasov had vanished. Some decision had been taken, but I had no idea what.

2

___

RUTH

The telephone rings twice and stops.

She is startled, even though she is expecting it. She looks at her watch. Twelve-eighteen. Why must it always be so late? Wearily she drags herself out of her chair, puts on her coat, scarf, fur hat and boots and quietly leaves the flat, locking the door behind her. Down in the elevator. Across the dimly lit lobby. (What business is it of the babushka's what she does at this time of night? She can think what she likes.) Out into the dark street, the cold air hitting her like a blow.

She and Andropov no longer meet in his office. There are no more telephone calls for her at the Institute, no official car arrives to collect her during working hours. Each night she waits for the eloquent, commanding silence after the second ring before she sets out into the freezing dark. Three blocks away, parked outside the Novostny Bank building, its exhaust congealing in the night air, the black limousine waits for her.

Andropov sits inside, smoking. She opens the door, gets in and is driven off into the night. Not a word is spoken between them, no greeting, no acknowledgement of her presence. Andropov ignores her until they are alone. Their meeting places vary in location but little in setting; anonymous rooms in unlived-in apartments scattered all over Moscow. She wonders what else they are used for.

It is like this most nights now.

★

Her question at the progress meeting has touched a secret nerve among the senior scientific staff at the Institute, and set off a response beyond her imagining. She finds anonymous notes tucked into her overall pocket, slipped inside copies of minutes of meetings left in her in-tray; one is hidden behind the flowerpot she keeps on her window sill. The text of each is similar: admiration at her courage in asking what others have never dared to ask. She is flattered but not beguiled.

Discretely her correspondents identify themselves. Secret smiles in the canteen, doors held open for her and a touch on the arm as she passes. The ladies' lavatory becomes an unexpected centre of revelation, glances, smiles, nods – a Masonic language of recognition. As she adjusts the clips in her hair, faces appear next to hers in the mirror and knowing looks are exchanged.

'They are behaving as I expected,' Andropov tells her. 'Encourage them.'

One night Leon Gromsky (he is an expert on explosive lenses), catches up with her as they leave the Institute. He whispers that he has been unable to sleep since her brave statement at the progress meeting. His conscience has been reawakened. He now questions their work at the Institute.

'We cannot create such a mighty weapon of destruction without establishing political limits to its use,' he says. He is not alone in this opinion, he tells her. There are others who share his doubts and are willing to join them.

'Join what?' she asks, terrified at this unexpected level of involvement. She has never joined anything in her life. She hates joining.

He doesn't hear her question in his enthusiasm to enlist her support in a new cause. Gromsky is an enthusiast.

She tries to steer him away from the idea of any meeting of 'those of like mind.' She is ashamed of the deception she is practising, but how does she know Gromsky hasn't been set up by the secret police to trap her? (Later, Andropov puts her mind at rest on this point.) Gromsky brushes aside her objections. Her courage has aroused in him a sense of responsibility for what they are doing.

'Given the nature of our work, we cannot remain passive. We must act.'

She concedes to his request because Andropov has told her she must. Late one evening four of her colleagues from the Institute arrive separately at her apartment.

She listens to them talk, using the presence of her mother and son in the next room as an excuse for them to keep their voices down, privately terrified that her neighbours will report to the secret police the unusual noise in her flat and that suddenly the door will burst open and they will all be arrested. Twice during the evening she goes into the kitchen by herself, turns out the light and looks through the curtain at the street below. Once she opens her front door and peers into the corridor. She sees and hears nothing. Her absences go unnoticed by the others, who are gripped by the fever of their new-found freedom to speak their minds.

Buoyed up by their success, they agree to meet again. She does not remember what they said at their first meeting, only the excitement of their discussion. She herself has said little.

The next time four have become nine. There is hardly room for them in the flat. Her eyes and throat burn from the smoke of their cigarettes. She does not have enough glasses. Three of them have to drink vodka from cups.

'If the risks of meeting like this are to be justified,' says Leon Gromsky, 'and if we are to consolidate the position Ruth Marchenko has so courageously set up for us, then these gatherings must have some purpose. I propose a statement of aims.'

Andropov has already prepared her for this.

'Establish the common ground between you. It is important, at this stage, that first you talk, get used to each other. Then organize yourselves, make plans. There will be time for action later.'

She encourages them to talk. 'First we must organize ourselves,' she says. 'There will be time for action later.'

They are impressed by her wisdom.

Pavel Lykowski, whose youthful face conceals the most brilliant mind in the Institute, smiles at the possibility of future action. She wishes he would drink less at these meetings but she does not know how to broach the subject without sounding like his mother. She knows Pavel dislikes his mother.

Led by Alexei Tomasov, a researcher in her department, they agree the need for an agenda. What topics should they discuss? Prompted by her meeting with Andropov the night before (or was it earlier that morning?), she proposes they begin by discussing the implications of the scale of destruction caused by the explosions in Japan.

The importance of Hiroshima and Nagasaki, she tells them, is that they provide the only available evidence of the impact of nuclear explosions on concentrated areas of social and economic activity. (Why can't she says 'towns' or 'cities'? What's happening to her?) They have never before discussed among themselves the possible consequences on the *civilian* population of a nuclear explosion. If the information and analysis of Hiroshima and Nagasaki are correct (and they have no reasons to doubt the official reports, copies of which are in the Institute's library), then they are involved in a process that could lead to the deaths of many thousands of innocent people. A nuclear bomb is by its very nature indiscriminate.

Two meetings later the possibility of casualties from a single bomb has grown from a few thousand to millions in a war in which the exchange of nuclear weapons lasts only a few hours. Civilians will die, they agree, in increasing numbers because nuclear destruction cannot discriminate between military and civilian targets.

What can they do? They agree that, on the basis of the projections they are making, using the empirical evidence of Hiroshima and Nagasaki, they cannot remain indifferent in the face of the appalling truth that they now openly acknowledge to each other.

'Organize,' Gromsky says, echoing Andropov's words. 'Now is the time to organize.' (Organization is the Soviet solution to any circumstance.)

'And change the world,' Elizabeth Markarova whispers knowingly to Ruth. Is this cynicism? The voice of weary experience? Or a new-found belief?

There are murmurs of assent. No one knows what this means but it sounds right. It is what people in their position *ought* to be saying to each other.

'Create a movement, subvert and oppose, above all oppose,' someone says (who? Gromsky? Probably).

'Stop the murder of innocent people,' Lykowski shouts in support at this point. 'Change for ever the nuclear policy of the Soviet Union.'

He is hastily subdued by Tomasov and Gromsky, who are aware of Ruth's concerns about arousing the neighbours. Others take up the idea. Warn the world of the dangers it faces. Make a better, safer world. Banish nuclear weapons. Banish war. Nuclear energy as the servant of society, not its destroyer. They are carried away by their own enthusiasm and the vodka that they have brought, concealed in the folds of their overcoats, as they paint the future of their dreams.

Say no. Say no. We must teach the world how to say no.

Ruth is alarmed. They continue to talk and drink. In their heads they are fighting a war and winning. In reality, she sees this event running away with itself. What began as a lone voice of protest only a few days ago has grown with alarming speed into a rebellion that is straining to free itself of her (or of any) control. The conventional reserve which dictated the initial actions of herself and her colleagues has been discarded in favour of a reckless openness within the group that has formed around her. Sooner or later a careless word or an undisciplined act will betray them. She fears the brutal response of the secret police to any talk of opposition. She tells Andropov of her anxieties.

'Hold them back,' he says urgently. 'You must exercise control over them. That is your essential task now. You must succeed.'

This is the moment of greatest risk in his plan, when he is dependent solely on her to achieve what he wants. She feels inadequate and desperate. There is no one she can turn to. She tries her best to bring them back to reality.

'Courage,' her companions say, defying her efforts. They are beyond the reach of argument by now. 'We will win.'

'We will be betrayed,' she says. She reminds them of the powers of the secret police whose spies surround them.

They laugh at her fears. The secret police are buffoons, they reply. We will outwit them. Their task is of major importance, Gromsky tells her (he is drunk). They alone can save the world from destruction. That has become their mission. In their own country, they will be listened to because their skills as nuclear scientists cannot be replaced.

'Where are the other nuclear scientists in the Soviet Union?' Tomasov asks. 'Without us they can do nothing'. They will tell the state what to do and the state will have to obey. What a bargaining position. 'We are inviolate.'

Ruth knows, as they do, that other institutes are working on the bomb too. They are not inviolate. Far from it. She cannot hold them back, she tells Andropov. She bursts into tears of strain and despair.

'It is time to form a committee,' Andropov instructs. 'Give them a world they can understand. They are the creatures of committees. They will respond.'

Elizabeth Markarova is her ally. She whispers to Ruth one day in the ladies' lavatory, 'We must form a committee.' They agree that discipline must be imposed or the advantage they have gained will be lost; their energies will be wasted through disorganization, which is no doubt what the political authorities expect. With Markarova's help, during a difficult meeting, a committee is formed. Votes are taken. Roles are assigned. Energies that threatened to get out of hand are now channelled. There is even an 'agitation secretary', a concession to the possibility of future action. The vote goes against Pavel Lykowski for this role. He is inconsolable. Slowly some kind of order is restored. Ruth's anxieties diminish.

Further meetings are planned, other venues chosen. No longer will they risk always meeting at her apartment. A strategy paper will be presented, Gromsky says – he is now political secretary. The drafting has begun but like so much Soviet activity, it is already behind schedule. When completed, it will be discussed and agreed and will form the basis of the demands that they will put before the Institute's directorate.

There is heated discussion at this point and the committee threatens to divide into two camps, those who believe they must plan each stage with care, and the hotheads (Ruth is surprised that Tomasov supports Lykowski in this), who are all for action now. What action is unclear, but anything to keep the cause alive. Prudent counsels prevail.

Ruth is elected Comrade Chairman, an honour she tries to decline. Elizabeth Markarova deserves that honour, she argues. They will have none of it: her candidacy is put to the vote and she wins. The event now has a momentum of its own. She sees a new excitement in the faces of her companions, she senses the pitch of the emotions in their hearts, she feels the extraordinary energies that have been released.

She remains untouched by everything she says and hears. She performs her role for Andropov faultlessly. She feels hollow, empty and vulnerable. She is giving the performance of her life because she knows her life depends upon it.

★

He is taking her on a journey but where to she doesn't know and he does not tell her.

He arrives at their midnight meetings without papers (never even a briefcase) and he hands her none. He allows her to take no written notes. He insists they both commit everything to memory.

'There must be no evidence,' he says, 'to prove that these conversations have ever taken place.'

At each meeting he reveals the next stage in his complex design, the shape of which she cannot comprehend. It is like unfolding a map an inch at a time. Each day she knows the distance she has travelled, but she is denied a sense of direction or destination. He tells her what she needs to know, not what she wants to know. She has tried questioning him but he refuses to answer her. Now she has given that up. She accepts.

The routine has become predictable. He asks her to describe the latest activity of her 'group', as he calls it. Where did they meet? Who was there? Who said what? What decisions have they taken? This irritates her because she is certain he already knows what has gone on (she cannot bring herself to believe that he hasn't got an informant on the committee). Perhaps he asks for her account to test her commitment to him. She hates it but there is nothing she can do.

Then he gives her a prepared position for the next meeting and they rehearse the arguments. She dislikes the sublimation of her own identity that this act demands but she has travelled too far with him now to reject his script. Without his guidance she is disorientated and vulnerable. She does what he asks and she performs well, as he knows she will.

After each meeting with Andropov, she lies in bed trying to calm her disturbed mind into a short and troubled sleep (has Andropov no home to go to? Is that why he keeps her up so late?).

Why is he making her do this? What does he want to achieve? But she can find no answers (or none that makes any sense) and Andropov has offered no explanation. She is forced to accept his silence because her greater anxiety is that one night he will not summon her. Then she will have no script to guide her and the truth of her deceit, her inability to speak without his prompting (she still does not have any conviction about what she is doing) will be revealed to her colleagues at the Institute.

★

Once, without warning, Andropov comes to her apartment. He arrives at one o'clock in the morning, pressing the bell twice and terrifying her, while she is clearing up after an unexpected meeting of the committee. She is alarmed her friends will have seen Andropov as they leave the building. He is amused by her distress.

'I have played this game a long time,' he says. 'I can become invisible when I wish to.'

She begs him never to do this again and so far he has kept away. He has seen how his visit has distressed her. She sees his compliance as a sign of her importance to him but she is so exhausted from the strain of her deception that she is unable to make anything of this.

Andropov says he is pleased with their progress. The committee is doing its job well. She reminds him that the directorate has rejected every recommendation her committee has so far made. (She remembers the unfamiliar, shiny corridor, the knock on the door of the deputy director's office, the wait until the light changed from red to green, the formal greetings, *Comrade Deputy Director, Comrade Marchenko*, the splinter of wood on the leg of the chair on which she tore her stockings, the serrated edge of the paperknife he used to open her envelope, his concentration as he read the first page of the letter – 'Recommendations,' Gromsky had said, 'Demands,' Lykowski had shouted – her departure down the same empty corridor after his mumbled response that he will reply to her in due course, and then later the one-line letter of rejection.)

'Rejection,' Andropov says, 'is the only response they know.' The commissars do not know how to cope with the demands made of them. Their hope is that continual rejection will stifle the root of their opposition. He reminds her that it is her task to ensure that this does not happen. He asks after the progress of the list of demands Gromsky is preparing (she is surprised he doesn't refer to it as a policy document). She gives him the bad news that it is delayed. He tells her that keeping up the pressure is important. She must pursue Gromsky. He gives her a list of points for inclusion in the document.

He commends her own performance and reminds her of comments she has made during a recent meeting. She knows then that someone within the committee is Andropov's creature too, one of whose purposes, at least, is to report on her. She wonders if this man or woman knows she is simply the vehicle for Andropov's design. She assumes not. She is now even more confused about Andropov's role.

★

One night she takes her courage in her hands and asks Andropov once more why he is asking her to do this. Why is he stirring up this opposition within the Institute when he himself has said that its work is so important, that Soviet foreign policy calls for the manufacture of the Soviet nuclear bomb? What is the true purpose of this strange drama in which she finds herself playing so unexpectedly important a part? How does the creation of an opposition to nuclear development within the Soviet Union help the cause of damaging the processes of nuclear research in the West?

He turns towards her and smiles. The light from the lamp on the table beside him flashes momentarily across the lenses of his rimless glasses. The smoke from his cigarette clears from in front of his face and she sees his cold blue eyes staring at her. For a moment she suspects he is near to telling her and she waits, holding her breath. Will he pull back the black cover he has thrown over the cage of her life and reveal a chink of light? But his discipline reasserts itself and a brief smile is all he will concede. He says nothing. She must be content with his smile.

★

Now they appear to have entered a period of relative calm. For a while there are no new instructions, though Andropov insists they must continue to meet as before.

'The initial move has achieved its objectives,' Andropov tells her. What objectives? she wants to ask but doesn't.

His mood is expansive; he offers her a cigarette, something he has not done before. She wonders if he is finding reasons to prolong their meetings which now could be over in five minutes or less, as for the moment he seems to have little or nothing to say to her. But he keeps her there as long as before, usually up to an hour or more. The conversation moves away from the strict agenda of the early meetings. He asks after her mother and her son. At first she is suspicious and says little. Slowly she senses that his questions are genuine, that he wants to talk to her. She wonders why. Is it possible that he is lonely?

They are sitting in a pool of yellow light in the living room of a small apartment somewhere in the city. She has, as usual, no idea where they are tonight, and has given up trying to discover where he takes her. The curtains are pulled. They are alone. His driver waits in the car in the street many floors below. (How many? Seven? Eight? She can't remember). He smokes. Sometimes he offers her a cigarette. They don't drink anything, not even tea. She wonders if the apartment has a kettle. Outside she hears the distant noise of the city, a lorry plunging through melting snow in the street, the wail of a siren, a human cry, part curse, part despair, all the sounds of Moscow at night. Never before have they frightened her but now she starts at each sound.

Andropov is talking about the official reaction to her committee's latest demands. He calls it 'her' committee. She hates that. The political directorate at the Institute, he tells her, is puzzled by this prolonged upsurge of discontent about which they can do little. What has caused it? Why will it not go away? Why has their offer

131

of improved privileges (cheap rates to rent a summer dacha, better-quality winter coats at GUM, cheaper than those bought anywhere else in Moscow) had no effect? They are baffled by events. They have no idea what tactics to employ to quieten it down.

'What'll we do?' she asks.

'Wait,' he says. 'For the moment, we will do nothing. We must not add to their confusion – that will only make their response more rigid.'

'Do nothing for the present,' she tells her committee later. 'We have achieved our first objective, we have confused the directorate. Let's see how they react to their confusion. That may create new opportunities for us.'

There is some complaint at this, the more fiery members of the committee scenting blood and wanting to go for the kill.

'We have them on the run. We must push, push, push till they fall over. We have an opportunity now which will not recur.' (This is Lykowksi who, with all the skills of a politician, has ruthlessly promoted himself and his opinions. Sometimes she wonders if he is not an agent provocateur.)

She argues that the power of the authorities is absolute, they must never forget that, and that they are fooling themselves if they think they can push them over. After all, she says, hoping it is true, they are all responsible people and their demands are legitimate. They require a legitimate response. Fight orthodoxy with orthodoxy (Andropov's phrase) and not as a rabble. Their great asset, she reminds them (Andropov again) is that they are more organized than their opponents. That is their strength, which they must not squander. To her relief, and with support from Gromsky and Markarova, she wins the argument and restrains the hotheads.

She does not report this to Andropov but the following day he tells her: 'The authorities will never fall over. You were right to remind your colleagues of that.'

He is putting her on notice that every move she makes is watched, every word she speaks is recorded. Sometimes she finds the strain so great that she wants to scream the truth in the middle of a committee meeting. Then there flashes across her mind the faces of her mother and son and she knows that any revelation of her double life is impossible. The truth would condemn them as well as herself. There is no way out for her, as Andropov knows. She is locked into the deceit.

132

3

MONTY

'We nearly jumped out of our skins, guv, when the Old Bill rolled up. Gave us the shock of our lives.'

We were sitting disconsolately in a car outside the entrance to the building, waiting for Corless. Above us was the darkened window where, until a short while ago, a light behind a curtain had reassured us that Krasov was safe and sound. In the space of a few moments our world had been turned upside down.

'What the hell did the police want?'

'Search me, guv. All very quiet, like. No lights, no bells, nothing. Three cars and a Black Maria. A couple of bobbies posted front and back. Then these three uniformed officers go in through the front door, don't they? A minute later out they come with some poor sod under a blanket and they're away. All over in the blink of an eye. Nothing we could do about it, was there, sir?'

'Who was it, the local nick?'

'No, sir. The local swears blind they knew nothing was going on in their parish. I'm sure they didn't take our boy.'

I found a telephone box and rang the duty desk at Scotland Yard. I was given the runaround at once. There is no one more obtuse than a policeman who doesn't want to be helpful.

Foreign gentleman would he be, sir, with a name like that? Karsov, was it? Could I spell that, please? Nobody of that name, no, sir. Nothing in the duty book. Just a minute, sir. Sounds of a muffled conversation, one hand partly over the receiver. Yes, he could confirm someone had been brought in, Russian gentleman, Mr Krakoff by name. No, sir, he couldn't authorize that, he's being held incommunicado at present.

Nothing more after that, just round in circles, an impenetrable defence that left me furious at my impotence and apprehensive about what might happen now.

Corless turned up at midnight, wearing a dinner jacket. He had been angry when I had finally made contact and given him the news about Krasov. His temper hadn't cooled on the journey back to London.

'What an utter mess,' he said. 'What the hell were you doing with him anyway? You had no authority to take charge. Why didn't you get hold of me at once?'

I did my best to explain that I'd tried but he wasn't in a mood for listening.

'Where's Krasov now? Do we know who's got him?'

'Scotland Yard are holding him overnight.'

'You've asked to see him and some idiot in blue has said no? Is that right?'

'Out of bounds,' I said, shaking my head. 'Very unhelpful. Didn't want to know.'

'I'm going to make a telephone call,' Corless said impatiently.

But his contact, whoever he was, wouldn't oblige. The establishment he thought he'd joined still had him on probation. He didn't like that, especially since I was a witness to his rejection. (A setback to the growth industry of Corless mythology, not good for rising stars.) His mood darkened.

'Do you know what pisses me off?' he said, genuine bitterness in his voice. 'A man who is probably an active member of the Russian intelligence service and not the friendly journalist *some* of us imagined him to be' he glanced at me, 'is sitting in a nice warm cell a mile away from here, while all because of our bloody bureaucracy we're out here freezing our balls off unable to get our hands on him. No wonder this country is going to the dogs.' He pulled up the collar of his overcoat. 'Let's go and get a cup of tea. You can tell me the full story on the way.'

We walked to the cabbies' hut in Pont Street and got two cups of strong tea which we drank in the back of Corless's car. I told him as much as I knew.

★

'Christ!' Corless banged his gloved hand against the side of the car. 'We had him in our grasp and now we've lost him.'

He was sunk in gloom. Krasov was a sleeper, he said. He'd served his years as a journalist, established himself so well that when the call came we were looking the other way. He'd been wrong about Krasov. We'd all been wrong about Krasov.

'The Soviets need to contact their source in Cambridge. Who better for the job than our friendly Russian? He spins some yarn about being afraid to go home and we all fall for it. Minutes later he's getting soup and sympathy in the home of his target. Half an hour with Stevens and the deed, whatever it is, is done. Next day he's back in town, we shelter him for the weekend and as the time comes for a move, Scotland Yard take over and hand him back to his own people the following day and we can't touch him. All very neat, thank you very much. We've been set up, good and proper, that's for sure.'

It was meant to hurt and it did.

'Nothing more we can do tonight,' he said. 'We've lost this round. Let's get some sleep. We'll meet again at eight and see if we can retrieve something then.'

The light of day didn't make things better. Colin Maitland put his head round the door. Rupert had summoned him at dawn from the depths of Sussex.

'Our boy's in the embassy, Rupert. First thing this morning. Police escort all the way. Looked like royalty. The press are on to it, I'm afraid. Someone tipped them off.'

Corless's secretary came in (another early-morning telephone call to her flat in Putney). 'I got on to Northolt, sir. There's an Aeroflot plane leaving at two-thirty.'

'That's the one they'll be going for,' Corless said, suddenly animated. 'That gives us five hours.'

'Do you want me to get the car, sir?'

'Better still, Maureen,' he said, scribbling a number on a piece of paper and giving it to her, 'see if you can raise Willy Glover, will you? Say I need to speak to him urgently.'

'You won't be popular,' Maitland said. 'Glover's spending the weekend with David Iredale.'

'I'm not in this to be popular,' Corless snapped. 'I'm sure Glover will think national security's more important that slaughtering birds on Iredale's estate.'

The buzzer went on Corless's desk.

'Mr Glover for you, sir.'

It was a fairly stilted conversation and Corless didn't get his way at first. But he stuck to his point, Glover gave in and said he'd be with us by eleven. He was senior to Corless and he had the clout Rupert so obviously lacked. Rupert's idea, I imagined, was to get him to sanction his scheme, whatever it was.

Corless put the telephone down and we heard Maureen's voice on the intercom.

'I've put the car on standby all day. We'll pick up Mr Glover at Victoria.'

'Thank you, Maureen.' Corless looked at his watch. 'Maybe there's a chance we can pull something out of the bag.' He pressed the buzzer again. 'Maureen. Some of us missed our breakfast. We'd love one of your famous cups of tea. And any chance of a piece of toast, Mr Maitland asks?'

★

'This had better be good, Rupert.' In his tweed suit Glover looked more like a country squire than a senior civil servant, what Corless in the days before his elevation had called weekend fancy dress but which now he copied slavishly. 'David Iredale doesn't like his guests being called away when he's asked them down for a shoot.'

Corless said he hoped Lord Iredale would accept his apologies for the inconvenience. If he hadn't judged it important, he would never have asked for the meeting. He reported that he had evidence that Krasov had been in Cambridge, in contact with a senior British nuclear scientist already suspected of working with the Russians. He wanted an order to prevent Krasov from leaving the country, pending further enquiries. The Russian was to be arrested and handed over to SOVINT for questioning.

'No can do, Rupert. Sorry.'

'Why not?' Corless was horrified.

'Number of reasons. One. We've no evidence he's done anything wrong. Two. They informed us an hour ago that Krasov is seriously ill and must return to Moscow for immediate medical treatment.'

'For God's sake, Willy, they're shooting a line. You don't believe it, do you?'

'We offered them medical facilities here, but the embassy spokesman said Krasov requires specialist treatment only available in Moscow. We have naturally accepted their judgement in the matter.'

'Aren't you surprised that a man who is perfectly healthy one minute should fall so desperately ill the next, Willy? Doesn't it make you ask questions? Doesn't it stink?'

'Not our job to question the competent medical authorities,' Glover said. 'The Soviets have their own doctor, and he has made the diagnosis. Krasov's health is a matter for them.'

'Do you think Krasov's collapse might have been engineered with the use of drugs administered under duress?'

'We have no evidence for that. We cannot act on supposition, however convenient it might be to do so. Our contacts at the Soviet embassy have assured us that Krasov will receive the very best medical attention in Moscow. They hope he will be back at his desk before long.'

'You let them say that, Willy? You let them get away with it?'

'What grounds do I have for not believing them? Certainly not the extravagant story you've spun me.'

'Krasov was perfectly fit when he left Scotland Yard a few hours ago. There was nothing the matter with him. Do you want me to produce witnesses?'

'Got to take the Soviets' word for it, old boy. We can't risk a damaging political incident out of this, you know.'

Corless was controlling his anger only by the skin of his teeth.

'We're now almost certain Krasov is a Soviet intelligence officer. It is our belief that he may be taking British nuclear secrets back to Moscow with him. Are you still prepared to let him go?'

'Come on, Rupert. You can do better than that.'

'I want an answer, Willy.'

'I can't stop him, and you know I can't.'

We were kicking against an invisible wall. There is nothing so smug nor self-assured as an official working within the strict guidelines of the rule book. Willy Glover did not put a foot wrong that morning and we got nowhere. The armour of the rule book was impenetrable. Corless threw up his hands in despair.

We stood helplessly on the sidelines while Krasov was taken away. Our department's efforts to prevent the Russian embassy removing him, drugged and strapped to a stretcher as reported by Northolt security officers, 'seriously ill' according to a Russian press officer when only twenty-four hours earlier he had been in the best of health, had failed utterly. But what depressed us most was the hostility we met from our own side.

'Soviets one, SOVINT nil,' Adrian Gardner said. There was a general reluctance to go home on this wet and depressing Sunday afternoon. We had suffered our first defeat and we knew it. The trouble was, we didn't know what to do about it.

4

RUTH

Miskin has disappeared from her life. The last communication between them was a brief exchange as they passed unexpectedly in a corridor the morning after she asked her question about the security measures in D4.

'We must stay away from each other,' was his whispered instruction. 'It is too dangerous to meet.'

He has kept his word. Since that moment she has not heard from him. This doesn't surprise her. Even if he betrayed no reaction on that first day of her unexpected outburst, she has spent enough time in his company to imagine his astonishment at seeing her play a role so out of character with the woman he knows, and he knows more about her than anyone else at the Institute.

When has he ever heard her express any of these opinions in private? When has she voiced any opinions at all? Where has this new passion come from? None of it fits, she can hear him saying. Her behaviour makes no sense.

Week follows week without any word from him. She interprets his silence as anger. If only they could meet, so he can have it out with her. She could give him some lie about her motives that might at least allow them to remain friends, even if the previous intimacy were now gone. (Is that in itself such a loss? Probably not.) Whatever happens, she is desperate not to lose Miskin.

Then at last he arranges a meeting. But as she leaves her apartment, her telephone rings, two short bursts, then silence. There is no mistaking the familiar urgency of Andropov's summons, nor any doubt about what she must do. How can she get hold of Miskin? She cannot telephone his home to postpone their meeting. (Contacting him at home has always been expressly forbidden. He does not want his wife to know of Ruth's existence.) She does not have

138

time to go to the rendezvous and tell him that she is summoned elsewhere. She will have to stand him up. But her heart is heavy and she is fearful of the consequences.

She knows the level of distress he will feel at her non-appearance, how in his confusion he will have allowed his good nature to be overruled by fantasies of disaster or conspiracy. His anger will burn away slowly inside him until a fire rages, bringing the risk of a sudden downward spiral into a depression that will release the voices he fears so much when he is rational and he listens to so assiduously when the madness takes him.

She hears from Miskin again. This time she leaves the apartment before any rival summons. He hardly glances at her when she gets into the car beside him. She is shocked by his appearance. He is very pale, there are deep rings under his eyes and the twitch on his right cheek is more pronounced. He drives fast out of Moscow, saying nothing. The city is a grey ghost in the distance when they turn off the road and Miskin rolls the car down a track to come to rest beneath the trees, well out of sight of the highway. This is not a meeting place she knows.

For some time he says nothing. He leans forward and rests his head on his hands, still gripping the wheel. She wants to touch him, to soothe his distress and tell him the truth. It takes all her strength to stay silent. When at last he speaks, his voice is worryingly calm.

'What happened the other night?'

'My mother was ill. I couldn't leave her.'

'I waited over an hour.'

'I'm sorry. You know I wouldn't do that deliberately.' It is the first time she has lied to him.

'I don't know anything any more.'

'What does that mean?'

'Whatever you want it to mean.'

'Yuri?' She wants to reach out and touch him but she is afraid to do anything.

'What's happened, Ruth? What am I to think? I hardly know you any more.'

She has prepared for this moment. So far Miskin is behaving as she'd expected. He is defensive, mystified, controlling his anger, but revealing the strain he is under. She has to gain control of the situation so she bursts into tears. Miskin hates tears: they bring out the instincts he wants to conceal. Expressing his humanity betrays a weakness he is afraid of. Tears can always move him.

'Oh, Yuri.' She has her handkerchief held tightly against her mouth.

'Ruth, please.'

He puts his arm around her and she leans her head against his shoulder and sobs. He holds her to him. Suddenly, he speaks, his voice almost strangled with emotion.

'Tell me his name. You must tell me his name.'

'Whose name?'

'Your lover's name. Who is he?'

'I haven't got a lover, Yuri.'

'I want to hear his name on your lips.' He has turned to face her, his expression showing how near the limit he is.

'Each night you leave your apartment very late, you meet a man in an official car, he takes you to different places all over the city, you stay with him for an hour or so, then you are driven home. Night after night I have followed you. You were with him three days ago when you should have been with me. You cannot expect me to believe that man is not your lover.'

'It isn't what you think it is,' she says, hating herself for her inability to speak the truth.

'Then deny it,' he says hoarsely.

'Would you believe me if I did?' she asks.

'How can you ask me that, Ruth?'

His mouth has dried with emotion and the words sound strange and unlike him.

'Can't you trust me after all these years?'

'Then tell me I'm wrong!' His voice is raised. He turns away from her and bangs the steering wheel with the flat of his hand. 'Tell me it isn't true.'

For an instant she thinks he is about to hit her and she is terrified. The night air is cold and she wraps her coat around herself.

'Take me home, please, Yuri.'

'No.'

His voice is like an explosion, a burst of pain from deep within him, his jealousy and suffering uncontrolled.

'Your lover is an intelligence officer. His name is Andropov. He is a diligent, unquestioning servant of the state, a man who will commit crimes at the instruction of those he serves. Ask him about

140

the blood on his hands, Ruth. Get him to tell you about the innocent men and women he has killed because he was instructed to do so. Then you will know you are sleeping with a murderer.'

'No, Yuri. No. That is not true.'

He shouts: 'What isn't true? That Andropov isn't a murderer? Or that he isn't your lover? Are you his whore, Ruth? Does he pay you when it is over? Do you have fur coats and hats and shoes and silk stockings? Is that how he buys your silence, your compliance in his crimes?'

She is sobbing now, real tears from deep within her.

'Tell me what is going on.'

The appeal in his voice has vanished. This is an order, not a request.

'I am seeing Andropov but it is not what you think.' It sounds so hollow that she is ashamed, and yet it is the truth.

His head falls forward on the steering wheel. She watches him almost physically deflate, as if her words have removed from him some property that up to now has kept him going.

He moans. She thinks he is saying: 'No, no, no,' but he speaks so quietly she can't be sure. She dares not say anything. She is so close to him and yet unable to help in any way. She feels at that moment not love for him – she doesn't think she has ever loved him – but sympathy, tenderness, a fellow feeling for another suffering being in this land of suffering. She is stronger than he is, she has always known that, and she wants to protect him. But he has rejected her and in that rejection he has withdrawn terrifyingly inside himself.

He is muttering to himself, meaningless phrases, words in no order, a growl from some demented inner being that is now, in front of her, struggling to assert its control of the mind of this poor man, a wild and dangerous force fastening him in its grip.

He turns towards her and though in the darkness she cannot see his expression, she senses that his battle against the voices is lost. He lets out a cry, a long, hollow exhalation, not just of breath leaving his body but of all hope pouring out of his soul. This is no longer the Miskin she knows. He has fought and lost. The demons have won.

★

The Miskin story is all round the Institute within twenty-four hours. He has been found wandering in the streets of Moscow; someone has taken him to a hospital where he has been diagnosed as suffering exhaustion from overwork. He is now being treated at a clinic outside Moscow.'

The story is believed (why shouldn't it be? She knows the authorities will never have the courage to admit that one of their senior scientists has gone mad but that is what everyone understands). The general comment is 'poor Miskin'. Very few people know much about him, he is acknowledged to be a private man, and in a day or two his absence is hardly mentioned. No one asks which clinic he is at nor if they should visit him. Miskin has vanished. Whatever is wrong with him, they all have to get on with their lives.

Within a week his name has been removed from his door. She knows he is never coming back. Why does she feel no guilt about this episode, only an intense relief? The secret of her relationship with Andropov is safe. She has survived again.

5

DANNY

'The Finns don't know about your visit,' Monty had warned, putting his finger to his lips. 'Nor does our embassy. You're to keep it that way. Not a peep to a soul.'

I knew next to nothing about Finland. I had a Finnish friend at Cambridge before the war, and one long and drunken night he had tried to explain to me the moral dilemma facing that distant country, and its relationship with its vast and powerful neighbour. I remembered little now of that evening except his warning that, if war came, the Finns would side with the Germans because Russia was their common enemy. They had done and they had lost. Russia now had its boot firmly on the neck of the Finns and there was nothing they could do about it. I had an uneasy feeling that they would be very unhappy if they knew why I was about to enter their country.

The train pushed on through the grey winter day. We passed through Danish customs without incident. Monty or someone had provided me with an alternative identity. I was a representative from an English printing company on my way to Finland to discuss the purchase of wood pulp.

'The Finns have trees,' Monty said, 'so why shouldn't we buy them?'

It was late morning when I boarded the ferry for the short journey across the Oresund from Copenhagen to Malmo. The bitter cold had intensified, a strong wind blowing down from the north over snow-laden lands. Ice was forming in the grey choppy waters. I wondered how long it would be before the ice-breakers came out.

From Malmo, the train went north. Slowly the snow-covered flatlands of southern Sweden gave way to thickly wooded country-side, broken by the occasional lake, frozen silver in the afternoon light, the only signs of life coming from the smoking chimneys of solitary factories.

'Paper mills,' I said to myself, trying to sound knowledgeable.

Soon I fell asleep, and in my dreams I relived my return to Berlin.

★

'*Schokolade? Zigaretten?*'

A child emerged from the ruins. He had an ancient, wizened face, pale and drawn with hunger and exhaustion and a body that would have fitted someone half his age. If I think of that child now my heart is torn, but at that time we were used to such sights and most of us were beyond feeling by then. Toby Milner referred to them cynically as the 'hope of the future', and we all knew what he meant.

'*Schokolade? Zigaretten?*'

I pushed the boy away. He retreated and then for some reason decided to follow me. He was undemanding, so I took no notice.

I let myself into the battered building (how it had remained upright and almost intact in that street of ruins always astonished me). The boy slipped in past me before I could stop him and ran ahead up the stairs. He stood beside me as I found the key and opened the door. The room was in darkness.

'Miriam?'

I turned on the light but there was no answer.

I could tell that Miriam had not been there for some days. The air seemed stale and there was already an untouched quality about the room.

I opened her wardrobe. Her clothes were still there, resting on sheets of newspaper she used as lining paper for the drawers and shelves. Wherever she had gone, it cannot have been planned, or she had not intended to be away for long because she had taken nothing with her.

By the gas ring there was a jug of milk which had gone bad. I found mildew on the remains of a loaf of bread. Behind me, the boy had found an opened packet of biscuits. I saw him take one and pocket the rest. It seemed pointless to deny him.

'*Herr Major.*'

Frau Gassmann was calling from the hallway. I heard her make her way slowly up the stairs. She came in, thinner than ever, her mouth opening wide as she struggled for breath. I greeted her but she waved me away, indicating with her hand that she could not speak yet. She sat down on a chair, her hand on her heaving chest. The emphysema that was killing her had worsened in the time I'd been away.

I watched the boy's reaction. He must have seen death many times in his young life. Perhaps he had never seen anyone dying before. He went up to her and touched her arm. She smiled briefly at him, covered his hand with hers, and continued her desperate struggle for breath.

'It happened a week ago,' Frau Gassmann said eventually. She burst into tears. 'Two days ago they brought me this.'

She gave me Miriam's handbag. I knew at once that she was one more innocent victim of a crime we were powerless to prevent. Every day, men and women were snatched from the streets by the Russians and every day we recorded the statistics. But where the victims went, what happened to them, remained unsolved. All we knew was that they never came back.

The random nature of the seizures added to the offence of the crime. Cars would stop, doors would open, hands would snatch their victim off the street – anyone, it didn't matter. We could never make out any discernible pattern. It was all over in seconds. As she screamed for help that was so seldom given and struggled briefly with her captors, Miriam would have known her fate. As a final assertion of her identity, before it was lost for ever, she would have thrown away her handbag. It was the unwritten law of the street that the finder would return it to where she lived, a last poignant message.

I tried to comfort Frau Gassmann. The boy stood by her, watching her tears, curiosity on his face. I saw him wipe a tear from her cheek with the sleeve of his coat in a brief and unexpected moment of compassion.

'She was very good to me,' Frau Gassmann said.

Three weeks earlier in this same room Miriam had given me a present which I had never opened. I went to my briefcase and found her parcel tucked in a corner. I unwrapped a silver-gilt frame and a photograph of Miriam, not as I had known her, but as a young girl of sixteen or seventeen, smiling shyly at the camera, blonde plaits framing her face, her eyes full of hope and expectation that all too soon would be taken from her. I wondered if this was how Miriam thought of herself, or wanted me to think of her.

'She would like you to have this,' I said to Frau Gassmann.

145

'No, no, it is yours,' she said, pushing it away. 'I cannot possibly take it. She gave it to you.'

I had no claim on Miriam's life. I remembered Frau Gassmann telling me that in the final days of the battle for Berlin she and Miriam had hidden in the cellar of the house, terrified that they would die, either crushed by falling masonry as a shell exploded above them, or suffocated in the dust clouds that each explosion released; or worse, raped and murdered by the Russian soldiers searching the cellars for surviving Germans.

They had expected their presence to be betrayed by Frau Gassmann's cough but no one came, no one shouted *Frau, komm*, no one pushed them up against a wall at rifle-point and stripped them of their being. They clung to each other in that stinking pit where they had spent so many days they had lost count, close to starving, deafened by the roar of shells and guns.

Then the awful sound of the bombardment died away, leaving in its place a desolate and echoing silence. The fighting was over, the nightmare ended. They had survived. They emerged into an unfamiliar world of total destruction. Houses, streets, all were skeletons and emptiness, dust and decay. They wept with emotion when they thought how they had managed to keep each other alive and maintain their sanity while all around them the landmarks of their world collapsed in ruins.

'Please take it,' I said. 'I know it is what Miriam would want.'

Frau Gassmann cried again and with a show of reluctance accepted the photograph. She looked at it, kissed it and cried once more. The gesture disgusted the boy and he turned away.

'She was so young,' she said. 'She had her life to live. Why didn't they take me? Mine is ending. A few days sooner, what does that matter? It is so cruel. So cruel.'

By now the boy was bored by her performance and was looking around the room for anything else he could steal. He found a packet of cigarettes in a drawer and that too disappeared into the pockets of his overcoat.

We locked the room and I helped Frau Gassmann downstairs.

'Will you come back?' she asked.

'Whenever I can,' I said.

We both knew that I was lying. We both knew, too, that in a few weeks Frau Gassmann would probably be dead as her lungs finally seized up and she could breathe no more.

'Goodbye, *Herr Major.*' She kissed me and watched me leave, clasping the photograph to her bosom.

'*Schokolade? Zigaretten?*'

Out in the street, the demands began again, more insistently this time, and echoed by the boy's friends, who had emerged from the dark ruins of the house opposite. They were a street gang, orphans, homeless, wandering from ruin to ruin, stealing what they could, living off the scraps of a civilization that itself was living off scraps. The only morality they knew was eat or die, and too many of them were dead already. The casualties of war continue long after the last shot has been fired.

I pushed the boy away but he persisted.

'Fuck you,' he said. 'Fuck you, English.'

As I walked away a hail of stones and broken masonry fell about me. 'The hope of the future,' I thought, as I wiped cement dust from my lips and brushed down my greatcoat with my hand.

★

'I've often wondered what you did all day,' Monty said as he threw himself down in the chair opposite my desk.

'Good God! What are you doing here?'

I was genuinely surprised to see him. He had given me no warning he was going to be in Berlin.

'Come to see you,' he said. 'What else could drag me to this hole?' He leaned forward conspiratorially but his voice boomed as usual. 'It's late. The pubs are open. Won't you show me this circle of hell?'

We ended up in a bar where the only occupants were a group of elderly Germans sitting in silent contemplation of their beer. It had little to recommend it but at least it was warm. Monty settled in a corner seat and I bought him a drink.

'How's tricks?' he asked.

'You didn't answer my telephone calls,' I said accusingly. 'You never got in touch after the business with Krasov.'

'*Mea culpa*, Danny. Sackcloth and ashes. *L'Affaire Krasov* was not our greatest moment. It was an almighty cock-up. Was there much about it here?'

'Kidnapping is a daily event in Berlin. No one takes much notice any more.'

'If Krasov had been taken by his own people to stop him changing sides, we'd have been in the clear,' Monty said bitterly. 'But it wasn't like that at all and that's what hurts.'

'What happened? What went wrong?' This was the official Monty I was dealing with, not the Cambridge Monty. The wrong man had turned up in Berlin and he had something to tell me I suspected I didn't want to hear.

'When we heard that a pathetic, drugged figure strapped to a stretcher had been lifted from the ambulance into the plane, we knew then what the Soviets wanted us to understand: that Krasov the would-be defector was being dragged back to Moscow against his will.'

'You told me you were sure Krasov wanted to stay in the West,' I said, trying not to sound accusing.

'That's what we originally thought, and that's the story the press reported.'

'Only it wasn't true?'

He shook his head. 'It was a Soviet trick and we fell for it. Krasov isn't the disaffected journalist he led us to believe he was. He's an officer in Soviet intelligence, and a willing player in a carefully organized deception. What we saw was all done for public consumption. The Soviets broke every rule in their book and played this one to the gallery.'

'Who was in the gallery they were playing to?'

'The Americans.'

It wasn't hard to guess the rest. The Soviets had humiliated us on our own patch by snatching him from our grasp in the most public way possible. Our security was shown to be hopeless. American confidence in us, always shaky, was now badly dented. Anglo-American unity was under threat and Monty and his people, I guessed, had been caught in the line of fire in the recriminations that followed Krasov's very public departure from London. When there is an unexpected reversal of policy, the policy-makers look for a scapegoat. Monty was a sitting target because he had let Krasov slip through his fingers. I began to understand his bitterness.

'It was all an act, Danny, a performance put on for the benefit of the press and the Yanks. The bastards ran rings around us. Made us look bloody idiots in our own backyard. Not good. Not good at all.'

There was no bravado in this account, only the pain of professional

148

humiliation and the hurt of personal betrayal. Krasov, after all, had been Monty's friend. I had some sympathy for his distress but why had he come to Berlin to tell me this?

'What are the bastards up to?'

What they're always up to, I wanted to say. Out to deceive us, confuse us, humiliate us, defeat us in any way they can. They're brutal opportunists. If we leave the door open a fraction of an inch, their hordes will pour through in an instant.

'No theories?' I asked.

'Theories galore,' he said grimly. 'But none that sticks.'

We finished our beer and at Monty's insistence went out. He wanted to walk, he said, he wanted to absorb the atmosphere. He asked me to point out where the Russian Zone began. He'd never been this close to the enemy before.

'So that's where the bastards are,' he said, growling into his beard. We looked across at the flickering lights of the Soviet Sector.

'What happens now?' I asked.

'God knows. There's an official enquiry but it won't resolve anything. The Department's under scrutiny. The Americans accuse us of leaking secrets to the Soviets. We've lost our form recently. The Soviets have made monkeys of us and now the Yanks are piling on the agony. It's not been a good few weeks for any of us. Who knows what's going to happen now? There are times when I feel like chucking the whole thing in, and this is one of them.'

This was Monty in an unexpectedly confiding mood. In the space of an hour or so he had revealed more about himself than he had since we were boys together.

'I'm in the shit, Danny,' he said. 'Well and truly up to my neck, as you can imagine. That's why I'm here. I need to talk to you. For God's sake, I'm even being blamed for the present crisis.'

Crisis, I asked? What crisis?

'Oh God, Danny,' he said. 'You don't know anything stuck out here in this infested backwater, do you?'

Immediately after Krasov's departure, he told me, they'd had a visit from an American political delegation led by Senator Shearing. There was a real expectation on both sides of the Atlantic that this might lead us to retie the knots that bound us to the Americans, revive our wartime collaboration, get all cosy about nuclear secrets again, all that. A lot of work had been done behind the scenes before the delegation left for Britain, especially by our people in

Washington, and there'd been a general feeling of optimism that something positive would come of this visit.

'God knows, we need their know-how and their dollars if we're not to bankrupt ourselves making our own bomb.'

But the Krasov business put a stop to that. It gave the anti-British brigade in the American camp all the ammunition they needed to say no to renewed collaboration. Because of foul-ups like Krasov, they wanted their nuclear secrets anywhere but near our slippery fingers. That argument won the day. No deal. No collaboration. We were on our own and likely to remain so. That was the worst news possible. We were going to have to build our own bomb now, and we were going to have to scrape the bottom of the barrel to find the money for it.

'Our relationship with the Americans is at an all-time low,' Monty said. 'Someone has to take the flak for that and it happens to be us. Our friends in high places appear to have vanished into thin air. The Department's feeling very exposed.'

Two British Army lorries went by, their wheels throwing up slush from the melting snow on the roads.

'In my bad moments I think the Russians and the Americans are conspiring against us. If it hadn't been for Krasov, we'd probably have access to American know-how today. The Soviet timing was perfect. It scuppered any hope of us and the Yanks getting cosy again.'

'Isn't that your answer?' I said. 'The Russians learned about the American visit. They wanted to make life difficult for us. They took Krasov off the shelf, dusted him down, set you up nicely and you fell for it. Round one to the Soviets.'

Monty wasn't listening. His mind was far away.

'Krasov was the genuine article,' he said. 'An old-style communist who'd lost his faith and wanted out. I wasn't wrong about that, Danny. He may have done as he was told, but I'm sure he was troubled by what he was asked to do.'

'Why did he agree to do it then?'

'He had to. They gave him no choice. I know his heart wasn't in it.'

That was the Cambridge Monty, my lifelong friend, showing me how much the betrayal had hurt. But the Monty who had come to Berlin was the Monty who worked for a secret department somewhere in Whitehall. What had his presence here to do with me?

Why was he telling me all this? Did he just want my sympathy? I determined to keep my distance. I had to avoid taking sides.

'It's the self-recrimination that's so painful,' Monty said. 'Reliving the times we spent together, remembering the conversations we had, wondering where I got it wrong.'

'We all get things wrong sometimes,' I said, not very helpfully.

Krasov had arrived in Moscow a bit of a hero, Monty was saying. They made a fuss of him, gave him a medal and a desk job. Nothing unexpected there, except no one in Horseferry Road believed he was being pensioned off. A few weeks go by when, out of the blue, there is uproar on the teleprinter. The wires are bristling with the news that Krasov's made contact with our people in Moscow (someone called Martineau), says he has important information he wants to give to Monty.

'After what happened in London, Martineau thinks this is a set-up and won't touch him. Nor will anyone else. Our reply was not interested. Corless slammed the door well and truly shut.'

But Krasov had reopened the wound. All the old doubts surfaced. Monty was in trouble again.

'You can't blame Corless,' I said. 'Not after what happened before.'

'What if we're wrong, Danny? What if last time the Russians did stop him defecting? Suppose this time it's genuine?'

'For God's sake, Monty. You have just said that Krasov is a Soviet intelligence officer. He works for the other side.'

'Not every Russian is bad. Circumstances change. Something might have happened. That's possible, isn't it? Maybe he's in some kind of danger and he's asking for help.'

Don't appeal to me, I wanted to say, only I didn't know how to without hurting him further. I can't help you. I can't even advise you. Better to face the truth and get it over with. The man's a communist and he's paid to work against us. Krasov was enemy, not friend.

'If you're so keen to know the answer, go to Moscow and ask him yourself,' I said impatiently. I wanted to bring him to his senses by making an absurd suggestion.

'He isn't in Moscow any more,' Monty said.

'Where is he?'

'Finland.'

'Go to Finland, then.'

'I can't.'

'Why not?'

'The Finns won't let me in.'

He wasn't going to ask, I knew that, just as I knew he wouldn't tell me why the Finns wouldn't let him into their country. He would never say: I want you to go, it's all arranged. Look, here's the currency, the tickets, I've cleared it with your commanding officer, though I was sure he had currency and tickets in his pocket and that he had seen my commanding officer before he'd arrived in my office. I would have to offer. Why would he expect me to do that? This was the official Monty playing the Cambridge card. I would answer his call now because he had answered mine in the past. We walked on in silence, while the memory of my debt to Monty, whose home had been my childhood refuge, worked its way through my consciousness, as he had known it would.

'Do your people know you're talking to me?'

'They told me to come to Berlin.'

'So it's official?'

'We want you to find Krasov,' he said, 'but we don't want you to tell the Finns that you're in their country looking for a Soviet intelligence officer who's on the run. It wouldn't go down too well.' He was silent for a while, lost in thought. 'All you have to do is find Krasov, ask him what he wants, see if he's the genuine article this time and bring the message back to me. Not too hard, is it?'

That was why I was sitting in Hanno Larsen's flat in Stockholm (whoever Hanno Larsen was) looking at the snow falling, waiting to go to the icy north to find a missing Russian. Suddenly I hated Cambridge and all it stood for in my life, which seemed to be all the difficult things: my relationship with my father, my unfinished degree, the advantage Monty was taking of our friendship and now the Krasov business, in which I had gone from casual bystander to major player without even being consulted. Bloody Cambridge. Would I never be free of its chains?

★

Larsen returned just before five. He did not explain where he had been. 'You are ready,' he said. We collected my things and Larsen drove to the harbour. It was snowing harder than before.

'It will be colder in Finland,' he said in his mournful voice. 'You will need this.'

152

He gave me a fur hat. As we got out of the car, the icy wind cut across the water and took my breath away.

'A world on its own,' Larsen said admiringly, looking up at the ferry. It was a mountainous ship, much larger than the surrounding buildings on the quayside, lit up brightly along the length of its hull. Through the portholes I could see the silhouettes of people moving.

'I wish you good business on your trip,' Larsen said. I wasn't sure if he was serious or not. We shook hands and I boarded the ferry.

I dropped my bag in my cabin and went to the dining room, drank some brandy to warm myself up, ate smoked fish and potatoes, had more brandy, this time with a group of Finns, some of whom could talk passable English. It was clearly their intention to spend the night in the bar.

A few brandies later, I went out on deck. The Baltic was iron-black, its surface thickening with ice. On either side we passed island after island, grey-black mounds, sometimes illuminated by lights, emerging like mysterious glistening creatures from the water. Clouds obscured the moon and stars and the night was very dark. The snow continued to fall, now driving furiously into our faces. The wind howled an accompaniment to the constant beat of the ship's engine. I shivered and turned in.

I awoke at dawn. The vibrations had died down and we had slowed. When I went up on deck, it was still very dark. A man next to me spoke in Swedish and pointed at the lights ahead of us. 'Helsinki,' he said.

Journey's end, I thought. Or nearly.

The ship was turning into the narrow entrance of the bay, navigating between two islands that stood like sentries guarding the city.

'They had guns there in the war,' my Swedish friend said. By now he had discovered I was English. 'If they've got any sense, they still do.'

We crept slowly towards our berth.

'A courtesy visit,' the Swede said, pointing out a Russian warship moored in the harbour. 'That's what they call it. A show of strength to keep the Finns in order, more likely. Poor bastards.'

It was indeed very cold, just as Larsen had warned. We walked off the ship, through the customs sheds and out into the freezing morning. It was still dark. I pulled my overcoat around me, burying my face in the collar. Lights danced in front of my eyes as the icy wind swept across the bay.

I had only a short walk to the Palace Hotel, whose frontage faced the harbour. I booked in, had something to eat, slept for a while. My instructions were to wait until I was contacted, though by whom I had no idea. It was still dark when I went out for a walk and a bitter wind whistled down the streets. I went up the Esplanadie, towards the centre of Helsinki, but the cold soon got the better of me and I fled into a bar in the station. It was smoky, crowded and warm. I saw two Russian sailors drinking in a corner.

I was on my second brandy and thawing out when a voice said: 'Long time no see.'

The American with whom I'd travelled from Berlin was smiling at me as he removed his fur hat, his gloves and scarf and laid them carefully on the floor under his chair.

'Warm in here,' he said. 'Good place to be on a day like this.' He extended his hand to me. 'We've not introduced ourselves. My name's Glenn Hammerson.'

6

MONTY

'Good God. What do you make of this, Monty?'

I caught the urgency in Adrian Gardner's voice. I got up wearily and went over to his desk. He handed me the decrypt he had been studying.

The message from Peter was unequivocal. There had been a serious explosion in the laboratory where the Soviets carried out experiments on a number of the complex technical processes which had to be mastered if they were to make an atomic bomb. Something had gone badly wrong. The building had been destroyed and lives lost. Peter was unable to tell us what had caused the accident, but that didn't matter. We had the news we needed. The Soviet nuclear programme had suffered a major setback.

Within twenty-four hours Martineau had verified that the laboratory was a wreck (he'd been out to see for himself) and was not likely to be back in service for many months. The early damage assessments from our SOVINT experts put the likely delay to the Soviet schedules at six months. Twenty-four hours later, when Corless reported to the Cabinet Committee, he was able to say that this estimate was too conservative. Closer examination of what Martineau was able to tell us about the devastation at D4 led to the view that the Soviets had probably suffered a catastrophic accident while experimenting with the casting of plutonium, a highly delicate and technical process. The revised view was that the setback could be as much as a year.

Morale in the Department soared. This was a much needed break in what had been a lean period. Corless re-established his own and Peter's credibility. Corless's luck turned once more. It was about this time that he became known as 'Lucky Corless', the man who could conjure victory out of defeat. It was an epithet that Adrian

155

Gardner and his faction found hard to oppose. Their star retreated. The Committee settled down once more. We were back at the centre of events.

As Corless reported at our next meeting: 'Best news we've had for ages.'

'I think we should minute that,' Arthur Gurney said, loyally writing in his pad as he spoke.

7

DANNY

Did I know about Senator Shearing's visit to London? Hammerson asked.

I'd read about it in the papers, I said, revealing nothing of Monty's briefing. But that was all.

I didn't know what happened?

Not a thing, no.

'Shearing was sent over to investigate your security. Washington is paranoid about these rumours that your people are betraying nuclear secrets to the Soviets. Up to the day he arrived, Shearing was giving you guys a clean bill of health. Then the Krasov business gave his opponents the chance they'd been waiting for and they made a meal of it. Shearing had no case after that and like a good politician he changed sides. Pro-Brit became anti-Brit. His report to the President was short and to the point. Don't trust the Limeys. Their security's full of holes.'

Everything he had said so far was consistent with Monty's version.

The timing, he added, was too good for coincidence. We had to give the Soviets best on that. Somehow they'd got to know about Shearing's visit ('probably a fellow-traveller hiding out somewhere in the structure'). It had to be in their interests to maintain the split between the Americans and the British. So they activated Krasov. Made the whole thing as public as they dared.

'What did they hope to gain by that?' I asked. Monty had been vague (deliberately so?) on Soviet motives.

Hammerson smiled. 'They wanted to show Shearing how easy it was to make fools of your security services. Our embassy gave Shearing the Krasov press cuttings on his arrival. The story they told was that you guys couldn't be trusted to fry an egg. The Reds got a walkover. What could be simpler?'

157

Krasov killed off any hope of working with the Americans. From the British point of view, that had to be seen as an enormous setback, while the Soviets would regard this split as a success.

'Some of us think Senator Shearing was wrong,' Hammerson was saying. 'We don't agree the UK is a leaky boat. We believe we should be working together against the Soviet threat, building bombs together, the whole works. We didn't like what the Soviets did to you guys in London. We think it was a fix, you got shafted and Shearing fell for it. We're here to get the evidence so we can tell Shearing he's dancing to a Soviet tune. That'll shake him. Then we'll get this freeze rescinded. Who better to tell us that but the man himself, Mr Krasov?'

'I thought Krasov was in Moscow,' I said. I was appalled that the Americans were on to Krasov. Had Monty told me everything he knew? Or only enough to get me to do what he wanted?

'Your people know damn well he's in Finland, and I guess you're here because you want to see him too.'

I could have argued with him, denied it, played the innocent, and where would it have got me? He would have been on my heels, dogging me every step of the way. Hammerson read my thoughts.

'Why don't we work together on this one?' he suggested. After all, he argued, we were both a long way from home, stuck out in hostile terrain, the enemy was everywhere around us and it made sense to employ the special relationship, otherwise we might both end up dead in the snow. He didn't fancy that and he didn't imagine I did either.

There didn't seem to be much sense in arguing. I wasn't sure that Monty would be pleased but there was nothing he could do about it. We shook hands and had another drink. Partners for as long as it took.

'Time to go,' Hammerson said, looking at his watch.

We set off down Mannerheimintie, the main street named after Finland's national hero, and turned left into Salomankatu. We were now in a residential area, the stone buildings imposing in their strength against the elements. Hammerson found the house he was looking for and rang the bell. The door opened and we were ushered quickly into a basement flat. In the smoky gloom I could make out three men.

'Mika?' Hammerson said cautiously.

One of the men got to his feet.

'Glenn.' He threw his arms round Hammerson.

'All well?'

'The police were here earlier. They were looking for some Russian sailors who'd overstayed their leave. They were probably drunk. Or dead.'

Hammerson introduced me as an Englishman he was working with. Mika appeared to accept his explanation of my presence.

'How is our Russian friend?'

'Impatient and hungry,' Mika said. 'He has a big appetite for a small man but he does not like what we give him to eat.'

'Let's put an end to his impatience before he starves to death,' Hammerson said. It was an order and Mika heard it as such.

'Everything is ready.'

'OK. Let's go.'

Mika led us out into a courtyard at the back of the building. We climbed into an old Russian lorry; one of his silent companions was to drive.

'Do they understand English?' Hammerson asked, indicating the two men in the front of the lorry.

'Not a word,' Mika said. 'It's all right. I know them both.'

'Have you had any problems?' Hammerson asked.

'There are too many Russians in our country at this moment. Security is tight. We have to be vigilant. I'll be glad when we say goodbye to the little Russian.'

'I brought you this.' Hammerson pulled a parcel out of his coat pocket and handed it to Mika, who tore off one corner of the wrapping to reveal bundles of dollars. 'A token of our appreciation.'

'Hard currency. My friend, I thank you.'

'Thank Uncle Sam, not me.'

'You are his messenger. I thank you. You will thank your uncle for me.'

Mika opened a panel in the floor of the lorry and dropped the parcel into it.

'Something's wrong, isn't it?'

Mika shrugged his shoulders. 'Sometimes I think yes, sometimes no. Nothing goes to plan in this crazy business. We both know that. This time, we have more problems than usual. Why? Bad luck? Bad timing? Bad people? If things go wrong it does not have to be a crisis.'

'What happened?'

'It was difficult crossing the border. Someone did not show when they should have done. Someone else did not follow instructions. The border guards became suspicious. We had dangerous moments. We were all right, nothing happened, but Krasov was scared. I was scared.'

'Is the network blown?'

'We don't think so, no.'

I had the impression he was nowhere near as confident as he wanted to appear. I was sure Hammerson felt the same.

'But you're not certain?'

'All we can be certain of is that if we are caught by the wrong people we will be shot, and if we are caught by the right people we will be imprisoned.'

It wasn't hard to guess who was who.

'Our network is for our people, Glenn, not yours. We lend it to you now because of what you have done for us. We are not mercenaries, working to the highest bidder.'

'We both know that, Mika.'

We drove on in silence. We had left Helsinki now and were out in the country, rolling plains deep with snow on either side of us and in the distance the first sign of hills.

'We go north first and then we go east,' Mika said to me. 'Towards the lakes. In the summer, this is where we sail. Now?' He looked gloomy. 'Now, it is a wilderness of snow and ice where we hide our Russian friend.'

'How well do you know Krasov?' I asked Hammerson.

'No one knows Krasov,' he said. 'Not even Krasov knows Krasov. He's a major in the Soviet military intelligence, at least we've established that now. He led you a dance in London because his cover was so good. He behaved like a journalist because that's what he's been for years. To his masters in Moscow, he was there as a one-task man: all he had to do was perform on the one occasion they told him to, and he did, with distinction. He's a man with a lot of charm and no morality, a dangerous cocktail.'

'What's your interest in him?' I asked.

Hammerson was surprised by the question. We may have agreed to work together, but did that mean he had to tell me everything?

'He wants to come and live in America,' he said with some reluctance. 'That's what he tells us, anyway.'

'Hasn't he sung that song before?' I said.

'I don't have official sanction to be here,' he said. 'I guess it's much the same for you too.' Before I could say anything, he added: 'Nobody wants to be seen in public holding hands with Krasov, but no one wants the other side to get him either. So they entrust him to people like you and me. Look for the written instruction sending us both here and you won't find any. If things go wrong, the people we work for can disown us. Gives you a good warm feeling, doesn't it, knowing that officially you don't exist?'

'He must have something special we all want,' I said.

'The ladies like him,' Hammerson said. 'And he plays the piano well. That should be enough for most people, shouldn't it?'

It was early afternoon but already darkness had fallen and I could no longer make out our surroundings. Hammerson appeared to sleep. Mika smiled at me from time to time but said nothing. We drove on steadily through the frozen countryside. Some hours later, the lorry slowed as we drove over a wooden bridge, expanses of ice on either side. I guessed it was a causeway to an island. Then on to solid ground once more, through a small birch wood until we came to a halt outside what looked like a farmhouse.

Mika helped Hammerson and myself down. I was stiff with cold. Hammerson banged his hands together to get the circulation moving.

'Come and meet our guest,' Mika said, leading the way into the house.

I was unprepared for the contrast between the darkness and cold of the world through which we had travelled, and the warmth and light of the room in which we stood. Brightly varnished wooden floors, walls and ceilings, almost orange in colour, reflected chandeliers that threw a glistening light around the room; mirrors and pictures adorned the walls. At the centre of it all was a large ceramic stove, a basket of recently cut logs beside it. Sitting beside the stove was Krasov.

He looked up as we came into the room.

'My friends,' he said. 'Here is man starving to death. Food in this country is uneatable. Be prepared not to live long.'

8

RUTH

Dawn.

Or what passes for dawn in this summer land without night. The sun is rising slowly. The sea remains a steely grey, encasing the shore. There is no movement anywhere, either outside the house or inside, and no sound: no waves breaking, no birds singing, no human voices, not even her own now. She has not said anything for some minutes and nor has Stevens.

But she knows that she must finish the story she is telling him; there must be an end to it. Only then will she be able to ask forgiveness for the wrong she has done. To leave without that would be intolerable, unthinkable.

She watches the sun rise inch by inch above the horizon and then she breaks the silence.

★

'The explosion occurred in the early hours of February the eighteenth,' she says. 'By eight o'clock that morning, we'd heard unofficially that D4, a laboratory on the outskirts of Moscow, had been damaged but we didn't know how badly nor if anyone was hurt. Our requests for information were met with silence.

'This is not unusual. We knew it would be some time before an official explanation was ready. Every event has to be reinvented to fit correctly within the ideological frame. But the continued official silence made us suspect that the damage to D4 must be serious. The truth was worse than we had feared.

'"All that's left is a hole in the ground,"' Alexei Tomasov told us after a secret night visit to the site of the laboratory, now sealed off, he said, behind a wooden fence which had been hastily erected and wrapped with barbed wire. Police with dogs patrolled the area.

'Then to his horror he saw that the fire had spread from D4 to a neighbouring block of flats. What had once been a five-storey building was now a blackened, eyeless skeleton, no windows, no doors, again sealed off and patrolled.'

(Suddenly she has a sense of déjà vu. She is listening intently to Alexei Tomasov describe what he has seen. She knows what he is saying. She has heard it all before. But when? *When?*)

'Alexei asked what happened on the night of the fire. He found few people willing to talk. Most shook their heads and said they thought it was an earthquake or a new war starting. Violent explosions had shaken the district. They were terrified.'

Was there more than one explosion? he asked.

There was a hell of a bang and the laboratory disappeared in a cloud of smoke, he was told. Not long after there was another explosion and the apartment block caught fire.

How bad was the second explosion?

You couldn't survive a blast like that, they said. The place burned out very quickly. It was badly built, done on the cheap like all the buildings round here. There'd been a fire in another similar block only a week or two before and that was a raging inferno in minutes – by the time the fire brigade got there it was gutted, nothing left.

How many people lived in the apartment block?

Sixty? Maybe more. No one was sure. About sixty. Old people. Pensioners. Veterans of the war.

What happened to them after the explosion?

Silence.

Were there any dead or injured? he asked cajolingly. If the place burned out quickly and the inhabitants were old people, then some of them must have been hurt.

They died, was the reply.

How many?

More shaking of heads. Impossible to say.

Ten? Twenty? Thirty?

The building was an inferno, the area was closed off. There were soldiers there, lorries, ambulances, firefighters. You couldn't get near the place.

Most of the pensioners died? he asked.

Most of them, yes.

And the survivors?

No one knew what happened to them or if they knew, no one

163

was telling. In their evasiveness Alexei read that the casualties were too high for anyone to dare mention the figure. He guessed twenty dead at least, possibly more.

It's the laboratory, isn't it? We've been saying for years they should move it. The things that go on there. It shouldn't be allowed in a civilian area.

Possibly, he said, matching their vagueness with his own. It was too early to be sure of anything yet.

'Then (she continues) we were dismayed to learn that some of our best technical staff had died in the fire. We had no idea why anyone should be working in the lab in the early hours of the morning.'

By now the fire is no longer simply an accident: it has become a disaster. Each day brings more questions. Why is the laboratory fenced off? Why are they prohibited from visiting the site? What were their own people doing there at that time of night? What could possibly have happened to cause an explosion of such magnitude? Without the official report, no one in authority is empowered to give any answers. The unease at the Institute grows. They are agreed that work on the development of the nuclear bomb has received a severe setback.

Ruth's committee meets secretly to discuss the accident. Their mood is sombre. Something has gone terribly wrong and they must find the cause. They are concerned that some mistake on their part may have killed their colleagues. They are frustrated by the official obstacles put in their way. Appeals to the director of the Institute for more information have no effect.

'The technicians in D4 were very experienced,' Tomasov says, 'which makes what happened all the more devastating.'

'Men like Miklos Khudiakov are irreplaceable,' Gromsky laments.

The materials they were dealing with, Tomasov reminds the comrade members of the committee, particularly plutonium, are both volatile and toxic. Something could have gone wrong. It needs only one small mishap to create a catastrophic accident.

Lykowski mocks him. The men who have died were their best technicians. Tomasov is casting a slur on their memories. Such men don't make elementary mistakes.

Tomasov replies testily: there was an explosion. The laboratory blew up. What is Lykowski's explanation?

But no one has an explanation because there are no details on which to base any hypothesis. Without evidence, without being allowed on to the site, the necessary investigation cannot take place. Speculation, Ruth tells them, only reminds them of their lack of knowledge and therefore achieves nothing. They must wait until the authorities issue their report and allow the necessary procedures to take place.

She sounds like Senior Technician Maximov reading from one of her lists of instructions. But she knows there is no alternative. She hopes they can curb their impatience and wait.

★

Four days later the official version of the accident is issued. There was a single explosion, it reads, set off deliberately by imperialist enemies of the state who have been caught and punished. Unfortunately, given the high wind that night and despite the valiant efforts of the fire services, flames were driven from the laboratory to the nearby apartment block, causing damage at a secondary site and minor injuries to some pensioners. The four technicians who died are heroes, they were working through that day and night to complete the state's tasks. We mourn their loss, the report exhorts, and we honour them for their selfless sacrifice.

No one believes this version of events because it fails to address any of the fundamental questions (there is nothing new in that). What could have caused such a violent explosion, with such devastating results? How could the fire have spread from the laboratory to the apartment block when there is an empty concrete expanse between the two buildings? Why should those on the spot report two or more explosions when the official report speaks of only one? Why were those men working at night when no night work was scheduled? Who are these unidentified 'enemies of the state' who have been captured?

Deputy Director Dimitriov calls a special meeting of all senior staff to set out new schedules to recover the time lost. The destruction of the laboratory is causing great disruption to their research, he reports. Not only has valuable experimental work been lost, the Institute now has no immediate access to equipment or a secure working area for the development of techniques for the casting of plutonium. The programme, already late, is now delayed still further. Plans are in preparation to reverse this situation. He asks Senior Technician Maximov to issue the new schedules.

It is an open secret that the new timetables are hopelessly unrealistic but there are no dissenting voices because they all know they are being asked to work to a political, not a scientific, agenda. The truth will come out at the appropriate moment when they will make the usual disclaimers: 'It was not my fault', 'No one could have foreseen the difficulties encountered', all the well-practised escape routes on which their working lives depend. Somewhere (somehow?) a culprit will be found, but not one of the Institute's scientists, who are too valuable to be blamed.

Ruth is impressed by how quickly arrangements are made for them to use another laboratory for the plutonium casting. Within a few days the next experiment is set up in D7. She pays an early-morning visit to inspect the preparations.

'Ruth. Ruth.'

Elizabeth Markarova, in some distress, is beckoning. 'Look. Over there. With the moustache. See him?' All this beneath her breath, a frenzied whisper. Silly, nervous woman.

'Who is he?' Ruth asks.

'I've no idea,' Elizabeth says, her whispers sharp with impatience. 'I don't care who he is – all that matters is he works *here*.'

Elizabeth pulls her away, out of sight of the white-coated man with the moustache. Their heads touch. 'Do you know what he said just now? I can't believe it. I can't bring myself to believe it.'

'Tell me.'

Elizabeth nervously reassures herself that she cannot be overheard. 'He said the space we are occupying here, in D7, was made ready a week before the accident. Do you know what that means, Ruth?'

She knows only too well. Actions like that cannot happen without official clearance. The conclusion she draws is ominous.

'Take no notice,' she says quickly, hoping that Elizabeth Markarova will be impressed by the authority in her voice. 'The man's a fool.'

'He said they were instructed to clear this area a *week* before.' Elizabeth repeats her message, urging Ruth to hear it.

'Wild talk. Ignore it.' She can see Elizabeth's confidence draining away.

'Do you think so?'

'There could have been any number of reasons for clearing the area,' she says dismissively.

'Don't you believe me?'

166

'I don't believe him.'

For the first time since the news broke, she feels frightened. If the white-coated man with the moustache is right, the evidence appears to support the theory that the explosion was not an accident. ('Enemies of the State', as Pavel Lykowski reminds them, is the code used when the authorities refuse to tell what they know. What alarms her more is that they are still not allowed to visit the site of D4.) There have already been murmurings of this among the committee, which she has done her best to control. Wild speculation, bred from the manipulation by the authorities of the information about the explosion, will cloud their judgement. This is the time for clear heads. They must discover what happened in D4 to prevent further loss of life. She is holding to the view that the responsibility is theirs, and for the moment they go along with her, accepting that it is too easy to become prey to extravagant ideas just because they do not yet know the true cause of the accident. But she knows that, without some breakthrough, she cannot hold them to this line much longer.

*

The breakdown in the discipline of the committee comes sooner than she had expected.

These men were murdered, Lykowski says with a certainty that shocks them.

Murdered? Who murdered them? Why? How?

An external agency placed a bomb in the laboratory and detonated it, he says.

Lykowski has neither evidence nor motive for such an assertion, Tomasov replies angrily. Lykowski points out the inability of the authorities to come up with any credible explanation of the cause of the accident and the director's refusal to help them. The official silence speaks volumes. What further evidence does he need?

The discussion that follows is unexpectedly bad-tempered. Pavel Lykowski sticks to his charge that this is an 'official' accident, which means it is murder by agents of the state acting under orders from whom: the KGB? The Central Committee? The Politburo? His theory of murder by official sanction is opposed on all sides.

'What about the apartment block?' Tomasov asks, switching targets. 'How do you explain that?'

'A second bomb was placed there,' Lykowski replies.

'You don't know that,' Gromsky says. 'What evidence do you

167

have? The fire could easily have spread from the laboratory to the block of flats.'

'Measure the distance between the laboratory and the apartment block. Sixty metres of concrete desert. Fire doesn't travel that distance unaided.'

'Are you saying these pensioners were murdered too?'

'It's the only possible explanation.'

'Sixty old people pose a threat to the state, do they?' Gromsky's attitude is that Lykowski is talking dangerous nonsense. Why should anyone want to blow up a building full of pensioners? He begs them to keep their heads and ignore Pavel's extravagant inventions.

'What possible purpose can the deaths of a lot of elderly veterans serve?' Elizabeth Markarova asks, now unconvinced.

'The murder of innocent people,' Lykowski explains, 'has a long history of justification in the Soviet Union. Are we not all familiar with the concept of the "small sacrifice" for the greater good? How much blood has been spilled, how many lives lost in this way?'

As Lykowski says this a memory passes before her like a shadow. It carries a truth she must recognize if she is to understand why this event is so familiar to her. But as she reaches for it, the ghost of the recollection slips away into darkness and out of her grasp.

'What greater good were these men and women sacrificed for?' Tomasov asks, his disbelief thinly disguised.

'Their murder is a warning to us,' Lykowski insists. 'The disaster at D4 is a reminder that the state is all-powerful and will not tolerate deviation from the official line.'

There is an immediate, noisy rejection of this view. It is too extreme. The state would not kill so many innocent people in order to tell a few scientists that from now on they must toe the official line. That assumption is absurd. There are many better ways to do that. Lykowski is shouted down. He shouts back. This senseless act is a declaration of war, he says. Let the hostilities begin. He at least is ready for the fight.

Gromsky takes a more cautious line. 'It is too easy to give in to paranoia,' he says, risking the accusation that he is on the side of the state. 'We must not imagine that every act has a sinister connotation, that in the Soviet Union an innocent explanation can no longer exist. Until there is hard evidence to the contrary, it must be seen for what we firmly believe it to be – an accident, albeit a terrible one.'

Tempers boil up and spill over. Gromsky and Tomasov both demand that Lykowski resign from the committee. His continued membership should be put to the vote. Before there can be a show of hands, Lykowski has physically attacked Tomasov and knocked him to the ground. The two men have to be forcibly separated from one another.

Ruth has said nothing so far but now she has to act. She knows it may already be too late to reconcile these two positions and that this quarrel could destroy their committee. She speaks as calmly as she can, hoping her voice will quell their hot tempers and that her words are those Andropov would choose. (If only he had written this scene for her.)

Their disagreement is not a sign of any fundamental division within the committee, she says, it is a measure of their insecurity, their nervousness at the inaction of the authorities in the face of their own unprecedented behaviour. Each day they wait for a blow to fall that never comes. She urges them to hold their nerve, not to do the work of the authorities and destroy themselves through their own quarrelling. Their cause is too important to think of failure.

Nerves are soothed and the discussion continues more calmly. Lykowski's position is reviewed and rejected. Lykowski walks out in a fury.

'Find the survivors and get them to tell you I am wrong,' he says as he leaves. 'I know that you won't.'

His words hang in the air long after the members of the committee have left and the room is empty. She has not moved since their departure. She feels exhausted, hollow and cold. Where does she stand in all this? She is closer to Lykowski than she wants to admit, and this makes her fearful. So much in their lives is the result of manipulation. Why shouldn't this explosion be one more act in a long and tarnished history of official lies and deception?

Then her imagination falters. She refuses to understand politics. She has shrunk her life to its essentials: her work, her mother, her son, their collective survival. She cannot comprehend the mind that can have ordered the murder of so many innocent people. What kind of person can have done that? What possible motive could they have? Then she wonders if the mind that can order the deaths of innocent people in a block of flats is so different from the mind that can order the dropping of an atomic bomb on a city centre.

9

DANNY

'This is Krasov,' the voice hissed in my ear. 'We must speak. It cannot wait.'

It was three in the morning. I had gone to bed soon after we had eaten and, exhausted, I had fallen into a deep sleep. I had awoken to Krasov's urgent entreaties to get up and a vigorous shaking. I put on some clothes and joined him downstairs. The fire in the stove was no more than a few glowing embers, but Krasov revived it and soon the heat was almost as strong as before.

'Where to begin? Is that not the question? What do you know?'

He was in a strangely animated mood. I wondered if he had been drinking. There was a bottle of vodka on a table by his elbow but it had hardly been touched. Maybe he had a bottle in his room. More likely his nervousness was due to the strain of being cooped up in the middle of nowhere, waiting for an event to take place over which he had no control.

'Monty told me his version of events.'

'You believed him?'

'Of course I did.'

'Monty, like all Englishmen,' he said, an unexpected bitterness in his voice, 'always speaks truth.'

'Tell me your version then,' I said.

'My version? Why not say, tell me truth, Krasov? Tell me truth?' He turned on me angrily, his voice rising.

'If you prefer that.'

'You think I tell lies because I am bloody communist.' His voice was shaking with emotion.

'For God's sake, Leo! Get on with it or I'm going back to bed.'

My irritation brought him to his senses. He got up, opened the stove and dropped in a couple more logs. His action took the sting

170

out of his anger. It seemed he was disappointed with my presence.

'I expected Monty would be here.'

'You can't be surprised he didn't come.'

'He sent you in his place?'

'Yes.' There seemed no point in denying it.

'Why? You do not work for him.'

'I'm here and I'm all you're going to get. Either you speak to me or I'm on the next boat out of Finland.'

'Monty is my friend. Do you believe that? I treat him badly. I betray our friendship.'

I could hear the beginnings of a long Russian lament, morbid reflections on the impossibility of friendship, the harshness of fate, ending in tearful embraces. I wanted none of it.

'What happened between you two is none of my business,' I said. 'Say what you want to say and I'll report it back to Monty.'

'It starts with my meeting with your father in Cambridge. I told him there was small but growing movement in Soviet Union of physicists against nuclear bomb. I knew that was his position too. I said he should take heart. Maybe soon good sense would win.'

I remembered my father's reaction as I entered his study and I doubted very much that Krasov had said anything of the kind.

'That's nonsense, Leo,' I said. 'You gave him news that upset him. We both know that.'

'That is what I told him.'

'That was a part of what you told him.'

He smiled. 'Now I understand why Monty send you. Sure. That was not all I say. I tell your father that an old friend of his was still alive but in trouble. She is nuclear physicist in Soviet Union. She is leader of anti-nuclear movement. Your father must support her from outside Soviet Union or she will die.'

'What kind of support?'

'He must lead anti-nuclear movement in West. He must get others to join in.'

'Who is this woman?'

'Her name is Marchenko. Your father knows her since many years. Perhaps he has not told you about her?'

A ghost from his past? Was that what Krasov had brought to my father's house in Cambridge all those weeks ago? Was that why he had looked so shocked?

'I tell your father that Marchenko is blackmailed by intelligence service. She must do what they tell her to do or first they will kill her mother, then her son, then her.'

'What did my father say?'

'He ask: what must she do to stay alive? I answer: the peace movement she has started must have international support from other physicists. Their voices must be loud enough for governments of the West to hear what they say and then to discuss nuclear treaties with Soviet government. That way Marchenko will be saved.'

'If your government wants to talk to ours, aren't there more established routes for unofficial contact?' I asked, making no attempt to disguise my scepticism.

'Is not government. Is not official,' he hissed at me angrily.

'Who is it?'

'How little you understand. Is opposition.'

'Political opposition to Stalin?'

'Yes.'

'Your story's too far-fetched for me, Leo. You'll have to do better.'

I saw his eyes burn with deep anger, the muscles in his cheeks tighten.

'Listen to me,' he snapped. 'Then maybe even you will understand what is happening.'

'Try me,' I said unhelpfully.

'There has been disaster to nuclear research in Soviet Union,' he was saying. 'Huge explosion in laboratory, radiation leaks, many people very sick, many people dead. Some of our best scientists are killed. This time Soviet programme is set back months, perhaps a year, is too soon to say. Many people are seeing how dangerous it is to make nuclear bomb. News of explosion is reported to Central Committee and suddenly there is disagreement. There is a challenge to Stalin. Behind closed doors of Kremlin, there is struggle for power between two groups, those who believe in nuclear weapons, and those who don't.'

'Who will win?' I asked.

'Is too soon to say,' he said. 'That is why I bring message for Monty. He will understand.'

'What is that message?'

'Everything must be done to support those who are against the development of nuclear weapons. Since I bring message from Marchenko to your father, much has changed. This is now fight between

172

old Russia and new Russia, the true revolution against those who are in power now. We must fight Stalin and his people because they are evil. We must bring them down. If we do not, there will be war between Soviet Russia and West, and many millions will die. Russia is my country but it is society gone mad, lives of human beings have no value. Our leaders are barbarians. They have no heart, no beliefs, they have only power.'

'Do you have any proof for any of this?' I asked.

That touched Krasov on the raw. He suddenly became very angry. 'You do not believe me, do you? You think me excitable Russian, yes?'

I drew in my breath: I wanted to say yes, you are excitable; no, I don't believe you. I wanted to ask, why are you telling me all this, what does it mean, what am I doing here at three in the morning in the middle of nowhere talking to a mad Russian? But on he raced.

'The world is now a very dangerous place,' he said. 'We have maybe few weeks, maybe month or two, when we can try to stop Soviet Union and West building these terrible weapons which will destroy us. That is appeal that you must take to Monty. This is our chance. He must help us – Marchenko, me, others – or maybe we are all destroyed.'

I looked at the man in the reflected light of the fire. It was too neat, too orderly, too coincidental. My acceptance of his story was dependent on too many events that I could not believe in. Little Krasov, I thought, to whom truth was a coin he tossed in the air. The trouble was, he didn't care whether it came down heads or tails, as long as he was safe.

10

RUTH

How much longer can she hold Stevens's attention? It is morning now, there are people on the beach. The day has begun. She must complete her story before her time runs out. She tells him about the meeting with Pavel, when he forced her to face the truth she could no longer avoid.

'You believe me, don't you? I can see you do, even though you won't admit it.'

'Pavel, please.'

'Tell me I'm right.'

He stares straight into her eyes. His skin is very pale, dusted with freckles the colour of his hair. But his eyes are dark and intense.

'Go on, say it. Say you believe me.'

'How can I admit something for which there is no evidence?' she asks.

'Evidence?' His laugh is full of bitterness. 'What about the historical evidence of consistently excessive behaviour? What about the evidence of crimes against the people? What about the betrayal of every principle on which our so-called glorious revolution was based? What about the way our lives have been stolen from us in return for lies and empty promises? You don't need me to prove anything to you, Ruth. All you need to do is open your eyes and see what's happened.'

But opening her eyes is what she has promised herself she will not do. Her task is to protect her mother and son – and herself, only because they will not survive without her.

'No, Pavel. No.' She turns away.

'Ruth.'

He grabs her arms as if to shake her. She tries to push him off but his grip is too strong. He forces her to face him.

'Listen to me, Ruth. Believe me. What I am saying is true.

174

Khudiakov and the others in D4 were murdered. So were the pensioners. I am sure of it.'

She breaks away from his grasp. 'You mustn't do this to me, Pavel. Please. No.'

'I have telephoned hospitals all over Moscow. No one can give me details of elderly patients with serious burns brought in during the early hours of the eighteenth of February for the simple reason that none were. I contacted the state mortuary. There were no unusual numbers of dead brought in that day. Sixty people or more have disappeared, Ruth. You can't close your eyes to that. Sixty old people have vanished.'

In her heart she believes him. She knows she is trapped in an event which is rapidly running out of her control. How she wishes it were possible to tell him so.

★

'Here,' Andropov says, tapping the glass partition with his lighter. 'Stop here.'

The car draws to a halt outside her apartment block and she gets out. He says nothing to her, he doesn't even bother to look at her, it's as if when she arrives home she no longer exists for him. He taps the partition once more and disappears into the night.

She looks at her watch. One-thirty. She does not go up to her flat. Unseen by the babushka (the view from her desk doesn't extend this far), she walks quickly round the corner where Tomasov is waiting. She gets into the car he has borrowed and together they drive off in the direction of D4.

Alexei has reconnoitred the area earlier in the evening and found a quiet street nearby where he can park out of sight of what remains of the laboratory. He takes Ruth to a vantage point, a low wall from behind which they can time the frequency of the patrol, a policeman with a dog every fourteen minutes.

'Time enough? If we're quick? Nothing will go wrong.'

Alexei shakes his head. Ruth will need more time. He has come prepared. He takes off his glasses and puts them carefully in an inside pocket. Then he takes out a bottle of vodka from his knapsack and splashes it over the old clothes he is wearing. Ruth pulls his woollen cap lower over his forehead. She smears some mud from the slush in the street on his face and clothes. With his torn coat, battered appearance and vodka bottle, he looks like a tramp.

'Ready?'

'Yes.'

She removes the Geiger counter from the canvas bag in which she has hidden it. Together they wait for the policeman. Alexei checks his watch.

'Ninety seconds.'

Alexei takes a swig from the bottle, spits it out and emerges from their hiding place. He walks drunkenly in the direction from which he expects the policeman to appear. He carries the vodka bottle in his hand, wrapped in a newspaper.

Ruth, out of sight behind the wall, hears barking, shouts from Alexei, another voice (the policeman), more barking, more shouting, more words, louder this time – they are coming this way. They pass by, so close she can hear the dog's paws scratching on the pavement as it pulls at its leash.

'Have a drink, why not?' Alexei's voice is raised, drunkenly persistent. 'There's more where this came from. How about you, dog? Have a drink yourself! What's your name, eh? Tell me your name.'

She counts the agreed ninety seconds under her breath, then emerges from her hiding place and runs to the iron gate that has been erected to prevent entry into the laboratory site. She climbs over (it is less difficult than she had imagined), then, trying desperately to balance herself on the uneven surface of the rubble, she stumbles towards the centre of the blast.

She stops, assesses her position (how dark it is, is she where she needs to be? Why can't she see better?), points the Geiger counter and switches on. The instant clicking almost deafens her. Terrified at the noise, she switches off the machine.

Take your time, Alexei has instructed her. Get as close to the centre as you can before you take any readings.

What about the noise?

No one will hear.

She didn't believe him then and she doesn't believe him now. She closes her eyes tightly and remains very still in an effort to control herself before finding the courage to start again.

Sweating and frightened, she switches on the Geiger counter again, takes the reading by the light of a small torch and copies it into her notebook. She is horrified at how high it is. How much plutonium can have been held on the site?

She switches off, gets up, starts forward, misses her footing and falls headlong. She drops the machine and it rolls away from her into the darkness.

Where is it?

She gets into a crouching position, too frightened to stand up and cautiously looks around, feeling for the counter with her left hand, then using the thin beam from her torch to stab into the darkness.

She can see nothing. She wants to cry with despair. If she does not get out of this awful place in time, she may be trapped here all night. The reading in her notebook has given her an unmistakable message about the dangers of staying too long in this place.

Be systematic, she says to herself. (Ruth the scientist.)

Which way did I fall?

Forward.

I had the machine in my left hand.

I must have thrown it to the left.

Over there. It must be over there.

She switches on the torch and metre by metre scans the area where she thinks it might be.

It takes her a valuable two minutes to locate the instrument. It is two metres away. She retrieves it carefully and blows the dust off it, rubbing the face of the gauge with her sleeve.

She looks at her watch. She's been inside for twelve minutes. Two minutes left. She must get out now, Alexei will be waiting, she will be overdue if she doesn't go now, her fall means it has taken longer than they'd planned. She walks towards the gate, too quickly – her feet slip and disturb the rubble. She freezes. (More delay.) Has anyone heard? She walks more carefully now, testing the ground before putting her weight down. Valuable seconds are passing.

Her heart stops. The guard is back, sitting by the gate, two, three metres away, warming his hands before a fire in a brazier, smoking a cigarette. The dog, off the lead, is drinking water noisily from a bowl.

Alexei never warned her of this. She is frightened and cold. Her teeth chatter and she shivers uncontrollably. What can she do? She turns slowly, careful to make no sound at all. If the dog were to worm his way under the gate, he'd smell her in a moment and she'd be done for.

She retreats silently into the darkness. There are no other exits. It is this gate or nothing. It will be all right, she says to herself. The guard will resume his patrol soon. Alexei will wait. He will have seen the guard. He will know she is trapped. He will wait for her. He must.

She stands in the darkness, a solitary figure amid so much desolation.

Suddenly the darkness falls in on her. She can see nothing. There is no light anywhere, only an endless and impenetrable blackness. She has no sense of the world around her. She has ceased to be. She and the darkness are one.

Where am I?

Where am I? a voice echoes.

What is happening to me?

What is happening?

In that instant the sky lights up, the light is brighter, sharper, clearer than any she has ever seen, illuminating every detail, however minute, with an extraordinary clarity. There is nothing that she cannot see. What is it they called this? What is the phrase she has read? 'The light of a thousand suns.'

Then the whistling starts, a distant, hollow sound, like the drawing of breath before a scream. In the instant of its life, the noise gathers strength and force as it approaches at enormous speed until she is surrounded, then swallowed up in the intensity of its thunder.

The history of the event she is witnessing lasts only milliseconds but she is able to distinguish the phases of its short life. First the light, then the screaming sound, now the breaking roar as firestorms fill the sky, burning the air around her. The Earth is screaming with the pain of the destruction wrought upon it as the air catches fire, mountains split, oceans evaporate and matter vaporizes. Everything burns.

Then the wind, the tempest. The storm drives her back with incredible force, she is flying backwards faster and faster towards the flames, disintegrating with the world she knows, mountain and flesh and bone together, all one again, primeval dust.

Where once there was substance, now there is nothing. Emptiness. A void. The history of the end of the world in a second or less.

This is what you did, the voice accuses. *This is what you did.*

What have I done? she asks. What have I done?

Her soul cries in anguish into the fire that consumes her.

The light has gone, the scream has vanished, the thunder has faded, the wind has passed, the flames have died. She is suspended in silence, an invisible witness. A huge grey cloud hangs over everything, its stinking poisons raining over the dead land beneath it, contaminating the emptiness. There is no life anywhere. No marks of life. Nothing. Only an empty graveyard hurtling through the endless night of eternity, trapped in the rhythms of the heavens.

Where am I? she cries again. Where am I?

You are in Hiroshima, the voice says before it too vanishes into the darkness and she is alone once more among the poisonous dissolution of the ruined planet. *See what you did.*

The moment of hallucination passes. Has she died? Gone mad? She opens her eyes. Consciousness returns. She touches her face: her eyes are still there, they have not become empty sockets; her nose, her mouth, her teeth. She is complete and alive (though her fingers are sticky with blood from a wound in her head). Perhaps nothing has happened, perhaps it was all a dream.

Perhaps.

She sees the gate, the glow of the brazier, the night sky with clouds and stars, the dog eating a bone, the policeman putting coals on his fire.

But somewhere, just out of reach, she hears a distant cry, *Hiroshima*, echoing in her mind.

How long before the guard starts his patrol again? Ten minutes? Fifteen? Every moment is like a century. She is desperate to be away from this awful place, back in the heart of the city again.

The guard has gone. She counts a hundred and twenty seconds and then goes carefully towards the gate. She cannot see if he is in the shadows waiting for her. She counts another minute. There is no sound except her heart beating. Now. She darts forward, climbs once more over the steel bars of the makeshift gate, drops down into the street, adopts the crouching position and runs as fast as she can.

'All right?' He has his arm round her. Good, faithful Alexei.

'Let's get out of here.'

'Get the readings?'

'Yes.'

'High?'

'It's terrible.

'What did I tell you?'

'What can they have been doing in there?'

Halfway into the city he stops the car by the side of the road, takes out the Geiger counter and ranges it over her body. It ticks aggressively. He tells her to have a bath when she gets back and to destroy her clothes.

'You're all right,' he says reassuringly, 'You weren't in there long enough.'

She knows that, but it is good to hear someone else say it.

11

DANNY

It was late afternoon. The snow had stopped some hours before but dark clouds hung low over us. Before long it would start to snow again. Mika and I were outside splitting logs by the light of a kerosene lamp.

'How do you find him?' Mika asked, resting his axe for a moment.

'Krasov? Frightened.'

'He has reason to be.'

He picked up the axe again and struck at the wood, splitting it neatly in two. I admired his skill. His pile of logs was much larger than mine.

'You must get him out as soon as you can. He'll crack up if he stays here much longer,' I said.

'Our people have seen Russian patrols in the woods. We cannot move him at present. It is too dangerous.'

'One day more?'

'Maybe two. Who knows?'

'It's too long.'

'Glenn is unhappy but he accepts the situation.'

'I'm not worried about Glenn.'

'There is more at stake than the sanity of one man,' Mika said.

I saw then, in the detachment of Mika's verdict, the roots of Krasov's despair. Only Hammerson and I valued him. For Mika and the others with him, Krasov was a parcel, and not a parcel they would ever have chosen to deliver. But Krasov was something they owed Hammerson, and that was why they turned on him the anger they felt at themselves for owing anyone anything, and then for having the debt called in.

I saw too that nothing I said carried any weight. I was powerless – another parcel, like Krasov, though of less value. We continued cutting logs in silence, the sound of our axes striking the wood echoing dully against the snow-laden trees that surrounded us.

'Were you a soldier?' Mika asked suddenly. 'Did you fight in the war?'

'Yes.' I hoped the shortness of my reply would put him off any more questions. It didn't.

'Where did you fight?'

'In the desert. Sicily. Normandy.'

'I cannot imagine dying on a beach.'

'It's no different from dying anywhere else. If you're lucky, it's quick; if you're not, it isn't.'

'I saw men die too,' he said.

I looked at him. Perhaps I had mistaken his deliberate way of speaking, his lack of familiarity with English, for coldness. But his questions revealed his search for common ground. Now we had found it. We had both fought, and we had both survived. The survivor always has a tale to tell.

'We called it the Winter War. We went into Karelia and forced the Russians out. Then they forced us back. We lost our land. There were many dead.'

'Is that why you hate the Russians?'

'It is one of the many reasons,' he said. 'To us, they are always the enemy. I cannot imagine a day when they will not be. That is the price for living too close to someone more powerful than yourself.'

He stopped talking and concentrated his energies on splitting logs. Then he said:

'Are you still in uniform?'

'Yes.'

'So, we are brother soldiers.' He smiled at me.

★

A small wooden building stood at one end of the house, a pile of logs to one side of the door. This, Mika explained, was the sauna.

We went into the room and undressed. There were towels piled high on a shelf. Mika, now naked, pointed to the door.

'First we wash ourselves and then we go into the steam room. After the steam, the snow. Come.'

We washed and then Mika handed me a towel. 'Spread this on the bench and sit on it. It is to prevent burns. In there is the steam.'

181

He pointed at the door. 'At first it is better to lie on the lower benches. It is cooler. As you get used to the heat you move higher. Are you ready?'

'Yes.'

He opened the door to the sauna and went in. I followed him and walked into a wall of heat. My eyes closed at once with the sheer intensity of it. Sweat broke from my body and I fought for breath, choking as the air was drawn out of me as I sought, mouth open, chest heaving, to breathe again. I put out my arms to keep my balance, searching like a blind man for something to hold on to.

The moment passed. My body adjusted and I breathed once more. I opened my eyes. In a corner, I could make out the scalding stones over which water had been poured. Steam continued to rise, but my discomfort was limited now. I stumbled towards a bench and threw myself down on its wet wooden surface.

Slowly the perspective of the room came into focus. There was wood everywhere, the light scrubbed spruce I had seen in the house. I could see Mika lying full length on the bench, his hands over his eyes, breathing deeply and slowly.

It was only then that I realized there was someone else in the sauna with us. Sitting opposite me was a young woman. She too was naked. Her body shone wetly in the dim light. She brushed her fair hair back from her face with her fingers and smiled at me. Then, with a scream, she opened the door and plunged out into the snow. I watched her go in disbelief.

She rolled in the snow, then she turned her back and gathered handfuls of snow and rubbed it over her body. It was an extraordinary performance, without guile or intent, wholly private and wondrous to observe.

She saw me watching her and laughed again, throwing snow up in the air so that it fell all over her. Then she ran back into the sauna and closed the door. She leaned towards me.

'My name is Tanya Alenius,' she said, and offered me her hand.

I was looking into the most beautiful blue eyes I had ever seen.

12

MONTY

Scrawled in red ink across the top of the letter were the words *R.C.*, *Do you know about this*? *W.G.* The unwritten coda to Willy Glover's question was ominously clear: if not, why not?

The typewritten letter now being passed round the table was addressed to a Dr Christopher Hall of the Engineering Department, Birmingham University, dated 26 February 1947 and signed by Geoffrey Stevens.

> I can't say how I know (forgive my lack of candour) but I
> have received information that some of our colleagues in the
> Soviet Union regard the dangers of an unregulated nuclear
> world with the same horror as we do.
>
> That may surprise you. All I can add is that I find the
> evidence compelling. I hope you will accept my word that
> this is truth not propaganda.
>
> I understand that some of these men and women are
> prepared to risk their careers (perhaps their lives?) for what
> they believe. They have stopped work on the Soviet bomb
> until their government agrees to their request for firm
> safeguards on the political control of nuclear weapons. Their
> courage and decisiveness puts our unresolved deliberations to
> shame.
>
> These Soviet physicists are appealing through me to
> their fellow scientists in the West for support. Without us,
> they fear they may be isolated and that could lead to their
> rapid extinction as an opposition. We cannot let that happen.
> We must add our voices to their cause because it is our cause
> too. We must use our energies to save these good people.
>
> I have been thinking for some time about forming an

association of physicists of like mind, under the banner of some kind of International Association for Peaceful Nuclear Collaboration. This would seem to be the moment to start. By using the brave image of these Soviet scientists, we can capture the imaginations of our co-physicists around the world. Maybe we will gather enough momentum to influence governments. Who knows? But try we must. For the safety of these courageous men and women in the Soviet Union, we must do something.

Will you be at the Smith Street meeting on Thursday? Would you have time for a drink afterwards? Do let me know. We could have a talk that evening before we return home.

'Do we know if Stevens spoke to Hall last week?' Gardner asked.

'They were seen leaving Smith Street together after the meeting,' Maitland said. 'So we must assume he did.'

'Did anything come of it?'

'We've no evidence so far, but that may not mean much,' said the ever-cautious Colin. 'The truth is, we don't know what happened.'

'Has Stevens sent any other letters like this?' Boys-Allen asked. 'How wide is he casting his net?'

'No others have come to hand,' Colin Maitland said. 'But that's not to say he hasn't written to his contacts.'

'He's bound to have written other letters,' Gardner said. 'My guess is there could be twenty more like this in circulation, possibly forty. Some of them will have gone to America. Stevens is a powerful figure in the scientific community here and on the other side of the Atlantic. He's one of the Government's main advisers on nuclear issues, knows all the leading players, particularly the Americans. They respect him for the work he did before the war.'

'He mentions forming some kind of association,' Maitland said. 'There could already be a groundswell of hostile opinion among our own scientific community which we haven't yet noticed, and this proposal could fly within days. There would be serious repercussions,' he warned, 'if this country's senior nuclear scientists created an effective lobby in defiance of government policy.'

'He'll need more than the voices of a few scientists to pose any threat to policy,' Guy Benton said. 'This kind of opposition is usually very amateur, all emotion and no sense.'

If Benton's rejection of the amateur was intended to reassure us, it didn't. Stevens was a man of standing whose opinions held considerable weight. Whatever he said would get listened to.

'I accept he's not in the Nils Bohr league,' Colin Maitland said. 'But he's not far behind. He'll be listened to.'

'What do we know about Hall?' Arthur Gurney asked. 'He's a new one on me.'

'Explosives expert.' Maitland consulted his notes. 'Very highly thought of. Did a lot of experimental work during the war. Worked with Barnes Wallis for a time. He's one of the men Willy Glover's trying to lure on to his nuclear programme. I am told that without Hall, making the bomb's going to be a damn sight more difficult.'

'Is he likely to be convinced by Stevens's argument?'

'I don't know enough about him to answer that,' Maitland said, sounding less than sure.

'Has Hall ever expressed any views similar to Stevens?'

'Not that we know of,' Colin said. 'That doesn't mean he hasn't, it means we don't know if he has.'

'So it's possible?'

'It's possible, yes.'

'There's a lot of moral uncertainty within the scientific community at present,' Arthur Gurney said. 'We've picked that up from a number of sources. They've seen the photographs and the films of the devastation of Hiroshima and Nagasaki and it's scared them half to death. Those images of molten corpses are very powerful, certainly enough to make any reasonable person think twice about taking part in a project to build a weapon of such indiscriminate destruction. There are real grounds for thinking that Stevens's appeal may suc-ceed. He could be pushing on doors that are already open to him.'

'What if a significant group of scientists were to agree with Stevens?' Guy Benton asked. 'What would happen then?'

'No scientists, no bomb,' Colin Maitland said bluntly.

'And if we have no bomb?'

'How can we play in the big boys' playground if we don't have the toys they have?'

There was silence while we contemplated life on the margins of international politics. It didn't appeal. I sensed a brief but unspoken yearning for the simple choices of past glories. How much simpler our lives had been when we had an empire: we knew our place in the world, and no one had exploded a nuclear device. Stevens's letter seemed to illustrate all the complications and dangers of the difficult, new post-war world.

★

A week later a newspaper article appeared in the press in Stevens's regular column. It was clear he was unable to keep his secret to himself – or that he had been instructed not to do so.

> News comes of citizens within the Soviet Union, scientists like myself, who are prepared to oppose their political masters over the moral issue of the building of nuclear weapons without safeguards for their use.
>
> These men and women have taken the courageous and unprecedented step of refusing to continue work on the nuclear programme until their government accedes to their demands. They are using their knowledge, their skills and their consciences to counterbalance the enormous weight of the all-powerful Soviet political machine. They are risking their lives for their beliefs.
>
> We must applaud these brave men and women as heroes and lend them our strongest support. We must add our voices to theirs until our chorus, the sentiments of ordinary people the world over, drowns out all other voices, particularly the strident thump of ideological anthems. We must set ourselves the task of rebuilding a world from which we have banished all weapons of mass destruction. If we can do this, and we must, we will have taken the first important step in liberating the world of war itself.

Later that same day the cutting appeared on Rupert's desk. There was the familiar red scrawl. Even upside down the instructions were clear.

Rupert, this must stop. Do something. W.G.

The battle lines were being drawn.

13

DANNY

We left on the second night.

One of the Finns who had accompanied us from Helsinki reported that a Russian patrol had been seen a few miles away, heading in our direction. Mika said it was no longer safe for us to stay and Hammerson agreed. It meant a change of plan about where Krasov was to be picked up but the contingency was in place.

'It ought to work,' Hammerson said to me. 'But you never know, do you?' It was the first time he'd shown less than full confidence in the enterprise.

There were six of us in the party: Krasov, Hammerson, myself, Mika and his two minders. Over our clothes we wore white suits, like those used by soldiers in the Winter War. Mika issued us with guns. Hammerson saw my surprise and said: 'Better safe than sorry. But I don't expect to use it.'

He was holding a German Luger admiringly. Mika gave him ammunition.

We piled into the lorry and drove back across the causeway and then on through the thickly wooded countryside. It was snowing again heavily now, and our progress was painfully slow. We passed no one, saw nothing. The land was deserted, empty except for an occasional animal, momentarily trapped in the glare of our headlights, eyes flashing like stars and then vanishing as it raced away into the night.

After two hours we stopped. There was a muttered conference in Finnish.

'This is as far as he can take us,' Mika told us. 'The road has become too dangerous.'

'We can't stop here,' Krasov said frantically.

'Now we go on foot.' Mika's expression wasn't encouraging. I

187

imagined he was worried about whether or not the diminutive Russian would last the journey. Krasov looked at him as if he were mad.

'Road is too dangerous, snow is up to our waist, and he tells us walk.' He leaned against the side of the lorry and groaned in misery. 'Here I am staying. I will not move. Here I will die.'

Mika unloaded skis from the lorry and handed them round. Hammerson took a pair for Krasov and fitted them on, whispering encouragement to him as he did so. There was something almost tender in the way Hammerson treated him. He was doing it out of affection and respect for the man, and Krasov appeared to respond.

'Keep together but not too close,' Mika instructed. He and the others had carbines slung over their backs.

We set off down a gentle incline, pushing our way through the winter skeletons of birch trees. I tried to imagine what it would be like in summer, islands of silver birch floating in green meadows on the side of a long rolling hill, under a wide blue sky with the soft grey water of the inland lakes stretching into the distance. But the thought did nothing to keep out the cold.

'We rest here,' Mika said some time later. We had reached a summer house deep in the woods. 'Then we begin the last leg of our journey.'

One of the minders started a fire while Mika gave us brandy from a flask. Slowly, our frozen bones came back to life. Krasov was exhausted, too tired even to complain. Hammerson looked after him like a child, finding him a corner where he could rest, wrapping him in a rug to keep warm, bringing him food.

I had lost track of time. I hardly knew whether it was day or night. The daylight was over so quickly it hardly seemed to matter. By now the wooden house was warm. I settled in a chair and slept intermittently. Krasov snored in his corner.

'He did well,' Hammerson said, indicating Krasov. 'You have to give the little guy his due. He's tougher than he looks. There's some strength in that body, despite its size.'

'Have you done this journey before?' I asked Hammerson. If this was to be our last night together, I was determined to find out as much as I could.

'Once. Some time ago now.' He seemed reluctant to say more. 'Krasov isn't their usual cargo. That's been the trouble all along. Their heart's not in this.'

'What is their usual cargo?'

'Balts.' He said. 'Estonians, Lithuanians, Latvians; not your genu-ine asshole Red like Krasov. Reds by coercion, the guys who can't swallow the ideology though it's all they're given to live on. The good guys. The opposition.'

'There isn't an opposition in a one-party state,' I said, rather too smartly.

'There is – it's underground,' Hammerson said. 'We call this the lifeline, the escape route for Balt nationalists. We bring them out when things get too hot. There are a number of these networks operating across the Baltic states, left over from the war. I guess, for the Balts, the war never ended.' He pointed at the sleeping forms of the three Finns. 'That's why they're edgy. Russia is the enemy and Krasov is Russian. This cargo smells.'

The cargo in question stirred and murmured something in Russian but did not wake up.

'Why did they agree to take him then?'

Hammerson smiled. 'I called in my marker.' It was all he would say.

I tried to question him about his involvement with these Baltic peoples. How did it start? When? Hammerson smiled through his evasion.

'It's a long story.'

'There's plenty of time.'

'I have a simple view of the world. You have to stand up for your beliefs. These people are oppressed by a system they didn't choose. They can't be what they want to be, what they have a right to be. In my book that's bad. I'm on the side of freedom. The guy who's taking it away from them is my enemy.'

'Isn't there more to it than that?'

'You tell me then.'

There was an edge to his voice which warned me off. For some reason I didn't understand, he wasn't going to tell me anything more. I changed the subject.

'What brings Mika into this?'

'The Finns had a hard time in the war. Mika lost a father and a brother. He can't forgive the Russians easily.'

'And Tanya?'

Hammerson laughed. 'You've met Tanya, have you? She's his sister.'

'What's she to do with all this?'

'Not much. Mika doesn't involve her unless he has to. She's a doctor. We needed a doctor to get Krasov across the border.'

'Where's she gone now?'

'Back to Helsinki, I guess. That's where she lives.'

I must have slept after that because the next thing I remember is Hammerson shaking me and saying: 'We're moving out, Danny. We're on our way.' He turned to Krasov. 'Last leg, my friend. Not far now. Imagine you are walking to America.'

I looked out of the window. It was very dark and the wind was blowing the snow into drifts. It was going to be a cold and difficult journey.

We set out in single file once more, crossing fields and forests. The sky had cleared and the moon was up, draining the landscape of colour but etching every outline black against the snow and making our shadows look like pools of darkness sliding silently across the ground.

We were following the edge of a forest, moving along the top of a sweeping hillside, keeping always within sight of the line of the trees so that, at the first sign of danger, we could slip back into the shadows.

I was the first to see the other skiers. They were below us, just above the base of the valley on the opposite side. There were four of them, visible only briefly as they too kept close to the line of the trees. But occasionally one, then another, would break out into the open, only to disappear again. At first I thought they were hunters looking for game. I could see the guns on their backs. Then I knew they were shadowing us, that we must be in their sights. They were still hunters but now we were the quarry. I called to Mika and pointed down the hill. He waved us back out of sight into the trees. He had taken his carbine off his shoulder.

'What's happening?' Krasov's anxieties returned.

'There are people down there,' I said, pointing. 'I don't know who they are.'

'Russians,' Mika said, scanning the valley through binoculars. 'Looking for us.'

'If we go back into the woods,' Hammerson said, 'we should lose them.'

'Too slow,' Mika said. 'We have a deadline for the rendezvous and it is only safe for our friends to wait a short time. We must

190

keep going, only faster. There is only one way now and that is forward.'

We started again, a greater urgency in all our actions. The slope of the hillside was in our favour and our speed improved. From time to time I looked down and though there were moments when I thought we had outrun our pursuers, always a figure reappeared, only to vanish again. They had found us and were not going to let us go.

'We won't make it at this rate,' I heard Hammerson say.

'We have to make it.' Mika was grim-faced.

But the decision was not to be ours to take. A branch above me shook with a sudden vibration and snow fell on to to the ground. I looked down the valley and saw a narrow arc of white light streaming silently towards us. I watched it snake up the hill, marvelling at the swift beauty of the line, before the muffled crackle of explosions reached us, like distant fireworks. Then the single line became a chorus as others joined it, lines of light that lived and died in seconds. It was an uncanny, almost surreal experience, the uneven patterns of the tracer bullets bursting out against the dark sky and then dying away, followed by the delayed sound of muffled crackles from deep in the valley. The trees around us echoed as bullets buried themselves in wood or whined uselessly away into the darkness beyond and shook with the explosions. Snow fell from the swaying branches above us.

'Looks like World War Three's begun,' Hammerson said. 'Just what we didn't want.'

The pattern of our response was professional. Hammerson and Mika were responsible for Krasov and they pulled him along as fast as he could go. The two minders, their carbines at the ready, were already crashing down into the valley, concealed in dead ground. They were to divert our attackers while we were to be given the chance to escape, even at the cost of their lives.

It was then a question of move and countermove, a deadly ballet of diversionary fire from the Finns while we pressed forward; the answering counter-attack from our pursuers. Then more fire from us down the hillside, while the two Finns changed their position, followed by another burst from them drawing answering fire from the Russians while we moved forward as fast as we could.

Our pursuers were not getting any closer, but nor were we escaping. It was as if we were inextricably joined to each other, Siamese twins each bent on driving the life out of the other.

There was a sudden cry from behind us. I turned to see Krasov fall forwards, sliding away from us over the rim of the ridge, his arms grabbing helplessly at the snow as he slithered backwards down into the hollow of dead ground below us. I thought he must have been shot. But as soon as he came to a halt he shouted for us again and we knew he was all right. Hammerson was already going after him, plunging through the snow, and when he reached Krasov he grabbed him by the shoulders and pulled him to his feet. Krasov appeared shaken but unhurt.

'Come on,' I heard Hammerson say. 'Climb. Climb.'

Mika had taken up a position behind a tree and was giving covering fire to Krasov and Hammerson. I watched them clamber up together, Hammerson encouraging Krasov forward as fast as he was able. For a moment the firing stopped and there was an eerie silence broken only by gasps for breath from Krasov.

'Help him,' Hammerson called to me. 'Give him a hand.'

The last few yards were up a steep snowbound slope to the ridge on which we stood. This part of their ascent was fully exposed to the view of our pursuers below. I secured my foothold and leaned over the edge, reaching down as far as I could. Krasov's progress was painstakingly slow and he was still too far away for me to get hold of him. He was finding it a very difficult climb and he kept losing his grip and sliding backwards into Hammerson's arms.

'OK, we'll try another way,' I heard Hammerson say.

He started climbing himself, diagonally this time, leaving Krasov where he was. He dug out footholds in the snow and made a platform for himself. Then he reached backwards, took Krasov's hand and pulled him up. Slowly, they came towards us, Hammerson leading the way, digging out the snow in a ragged staircase for the little Russian.

As they came fully into view, the moonlight making their dark outline easily visible against the snow, the arcs of light from down in the valley burst out again, chasing them as they zigzagged up the last yards of the slope. I was lying full length on the snow now, both arms reaching for Krasov. He was a few feet from me, struggling against the steep slope to find the grip that would drag him over the edge to safety. The marksmen below were finding their range and bullets started to crack all around us.

Then the streams of light found their quarry and converged on Hammerson, and with a cry he fell forward in the snow. With agonizing slowness he began to slide head first down the hillside. Krasov looked round and shouted for him. I grabbed his arm and pulled him to safety. Behind him, as the hillside gave way steeply, I saw Hammerson plunging downwards faster and faster, out of sight and out of range. I saw the Russians clambering towards his still form.

Krasov moaned in despair. I wanted to fire at the ant-like figures swarming up the hillside.

'No.' Mika grabbed my arm. 'No time for that. We have to go on.'

'We can't leave him there.'

'He's dead or dying. We can do nothing for him now.'

He pulled me after him, and then Krasov. With almost super-human strength he dragged us through the woods and down to the road. There, waiting for us, its engine turning over, a plume of exhaust visible in the night air, was a lorry. Two figures emerged and ran towards us. They spoke in Finnish to Mika who pointed at Krasov. They took him by the arms and bundled him into the lorry and drove off. It was all over in less than a minute. No time even for goodbye.

'Now we find Hammerson,' Mika said.

It took us more than an hour to climb back up the hill. The night was still clear but I could see no sign of our attackers. After a time we picked up one minder, then the other, both unharmed. From the expressions on their faces, they had enjoyed themselves. I wanted to know how they had got on but I was too breathless to ask Mika to translate for me. He seemed in no mood to talk.

We retraced our steps to the point where Hammerson had fallen. I could make out the course of his body as it fell down the snowy hillside. It had torn a path in the virgin snow. Carefully, we climbed down after him. The snow had drifted here and sometimes we fell in it up to our waists. As we went down, the minders indicated with casual sweeps of their carbines which way our attackers had gone. It seemed we were safe enough not to worry about cover.

We reached the bottom of the hill. There was no sign of Hammerson's body, though there were marks in the snow where he had come to rest. There were other marks, too, footmarks, imprinted in the snow. Our enemies had removed Hammerson.

'He must be still alive,' Mika said. 'They'd never bother with him dead. I do not like to think what they will do to him.'

He made it sound as if he were writing Hammerson's epitaph.

★

I was sliding out of control, my hands tearing at roots, branches, grass, anything that could stop my fall. But the roots came away, the branches broke and the wet grass gave me nothing to grip on. Faster and faster I fell, my body jarred and bruised as I bumped my way down the rocky surface of the hillside. I knew there was nothing I could do to stop myself and the certainty of what was happening terrified me. It seemed such a pointless way to end one's life.

I saw the sand below racing up to meet me and with what little consciousness I had left I braced myself for the impact, no time even to wonder if I would survive. But there was no shock, no sudden grinding stop as my bones and ligaments were crushed and torn by the weight of my own body: only a gentle deceleration, like being in a slow-motion film. I was standing upright on the sands, staring at the waiting ship only a hundred yards or so away and the thin line of soldiers snaking towards it.

Then the explosions came, bullets tearing up the sand dunes and bombs bursting all round. I saw the bodies of men disintegrate in front of me. One moment there were groups of soldiers, the next nothing but fire-scarred flesh and horror. I fell on my face, the grit of sand in my mouth, my hands tight around my head, trying desperately to shut out the horrifying sights and sounds of the battle and make myself invisible.

Through the smoke and the screams I heard a voice say: 'I cannot imagine dying on a beach.' And the dead and the dying on the beach rose up and turned their broken bodies towards me and mocked me with their laughter.

I woke up then, my body shaking with fear and my head still full of a noise I could not recognize. The bombs and the bullets had gone but I was in darkness and could see nothing. I could not remember where I was.

'Are you all right?'

Voices near me, unfamiliar voices. Hands came out of the darkness and touched me reassuringly on the face and shoulder. At least I knew I was alive. The high-pitched rattle of mocking laughter stopped.

Someone said: 'Don't turn the light on yet.'

I knew then what had happened and I did what I always did on these occasions. I murmured: 'I'm sorry. Sorry.'

A woman's voice asked: 'Do you want a drink?' She handed me a glass of water.

'Was I shouting?' I asked.

'Screaming.' It was the woman again. 'And hiding. You were face down on the bed.'

'I'm sorry.'

Someone switched on a light in the bedroom. I saw Mika and Tanya and the mess of the bed in which I had been sleeping. In my nightmare I had wrecked it.

'Are you all right now?'

I nodded in response. My throat was too dry to speak.

'It's three o'clock. Try to sleep. If you want anything, call.'

I didn't sleep again. I relived my life since the beginning of the war. But this time I was in command of the demons and they lay quiet.

★

'Does it happen often?'

It was morning. I was drinking tea in Tanya's apartment. I had no idea where Mika was.

'The nightmare? No. Not often.' That wasn't true. It happened more often than I dared admit to myself.

'What makes it happen?'

'If I knew that,' I said, 'I'd be able to control it.'

'What do you dream about?'

'The war mostly. Memories of war.'

'What stimulates those memories? We say we cannot remember something but we store every event of our lives in our minds; it is all there, waiting like an old film to be rerun some day. But with time these events sink deeper and deeper. They break up, fragment. They are not lost. They are only harder to find, more difficult to reassemble. The mechanism we have for retrieving those memories is not strong. It is not well-trained. It has difficulty in reaching deep enough.'

'It reaches deep enough with me.'

'These memories are recent. They are not buried. Something releases them within your mind, something deep within yourself that you would like to stay buried for ever. There is a trigger. What it is remains a mystery.'

'You're the doctor. What do you think?'

She laughed. 'I know what Freud would think. He would look at you and he would think to himself: guilt. That is it. English guilt.'

I wasn't sure if she meant it seriously or not.

'Why English guilt?'

'The English are born guilty. The first word they learn to say is sorry.'

'I don't feel guilty.'

'You think you don't feel guilty.'

'I've nothing to be guilty about.'

'You think you have nothing to be guilty about.'

'Are you suggesting a course of psychoanalysis?'

'I am suggesting nothing. I am trying to make you laugh.'

She was laughing herself, her head thrown back and her body arching away from me. I wanted to reach out and touch her, to take her in my arms and hold her to me. I did not want this moment to pass.

'Is that better?' Her face was close to mine, her smile still there. 'You looked so worried just now.'

'I'm sorry.'

'You see? You apologize. You are always sorry, you English. Even when it's not your fault. It is in your nature.'

We laughed again and she poured me some more tea.

'What happens now?' I asked.

'What you are really asking is where is Mika.'

'I don't want to be a burden to you.'

'I am pleased you are here,' she said, and it sounded genuine. 'Mika wants you to stay a few days until it is quiet once more. Then you will be able to leave.'

'Will I see Mika again?'

'Probably not. He will telephone with instructions about your departure. That is all.'

We talked on through the morning. She told me she had trained to be a doctor before the war and had worked in casualty stations near the front line during the Winter War. She had seen men die, but she had expected that. What had distressed her was the terrible nature of the dying she witnessed, the dreadful injuries men inflicted on one another and how the wounded could live on though their bodies were shattered beyond repair. Sometimes she had willed her patients to die to release them from pain.

'Sometimes,' she said, 'I wanted the power to kill, to put the poor creatures out of their misery.'

'Do your memories of that time come back to haunt you?' I asked.

196

'No more.'

'I envy you.'

'All that is over now. I have made a new life. Those memories are are under my control. I bury them in my new experiences with my mothers and their babies.'

'But you still help Mika.'

'Mika is all of my family I have left. He knows I think what he is doing is wrong.'

'He is fighting for a cause he believes in.'

'No, he is fighting for revenge, he is fighting because that is all he knows and he cannot give it up. Perhaps you are too. Perhaps that is why you have nightmares.'

I wanted to tell her about myself then, but before I could say anything, she said: 'Come. It is dark again now. It is safe to go out. I will show you this city where I live.'

I have never known a city whose nature through the seasons matched that of its people more closely than Helsinki. In winter, deprived of the light, it is a dour place, its buildings granite-hard and grey, its people concentrating all their energies on outfacing the long days of darkness and cold. In summer, when light rules unopposed, the streets are never quiet, whatever the hour. A kind of summer madness takes over, a real coming to life after the rigours of winter. Even the houses seem changed, the greens, blues, yellows and reds of their painted walls making the streets seemed decked with enormous flags.

But the festival of summer is short-lived: soon after midsummer, the days start to shorten again, the extraordinary warmth of the Gulf Stream ebbs away and the long journey into the darkness and the cold begins once more.

But I love that city. I love its intimacy, I love the decorations on the buildings, each carved stone or shaped brick expressing a sense of the country and its people and their slow fight for independence. I love its Russianness, the beech trees and the Chekhovian houses in the diplomatic quarter. But most of all I love the water that surrounds it, so green and inviting in the summer months, so grey and treacherous in winter.

It was on that cold and blustery afternoon that I fell in love with the city and in my mind, Tanya and the city became one.

★

'What will you do now?'

Mika had telephoned earlier. Arrangements for my departure had been made. I had picked up my ticket from the ferry office. In a few hours I would be on my way. Tanya was in the kitchen making me something to eat before I left.

'I go back the way I came,' I said.

'Home?'

She had her back to me as she stirred something in a saucepan.

'Berlin isn't home. Berlin is where I work.'

At that moment Berlin had no reality. It was a distant city on the map whose streets I didn't know, whose people I had never met, somewhere I never wanted to see again.

'What do you do there?'

'I ask the locals questions. If they give the right answers, they get a tick against their names, if they don't, a cross. Something like that.'

We had been together for more than forty-eight hours. In that time we had only touched when she had taken my arm in the street. Now, in a few hours, we would say goodbye and I would probably never see her again.

'You don't sound happy about it.'

'I hate it.'

The words were out before I knew what I had said. Tanya turned towards me at once.

'Since I met you that is the first time you ever tell me how you feel about anything. Why are you so afraid of saying what you feel?'

That's when the confession began. I told her things I didn't even know I knew or thought or felt, things that had been buried deep in me for a long time. It was like talking about someone else, someone whose existence I would rather not have owned up to.

I talked about the war, about those few but soul-destroying moments of fear when you think your life is about to end, and the humiliating sense of relief when you know you are still alive. How the ordinariness of life, everyday sights and sounds – the sun rising, a bird singing, rain falling – suddenly become more precious than gold. I described the humour and the boredom of war, the way that fighting with men over weeks and months changes you so that afterwards, when the war is over, you are no longer who you were before, and how sometimes you don't know who you are any longer. I told her about my father, about the paradox of his detachment from me and yet what I felt to be his need of me to fulfil his idea

198

of what I should be. How I would always fail him in that respect, and how that sense of failure shamed me, since I longed for him to accept what I had become.

Tanya said very little. She didn't need to. The words poured out of me. At some point we ate something, I can't remember what it was; we drank, and I talked. Once I looked at my watch but she covered the face with her hand.

'It doesn't matter,' she said. 'This is more important.'

It was after midnight when I stopped, and the ferry had sailed two hours before.

'Why did you let me do that?' I asked.

'Once you started,' she said, smiling, 'I don't think anyone could have stopped you.'

'And now?'

'I think you have to stay another night.'

She bent towards me, put her hands on my face and kissed me. I took her in my arms and felt the weight of her body against mine.

'Why did you not do this earlier?' she asked after a while. There was nothing I could say, except confess my weakness that this was what I had wanted from the moment I had first seen her.

'But I thought you did not like me,' she said, between kisses. After all, you have seen me naked. I have not met many men like that, you know.'

All the time beneath the surface lay her laughter, the gentle mockery both of me and of herself.

'Then I thought you did not like women.' She laughed again. 'I have heard dreadful stories about your English schools. Then I listened to you and I knew why. You are afraid. Not of guns and bullets, I am sure you are a brave man. But you are afraid of yourself. Of the person you have become. The bad dreams will not stop until you accept who you are.'

Her hands were on my face, soothing me, drawing the pain out of me.

'You are like a man frozen. So I have to make the first move.' More laughter. 'We are not used to that in our country. Finnish girls are shy. But I could not let you go away to Berlin without telling you that I have fallen in love with you. Will you tell me that you do not hate me for saying that? Or will you look at me like a sphinx for ever?'

★

199

We lay together in the dark.

'What happens next?' I asked.

'For most men that would be enough for now. Perhaps with the English it is different. I have never made love to an Englishman before.'

'And . . . us?'

'In a few hours you will catch a ferry and go back to your Germans and their questions, and I will go back to my women and their babies.'

'We say goodbye and that's it?'

'What else can we do?'

'But—' I was confused. 'You said you loved me.'

'You never said you loved me.' It was neither a reproof nor a question. It was a simple statement of fact.

'I'm sorry.'

'No,' she said, sitting up and leaning over me. 'No guilt. No sorry. I have said I love you. I have shown I love you. You are here beside me now, in my bed, this is my body you have made love to, this is my heart that is beating here,' and she took my hand and held it to her breast.

She put her arms on my shoulders and pushed me back into the pillows.

'You have shown me that you love me too, I know that. I would like to hear you say it, but I know it is difficult for you. I will have to believe in your silence.'

I tried to put my arms around her but she pushed me away. For the first time I saw that behind the laughter, there was uncertainty too.

I looked into her blue eyes, saw her soft golden hair falling around her face and felt the warmth of her body over mine. In that moment I experienced an intensity of feeling stronger than anything I had known before. Then something broke inside me, and I felt like I was bursting out of the restraint that had held me captive all my life. For the first time I became someone I could recognize without shame, someone I could face without fear. I had discovered myself in her embrace.

'Tanya.'

All the love and emotion that I had withheld from others all my life poured out of me then. I told her that I loved her, that I had never loved anyone else; that with her I was complete, whole; that with her I was someone I had not believed I could ever be.

She held me in the dark, speaking to me in Finnish. I could not understand the words but I sensed what she was saying, and I wanted to weep with happiness.

'In the war,' she said later, 'I learned to ignore the future. Remembering yesterday meant that I was still alive. And there was *now*, what I was doing, where I was doing it, that meant I was alive too. But I never thought about anything after that because I could never be sure that I would be there to live through it. Be happy now. That is what matters. It is a useful lesson.'

'I can't leave you like this. I can't walk out of here not knowing if I will ever see you again.'

'I don't want you to. It would break my heart if you did. But I do not know what to say.'

Nor did I. Our lives were being pulled apart before they had a chance to come together. It seemed impossible, wrong.

'I will come back. As soon as I can.'

'No,' she said. 'We both know that will not be possible. Don't say it. Don't think it.'

'I won't go then.'

'Stay here and live with me? I would like that, but it is impossible. It is not safe for you here. The Russians will soon know that Mika was involved in Krasov's escape. They will put pressure on our government — they are expert at that — and before long the police will start to look and it is not hard to find an Englishman in Helsinki, even in winter.'

'I will write to you, every day, every week, twice a day. You will be drowned in a sea of my letters.'

She laughed and put her fingers to my lips.

'No,' she said. 'We will not write to each other. We do not need letters to remind us of what we already know.'

'What can we do?'

'You will go away now. Don't come back in the winter. Don't write to me. Don't send messages. Remember me, and I will remember you. We will be together in our minds. Come back in the summer. One day there will be a knock at the door and I will open it and you will be there. We will go to the lakes. There I will look after you and love you and you will love me. That is when we will start our life together.'

She traced the contours of my face with her fingers.

'I will wait a year,' she said. 'If you do not come back in a year, then I will know that you no longer want me.'

I told her that was impossible, I would always love her. I would say her name a thousand times a day and when the days grew longer I would return.

'I will wait a year,' she said again. 'Not a single day more.'

PART THREE

1

DANNY

I left the army in March to work for Charlie Faulkner. The disease that had begun to cripple him since we'd first met had struck another blow at the end of January, and by the time I joined him in Eccleston Street he was in a wheelchair. Each morning, at nine sharp, his chauffeur Thomas would bring the Rolls to a halt outside the office and Charlie would be delivered into the hands of the redoubtable Beryl, who had been with him since his early days in Manchester.

On Mondays we would have what Charlie called his 'prayer meeting'. We would analyse the political news in the Sunday papers, review the past week's events and refine our own timetable of work for the coming week. Each Monday afternoon, Charlie was driven to South Street for his regular meeting with Watson-Jones. We never knew what was said there nor how much of our work was influenced by their discussion. We imagined that some hard talking had gone on about spheres of influence and that Charlie had won. Whether that was true or not, it was what we wanted to believe, and Charlie never did anything to discourage us. Watson-Jones never came to Eccleston Street.

Charlie's great gift was his memory. He would sit listening to us, head bowed, drawing star shapes in pencil on a pad, never taking notes. That did not prevent him from recalling with alarming accuracy conversations that might have taken place a week or more before, when we had made promises which for some reason or other were now not being met. We learned a number of lessons in the early days. It was simply not worth arousing the other side of Charlie Faulkner, when the sophistication he had acquired during his years in London was ditched in favour of what Beryl described as his 'plain face'. He could be downright crude if he chose, but you were never left in any doubt about what he wanted or where he stood, and when you delivered he was never short in his praise.

There were three of us besides Beryl: myself and two researchers, Roger Blake and Tony Meadows, both recently down from Oxford, too young to have fought in the war. They were the writers on the team ('my bright young men', as Charlie called them) drafting speeches for Watson-Jones, creating the copy for the newsletter we established, packaging the endless research projects into pamphlets and reports. I was what Charlie described as the 'team leader', by dint of my age and experience, though I was the oldest by only three or four years. I was never excluded from any political discussion, but I found I never had very much to say, and I don't think Charlie expected me to contribute. But once a course of action had been decided, he looked to me to make it happen.

It was an unlikely structure, but it worked because we were all 'Charlie's boys'. He was the driving force in our lives, a man even then in his last years with a quite extraordinary level of energy and commitment. We soon understood why Beryl had spent her life with him. If you got on with Charlie – and many didn't – you came to love him. I wasn't alone in wishing I'd known him in his prime.

★

I found those first weeks of civilian life very difficult. As the train pulled out of Charlottenburg station I had imagined I would be able to cast off the taste and smell of Berlin and all that it represented in my life, but memories of my time in occupied Germany persisted. I felt uncomfortable, uprooted, unable to settle. I was haunted by the despairing faces of the Germans I'd rejected in the months I'd been there. The London I returned to was not the city I had known in the past. Many of the landmarks had gone, obliterated for ever in the bombing, but the changes went deeper as I and others like me tried to reassemble our lives. Wartime privations continued though we were no longer at war. Our experiences in uniform made the customs and attitudes of the society we had fought to preserve seem hopelessly out of date. We searched for new certainties, only to find they were not there. If we wanted them, we would have to make them ourselves. It was a mystifying and unsettling time, made stranger because I no longer had the comforting support of khaki and rank to sustain the decisions I needed to take. All of a sudden

I was on my own. It was what I had wanted, but coming to terms with it was nowhere near as straightforward as I had expected.

I rented a small flat in Strutton Ground, near Great Smith Street in Westminster, three rooms above a cobbler. I got to know Manny Leman and his long-suffering wife Esther because Manny, a Latvian Jew who had been brought to this country when he was ten, was unashamedly curious.

'What you do in your work, then, guv?' he would ask. 'Sounds like an easy life to me, reading and writing all day.'

'Leave the poor man alone,' Esther would call out from the depths behind the shop. 'He's got better things to do than listen to you.'

'This is man-to-man talk,' Manny would shout above the noise of his machinery. 'You stick to your kitchen, woman.' He would wink at me and continue to ask questions.

Esther would emerge with her shopping basket. 'He's a terrible man. Don't listen to him,' she'd say to me. 'I don't know why I married him.'

They had a son, Joe, who was the fulfilment of all their dreams. He was a brilliant linguist and had won a scholarship to Cambridge to read Russian. 'He make 'is mark, that boy, I tell you,' Manny said, working on a leather sole. 'Where all those brains come from, I never know, not from his mother and me, that's for sure.'

They were good to me, Esther particularly, looking after me while her son was away, feeding me, taking messages, doing my washing, cleaning the flat when she thought it needed to be cleaned. She never said much, but sometimes when Manny was busy in the shop she would ask me into her kitchen for a cup of tea and she would listen to me talk, nodding, encouraging me to continue. I sometimes imagined she was the mother I had lost when I was thirteen. I know she saw me as an orphan, someone who needed caring for and that was the role God had created for her, to care for the men in her life. I was simply a late arrival.

★

I saw little of my father after my return from Berlin. On the rare occasions I went to Cambridge he appeared withdrawn and preoccupied. He never mentioned Krasov's visit nor its aftermath and nor, loyally, did Celia. But I detected a new urgency in his newspaper articles. He was openly arguing for the international scientific community to organize itself in opposition to the use of nuclear weapons by governments. He wanted to see set up a new, politically neutral international authority into whose control governments would surrender these weapons. His vision was idealistic and hopelessly impractical. I read the occasional flurries of outrage his increasingly radical opinions stimulated in the letter columns of his newspaper. If the letters illustrated anything, it was how isolated he was in his views.

My father sat on a number of Government scientific committees but he seldom got in touch with me when he was in London. When we did meet, he asked no questions about my job. He disapproved of my working for Watson-Jones ('very third-rate man, can't think what you see in him' was his only comment when I told him what I planned to do after leaving the army), and he wanted his disapproval to hurt, and it did. I was affected by his silence and he knew it. In the few conversations we had together, he steered well away from any endorsement of the life I had chosen. In return, I stayed away from Cambridge.

I never told him about my trip to Finland nor that I had seen Krasov. The heightened atmosphere of that strange night meeting lost its threat on my return home. Sitting in my office in Eccleston Street, the urgency and importance of what he had said looked very small and its truth was questionable. Had Krasov really said those words? I convinced myself he had, but I felt increasingly that his real purpose had been to emphasize his own importance, to show that he still counted. There were moments when my anger with my father almost prompted me to tell him who Krasov was and what he had done, but I didn't, not least because I doubted if my father would have let himself understand what I was talking about. Krasov wasn't a weapon to use against him.

★

Perhaps it was more in my mind than anything else, but I felt that my relationship with Monty was strained. He had telephoned me when I got back from Helsinki, to fix a time when he would come to Berlin to discuss my Finnish visit. But he cancelled each arrangement we made and when I pressed him he had changed his mind. 'Put it on paper,' he said. 'Tell me what you think.'

I was left with the impression that he had lost interest, that the importance Krasov had assumed a few weeks before had been overtaken by events I knew nothing of, relegating me to a reminder of a past whose relevance had faded. I was irritated because Finland seemed no longer to matter to him, while to me the country had become the embodiment of all my dreams.

I kept my report to Monty as brief as I could make it.

Go to Finland, find Krasov, was my brief. Ask him what he wants. Judge whether he's genuine or not. I did as you instructed.

Krasov's story is easy to summarize. During his short visit to Cambridge in January he told my father that a Soviet nuclear scientist whom he claims my father knows (please check this, a woman called Ruth Marchenko) had been blackmailed by the Soviet intelligence service to put pressure on my father to organize international support for a group of dissident scientists within the Soviet Union, who were refusing to work on the Soviet bomb. (What form that pressure took he wouldn't say.)

By the time I caught up with Krasov in Finland, his story had moved on. There was now, he claimed, the possibility of momentous political change within the Soviet Union. In the weeks since his meeting in Cambridge, the Russians had suffered a major setback in their own nuclear programme (a laboratory had exploded) and this disaster had encouraged a countermove by a kind of peace party that, from within the Central Committee, was now challenging Stalin's leadership. (Have you ever heard a whisper about opposition to Stalin?)

If this group was to win (I was left in doubt about where his own hopes lay), the West had to seize the opportunity with both hands to negotiate a non-nuclear treaty with the Soviets. To carry conviction, the louder the anti-nuclear outcry in the West, the greater the chance that a sane government would emerge in Russia and with it a genuine opportunity for a lasting post-war peace. He begged me to tell you this and to urge my father to redouble his efforts in support of moving international opinion against the bomb.

Is that plausible? He told me a tall story and in his heart he knew it. Every time I challenged him on a detail, he lost his temper. Krasov is a congenital liar. He will defend to the death that what he tells you at the time is true. But if circumstances demand it, he'll deny his own words an hour later. He doesn't understand what truth is.

Should you respond? Unless I've missed something (and I could have) you're better off washing your hands of him. My judgement is that the man has an overdeveloped sense of his own importance, and he's a troublemaker. Stay away, Monty. That's my advice. Let him stew with the Americans. See what they make of him.

I know Monty got the letter because he telephoned to tell me so. He said he understood how difficult it must have been for me in Finland, on my own like that. (No mention of Hammerson. I wondered if he knew.) He was grateful for what I had done. (What had I done, I wondered? but he didn't say.) I asked if he wanted to meet to discuss what I'd written. No need, he said, the matter was closed now, he had moved on to other things. New times, new agendas. We would get together soon enough, have a pint and a bite to eat, talk it all through. He'd get in touch when I was back in London, I could be sure of that. *Auf Wiedersehen.*

He didn't get in touch after my return from Berlin, and I found it difficult to make contact with him. When we finally met for a drink in a gloomy pub in Whitehall, he arrived late, apologetic and distracted, his attention clearly somewhere else.

'Krasov's with the Americans now,' he said. 'No doubt he's spinning them a few yarns.'

'Will they believe them?'

'God knows,' he said. 'It depends how much they want to believe him. They've not had much luck with defectors recently.'

I took that to mean he hoped they'd buy what Krasov had to sell, however dubious the merchandise. He seemed oddly amused at the prospect. Was ensuring the Americans bought counterfeit goods his payback for the humiliation he'd suffered after Senator Shearing's visit? If that was so, had he got me to Finland to ensure that Krasov the liar got to America?

'What about Krasov's opposition theory?' I asked, keeping a lid on my suspicion that Monty was using Krasov for his own private revenge on the Americans. (Surely this was too extreme?) 'Rivals to Stalin?'

This was the only element in Krasov's story that might have had a grain of truth about it.

'That?' Was it my imagination or was Monty being deliberately evasive? 'Baloney. Don't believe a word of it. Our people in Moscow took one look at it and laughed their heads off.'

Somewhere in the snowy wastes of that distant land we had faced Soviet bullets, Hammerson had been wounded and captured, Krasov had escaped by the skin of his teeth, we had all lived briefly at the edge of our lives and for what? The risks we had taken had achieved nothing. Finland was a pointless exercise. It was a bleak moment in our relationship.

'I'm sorry,' Monty said, looking at his watch. 'I've got to be somewhere else. The enemy never sleeps.'

'You're OK, are you?' I asked as we got up to leave. I remembered his remarks as we walked through the melting snow on a cold Berlin night. *I'm in the shit, Danny. Well and truly up to my neck.* What had become of all that anxiety?

'I'm all right,' Monty said. 'Just about. I'll be in touch.'

I telephoned him a couple of times after that but when we talked he again seemed preoccupied, and though we made arrangements to meet, he left messages cancelling on both occasions. I didn't see him for a while.

★

And Hammerson? For months afterwards I kept seeing his fall through the snow, his inert body gathering speed as it slid down the hill. Was he alive? I prayed so. Was anything being done to release him? My one attempt to find out, through an American military contact in Berlin, met with puzzlement and incomprehension. Major Hammerson had been recalled to Washington; no one knew when he was due back in Berlin. Was it a conspiracy of silence? I imagined that the Americans were so terrified the Russians might hold one of their serving officers in captivity that they had decided to make Hammerson invisible.

The memory I couldn't get rid of was of that last fateful night journey through the snow, Hammerson attending to Krasov, befriending the man, caring for him, encouraging him. Was that out of duty? Was he acting in the interests of those who employed him? No, it was more than that, it was the nature of the man himself. I had been startled by the ferocity of his anti-Soviet sentiments, mostly because I found they had an echo in my own beliefs that I had never faced up to. I envied him his simplicity, his fearlessness, his certainty that what he said and did was right.

Now he was gone, and I held the secret of what had happened to him. Some nights the memory tormented me. His face would

211

look up from the snow, blood-spattered and bruised, and appeal to me.

Help me, Danny. Help me, please.

His hands would reach out to drag me into the dark prison of his world and I would wake up, startled and sweating, the images rising up in the darkness and taking all hope of sleep from me.

★

I had left Helsinki with nothing of Tanya's, though I had asked her for a photograph.

'I need nothing to remind me of you. Why should you need something from me?' she had said with an impeccable if frustrating logic. I had wanted to argue the point until I saw that she would not change her mind.

'If you can recall me in your mind,' she had said later, 'you will not need anything else. If you can't, then having something of mine will not help.'

I admired her fatalism and regretted it. But as the weeks went by, I saw that she was right. If I concentrated I could recall exactly how she was, how she had looked, the sound of her voice and her laugh, what we had done together. Slowly but irrevocably an image of Tanya emerged and stayed with me, a companion in everything I did. For the first time I recognized the places in my life where I was incomplete and I was able to measure my incompleteness. It was a shock to see how much of a delusion my own sense of self-reliance was. I longed for her desperately but there seemed no likelihood that I would be able to see her again.

As the spring slowly broke the icy grip of winter, the possibility of getting back to Finland had all the permanence of a dream on waking.

2

RUTH

'Remember me?'

It is not the voice she expects when she picks up the telephone, but it is a voice she knows. An alarm is triggered deep in her memory and a discipline she hasn't used for years moves automatically into place.

'How are you?'

'I'm home again.'

No names, no dates, no times, no places. Those were the rules, she tells Stevens, as she continues her story. Give them nothing to work on, the secret listeners on the wire. Play the game and you might stay alive, though in those terrible times (how many years ago? Eight? Nine?), anonymity had provided no certainties.

'It's good to hear your voice again.' The code is still intact. He will be pleased about that.

'We'll meet soon, won't we?'

Somehow he will get a message to her with instructions for their meeting place. How careful he is. But then he works for the secret forces of the state.

'I'd like that.'

Little Krasov is back in her life.

★

'Little Krasov' (she tells Stevens), 'the boy with the large head and the small body – not weak, just misshapen until he was fifteen when his body filled out, though he was always small. We girls teased him but we protected him too, in our neighbourhood, at school, in the Young Communist League and afterwards when he joined the Moscow Engineering Academy. He was our mascot, our constant companion, and to us he always remained Little Krasov.'

She remembers the boastful stories he made up at school when he was teased about the hours he spent in the company of the girls in their neighbourhood.

'His defence was to keep the boys intoxicated with stories of seeing us naked, how he could wander in and out of our bedrooms unnoticed because he was Little Krasov. Sometimes he would produce sheets of paper on which he had sketched us – we were his "life models", he said as he passed the drawings around. We all knew he traced these from a book he found. We laughed when we saw his drawings. None of us had bodies like that. Oh, the things he had seen, the things he had done. He would roll his enormous eyes, the boys would jeer and shout and punch each other, but in their hearts they knew Little Krasov had been where they did not yet have the courage to go, and that was the basis of his protected status.'

After graduating from the academy he went to work on an engineering project in the Ukraine, and she lost touch with him. For years they had little news of each other. When he turned up in her life again, a year after the war had begun, he was no longer an engineer. He now worked, he told her, for military intelligence. He had been trained at a special school run by the Red Army general staff, he had learned English (and other skills he did not tell her about) and he was waiting for the final approval of his posting to London from the Foreign Branch of the Central Committee. He would be working as a journalist for Tass. There was important work to be done and he was anxious to do it.

Little Krasov an agent of the state? That was hard to believe. She remembered a time when Little Krasov refused to join the Party. 'It's another of your stories,' she says when he tells her of his departure for London. 'I can't believe in Little Krasov working for the state.'

'Why not?' he said, his finger to his lips.

'Is that what you believe in now?' she asks, ignoring his gesture for discretion. You cannot change the habits learned in your youth. She has never been discreet with him.

'I am afraid even to think what I believe.'

Then he had gone to London and she had lost contact again. Years pass. She doesn't forget Little Krasov but she has her own life to get on with. He never writes to her. If he returns to Moscow in that time (surely he must have) he has never got in touch. Now he has contacted her and she knows London is over, he is back in

Moscow and he wants to see her. She is pleased about that. It is always good to see an old friend. But she knows Little Krasov. Nothing is without a purpose. If he has made contact now it is because he wants something from her. An old instinct revived by Krasov's telephone call puts her on her guard.

★

He is waiting for her outside the Lux Hotel, dressed in black as usual. She recognizes the faithful worn overcoat with the tattered astrakhan collar. He kisses her and puts his arm through hers. They cross the road and to her surprise, he guides her to the waiting room of Hospital 22, a large echoing hall, filled with rows of people patiently waiting. Around them, like flies buzzing over carrion, the nurses and doctors walk up and down, giving the impression of continuous activity. But the crowd never gets smaller, the number of occupied chairs never diminishes. As names are called and men and women shuffle in and out, newcomers appear at the door and take their places.

Why here? she wants to ask, but before she can say anything he has read her thoughts.

'It's crowded,' he says, his huge eyes working their strange magic once again. 'Our presence won't be questioned, we can talk undisturbed for as long as we like. Who would think of looking for us in a hospital waiting room? And it's warm in here.'

They choose two seats near the back of the waiting area. Krasov takes out a flask of tea and a sandwich from a bag he carries and offers both to Ruth. All around them food is being eaten by men and women who know they must keep their strength up while they wait hours, perhaps even days, for the treatment they need.

'It helps us blend with our surroundings,' he says, smiling. 'Besides, I'm hungry.' He takes her hand suddenly and speaks with an unexpected urgency. 'We do not have much time, Ruth. You must believe everything I say. In the past I have lied too often, sometimes to those I love. Now I must redeem myself by speaking the truth.'

The emotional intensity, the way he can shrink the world until it contains only the two of them, the power of those huge dark eyes, the danger and excitement of his presence: that is the Little Krasov she remembers. Memories of old times return. How long since they last met? Three years or more?

'Five.'

He talks to her about his time in London and makes her laugh with his descriptions of the English. But she knows that he has not asked her to this hospital waiting room to listen to his jokes. He has another, more serious purpose, which must wait until he is ready to tell her.

'Did you ever meet my friend Gregor?' he asks. 'We were students together at the Engineering Academy.'

She shakes her head. It is not a name she knows.

'I want to tell you about him.'

In the last year of the war, he says, Gregor Bakov worked as a military planner on the general staff. He was a member of the team that devised the final push by the Red Army through Eastern Europe to Berlin. He saw first-hand that there were two agendas: the need to achieve a military victory and how that military victory was to be exploited for political purposes. Bakov as a loyal Party member had no objection to the race to Berlin bringing the Soviet Union political advantage once the war was over. But he had fought at Stalingrad, he had witnessed the appalling slaughter of men and women there and when the battle was over, he resolved he would oppose any act which put the lives of Soviet soldiers at greater risk than was necessary.

He watched as the strategic objectives of the military planners were overruled by the political commissariat. He saw how corners were cut for political ends, how risks were to be taken in the campaign in order to extend the borders of Russian influence. He realized that these tactics took no account of the welfare of the troops, that Soviet lives would be thrown away to ensure that the Russians reached Berlin well before the Americans and the British. He remembered the sickening images of the dead in Stalingrad, frozen in grotesque postures, every corpse in that city a dreadful, silent plea that such a conflict might never again take place. It was intolerable now to be taking part, on this last crusade of the war, in the unnecessary slaughter of his fellow citizens. Soldiers were men, not animals.

'For the sake of saving human lives, Bakov knew he had to do something.'

His distress brought him to the brink of suicide. The only result of putting a gun to his head would be his removal from the planning committee. He would be quickly replaced, the policy he opposed would continue and the lives of the men he wanted to save would still be wasted. Suicide would achieve nothing. Should he make a lone protest? Should he refuse to take part in the planning exercise? That would bring about his own arrest and trial, no better than suicide.

Days of desperation followed as he sought a solution. Then came inspiration. He would inform Russia's allies, the Americans, of the secret Red Army plans. In the debate in his mind, he repeated the word *allies* again and again, to convince himself he was not acting as a traitor. If they were made aware of Soviet intentions, perhaps the West would find a way of exercising some restraining influence. They were, after all, still fighting together for the defeat of a common enemy. With the information he would provide, the allies would argue Bakov's case for him and the Soviet High Command might be forced to change their plans, to slow down, and fewer lives would be lost.

'He saw the passing of information to the West about Russian military intentions as a patriotic act, not a betrayal.'

Early one morning, his briefcase full of secret papers snatched from the cabinets in his office, Bakov went to the American embassy. He showed them some of the documents in his possession and explained their importance. He waited for their response. Calmly, they gathered up the papers without looking at them and replaced them in his briefcase. He begged them to listen to what he had to say. But the American officials on duty at that hour were unmoved by his appeals.

'The Americans thought he was a plant. That's why they refused him. Nothing he could say or do would shift them.'

Taking him by both arms, they escorted him to the door of the embassy building. A military policeman pushed him out into the street, knocking his fur hat off in the process. Bakov watched it roll down the embassy steps and with it went all his hopes.

He was distraught. He now had less than ninety minutes in which to return the papers or the alarm would be raised. He had planned for many contingencies but never that his gift would be refused. He wandered disconsolately through the dark and deserted Moscow streets. Then, by the Embankment, his fate gave him a second chance.

'He sees a figure coming out of a building in the diplomatic compound. He notices the furtive movements, so similar to his own, looking both ways to make sure the coast is clear before he emerges into the street. Then, head buried in the upturned collar of his

217

greatcoat, the figure hurries away in the darkness. Is it Bakov's imagination or does the man look up at a window for a brief moment? Does a curtain move? Is there a woman's face behind the curtain? He will never be sure.

'From his hiding place in the doorway of a building, he recognizes the hurrying figure as Major Martineau, one of the military attachés at the British embassy whom he met at a reception some months before. Bakov hurries after him. He introduces himself, reminds him where they met and as they hurry on together, Bakov breathlessly explains what he has in his briefcase.

'Martineau asks Bakov to accompany him to his flat. There is a great risk but by now Bakov is so desperate he does not care.

'"Not a sound," Martineau whispers as he puts his key in the lock. "My wife is asleep. I am on night duty at present." He lies without a hint of difficulty but Bakov is too ridden with anxiety to notice.'

Martineau takes him into the bathroom, signalling that Bakov is to say nothing. Then he turns on the tap and lets it run. Now, he says, it is safe to speak. Bakov opens his case and hands over a few of the papers. It takes Martineau only a few moments to realize their importance. He fetches a camera and photographs the sample, and then makes an arrangement to meet Bakov at a safe house in Moscow later that evening.

'How will I know you?' Martineau asks.

'My name,' Bakov says, 'is Peter the Great.'

Martineau shakes Bakov's hand and sends him away to return the papers before their absence can be discovered. The meeting in his apartment has taken less than ten minutes.

'That is how the British got Peter the Great,' Krasov says. 'Whether they understand what they have got is another matter altogether. But as a source of information about the Soviet Union, Peter is unrivalled.'

For the last months of the war the deception worked, and secret Russian military plans were regularly despatched to the British. What use they made of them Bakov never knew, but he had to assume that his acts were saving the lives of his fellow citizens. Then, in the second week of March 1945, Bakov sensed he was being watched. It was nothing overt, just an instinct, though about what he was unable to say. He aborted a planned meeting for a handover of documents at the safe house.

Martineau had no contact with him for a week. When Bakov did reappear, he said, 'We are nearing the end.'

Martineau imagined he meant the end of the war, but Bakov said: 'They suspect me. If I am caught they will execute me. I can die in the knowledge that I achieved something. Be patient. You may think he is dead, but he will be resurrected. Peter will never die.' He shook Martineau's hand. 'Thank you for believing in me. You are a good man.'

Martineau never saw Bakov again. Two days later he was arrested by the KGB, given a summary trial and was already dead on the day the war ended. But before his arrest, he had secretly passed on responsibility for Peter the Great to Ivan Ulanov, an expert in the design of electronic navigational devices for shells and missiles. He had been a fellow student with Bakov and he too had his own reasons for hating the regime for which he worked. His parents, both teachers, had been arrested in 1938 on invented charges of conspiracy against the state (Bakov's father taught English and copies of the novels of Charles Dickens had been found in his apartment, sufficient proof of treachery at that time). Both had been sent to concentration camps and he had never seen them again. His exhilaration rapidly turned to terror when he learned of Bakov's arrest and trial.

For weeks Ulanov could bring himself to do nothing. This was the time of Peter's silence. In an attempt to regain his courage, Ulanov took to following Martineau. He got to know the daily pattern of his movements, his rota at the embassy. He became an expert in what he called 'Martineau's nocturnal habits', his visits to the dark-haired wife of a French consular official. He rehearsed his meeting with Martineau a hundred times. Then, early one morning, he caught up with the scurrying figure of the military attaché, handed him a briefcase and said only one word before walking quickly away: 'Peter.' Peter the Great had come back to life. Bakov's faith was vindicated.

By December 1945, the ever-vigilant KGB had caught Ulanov, but before his arrest he had recruited Joseph Militarossian who, months later, brought in Boris Shtemenko. Peter was passed from hand to hand. The flow of intelligence may stutter occasionally but it does not stop, but nor does the line of corpses of those associated with it. All of them, she knows, are Little Krasov's friends.

It is dark outside now; the windows have turned black while Little

Krasov has been talking. The hall is flooded with an icy blue light. From time to time she is dimly aware of names being called and of figures shuffling past her to be directed down ill-lit corridors by sour-faced nurses with the doughy complexions of camp guards.

Krasov is pouring more tea from the flask. Why is he telling me about Peter the Great? What am I to do with all this? Could it be a trap? She controls a sudden wave of paranoia. She has known Little Krasov all her life – surely they have been through too much together for him to betray her now? Then she remembers it is years since she last saw him. In that time, what might have happened to him that she does not know about?

She looks at the small dark man next to her, leaning forward as he speaks to touch her hand, she hears the urgency in his deep voice as the story unfolds, she remembers the adventures of their childhood and youth, she sees the Krasov she has always known. How could he lie to her when they have shared so much? She must be patient and wait for him to explain why he has to tell her this story. Then she will make her judgement or, perhaps, by then no judgement will be necessary.

Suddenly the lights fail and the hall is plunged in darkness. 'How many times this week?' someone says in the row behind her, and groans of complaint follow at yet another power failure. 'What's happening to this country?'

Within seconds lighters and matches flare. Grotesque, moving shapes are projected on to the walls and ceiling: huge heads, distended bodies, insect-like arms, a world of deformity. Then, where before voices could be heard in conversation, a whispering begins, a rising sibilant sound, the soft Russian *s* like fingertips sliding across velvet.

Krasov, holding his lighter in his hand, his face illuminated by the blue flame, continues his story undeterred.

'Why I am telling you this? That's what you want to know, isn't it? Why should Little Krasov reappear in your life after so many years to tell you these dreadful things about people you don't know?' He leans closer to her; she can feel his breath on her cheek and see the flame of his lighter reflected in his eyes. 'I am your friend, Ruth. Your loving friend. I have brought you here to warn you.'

My life is too simple to need warnings, she wants to say. It revolves around my son, my mother and my work. How carefully I have avoided any other involvement.

'Warn me about what?' she asks.

'I attend committees, read reports, see documents. I keep my eyes and ears open, Ruth. Perhaps that is why I have lived so long. I beg you to be careful.'

His words terrify her even though he has told her nothing concrete.

'I am not involved in anything,' she says. Denial is an instinct, a protective second nature.

'Madness has corrupted our lives,' he says. 'A name on a piece of paper can put your life at risk. Your name came up in a secret report on the explosion in D4.'

She must test him now. See how much he knows.

'The official report exonerated the Institute of any blame.'

'You didn't believe what you read and nor did I. The explosion wasn't an accident. A decision was taken at a high level to damage the laboratory and to blow up the apartment block.'

'And kill all those old people?'

'That was all part of the plan, yes.'

'Why?'

'We want the British and the Americans to believe we cannot master the techniques needed to make nuclear weapons. We want them to think we are falling further behind in the race to make our atomic bomb. Now do you understand?'

She shakes her head. 'No,' she says, 'that can't be so.' But of course, Little Krasov's story fits.

'The explosion destroyed everything within a large area. The laboratory and the apartment block are sealed off and guarded. To deceive the West the impact must appear larger and more damaging than it was. Peter has told them we have suffered a catastrophe.'

'Why kill old people?' she asks, maintaining the pretence.

'To confuse our enemies. You could say they served their country in the way they died.'

As he speaks his face disappears into the darkness. He has moved his hand and the flame of the cigarette lighter flickers.

'What did the report say about me, Leo?' At last she finds the strength to ask what she so wants, but fears, to know.

'It said that you were fully aware of what was to happen and had made sure that no research of any value was lost in the explosion. It expresses the fear that you may tell Professor Stevens the truth about what happened.'

'Why should I do that?'

'Because you were once his lover.'

If this whole business with Stevens goes wrong, he is saying, you will not escape. Your name is there, on a list, ready to have a black cross marked against it.

'I knew nothing of all this, Leo. Nothing. Believe me.'

'I do believe you, Ruth.' His deep black eyes stare at her out of the gloom. 'You are involved with powerful and dangerous forces. You have your protectors now, but if they should slip, then you will be alone, facing a power you cannot even imagine. Take care, Ruth. That is what I came to say. Trust no one. You must beware for your own protection. If I knew more I would tell you.'

This is why they are huddled close together in a hospital waiting room talking in whispers, surrounded by little flickering lights. He does not know about Andropov (or she assumes he doesn't know) but he is warning her that to reduce her life to its essentials is not as effective as she believes it is.

At that moment, the power is restored and the lights come on again. There are ragged cheers around the room, a few handclaps. She looks at him and sees his saucer eyes are fixed on her; his hands, still outstretched, are trembling.

It is an act of conscience. The proof that Little Krasov will always be her friend. The thought of it strengthens her in her moment of distress. She wonders how could she have doubted him so. She knows now why he is telling her so much. Krasov is leaving Russia for ever. He has come to say goodbye and he wants her blessing before his departure.

'I am leaving Moscow,' he is saying. 'Going far away. It is unlikely we will ever see each other again.'

She sees the sadness illuminated in his expression, she feels the tight grip of his hand on her arm.

'Where are you going?' she whispers.

'I dare not say, even to you.'

He does not want to hide the truth from her. The motive for his refusal is that even in this act of farewell he wants to protect her. If she knows his secret then she becomes vulnerable. He would never place her own safety in jeopardy. Knowing that, she does not persist with her question. Now she is convinced he is telling the truth.

'Oh Leo, Leo.'

There are tears in her eyes. When he has gone she will be truly alone. He holds her in his arms as she cries, clinging to him with all the strength she can muster.

'Ruth, please.'

Goodbye, my friend, goodbye, she wants to say, but she finds she cannot say anything.

3

MONTY

The few short weeks in March and April were the glory days of Peter's career. He was our eyes and ears as the crisis developed in the Institute of Nuclear Research. His intelligence was unsurpassed in its clarity and the momentous nature of its content. There were times when Horseferry Road was closer to Moscow than to Westminster Abbey.

Our astonishment at Peter's report of Marchenko's challenge to the Institute's safety policy turned to incredulity when, not long after, a group of like-minded scientists formed themselves around her into a small but effective opposition to Soviet nuclear research. Their tactics had pushed an already seriously delayed programme to the edge of crisis when their laboratory exploded and the setback became a disaster. Within days they faced their directorate with an ultimatum. Without major concessions on the issue of the political control of nuclear weapons, they were no longer willing to work on the nuclear bomb project. It was an unprecedented challenge by a small group of scientists against the authority of the Soviet State. We waited anxiously for Peter to report that the Soviet system had taken its revenge in the usual manner. Days passed but nothing happened.

Who were these courageous men and women whose actions had the power to hold the Soviet Union to ransom? We trawled the Registry for information. Our findings were thin. We discovered next to nothing about Marchenko, Markarova, Gromsky, Tomasov, Lykowski and the others. We put the word out to our SOVINT network in the universities and fared not much better. We were given one or two articles from pre-war scientific journals that Tomasov and Gromsky had written, but these were juvenile pieces and no guide to their politics, their resolve or their present positions

224

in the Institute. Marchenko's group was the new generation of post-war Soviet scientists, many of whom had come to prominence in wartime research programmes, a period when international scientific conferences (now essential intelligence-gathering grounds in the post-war world) had ceased to exist. New reputations had been made away from the spotlight and we knew little or nothing about them.

'Why don't they arrest and imprison the ringleaders?' Adrian Gardner asked as Peter reported that Marchenko's group had survived another day. 'What's going on?'

Surely the political authorities couldn't be in two minds about how to cope with Marchenko and her friends? The Soviets were not known for their slowness in repressing what they described as deviant activity.

'If this goes on much longer,' Colin Maitland said as the challenge began the third week of its life and work on the bomb (Peter told us) was rapidly coming to a complete halt, 'the Soviets will hand the nuclear race to us on a plate. That's what mystifies me. I can't believe they've given up the fight for their own bomb. There has to be an explanation for what's going on.'

★

'Maybe we're expecting more of Marchenko and her people than they can deliver,' Arthur Gurney said during one of our daily conferences about the situation in Moscow. His unexpectedly reductionist mood was, I supposed, intended to counterbalance the wildly speculative theories that grew out of our lack of knowledge; an attempt to bring us back to earth.

'Why shouldn't their action be no more and no less than genuine revulsion at the task they've undertaken? Put yourself in their shoes. They're intelligent people, patriotic Russians, not necessarily members of the Party but still committed to working on a highly secret project. Progressively they become aware of the terrifying consequences of what they're being asked to do. They realize that one slip of the finger could destroy all civilization and turn the planet into dust and ashes. Can you blame them for taking a stand against that madness?

Arthur warmed to his theme. The event itself was clear and unambiguous, its meaning eluded us only because we'd got our focus wrong.

'The Institute's team asks for certain safeguards to be put in place to protect their own technicians because of the hazardous nature of the work they are being asked to undertake. The directorate denies there is any need for safeguards. So what does our gang do? They down tools. At root, it's as simple as that. The revolt is a spontaneous event, unplanned, an expression of basic human decency. It has no significance outside itself. It is what it is, no more, no less.'

'Oh God,' Adrian Gardner whispered to me, 'he'll be saying the Soviets are like the rest of us next.'

'After all,' Arthur Gurney concluded, 'the Russians are no different from the rest of us, are they?'

'As far as I'm concerned,' Gardner said spikily, 'your average Soviet is two whiskers short of a savage.'

While we admired Peter's bravery and the courage of Marchenko and her colleagues, the question we came back to, and on which all our speculation stumbled, was the baffling inaction of the Soviet authorities.

'God knows,' Colin Maitland said, 'they've got the means to do what they please and they're not short of experience in stamping out what they don't like.'

It appeared the resistance was being allowed to develop its own momentum. Had we read the Russians wrong?

Some of us (Gardner, Boys–Allen, myself) believed the authorities were in a state of paralysis because they did not know how to cope with the situation. Faced with a genuine crisis in a totally unexpected quarter (the Institute's team was an elite whose privileges were intended to undermine any remaining moral scruple) they had looked in the rule book for guidance and had found none. Others (Maitland, Gurney, Guy Benton) took a more alarmist view. Their argument was based on the impossibility of the Soviet system *not* reacting to crush this outburst of individualism.

'If the state does nothing,' Arthur Gurney said with unexpected passion, 'It sows the seeds of its own destruction. The Soviet Union is a repressive society. Their leaders know they can't let the pressure off anywhere. Their survival demands a reaction.'

Martineau, speaking to us on a crackling but secure line from the embassy in Moscow, confirmed that the authorities had succeeded in maintaining a news blackout. No one knew that anything was going on at the Institute.

'Surely people know about the explosion, don't they? After all, there's a gaping hole where there used to be a building.'

'People here ignore what they know,' Martineau said cryptically. 'They look the other way, pretend it hasn't happened. Nothing unusual in that. It's standard Soviet practice. Say nothing, see nothing, think nothing if you want to stay alive.'

What about unofficial sources? we asked, going for another angle. Was there no gossip about the Institute?

No, he said, none of his Russian contacts (and he was well connected, we knew) had heard so much as a whisper.

Was there any evidence that the scientists had talked outside their own circle? Not as far as he knew. 'They're an isolated group socially. They keep themselves to themselves. That's always been their way. That shouldn't surprise you. They're given a lot of privileges and consequently they're unpopular. I'm not sure there are that many people who would listen to them sympathetically, even if they did want to talk. More to the point, when they get home they're frightened. Fear is the best security measure there is. Ask anyone here.'

He shared our view that the silence was deliberate and well managed. Soviet practice, he confirmed, was to seal off any area of difficulty and deprive it of oxygen. He agreed that the failure of the authorities to take action was surprising, but the Institute was probably the last place anyone expected something like this to happen.

How did Martineau react to the idea that Marchenko and her group had powerful protection? Didn't their continued survival argue that someone high up in the political apparatus had sanctioned a policy of non-intervention, even if only to buy time to resolve the issue of what to do?

'I wouldn't be too sure about that. Logic isn't a reliable guide to the Soviet system. There are countless examples where it simply doesn't work. This could be one of them. I wouldn't bet on a conspiracy or on protection, I really wouldn't.'

'How do you explain this phenomenon, then?'

'Left hand ignorant of the right, that sort of thing. The Soviets are chronically inefficient. Nothing more sinister than that, probably. Who knows?'

★

'The atomic bomb is the cornerstone of an expansionist Soviet foreign policy.' Adrian Gardner was standing in front of the blackboard, chalk in hand. 'So what happens when their nuclear programme comes shuddering to a halt, an event which strikes a blow right at the heart of Soviet ambition? Do they suppress the dissent? Eliminate the ringleaders? Shift their foreign policy? Quite the reverse. They stand by and do nothing. That's where we trip up every time.'

It was late. The room in Horseferry Road was full of smoke, the table littered with uncleared teacups and unemptied ashtrays. We were tired and despondent. It had been a long and unproductive day and we wanted to go home. Outside, the wind blew gusts of heavy rain against the windows. The room felt cold.

'If this rebellion had taken place at a steel plant,' he continued, 'it would have been stamped out long ago and the ringleaders imprisoned, if not executed.'

Boys-Allen knocked out his pipe loudly against the ashtray.

'Can anyone find me a precedent for a lenient response by the Soviets to any kind of serious dissent?' Adrian asked. He looked around the table. 'The answer's no because there isn't one. So where does that leave us? This event has got someone's seal of approval stamped all over it. Whose it is and why I have no idea. But I'm damn sure Marchenko would be dead by now if she didn't have powerful protection. There's no other possible explanation for this revolt lasting so long.'

'A member of the Central Committee or the Politburo?' Guy Benton said. 'To be effective it would have to be someone at that level and that's hardly likely, is it?'

'Why not a senior member of the military?' Adrian argued. 'A disillusioned general or marshal would have the authority and the organization to provide protection.'

Our imaginations stirred. The continued survival of a small group of scientists as evidence of a secret power struggle inside the Soviet Union, of which so far we had only a peripheral glimpse? A revolt within the military? It had its attraction but not all of us were sold on it yet.

'Peter paints the creation of Marchenko's committee and all its subsequent acts as spontaneous events,' Boys-Allen said. 'Their rebellion is self-generating. A sudden awakening of conscience, stemming from Marchenko's question, which came right out of the blue but which struck a chord. That doesn't sound like acting under instruction to me. Far too chancy.'

'I'm pretty sure Marchenko and the others are probably unaware of any larger context,' Adrian Gardner said. 'But their ignorance doesn't invalidate my theory. Their anonymous protector manipulates them by playing on their doubts.'

'What doubts?' Guy Benton asked.

'Whether or not they should engage in the manufacture of atomic bombs.'

'How do you know they've had doubts?'

'You can't look at newsreel footage of Hiroshima and Nagasaki and not ask if this is the future we want,' Arthur Gurney said quietly.

'Spontaneous events like this simply don't happen in the Soviet system,' Adrian said. 'The social lid's too tightly bolted down. The continued life of this group is a measure of someone's ambition.'

'Where's the motive, Adrian?' Guy Benton asked. 'Suppose Marchenko has powerful protectors. Why go to such lengths? What do they hope to gain by all this?'

'Think of owning that power base,' Adrian Gardner said. 'The heart of the Soviet nuclear programme in your control. The lives of key scientists in your hands. The future of the most strategically important development in Soviet military research under your command. The key to Soviet post-war ambition. You could bargain your way to the top with that one, couldn't you?'

A platform for a *coup d'état*? Was that what we were seeing? The birth of an event of enormous historical importance? Could this be the first crack in the Soviet system, one that might ultimately bring it all down?

'Rivals to Stalin,' Colin Maitland said. A feeling of excitement, tinged with disbelief, began to gather. 'Men and women who might be prepared to oppose him if the issue were big enough. If this was a plot by, say, a group of senior military commanders fundamentally opposed to the use of nuclear weapons, who might lead it, what are their chances of success?'

We reached once more for our Registry records, searching through the gallery of senior Soviet figures for even a whisper of evidence that might suggest such a possible leader. We came up with the usual catalogue of cynics, careerists and fanatics. Marshal Vasilevsky. General Zakharov. Politicians like Molotov, Beria, Abakumov, Zhdanov, Zorin. We knew that Stalin feared challenges to his authority (why else would he change his government so often? The removal from office of a potential threat, whether real or imagined, was a conventional Soviet tactic). We searched our archives for anything, however trivial, to suggest that one of them might be prepared to stand against him.

Two days later Peter told us that the explosion in D4 had acted as the catalyst in bringing together a band of senior politicians and members of the military into an ad hoc opposition to Stalin. They were firmly set against the development and use of nuclear weapons. They believed it was essential that an accommodation with the West be reached, and soon. Behind the walls of the Kremlin a major power struggle was going on.

Suddenly it seemed as though we had the advantage. The question was, what were we going to do about it?

4

RUTH

Somewhere in the depths of the night a clock strikes two. Andropov checks his watch. He has his back to her. If she were to creep out of the room now, would he notice her absence? For the last hour he has said almost nothing: she has sat there waiting, exhausted, trying to find the courage to ask the one question that controls her waking mind.

Andropov the Silent.

'May I remove my jacket?'

His question startles her. He has never before asked her permission to do anything.

'As you please.'

She watches him unbutton the tunic and hang it carefully over the back of a chair, brushing something off the sleeve as he does so. He loosens his tie. He sits down opposite her again. There are damp patches on his shirt and small beads of sweat along his hairline. It is a warm night, but not that warm.

'Would you like me to open a window?' she asks.

He shakes his head. His hands are on the table in front of him, the fingers laced together, eyes cast down. He is very still. His behaviour is unusual and that disturbs her.

'What is your opinion of what we are doing?' he asks.

A harmless question. Except he has never asked a question like it in all the time she has been meeting him. Now he has asked her two questions in a matter of seconds.

'I do as I am instructed,' she says defensively. 'I have no views.'

'Put aside the rules for a few minutes.'

If she did not know better she would say he was asking her to drop the deference she adopts at their meetings, to break her private refusal to discuss anything with him and ignore the instruction she

231

gives herself, that she must do what he wants and give him nothing else.

'Why?'

'It is very late. We are alone here. Let us be our true selves for once.'

Andropov the Alone. Of course. Perhaps he has no wife, no girlfriend, no parents, no one to share anything with. Perhaps he wants her now to play the role of confidante. She feels her sympathy rising and fights it back as she remembers Miskin's terrifying accusation that Andropov was her lover.

'If I was myself I would be home in bed.'

He lights a cigarette, then offers her one. She declines. He blows out smoke and says: 'You are free to go. The driver has instructions to take you home.'

The familiar cold tone she prefers. A moment of potential embarrassment has passed.

'Thank you.'

She turns towards the door, gathering her coat. This is the first time he has let her go without accompanying her.

'If you have any questions,' he says, 'I am prepared to answer them.'

A last chance to know more. Should she take it? Should she leave? The only question that matters bursts into her mind but she is still too frightened to ask. She stands by the door, undecided.

'Why do you keep me here like this? You could have let me go an hour ago.'

She looks at him carefully. His face is very white and there are dark patches under his eyes. For the first time she sees how young he is – early thirties, possibly even younger – an unlined face, fine blond hair cut short, white hands, the raised knots of lavender veins, pale blue-grey eyes behind tinted glasses. Is this the man Miskin described as having blood on his hands, a murderer?

'I have been trying to find the courage to speak to you,' he says.

'When you bring me here, I am your prisoner. You can say what you like.' Why should she help him? None of this is her doing. All she wants is to be at home in bed.

'Dr Marchenko.'

His hands tighten their grip, the veins protrude still further with the strain.

'Yes?'

232

'Sit down.'

An entreaty, not a command. So the moment hasn't passed. She sits down. The act of returning to the table is her signal of assent to his request.

'Are there secret microphones here?' she asks.

He shakes his head. 'My people sweep each apartment half an hour before we use it. If there were anything they would have discovered it by now. Nobody is listening to us.'

Nobody is listening. How many times in her life has she heard that phrase? Somewhere, she knows, someone is listening to the beating of her heart.

'I do have a question.'

He is wary, tense, alerted by her tone of voice. She knows he wants to talk about himself but she cannot let him do that. She must know whether Miskin's warning is true or not.

'The explosion in D4 can't have been an accident,' she says firmly.

'Why not?' Eyes still cast down. He refuses to look at her.

'I know which of our experiments is dangerous. Nothing we have been doing recently could possibly have caused that sort of damage if it had gone wrong. It was a massive explosion. There is therefore only one conclusion to draw.'

'The official report concludes otherwise,' he says sullenly.

'Why don't we speak the truth for once?' she says. 'No one can hear us. There will be no evidence this conversation ever took place. Everything we say will be deniable. Yet in our hearts we will know we have once faced each other as we are.'

He blinks frantically. A shadow seems to pass over his face. She has called his bluff.

'I see the official version won't satisfy you.' He lights another cigarette. He looks up at her, taking off his glasses to clean them on his handkerchief. Anything to avoid looking at her directly.

'Answer my question,' she says. She has become the interrogator now.

He plays with the cigarette lighter in his hand. She watches him turning it over and over, polishing the steel case with his thumb. He is searching for the courage to tell her what he knows, or the lie to conceal what he has done.

'The explosion in D4 had nothing to do with the experiment that was being conducted. A bomb was placed in an air vent and timed to go off in the early hours of the morning.'

'Why?' she asks.

'The intention was to damage the place. Break a few windows. Blow in a door. Make it look as if something had gone wrong.'

'Instead of which the laboratory was razed to the ground and months of vital work were lost.'

'Mistakes were made,' he says coldly.

'And people died,' she says.

'Building a nuclear bomb is a dangerous business.'

I had nothing to do with it, he's saying. Andropov the Innocent?

'How could anyone justify the destruction of even a corner of the laboratory? What possible purpose could that serve?'

He puts his head in his hands. It is the first sign of weakness he has ever shown her. Is he at the limit of his strength, or is he simply acting remorseful to impress her?

'In order to conceal their own inability to deal with the problem at the Institute, the political authorities put out a rumour that your resistance was crumbling. I assured my superiors that there was no danger of your protest collapsing. For their own reasons, they chose to ignore me and put their faith in the political commissars. Some form of action, they argued, was needed to revive your flagging morale. They wanted concrete evidence of the volatile nature of the process of making nuclear bombs. They wanted proof of how dangerous it was, proof that was undeniable. They devised the idea that an explosion in the laboratory would strengthen your opposition to the development of the bomb.'

'Why?' She is incredulous.

'The damage would illustrate how precarious this process is.'

Still she is mystified. 'You created the Institute's opposition to the bomb,' she says. 'You wrote the script and you have won the argument. We are your creatures. We have done as you instructed. How could you let such a thing happen?'

'We are not alone in this. Others, interests are involved. We are both part of something larger.'

It is out of my control, that is what he is saying. Is he warning her too? Krasov was right. If Andropov is involved with others, then so is she. Now she knows how her name appeared on papers Krasov has read.

'Part of what?'

'Even if I knew I would not tell you that.'

'But you allow yourself to be manipulated by these people you won't name.'

'We are only manipulated if we are forced to do something we don't believe in. That's the question I asked you. For weeks now I have fed you a script which argues that to build nuclear weapons without secure international safeguards for their control is wrong. That is the basis of your opposition. Have we been successful because you did as you were told? Or do you actually believe in the arguments you professed were your own?'

She knows she is no longer the naive woman who stood up in the lecture theatre (how many weeks ago? It seems like another life) and quoted statistics she had learned off by heart. Andropov still gives her the script but the voice is no longer his alone. The words he has given her have opened her eyes and the arguments have convinced her. That and the terrible experience amid the destruction at D4, where that night statistics became truth and the truth overwhelmed her, all that has given her an authority and a certainty she has never possessed before.

'Is what we are doing right?' he asks again.

'Yes. Yes,' she says urgently.

She prefers Andropov without doubts, the man who only gives her certainties, who questions nothing. It is easier to deal with conviction.

'You believe in it?' he asks.

'Yes.'

'There is a price we cannot afford to pay.'

'What is that?'

She is drawn in now, there is no going back. She justifies her reply by telling herself that this might be the only opportunity she will ever have to discover the nature of the man in whose power she finds herself.

'The destruction of everything we have worked so hard for.' Still she does not understand. He sees her questioning gaze, her frown. She does not know what he is working for. 'The creation of a new society.'

'You believe in that?' she asks. She is surprised at his innocence.

'A new order, a new civilization, yes. My father sacrificed himself for it when I was young. He was a Hero of the Soviet Union. I would do the same. I have always believed that we must strive for a new way of life. That is why what we are doing is so important.'

Andropov the Patriot. More than that. Andropov the Guardian of the Flame of Righteousness.

'The problem is, we have lost our way on the path to the new world. The ultimate victory of the people will not be possible until we have found again the roots of belief that inspired our fathers to break with the past and begin this giant social experiment.'

He lights another cigarette. The world outside the apartment has vanished. There is no one alive except her and Andropov and these confessions.

'Didn't you have dreams when you were young?' he asks. 'Didn't you believe in the possibility of changing the world? Don't you still?'

Andropov the Idealist.

Has she ever believed in anything? The selfishness of youth blinded her to the privileges brought by her father's position in the Party. Didn't everyone live like that? Then she fell in love. In the arms of an English scientist in a hotel bedroom in Leiden, she discovered how hollow the values were on which her life was dependent. On her return to Moscow she divided her self into real and apparent, and since then the real has been buried along with all her memories, her true feelings, and she has lived the false life of the apparent. Long ago love destroyed any possibility of her belief in Marxist ideology. No faith has replaced it, only a powerful instinct to survive.

'I was neither believer nor unbeliever,' says Ruth the Apparent. 'I have never questioned anything. This is the life I know, the society to which I belong. As a scientist I am a part of the giant experiment. I never see myself in any other role.'

'I was a Young Pioneer.'

The first piece of autobiography. Andropov the Idealist, his emotional needs satisfied by the Party and its organizations, its philosophy, its pageants, its rituals, its supreme mastery of young hearts and minds that so cleverly conceal the vacuum within. She sees him, shirt off, body wet with effort, the young man in the posters of her youth, working on the land alongside its peasants, believing that every swing of the axe is another blow against the old world.

When had the deception been discovered, his beliefs shattered? When had he lost his faith?

'I never believed the stories about the privileged,' he says. 'I thought they were put about by our class enemies. I denied them fervently. We had created a society of equals where privilege no longer existed. That was why I joined the Party. We were all one.'

'Then you discovered the stories were true,' she says.

He stares at her. Suddenly his blue-grey eyes no longer reflect her questions back at her; she can see through them, into his heart. The yearning for belief has not left him.

'I wanted to be a scientist,' he says. 'That was my ambition. I came to Moscow to study. I fell in love with the daughter of a Party official.'

'I was the daughter of a Party official.' she says.

'She took me to her home and I saw the corruption at the highest level. Everything I had denied was true.'

Andropov the Betrayed. The loss of faith. That was it, the admission she has fought so hard for. But now she has it, what can she do with it?

'Was it so very terrible?' she asks, thinking of the life her father's position had provided, the larger apartment, the dacha in the country, the plentiful supplies of food, the official cars. Was that corruption or just reward?

'To discover your belief is hollow? To possess something of value on which your whole life is based, only to have it taken away from you, to end up with less than before? Can you imagine the emptiness?'

Andropov the man who lost his ideals. Why has she never had ideals herself? Is there something deficient in her life, in the narrowness of its focus − her work, her mother, her son?

'I had nothing else in my life. When my faith was stolen, a terrible wrong was committed.'

She sees then who he is, she sees with a piercing clarity the twisted purpose behind everything that Andropov is doing. He is Andropov the Puritan, his self-appointed task to be the watchdog of the Party's ideals, to use whatever power he has to rekindle the flame of purity that had once burned so fiercely within him. He is yearning for certainties; he is ready to be consumed by a fire greater than himself. How easily he can be used by those with darker purposes, who exploit the emptiness within him. He has become their creature without knowing what is happening to him. Andropov the Fanatic.

'My parents were peasants. They believed in the dream of true socialism. My mother died of starvation when our smallholding was absorbed into a collective farm. You see now what we are fighting against? How we must resist the corruption that surrounds us?'

237

'We?' she says weakly. Andropov smiles.

'We are in this together now,' he says. 'We know too much about each other not to be comrades in arms.'

His words make her shiver. He is warning her. Miskin was right. Her heart sinks.

Andropov the Enemy. No, much more dangerous than that.

Andropov the Ally.

5

DANNY

Tony Meadows and I were looking through the early edition of the *Evening Standard* when Beryl put her head round my door.

'Charlie's been on the blower, Danny,' she said. 'He's with Mr Watson-Jones' (In all the time I knew her, Beryl never called him Simon.) 'He wants you to drop everything and join them. Thomas will take you over. He's waiting outside now.'

Was it Charlie or Watson-Jones who didn't want me leaning my bike against the railing outside the house in South Street?

I sat in the back of the Rolls and tried to work out why I'd been summoned. Charlie never discussed his weekly meetings with Watson-Jones; we assumed the agenda was about political management, which was nothing to do with the day-to-day workings of Eccleston Street. One of the earliest lessons I learned was that Charlie liked to keep the compartments of his life separate. Manchester and London never met, nor did home and politics. Charlie had a wife, but we knew nothing about her and never met her. It would take a lot to make him break this particular habit.

If Watson-Jones wanted my presence, there had to be a reason, however unpredictable he might be (Beryl's phrase), or unmanageable (Charlie's phrase, overheard once). That's where I came unstuck. After years in the army I might know little about politics but I was beginning to know Watson-Jones. He did nothing without a reason though his motives were sometimes obscure. Perhaps he wanted me there to observe, to listen; perhaps he wanted to prepare me for something in the future. Throughout the short journey I could not get rid of the uneasy feeling that he wanted something I would be reluctant to give. By the time I reached South Street I was on my guard.

Meredith answered the door. 'They're waiting for you, Danny.'

She looked pale and thinner than when I had last seen her. But her smile was as broad as I remembered it, and her welcome as warm. I would have preferred to have spent the afternoon talking to her than sitting in the study listening to her husband.

'Go on in. I'll bring some tea before long.'

I knocked on the study door and went in.

'Danny. Good of you to come. Sit yourself down. Charlie here and I were having a talk. We thought you could help us.'

I looked at Charlie. He didn't seem too pleased but his expression gave little away. I was sure it had not been his idea to summon me to South Street and he'd rather I wasn't there.

'We're reviewing progress, Danny. Prudent after nearly three months of operation, don't you think? How we're doing, where we're going, that sort of thing. Yes?'

I nodded my approval as I was expected to do. It allowed Watson-Jones time for one of his pauses.

'We've been looking at the newsletter.' Copies were spread all over the dining-room table. 'I was saying to Charlie here, jolly good, off to a strong start, well done to you and the boys. Well done.'

I knew the Watson-Jones style by now. Start with praise, soften up the resistance, get your opponent's eye off the ball (there were only friends or enemies in Simon's world and sometimes they changed sides with breathtaking speed), then go in with the big stick when they're least expecting it. I tensed myself for the blow. When it came it wasn't from any direction I'd expected.

'One observation though.' He had stationed himself at the table, arms outstretched, head thrust forward, surveying the newsletters as if he was searching for a typographical error. 'I'm not seeing enough anti-Soviet material. Nowhere near enough. We're letting the Reds off the hook. That's bad, Charlie. This isn't the time to go soft on the Soviets.'

That was it. He wanted me to hear his criticism of Charlie. He was sure Charlie would filter his objections when he reported the meeting to me. I was there to witness the full strength of his displeasure.

'That's a bit hard, Simon,' Charlie said. I was surprised at the lack of edge to his response.

'They're the enemy, Charlie. Bad, evil people.' He had come back into the centre of the room now and was standing in front of Charlie and myself. 'We've got to kick them where it hurts. That's what we're after, isn't it? Getting back at the bastards. You agree with that, don't you, Danny?'

This was the first crack in the relationship between Charlie Faulkner and Watson-Jones since I'd started working with them. Watson-Jones wasn't interested in my opinion. What he wanted was me as his man in the office, someone to keep Charlie up to the mark. I was being asked quite openly to change sides. I was surprised Watson-Jones imagined I would.

'Don't get me wrong. Lots of good stuff here,' he said, not waiting for me to reply. 'The economy. Beveridge. Education.' He gestured towards the table. 'Solid issues, all of them. But think back to the early days, Charlie. Remember what excited us then? We wanted to tell the truth about the Soviets. That's what I'm after, Charlie. Red lights for danger. I'm looking for the signs but I'm not seeing any.'

In a way I wasn't surprised at his criticism. Charlie had sold the venture to me because he'd agreed with my warnings about the Russians. Apart from Monty, Watson-Jones and Charlie Faulkner were the only people to take seriously the view I'd come to adopt in Berlin. Initially, when I started at Eccleston Street, I had been disappointed that the Soviet Union had featured so little in what we were doing. I hadn't thought it right then, certainly not while I was learning the ropes, to raise my concerns. Now it seemed Simon had got there before me. I had a sneaking suspicion he was right. The newsletter *was* soft on the Soviets. We could have hit much harder. But I wasn't here to show my disloyalty to Charlie. This wasn't going to be an easy meeting.

'While we were off fighting the Nazis,' Watson-Jones said, getting into his stride, his voice rising with feeling, 'The communists were slipping their people in here, not just the trades unions, left-wing groups, that's old hat, but the upper echelons, the universities, the civil service, our intelligence services, the army, the police force.'

'That's propaganda, Simon. You've got no reliable evidence to support that view.'

'Soviet sympathizers are littered throughout this damned socialist country. That's the point. The danger's here, now, all around us, everywhere. We're no longer safe in our own beds. The bastards are taking over.'

It was an extraordinary assertion, one I assumed Charlie would reject. To my surprise he didn't. His reply was defensive.

'We can't invent news for the sake of it,' Charlie said stiffly.

'I know it's hard, Charlie, and you've done a great job, you and the boys.' His words were silky, disingenuous. He was leading Charlie somewhere, I couldn't tell where but I sensed it was dangerous. 'The dangers we saw haven't gone away, they've got worse, much worse. We've got to wake up the world, Charlie. That's our mission. Alert them to the true nature of the Soviet beast. The enemy banging his rifle butt on the door is threatening enough. But some of them have slipped through the crack, and that's worse. If we close our eyes to what's happening, we're guilty of helping the enemy's cause.'

If there was to be an explosion, this was the moment. Watson-Jones's challenge was aimed at the heart of Charlie's decency. He was asking him to be someone he wasn't. I couldn't understand Simon's purpose. Charlie wasn't a man to be pushed around in this way, which is why Simon had wanted him to run Eccleston Street in the first place. How could Simon imagine Charlie would cave in and agree to something he already knew he'd never do?

'What do you suggest?' The voice was ice-cold, the body perfectly still, the eyes looked up from the wheelchair directly at Simon. The challenge was returned.

'Dig deeper, Charlie. Look harder.'

'Dig where?'

I could see Charlie was going to express his displeasure at being rapped over the knuckles in my presence by making Watson-Jones spell out every inch of the way he wanted us to go. But he wasn't about to lose his temper. I admired his self-restraint and wondered if it was the right tactic.

'The country is spilling over with spies, subversives, sympathizers, men and women who, if Stalin knocked at the door, would ask him in for a cup of tea, and nobody's doing anything about it. We need names, dates, facts, unarguable evidence.'

'We're publishing a political newsletter, Simon, not an investigative broadsheet.'

'I want to see the flag flown, Charlie. I want the world to know our newsletter is patriotic, what we write is for the good of the country. I want every sentence to declare unequivocally where we stand on the Soviet issue.'

('The man's mad,' Charlie said to me on the way back to Eccleston Street. 'Obsessed. He's lost all sense of proportion.' Somehow he didn't sound very confident about it.)

'Don't nudge the reader in the ribs, Charlie. Shove a pointed instrument up him till he bleeds. Look at this, our headlines should shout. Look at that. Look at the truth.' He paused a moment to draw breath, then went on. 'We've got to shock him out of his complacency. Make sure he sees the Soviets are here, standing in the bus queue beside us, not somewhere out of sight across the sea. We've got to bring our people to their senses. Get the urgency of our message across.'

('Get him to hate the Reds and vote Tory,' Charlie said later. 'Simon's recipe for peace of mind.')

'You and the boys can do it, Charlie. I know you can.'

Smiles, bangs on the arm, warm encouragement and we were ushered out into the afternoon and the waiting Thomas. Not even time for tea and another word with Meredith.

'If you're wondering what that was,' Charlie said as the Rolls turned into South Audley Street, 'it was a bollocking by any other name.'

'What can you do about it?' I asked.

'Simon's the paymaster, which limits our freedom to act independently. But he's wrong, the Soviets aren't lurking under every stone as he wants us to believe. They aren't waiting to take over the country as Simon implies. That's dangerous nonsense. If we don't keep some kind of balance, our readers will ignore what we say, and that will be worse still.'

Charlie was thoughtful as we rounded Hyde Park Corner on our way back to Victoria.

'We'll do something in the next issue. Tony will write a piece about new times, new enemies. The need to be watchful. Warning signs of danger. How to police the peace. That'll keep Simon happy and out of our hair for a while. In the meantime something else will come up to take his interest.'

I hoped he was right. I couldn't get rid of the feeling that there was more to Simon's position than Charlie recognized, and we that we hadn't heard the last of it by any means.

★

AN EXEMPLARY DEATH

When we can recall the deaths of so many millions of people all too recently, what possible significance can one more death have? Philip Ridout was not a military or political leader. He was unknown outside his profession. He left no body of achievement by which he can be judged. He was a young man, at the beginning of a career in physics. All he had was promise. What his early death denies us is the gift of that promise. How many of us, in these post-wars years, can think back with sadness on promise lost for ever on the battlefield?

Ridout spent his short life at Cambridge working to acquire knowledge that would benefit mankind. He approached the inherent dangers of nuclear physics with all the energy and enthusiasm of youth. He shared with all great scientists that rare intuition that directs one instinctively towards the right solutions to the problems one encounters. It was a privilege to work with such an original mind.

During the years we worked together at Cambridge, Ridout had become convinced that nuclear energy was too dangerous to be entrusted to politicians. Only the scientist can understand the true nature of this elemental force we have released into the world, he argued. In the last weeks of his life he talked continually of the choice society has to make between destroying civilization or renouncing the weapons of war.

Let us commemorate this young man's death by making a permanent monument to his courage and his vision by ensuring that the ultimate power of nuclear weapons is not abused by those who govern us. Then Philip Ridout's life will not have been in vain.

★

I read my father's piece on Philip Ridout's death with growing anger. How could he so misrepresent Ridout's view on the need to build up our arsenal of nuclear weapons against the ever-present threats of the enemy? He must have known that Ridout believed in what he was doing, that in the last months of his life he used all his remaining energies to try to complete the task he had undertaken. He had a clear vision, as men facing the inevitability of their own death often do, which was that the Soviets were a dangerous enemy and that force should be met with force. Ridout was a scientist, not a humanitarian.

Now my father was using his death to promote a different and contradictory point of view. He was betraying Ridout's political position. He must have known better than anyone that Ridout saw the Russians as the enemy who had to be defeated and that the only weapon they understood was force.

My father had knowingly distorted the truth. I wondered what could have brought him to that.

★

'That wasn't the real Philip talking,' my father said. 'What I wrote was consistent with the views he held all the time we worked together, when he was fit. My piece was true to the man as I knew him. His illness changed him.'

We were having a drink at his club. My father had telephoned earlier in the day to say that he was staying overnight in London, and why didn't we have dinner? It was an unexpected overture and I had agreed. We had got on to the subject of Ridout almost at once. I said how sorry I was about his death, my father repeated how serious a loss he was to British science and then I had thoughtlessly raised the issue of Ridout's political views.

'When I saw him in Addenbrooke's he was strongly in favour of building up our nuclear armoury against the Soviets. He saw them as a real threat.'

That had elicited the unanswerable assertion from my father that he knew Ridout better than I did and that any changes in his views were the aberrations of a dying man. Once I might have pursued the argument; now I preferred to drop the matter. There was no point in quarrelling this early in the evening.

'Now you're back in London, do you see much of Monty?' he asked me later over dinner.

'Not as much as I'd expected,' I said. 'He's always busy.'

'You don't know what he's doing in Cambridge, then?'

'I had no idea he was in Cambridge.'

'I've seen him a few times over recent weeks. Not to speak to. I thought you might know what he's up to.'

'He never talks about his job.'

I realized my mistake the moment I opened my mouth. My father had wanted my opinion on something that was clearly troubling him (why else would he have brought the subject up?), and, without thinking, out of perverse habit, I had rejected him. His question had held the promise of an intimacy that was now as remote as ever. I had been both hasty and foolish. The moment had come and gone and I was unable to do anything about it.

245

The conversation after that was desultory and pointless. We both knew an opportunity had been lost and neither knew how to make a new approach. We kept away from any topic of substance.

As I walked back to Strutton Ground, I was unable to clear my mind of my father's question about Monty. Why was he interested in him? He never had been before.

Monty was in Cambridge, his remark told me, for days at a time, possibly longer. No wonder I hadn't seen much of him since my return to London. What was he doing there? Was he watching my father? Was he working on the basis that what Krasov had told me was true? I felt a sudden pang of guilt. I had assumed that Monty had accepted my verdict on that long night's meeting and I had interpreted his reluctance to talk about it and his absence from my life as confirmation. Now I was faced with the awful thought that perhaps my assumptions were wholly wrong and the opposite was true. What if Monty had believed every word Krasov said? What if my father was now under suspicion of dealing with the Russians? If that was so, I knew only too well who was responsible for placing him in this position.

6

RUTH

She watches the procession pass by. The coffin is carried by four elderly men in black overcoats, followed by a silently weeping woman holding a bunch of white flowers and supported by two young men, presumably her sons. No mourners. No friends. No players from any part of the life just ended. A last journey of true loneliness.

How different from the hollow stage management of her father's funeral, when he was escorted to his grave by an honour guard of senior Party officials. Her brother walked behind the coffin carrying a huge, garlanded photograph of a man she hardly recognized, taken many years before when his hair still fell over his forehead. Ranks of politicians and officials in black hats and coats followed, whispering to each other, the hypocrisy of their show of public grief striking her with as much force as the driving wind on that bitterly cold December morning. Her father had fought with so many of them during his life. Now they were walking to his grave to satisfy themselves that he was well and truly dead.

The small procession has stopped near a group of ancient, wind-torn gravestones. They are preparing for the burial. She shudders. How long before her mother is carried in a box and lowered into the ground, while flowers are dropped on to the wooden surface of the coffin and the cold earth is shovelled over her too? Will she be mourned by only her daughter and her grandson?

As she checks the directions given her by the keeper of the cemetery (she knows that he will already have reported her presence to someone in authority) she notices the silhouette of a man by the iron gates. He is too far away to be identifiable but his presence disturbs her. What is he doing in this unkempt garden of the dead? Is he watching her? Following her? She experiences an all too familiar spiral of fear.

The grave is newly dug; there is no tombstone and probably never

247

will be, nor any name board to identify whose body lies there. A single bunch of dried flowers has been placed at the head of the grave, or what she imagines is the head, and attached to it a card with a scrawled signature. She bends to read it.

My beloved Miklos. Farewell.

Miklos Khudiakov. Tall, thin, balding, with delicate white hands and a studious expression. He would listen with infinite patience to her requests. When he spoke it was always thoughtfully and practically. Now he was dead, killed by a bomb, and he would never be able to help her again.

She feels rage burning within her and she closes her eyes. Can the dead renew the living? Can she draw the strength she needs from the fact that his damaged body lies under the earth? She is in pain, suffering outrage at the crime that has been committed, frustrated that there can be no justice, no righting of wrongs, no moment of judgement for the guilty.

Tears spring to her eyes and she weeps openly. No one can see. No one can hear. She lets herself go, sobbing as if Miklos Khudiakov were her husband or her son. She cries for him, his wife and children, for herself, her mother and her son, for her life without Stevens, for Miskin.

'Are you all right?'

She turns round, terrified at the sound of a voice.

'Pavel! You gave me a fright.'

'I didn't mean to startle you. I'm sorry.'

She blows her nose and wipes her eyes. She does not want him to see her like this.

'He's left a widow and three small children,' Lykowski says, pushing at the earth with the toe of his shoe. 'I wonder what will happen to them?'

She cannot think of the woman whose handwriting is on the card at her feet. It is too much to bear.

'What are you doing here?' she asks.

Is it her imagination or does he hesitate before he speaks?

'I have been wanting to talk to you for days. I could never find you alone. That is why I followed you.'

She is not convinced by his explanation. This is not the Pavel she knows, a young man full of emotional fervour, secure in the simplicity of his beliefs. He is hesitant, nervous, without any sign of the assurance she has previously found to be unwavering.

'You can say what you like,' she says. 'Only the dead can hear. I am sure they have better things to do than listen to us.'

He smiles, but his eyes don't meet hers. When he offers her a cigarette his hand shakes. She refuses. He takes one for himself and lights it, cupping both hands around the lighter. She watches the smoke drift away on the clear morning air.

'Poor Miklos,' he says. 'How we will miss him.'

Is he nervous because of what he wants to tell her? Or is he there to betray her? Will the secret police step out from behind the battered gravestones or from the shadows of the fir trees, and drag her to the airless basement in the Lubyanka where she will be forced to bargain for her life?

'What happens now?' he asks.

That is the question she has been asking herself ever since she heard from Andropov and Little Krasov that the explosion in D4 was not an accident. It is the reason she is standing now beside the grave of a young man who died in that explosion. The knowledge she seeks is not to be found in the mound of earth before her, but in the private territory of her mind. She must stand before Miklos's grave and remind herself that he is dead, and find the strength to fight. How easy it is to accept the inevitability of what happens, to shrug your shoulders in defiance of what you know and get on with your own life. How hard to find the courage to oppose what you know to be wrong.

'What can we do?'

This time their eyes meet. She reads the simple appeal in his expression. He is more frightened than she is. She is angry with herself for misjudging him. She takes his hand in hers.

'We will have to face the truth sooner or later,' she says.

'Nothing went wrong that night.' She feels his hand tighten in hers. They are allies in their secret knowledge. 'The explosion was not an accident. Miklos did not make a mistake. He was murdered,' he says. 'The pensioners too. They were all murdered.'

'How can you be sure?' she asks. She is not challenging him. She is looking for reassurance. He will know from her expression and the pressure of her hand that she has reached the same conclusion. What he says next shocks her when she thinks of the risks he must have taken.

'I've checked the D4 worksheets for the past three months. Nothing they were working on could have caused an explosion on that scale, it's not scientifically possible. They weren't so behind schedule that they needed to work at night to catch up. Yet Miklos and his colleagues died at three in the morning.'

'Do you know why they were working that night?'

'They were instructed to do so.' He hands her the familiar carbon copy of the worksheet they have to fill before the laboratory will act on their behalf. 'See who signed it?'

Miskin. Miskin signed it. She cannot believe this. Miskin could not have told Khudiakov to work that night.

'Miskin never signed worksheets. We both know that.'

'It's his signature, isn't it?'

'Or a forgery.'

'All Khudiakov would have looked for is a signature on the sheet. No one ever reads who signs these papers.'

She holds the forgery as if it might contaminate her.

'There's something else.' He digs in the pocket of his overcoat and hands her a piece of paper. 'I've calculated how strong the explosion would have to have been to carry all the way from from D4 to the block of flats. It must have been enormous. I'm sure there was a separate explosion in the flats, soon after the damage had been done in D4. It's the only possible explanation.'

She takes the paper from him and checks the calculations. He is right, of course, as she knew he would be. It fits. It all fits. What can she say?

In the distance, the burial is over. The pall-bearers are shaking hands with the widow and moving away. How many at her father's funeral knew the secret of her mother's dignity, so praised in the *Pravda* report? She didn't cry that day because after the years of her father's persistent infidelities there was nothing left to cry for. The marriage had been held together by her mother's respect for convention and her courage. The man so lauded in death had in more than twenty years of marriage made her mother's life almost intolerable.

'You're right.' She says it so quietly she wonders if he has heard.

'I began to despair of anyone listening to me.'

'I believe everything you say is true.'

'Why did it happen?' he asks. He can't keep still. He fiddles with the pockets of his overcoat, his scarf, his fur hat, incessant nervous movements. 'That's what I cannot understand. Why kill a man like Khudiakov on whom we all depended? Why kill those old people?

They never did anyone any harm. What's going on, Ruth? Sometimes I think I'm going mad.'

'If I knew I'd tell you.' That's not true. If she tells him what she knows she will reveal her sources and then she will put her own life in jeopardy. 'Explanations are beyond me.'

He turns his back to her, pretending to survey the cemetery. He is making sure they are not being watched.

'At least we know what happened.'

'What's the point of knowing the truth if we are powerless to act on it?' The bitterness in her voice surprises him.

'Are you saying we should do nothing?' He sounds incredulous.

'Even if we knew the names of those who are behind all this, how can we avenge Miklos Khudiakov's death? If we move a finger, who will suffer? His wife and children. Can you live with the thought of what might happen to them? We're powerless, Pavel. Surely you see that?'

'I won't accept that.' He is angry with her, his face mottled with red spots which mingle with his ginger freckles. 'A great wrong has been committed, Ruth. We can't leave it there.'

'We have to, Pavel. We have no power. There's nothing we can do.'

'Why did you come here today to visit Miklos's grave?'

She says nothing, too afraid and distressed to speak.

'I found you weeping by his grave, Ruth. You were weeping for the wrong of it all. That was why you came. To find the strength to continue in the face of it all.'

'No.' He has taken hold of her arms. She pushes him away. 'I should never have come here. It was a mistake.' Tears burst from her suddenly. She is desperate, confused, 'I don't know what I am doing here. Go away, Pavel. Leave me, leave me alone.'

She turns from him and runs away,

7

MONTY

Horseferry Road was gripped by the idea of a *coup d'état* in Moscow.
The work of the Department was inspired by the hope that one day
(and the sooner the better) the Soviet empire would collapse. The
possibility of a popular revolt, the people rising up in arms against
their oppressors, was remote. We had come to accept that the Soviet
citizen had been stunned into acceptance of the status quo, his
responses to the aberrations of Soviet policy numbed by years of
terror and crisis.

'They've been scared out of their wits and they won't move a
muscle to help anyone,' we had learned at one of our periodic
briefings by our experts in Oxford. 'Don't hold your breath for
a popular uprising, there won't be one. Look instead for the
power bases. If there is to be a new revolution, that is where it will
start.'

Opposition, we were told, would come from within the Soviet
leadership, from those who believed they were losing their power
base or that the government's policies were no longer sustainable.
We should keep our eyes open for signs of ranks being broken, of
political ambition being brutally curtailed, of serious disagreements
within the Politburo. We watched, waited, and then came Marchenko. Not what we had expected but when we came to think about
it, we weren't sure what we had expected.

The analysts set to work on the revolt in the Institute of Nuclear
Research. Had the prevailing social and economic conditions in the
Soviet Union reached the point where we were witnessing the
beginning of social breakdown? we wanted to know. Would Stalin's
removal by his own people usher in a truly new world? Would we
soon be able to settle down to the real task of creating a post-war
society that could offer a total break with the past, a rejection of

war and the new deadly weapons of war? These were tempting hypotheses to consider.

We pinned the names of our targets to a board on the wall in Arthur Gurney's office: Voroshilov, Molotov, Beria, Malenkov and others. We scanned photographs from the news agencies of recent state events, ticking off the names of the sombre figures on the podiums. We compared lists of names in *Pravda* reports of official meetings. We read transcripts of broadcasts from Radio Moscow. We reviewed Martineau's briefings for the last six months.

'You'll be surprised how much good information lies in front of our eyes only we never see it,' Colin Maitland said to encourage us after a particularly bleak day. His remarks did little to relieve our frustration. What we were looking for, he reminded us, were convergences, coincidences, missing names, names unexpectedly linked by presence or absence, a senior commander with a member of the Politburo, the head of the KGB with a member of the Central Committee or the Supreme Soviet. But if the links were there, they evaded us.

One by one the names on the board were eliminated. After five days we were left with three names, two members of the Politburo and a general. Martineau helped us clear the politicians; one was ill (over eighty and in hospital suffering from cancer of the liver) while the other, a deputy from Tashkent, was abroad (a member of a Foreign Affairs Committee mission to Tito in Yugoslavia). That left one last name, General Alexei Kosintzev, a military commander unknown to all of us. It was not the conclusion to the exercise we had expected, nor did it fill us with jubilation.

Kosintzev was Ukrainian, a young commander (mid-forties) of a tank regiment, a professional soldier all his life. He had fought against the Romanians at Stalingrad as part of General Eremenko's army, before being seriously wounded with a crushed pelvis when the car in which he was travelling overturned during a German mortar attack. He had recovered to take his part in the last campaign of the war and he had been one of the first to arrive in Berlin. After the war he had served on the Allied Commission for a time and was known to the British and American military as an ambitious and intelligent officer, if abrasive in manner. A disciplinarian, he was not liked but respected.

He had made his reputation during the war and was regarded as one of the brightest of the coming generation of military commanders. Cautious, calculating, a good administrator, a soldier whose bravery drew great respect from his men – these were the recurring epithets used to describe him. That was where the problem lay. Similar descriptions applied to others like him. Kosintzev was strictly second-division, a face too young to be seen at the front of the podium, one of a number of future front runners. The problem was, at this moment in time he did not carry any power or authority (so the analysis ran), so how could he pose any threat to the political hierarchy?

'Where's the leverage with a tank regiment that's not even stationed anywhere near Moscow?' Corless asked, impatient that our activities had yielded little of any value. 'Kosintzev's a professional soldier who's managed his career well. He may get to the top but not for years yet. We've no evidence of any political activity, no confrontation with Party officials, no deviation from Marxist ideology, and nor would we expect any. He's a Party member by default because those are the rules he must obey. Men like that don't lead revolts against authority because authority is the goal they've set their heart on achieving.'

We went back to our SOVINT advisers, calling for anything we could get. They returned the expected verdict that Kosintzev was a determined and loyal officer who had neither the military prestige nor the political power base to be the focus of any kind of opposition. By now I agreed with Boys-Allen that our search had sent us haring off in the wrong direction and if we spent much more on this investigation, we'd be up to our necks in something evil-smelling and sticky. Better to call it a day now – and try another tack. The amateur psychiatrists among us – Adrian Gardner and Guy Benton – would have none of it. They insisted on a further investigation, looking for psychological reasons for a Kosintzev revolt. Couldn't he harbour grudges against that authority, they argued, which his 'correct behaviour' might conceal? Perhaps he had suffered experiences that had undermined his moral position. His injury at Stalingrad? A failure to win promotion? A bitterness at favours granted to others?

'My guess is he thanked his lucky stars he got a crushed pelvis and not a bullet in the head and spent most of that campaign in hospital,' Boys-Allen said to general agreement. 'We wouldn't be talking about him today if he hadn't.'

Adrian Gardner was undeterred: how about psychological damage caused by the appalling casualties his regiment had suffered in the battle for Stalingrad?

'Show me a Russian commander who loses sleep over the cost of victory,' Arthur Gurney said dismissively. From the limited analysis we had conducted, he said, the subject was clean and he couldn't see that situation being reversed.

We were depressed at Kosintzev's unlikely casting in the role of opponent to the regime. Was this a case of mistaken identity? Had we got the wrong man? Should we start all over again, from a different angle this time – and if so, which angle? Yet despite our doubts, we couldn't quite dismiss Kosintzev: he was still a member of the military elite – an insider – and his regiment provided some kind of power base.

'On the surface he doesn't look like our man,' Colin said. 'But maybe he has a dark secret. If so, we must uncover it.'

Looking for what Adrian Gardner cynically described as 'a second-rate needle in a collectivized Soviet haystack', we went in search of Kosintzev's secret. Almost on cue, Martineau reported that Kosintzev had done a disappearing act. His regiment was on manoeuvres on the Polish border but he wasn't with them. He didn't attend the bimonthly regional commanders' meeting in Moscow. Our hopes rose. Was he on secondment at a military academy? we asked cautiously. No sign of him there, apparently. Martineau located his apartment in Moscow. Empty. No one had been seen entering or leaving for ten days or more. Kosintzev was nowhere to be seen. Perhaps he was our man after all.

'Generals don't disappear,' Corless said, dismissing as fanciful the idea that our inability to find Kosintsev implied anything other than our own inefficiency. 'They retire or they die. Kosintzev is too young to retire and we've no evidence he's dead. On that basis alone, he can be found. Find him.'

Hardly had he spoken than Kosintzev was back ('lucky Corless') tanned and fit, at a meeting of the Military Policy Review Committee. His wife and two sons reappeared in his Moscow apartment. They too were tanned. Kosintzev's absence could be easily explained, Martineau told us shamefacedly. He had been on holiday at the Black Sea. Our hopes dissolved. He didn't stay long at the military conference. He flew back to rejoin his regiment on the Polish border. We couldn't build a conspiracy on that.

★

Two weeks went by. Kosintzev was fading ingloriously into one of the many 'might-have-been' cases in the filing cabinets of the Registry when an extraordinary and apparently unconnected event took place. A young soldier, on leave from his regiment, was queuing with hundreds of others outside Lenin's tomb in Red Square when he suddenly stepped out of the line, turned to face the crowd, pulled a revolver from his overcoat pocket and shouted something incoherent. Then he put the gun to his head and blew his brains out.

Although it was a very public suicide, it was not reported in the Soviet newspapers but it was seen on the front pages of the Western press, its cause the source of much speculation but no definite conclusions. (A tourist had taken a photograph of the crumpled body before the guards got to it and had then, despite aggressive tactics by the secret police, successfully smuggled it out of the Soviet Union.) Peter had nothing to say about it, but Martineau came up with an unexpected link that brought new life to our investigations.

Suicide soldier in K's regiment, his encoded wire read. If there was any connection between the suicide and our discovery of Kosintzev, we had no idea what it was but the wire was enough to make us reach for the file once more. Martineau did a good job for us, sending back secret photographs of the funeral: the grieving mother at the graveside, the young soldier's brothers, other relatives (we presumed) and friends and there, in spite of the grainy quality of the photograph, beside the dead man's mother we saw, Kosintzev in uniform, who, Martineau told us, had flown to Moscow for the funeral.

After the funeral, Kosintzev did not return at once to his regiment as we had expected. He stayed in Moscow. In the next forty-eight hours he made two visits to the Kremlin. On each occasion he was unaccompanied, though there was nothing sinister in that. Each visit lasted an hour.

We chewed our pencils and puzzled it over. A young soldier kills himself while on leave; his general flies back to attend his funeral. Why? A gesture, the good general associating himself with his men? If it had been an accident, a death in the course of duty, we could understand Kosintzev's presence. But this was suicide. Kosintzev's behaviour was unusual.

'Perhaps something has happened, some event, which caused this poor young man to kill himself. You could explain Kosintzev's

256

presence as a gesture of solidarity, a protest – dignified, correct, but a protest none the less.'

It was a possible, if unlikely, reading, awakening echoes of Maitland's 'dark secrets'. We put forward possible reasons for the suicide. Homosexuality. Depression. Incidents of bullying (upgraded to racial bullying – the young man was a Muslim from Azerbaijan, we had learned). We were about to give up when Martineau sent us a cutting from the pages of *Isvestia*.

> Memorial to those who died on 18 February.
> To all those names we add one more in sorrow.
> How long before the list lengthens?
> Patriots of the 24th Tank Regiment.

'February the eighteenth was the day on which the Soviet research laboratory went up in flames,' Colin Maitland reminded us, 'according to Peter.'

What possible connection could the 24th Tank Regiment have with an accident in a Soviet nuclear laboratory in a suburb of Moscow? If there were connections (and there were cynics among us), this was really going over the top, too bizarre to carry credibility. We were baffled. Over the next four days, with Martineau's help, some facts emerged.

The 24th Tank Regiment, under Kosintzev's command, had been stationed in the Russian Sector of Berlin. That was not difficult to establish. Their tour of duty came to an end on 14 February. On that day they began the laborious process of packing up to return to their barracks outside Moscow. We got confirmation of this from the British High Command in Berlin.

Kosintzev had made his last official appearance at the Allied Commission on 12 February. That was a matter of record. He had then flown back to Moscow, in advance of his men, and two days later had gone on leave – he had mentioned to Martineau at a party on 15 February that he was going to the Black Sea. His second in command, Gerenko, who had accompanied him to Moscow, stayed behind with an advance party preparing the barracks.

Had there been any accounts or rumours of an accident around that time involving the military, we asked Martineau, as we tried to identify 'those who died on 18 February'? No, came the reply. None. *Apart from D4 explosion, night of February 18 quiet.*

Unexpectedly, Boys-Allen put forward a theory that gained sup-

257

port throughout the day. 'Solidarity,' he said, suddenly. 'That's the connection. Maybe the parents of some of the soldiers in the Twenty-fourth Tank Regiment died in the fire at the apartment block,' he argued.

'How do you explain the phrase "To all those names we add one more in sorrow"?' Guy Benton asked.

'We know many died in the accident. Perhaps a few survived, badly burned. Maybe the father or mother of one of them has died within the last week of injuries received that night.'

We put the question to Martineau. 'Any reports of old age pensioners dying in the last ten days of burns received on the eighteenth of February?'

'That's a tricky one,' Colin said as he watched the cipher clerk encode the message for the teleprinter. Two days of silence followed. Then: *No survivors of fire on 18 February. Official report appears true.*

Whoever the Patriots of the 24th Tank Regiment might be, it appeared their secret was secure.

8

DANNY

The telephone jarred me from the depths of sleep. My watch said it was ten to seven.

'I need you in the office as soon as you can make it – half an hour at the latest,' Charlie said, sounding hoarse with exhaustion. 'Something's come up.'

Charlie and Simon were both waiting for me when I arrived in Eccleston Street, a copy of a political weekly open in front of them.

'Read this first,' Charlie said. 'Then we'll talk.' He handed me the paper. Someone, I presumed it was Simon, had underscored some of the comments in the article on Watson-Jones by a Tory backbench MP I'd never heard of called Nathaniel Naismith.

Watson-Jones was a dangerous warmonger, I read. There was a consistently bellicose line throughout his speeches and in the columns of *Front Line*, the political newsletter he published. The Soviet Union was portrayed as more villainous than Nazi Germany, a threat to the free world that could be resisted only by rearmament on an unprecedented scale. Was this a truly held belief or were murkier motives at work? We were reminded that money was not something Watson-Jones had much of before his marriage to the American heiress, Meredith Devereaux. The Devereaux fortune came from the profits of an American aeronautics company which held a number of lucrative government defence contracts. Hardly surprising that Watson-Jones was such a staunch supporter of major rearmament in the West. He had more than just the national interest to promote.

It was a devastating attack, the writing full of anger and loathing. There was little doubt Naismith meant business, though what kind of business wasn't clear.

'Who's Naismith?' I asked.

'A maverick Yorkshireman,' Simon said. 'Likes to be known as

259

a bit of a rebel. He hangs on to the Party whip by the skin of his teeth. I wouldn't count him as a friend.'

'This is heavyweight stuff,' I said. 'There has to be more to it than personal dislike.'

'What did I say, Charlie?' Watson-Jones nodded furiously at me, endorsing my view. 'There's a conspiracy. Someone's got it in for me and I want to know who.'

Charlie looked exhausted. I guessed he'd been woken up a lot earlier than I had. I felt guilty. I hadn't meant to feed Watson-Jones's paranoia.

'We've no grounds for thinking that,' Charlie said with great control. 'None whatsoever.'

'The evidence is here, Charlie. In black and white. Every damn word of it.' Watson-Jones waved the magazine in front of him. 'This man wants my head, not for himself – he hasn't got the gumption – but because someone has put him up to it.' He turned away to look out of the window. 'Where the hell is Gelfmann?'

'He's on his way,' Charlie said. 'He said he'd get here as soon as he could.'

'Why can't he be here when I want him? I'm paying him enough.'

In our previous meetings, Watson-Jones had always impressed me with his self-control. There was a coolness about him that encouraged the belief he'd be effective in a crisis. That was gone now. He betrayed his tension through a succession of nervous gestures while his words fell over each other in the fight to make some sense of what had happened. There wasn't even a pretence of coolness now. We were seeing the man as he was, not the man he had invented. It didn't fill me with confidence.

'Is Naismith important?' I asked. 'Does his opinion matter?'

'Good God, no. The man's a nonentity,' Watson-Jones said quickly. 'Nobody gives a damn what he thinks.'

'The editor of this rag takes a different view,' Charlie said.

'Whose side are you on, Charlie? His or mine?'

'For God's sake, Simon.'

'I'm under great strain,' he said, taking a deep breath and attempting some semblance of self-control. 'I've got to believe Naismith didn't write this piece off his own bat. It's not his style. That means it's a put-up job. We have to find out who's behind him and what they've after. Then we have to put a stop to it before any more damage is done.'

'Have you any idea who that might be?' I got the message that Charlie didn't believe in conspiracy theories. His hint was lost on Watson-Jones.

'I'm baffled,' Watson-Jones said. 'I don't expect to be liked by everyone, but there's no evidence I can think of to suggest this was in the wind.' He looked down at the magazine. 'There's something else, too. If a political editor wants a controversial piece, he gets someone with a reputation to write it. Weight is essential to credibility. Naismith's a cantankerous old bugger who bores everyone rigid with his unending tales of how things are managed better in Yorkshire. He's not got the standing for this sort of thing.'

'In that case,' Charlie said, 'no one's going to take this piece seriously. If we ignore it, it will fade away in its own good time.'

That touched Watson-Jones on a raw nerve. 'Read what he's said about me and you'll see why I can't let the bastard get away with it.'

'We've both read it, Simon,' Charlie said coldly. 'More than once.'

'It's lies, Charlie.' Watson-Jones was shouting again now. 'I don't like people spreading lies about me. Is that understood?'

'All right,' I said, trying to steer a course between them. 'It's malicious. Let's look at how we handle it.'

'Gelfmann should be here by now,' Watson-Jones said, with signs of growing irritation. 'I shall sue if he lets me.'

Charlie gave me a despairing look.

'Why not let others come to your defence?' I said. 'MPs who mean something to the public. The big boys. Get them to speak for you. I am sure we can rally the troops to put the boot into Naismith. It might be more effective that way.'

'Danny's right, Simon. Leave this thing with us and we'll sort it out for you. No harm done.'

'No.' Watson-Jones was adamant. 'I want blood.'

'I think that's very unwise.'

'You'd think differently if you were the victim of smears like these.'

'You're falling into his trap,' Charlie said. 'If you show him it hurts, he'll know he's hit the target. Show some dignity and take no notice.'

'I am not going to be pushed around by some little bastard from Barnsley, Charlie.'

We heard the doorbell ring. 'That'll be Gelfmann,' Charlie said. 'Let him in, will you, Danny?'

I'd met Gelfmann before. He'd struck me as a competent solicitor, though too much in awe of Watson-Jones. He looked hot and breathless.

'Couldn't get a taxi for love nor money,' he said. 'Had to run most of the way. I came as fast as I could. Hardly had time for a shave. I gather there's a flap on.'

'How much do you know?'

'Only what Charlie told me on the telephone and that wasn't much.'

'A Tory MP has gone into print attacking Simon,' I said. 'Not surprisingly he's taking it badly.'

'Bound to,' Gelfmann said, mopping his head and face with a large handkerchief. 'Bound to.'

'We've got to put it right for him.'

'I take it that's an instruction?' Gelfmann asked. We were standing outside Charlie's room.

'Yes,' I said. 'He's very upset. The first task is to calm him down and do nothing precipitate. This is cooling-off time. So, no decisions, just options.'

'I'm your man,' Gelfmann said conspiratorially. 'Count on me.'

I led the way in. Gelfmann didn't exactly fill me with confidence. I didn't know why Watson-Jones used him.

'Christ, Bernard,' Watson-Jones said. 'You took your time.'

'No cabs, Simon. Sorry.'

'You should have run.'

'I did. It nearly killed me.'

'Well, don't die on me yet. You've got work to do. Read this and then tell me what I can do.'

Charlie beckoned me. I leaned across the desk as he whispered: 'We've got to work out how we keep this problem under control. I'll speak to you when Simon's gone. Nothing of importance is going to be decided now. I'll see to that.'

I left them to it. I trusted Charlie, and I hoped in the end Simon would too. He always said Charlie was a wise old bird. Now he had to show whether he meant it or not.

★

We had a few phone calls during the morning, all from well-wishers expressing astonishment at Naismith's outburst. No one was any the wiser about the motive, and Naismith himself had gone to ground. I thought the papers would be on to us but for a few hours at least they ignored us, and I was thankful they did. Gelfmann stayed until mid-morning. Simon spent another half-hour with Charlie after that, then I saw him leave just before twelve. Charlie lent him Thomas and the Rolls to take him to the House. When Charlie's buzzer went soon after I raced upstairs with my papers. Beryl stopped me before I went in.

'He's not well, dear. I want him to go home but he won't listen to me. He's not up to all this, not in his state. Will you say something? He may listen to you.'

I said I doubted I'd succeed where she'd failed and went in. Charlie looked frail, his face a leaden grey and his body sunk into his wheelchair in exhaustion. For the first time I saw that his spirits were low too. I wondered if Watson-Jones had thought what all this might do for Charlie's health.

'How did it go?' I asked.

'What with Simon's paranoia and Gelfmann's willingness to roll over and agree with every crackpot idea he comes up with, not well. I despair of Gelfmann. Simon naturally won't hear a word against him. We managed to avoid taking any decisions, so I suppose we can count that a plus. Jesus, I'm tired.'

'Why don't you take a break? I can come back later.'

'For God's sake, that's Beryl talking. Don't listen to her, the woman's fussing over nothing. I'd far rather talk it over with you than brood on my own but she doesn't seem to understand that.' He smiled at me. 'What I need is a large gin.'

'What's the damage?' I asked, pouring a drink for both of us.

'Naismith's been very clever. He knows what he's talking about and he's hit where it hurts. He pours doubt over Simon's probity, painting him as a man not to be trusted. That suggests he's not trying to destroy him, so much as discredit him. His aim is to wound, not kill.'

'Do you agree with Simon that someone's behind it?'

'I can't see Naismith doing this on his own because I can't see what he's got to gain. But I can't see any grounds for a conspiracy either. Simon may speak his mind on some issues but he doesn't upset the top brass in the Party. I've seen to that, and I know the

Party managers rate him. He's able, ambitious – they like that. Goes a bit too far sometimes but his heart's in the right place, so small excesses are easily forgiven. A man to watch. That's the verdict.'

'Until today.'

Charlie pulled himself together then. It was a huge physical effort, and gave me an insight into how ill he really was.

'Until today, yes. Something seems to have gone badly wrong and I've missed it. That's what's worrying me. This is about silencing Simon. The problem is, I don't know what needs to be silenced. I fear I'm losing my touch.'

★

It was a warm afternoon as I cycled over Chelsea Bridge, down Prince of Wales Drive and into the heart of Battersea. I couldn't get rid of the thought that this incident had come about because Simon was being unfaithful to Charlie: that some opportunity had come up, he had seized it and got in over his head before he had time to talk it over with Charlie. That was the charitable explanation. Now his actions had blown up in his face, he had to keep any knowledge of it away from Eccleston Street. That explained his angry posturing, outrage and hurt vanity. He'd cleverly offered no opinions as to why all this had happened. If I was right, we were going to get no real help from Simon, but a series of blustering performances to keep us off the scent.

'What do we do now?' I'd asked Charlie as we reviewed the situation. I didn't mention my theory to him because I knew his loyalty to Simon wouldn't let him agree.

'The only person who's likely to tell us anything is Naismith,' he'd said, giving me the address of a flat in Battersea. 'See if you can make him talk. If he's not in, wait. I don't want to hear from you until you've cornered him.'

Naismith wasn't in when I arrived at his flat, or at least no one answered the doorbell. There was a café opposite and I went in and read the paper. I'd had a good round of spam, sausages in gravy and fried bread by the time a woman showed up about three, but there was no sign of Naismith until well after five by which time I had drunk more cups of tea than was good for me. I went across the road and rang the bell. The woman answered and I asked for Naismith.

'Who are you, dear, the press? I can't make him come to the door if you won't tell me who you are.'

'I'm a friend of Charlie Faulkner's.'

She went in, leaving me on the doorstep. The door was opened a couple of minutes later by a small round man in his early sixties, balding and with a florid face. He had taken off his jacket, his stiff collar and tie. He stood before me, bright red braces holding up dull brown tweed trousers, the top of his shirt open where the stud had been. He had undone his cuff links and rolled up his shirt-sleeves to the elbow.

'Old Charlie Faulkner sent you, did 'e?' He spoke with a strong Yorkshire accent.

'That's right. I work for him.'

'You'd better come in then, lad. We go back a long way, Charlie and I do. Cup o' tea?'

'No thanks.'

'This lassie makes a grand cup o' tea. I'll have a cuppa, Vi. Sit yourself down. Now then, what's all this about?'

'I read your piece about Watson-Jones. You were pretty hard on him.'

'Toffee-nosed bastard. 'Bout time someone put 'im in 'is place. I've been a member of the 'Ouse of Commons for more than twenty-five years and 'e won't so much as give me the time of day. I've no liking for the man. I can't say plainer than that.'

'Why put your dislike in print?'

'Free country. I can say what I like about who I please within the law. That's what we were fighting for, wasn't it, lad? Freedom of speech. You said you worked for Charlie Faulkner. Seems to me you're carrying the flag for Watson-Jones.'

'I'm here on Watson-Jones's behalf.'

'Then I've nothing more to say to you, son. Good day.' He got to his feet.

'I think we've got things to talk about,' I said weakly.

'I don't give a horse's arse what you think, lad. I want you out of 'ere now. Do I make myself clear?'

The woman who'd opened the door reappeared, holding a mug of tea. 'I'd hear the young man out, Nat,' she said. 'It never harms to listen.'

She came into the room and sat down on the sofa. She patted the seat for Naismith to sit next to her. 'His bark's worse than his bite, dear, don't mind that. I expect you're something to do with Mr Watson-Jones, are you, dear? Yes, I thought so. Money, Nat.

Money and power have been in bed together since the world began. Never spit at money, I say, if you know what's good for you. Now come and sit down, Nat, and stop being a silly boy.'

'Women,' Naismith said to me. But he sat down none the less and took his mug of tea.

'My name's Vi, dear. You can call me Vi. Everyone does.'

Her comforting, motherly appearance and the sweetness of her smile made her an unlikely ally. I sat down and began again.

'I wondered why you wrote that article,' I said.

'Never 'ad to work for anything in 'is life,' Naismith said. 'Born with so many silver spoons in 'is mouth it's a wonder 'e didn't choke to death in 'is 'igh chair. 'E's everything I despise, that man.'

'Now, that's not right, Nat, is it?' Vi turned to me. 'He likes to think he's a great hater, does Nat. But he's a real Cadbury when you get to know him. Hard on the outside and all soft and gooey inside. Aren't you, love?'

'You keep your mouth shut, Vi.'

'Nat.' A silent battle of wills was going on. I waited. 'Why not tell the young man what happened,' she said.

Naismith gave her a look which was a mixture of affection and despair. 'It wasn't my idea, that piece, I'll admit that. I was asked to write it.'

'Who asked you?'

'I don't tell tales out of school, lad.'

I didn't like Naismith. He was too pleased with himself to listen to any opinion that didn't agree with his. What baffled me was how a sweet woman like Vi could put up with his bluster.

'What are you after, dear?' Vi asked. 'You want something, don't you? I can tell. You aren't Sagittarius, are you?'

'Have you seen this article?' I asked.

Vi shook her head. 'All this politics stuff goes right over my head, dear. I leave all that to his lordship here.'

'It takes an axe to Watson-Jones. Blood all over the place. You can't expect him to ignore it. He's not that kind of man. You know he'll come after you and anyone else involved. He's got the money and the will and you've made him angry enough. I can't believe that's what you want him to do.'

'I 'ardly started in that piece,' Naismith said. 'I could say 'ell of a lot more in the 'Ouse and there's bugger all you could do about that.'

266

'He'll come after you outside the House. That's what his lawyers are advising.' It was a reckless statement, but I had to puncture Naismith's confidence somehow if I was to scare him into telling me who was behind the article and why.

''E can do what 'e likes. I'll be ready for 'im.'

It was bravado and Yorkshire stubbornness, I was sure, but I didn't know how to shake it. I appealed to Vi. If there was a weakness in his armoury, I hoped it was her.

'I'm here to see if we can close this thing down as quickly and quietly as we can,' I said, trying to sound conciliatory. 'Surely you can see the sense in that?'

'I knew you and I were going to get along,' Vi said. 'As soon as I saw you I did. Are you Taurus, then?'

'You tell your boss 'e can do what 'e likes,' Naismith said, raising his voice. He was angry with me now. 'So long as 'is wife lets 'im use 'er money.' He turned to Vi. 'What kind of a man is that, eh? Sponges off 'is wife.' I could hear disgust in his voice. That sort of thing wasn't done in Yorkshire.

'You come with something up your sleeve, don't you, dear,' Vi said, responding to my overtures. 'It's us, isn't it? Me and this old hunk of Yorkshire pudding. I'm his fancy woman, dear, and I don't mind who knows it. I care for the old bugger, which is more can be said for that Lady Muck in Yorkshire, I can tell you. I've looked after this old man for years now and I'm too old to be hurt by what anyone thinks.'

'Are you?' I asked Naismith, hoping I sounded unscrupulous and threatening. He took his time to reply. Putting Vi in the firing line was not what he was after.

'I'll be frank with you, lad. There's many people know about Vi. It's one of those secrets you get about Westminster. Everyone knows and nobody says. I'm not the only one, I can tell you. It would make your blood run cold if you knew the things I know.' He was sounding chummy now – we were all boys together, we could keep our locker-room secrets dark, couldn't we? 'If I could 'ave married her all those years ago, I would.'

'Get away with you,' Vi said teasingly.

'But I couldn't and that's a fact. Least, not without giving up my seat. So Vi and me, we came to an understanding. That's all. No 'arm in that, is there?'

His change of tone told me he feared that the rules of the club he'd joined so long before might not be shared by younger men like Watson-Jones. The cosy certainties he'd lived by could now be undermined, if not destroyed, by the harsher realities of the post-war world. Naismith was on soft ground. It was the only opening he'd given me, so I took it.

'Watson-Jones is one of the new breed,' I said, hoping I sounded convincing. 'The old loyalties don't apply any more. The world's changing.'

'Aye, lad. And not for the better, either.'

'People like him are making the rules now.'

'That's what I'm told and I don't like it.'

'This isn't your quarrel, is it?' I said. 'We both know that. Why not let those who want to pick a fight with him come out of the shadows to face him on their own?'

'What are you saying, lad?'

'I'll guarantee Watson-Jones's silence if you tell me who's behind this business.'

'Very clever, lad. Very nice.' He smiled indulgently at me.

'What about it?'

'That might put me in the clear with you, lad, but I'm in the shit with them, aren't I?'

'So there is someone behind all this?'

'I'm not telling you anything you don't know.'

'No deal then?' It was an appeal and he took it as such.

'Not that I can see, son, no.'

'That doesn't seem right to me,' Vi said. 'My stars said I'd meet a handsome stranger today and he and I would get along.'

'Then your bloody 'oroscope made a cock-up this time, didn't it, girl?' It was said with affection. Naismith put his arm round her shoulder and pulled her, unresisting, against him. 'You wouldn't want to hurt my little girl, would you?'

'If I don't go back to Watson-Jones with something,' I said, my exasperation breaking through, 'he'll come after you like an elephant gone mad. I can't stop him.'

'I may have been a fool to put my name to this piece but if I say any more I'll make an even bigger fool of myself. There's too much at stake for that. I'd like to help Charlie, 'e's a good man even if 'e does support the wrong cricket team. But there's now I can do for you, lad. You'll have to leave here empty-'anded.'

He'd called my bluff and there was nothing I could do about it.

I rang Charlie as soon as I got back to Strutton Ground. He sounded distant and reluctant to talk.

'If you've got someone with you,' I said, 'I can ring back later.'

I sensed a moment of hesitation. I was sure he was not alone. Perhaps Watson-Jones was with him again.

'No. Go ahead.'

I explained I had had no luck with Naismith. 'He won't talk. But he admitted he wrote this thing for a favour. So we know there is someone behind it, though not who.'

'Progress,' Charlie said. 'Good. Sleep on it. We'll talk about it in the morning.'

I was dismissed. It wasn't like Charlie to do that. I put it down to exhaustion and the illness. If anyone had an excuse to be short-tempered after a day like this, Charlie did.

I rang Sylvia Carr and she suggested I go to her flat for a drink, 'though God knows why you think I should be able to help you.'

'I want you to help me for Charlie's sake,' I said when I got there.

'What did old Charlie ever do for me except say no?' It wasn't a question to which she expected an answer. I asked her if she'd read the article about Watson-Jones. She hadn't and she took great delight in my description of it.

'Why didn't they ask me to write it?' she asked. 'I'd have done a far better job.'

'It wasn't Naismith's idea. Someone put him up to it.'

'How do you know?'

'I've talked to him. He admitted as much.'

'Then why have you come to me?'

'Who might have talked to Naismith?'

'How should I know?'

'These are your people, Sylvia. You're part of their world. You know your way around them. I don't.'

'Meaning I've been to bed with too many of them, is that it? I'm sorry. That was cheap and uncalled for.'

'Someone struck a bargain with Naismith. Help us and we'll help you. That's why he won't talk.'

'We all know what Naismith's after. He's been waiting for years with his tongue hanging out. Arise, Sir Nat.'

'Who has the power to deliver that?'

'Who has the power to make Naismith believe he can deliver? That's the real question.' I waited for her to answer. 'Senior members

269

of the Party. A Party grandee in the Lords. Very senior civil servants. Someone with connections or influence, a route to the decision-makers. It's a pretty messy business, Dan, whatever the public face. A lot of mutual backslapping goes on.'

'I need names,' I said.

'I know you do,' she said.

'They're your friends.'

'You make it sound as if I'd committed an offence.'

'I didn't mean to.'

'You're an unlikely sleuth,' Sylvia said. 'And I'm no Watson to your Holmes.'

'Will you help me?'

She kissed me lightly on the cheek. 'All right, darling, you'll see I'm a woman who keeps her word. I'll see if I can find your villain for you. But I'm promising nothing.'

9

MONTY

'Why in God's name waste time on an unknown general who poses as much of a threat to the future of the Soviet regime as a cold in the head?' Rupert said angrily at the start of our weekly meeting. 'He's far too low down the pecking order to count.'

We were in for a bollocking and we got it. Time wasted, resources squandered, getting nowhere, blind alleys. We weren't spared the full force of Corless's frustration.

'The Soviets have suffered a massive setback through the explosion at their laboratory. Maybe there's an opposition to Stalin, maybe there isn't. My masters want to know what's going on inside the Soviet Union. Who's hard, who's soft on the nuclear issue. When I come to this Committee for answers, what do I find? You're running around like headless chickens after a second-rate general no one's heard of. Well, that isn't good enough.'

We were instructed to redirect our scant resources into a search for credible opponents to the system, and to come up with answers rapidly. Wearily we returned to our rooms, reopened the files and began a new investigation. Mysterious dates, suicidal soldiers and commanders of tank regiments were out of bounds.

'We're victims of Rupert's theory of the immaculate conception,' Adrian Gardner said with more bitterness than usual. 'Cock-up begets cock-up.'

A day later *The Times*'s Moscow correspondent reported the accident in laboratory D4, and there was immediate public speculation about the impact of this on the Soviet bomb and whether the subsequent delay (estimated, as we knew it would be, by Professor Stevens and others at between six months and a year) would create any political opportunities. Stevens wrote a piece arguing that our national energies would be better deployed using this unexpected event to reach agreement with the Soviets on the total banning of nuclear weapons than joining an arms race in which our participation would probably come close to bankrupting us.

Corless's anger erupted again. 'This is one of the men responsible for setting up the infrastructure to make the British atomic bomb.' He banged the flat of his hand on the opened page of the newspaper. 'Reading this, anyone would think he worked for the Soviets.' He looked round the room in fury. 'Now, I wonder where I've heard that before?'

Within hours we learned on the Whitehall grapevine that Stevens's theme found favour with those Ministers who opposed the level of expenditure on nuclear research, and they were looking at ways to exploit this new situation. Large sections of the opposition were displeased. Among the more vocal was Watson-Jones, who saw the building of a British bomb as an essential condition if there were to be any hope of permanent peace in Europe. The Oxford Union held a debate: that 'This House believes that now is the time to negotiate a nuclear treaty with the Soviet Union', and the surprisingly high majority in favour was front-page news in the national press. At a deeper level, what we were hearing was a heart-felt cry for some kind of certainty in what looked to be a very uncertain world; for the removal of a new and terrifying threat to our lives.

★

I returned to my flat one evening in a mood of exhausted frustration after a day that had got us nowhere, and dug out the report I had asked Danny to write after his visit to Finland.

His verdict on Krasov was uncompromising. The man was a liar and should be neither believed nor trusted. Whatever he told us should be viewed with the utmost scepticism. However much it hurt, it was a judgement I had to sympathize with. I reviewed the evidence once more, this time with the cold eye Danny demanded.

It was hard to accept that our assessment of the damage to the Soviet research programme was not true. A hole in the ground was a hole in the ground, and first Martineau and now *The Times* had confirmed it was there. Dead scientists and technicians could not spring back to life. It would take some time to rebuild D4. But was this the only laboratory where such experiments could be carried out? If the accident had been caused by the Soviets getting it wrong, didn't they possess the will and the resources to get it right? Wasn't it reasonable to suppose that we might be placing too much importance on a single event, that our reading of Soviet psychology at this moment might be wrong-headed? The Soviets were always at their most dangerous when they thought they were in a weak position.

I was on surer ground when it came to the question of an opposition. If the political analysts thought the conditions were unhelpful and we were unable to find a single candidate (apart from General Kosintzev) around whose leadership an opposition might emerge, couldn't this mean that in all probability there *was* no opposition? It was possible to argue that our enthusiasm for the idea of a new leader was a direct response to our growing distrust of Stalin.

What was unsettling about this analysis was that some weeks after Danny's meeting with Krasov, Peter had himself confirmed the points in Krasov's statement that I was now challenging. That was where the difficulty arose. Our trust in Peter was rightly sustained by the continued quality of his intelligence. Again and again, as Corless argued relentlessly in his defence, Peter had proved to be right. The only blot on an otherwise near-perfect record was his accusation against Stevens, and the jury was still out on that one. Krasov's credibility might not exist, but casting doubt on Peter was going to be next to impossible, particularly if Krasov was the source of the doubt.

The deeper I went, the more I became aware of an uncomfortable truth. The notion that because the Soviets were weakened by the damage to their nuclear programme, they now might be prepared to bargain with the West, even to negotiate a non-nuclear treaty, had little basis in fact. We had no firm evidence that this was so, only a carefully placed suggestion originating from Krasov and confirmed by Peter.

The theory had been cleverly planted on us, my sceptical interpretation went, and it had taken root, as no doubt our enemies had hoped it would, sustained by the verifiable evidence of the destruction of a laboratory. On that firm but narrow base, we had allowed ourselves (deceived ourselves?) to build a dangerously top-heavy construction of theories on which we were now acting *as if they were fact*. We wanted a way out of our own nuclear dilemma, and events in Moscow appeared to provide such a route. It was all too well timed, too neat and tidy. It had none of the roughness of reality, the jagged edges of actual events. In the midst of it all there was something I couldn't put my finger on.

An hour later my anxieties had formed into a theory, the shape of which was as unexpected as the logic was inescapable and frightening. We were only too ready to believe that the Russians were in trouble and keen to negotiate because of our own reluctance to build a nuclear bomb. Look at the economic drain on an already exhausted country, the argument went, made worse by the American refusal to share their knowledge with us. How much easier and cheaper not to have to build the damn thing at all. What Peter told us about the delay to the Soviet programme and the possibility of internal opposition to the bomb was what we wanted to hear. The intelligence he passed us added up to a solution to *our* problem. That was where we were going wrong. With Peter's encouragement, we were thinking about ourselves and forgetting the Soviets. All of a sudden I had the impression that we were being deceived into lowering our guard long before the bell had gone for the end of the round.

10

RUTH

She begs him not to do this but by now his anger is so aroused that she cannot stop him, he cannot stop himself. He drives on into the countryside, through deserted villages she has never visited before, past a factory, its enormous chimneys raining black silt into the afternoon air so that the buildings, the fields, the trees, even the stagnant water in a small lake are all black. She sees no one, no living being, on this silent drive to wherever it is he is taking her. It is a dead landscape on a desolate planet.

They stop at the edge of a forest. He gets out of the car, puts on a pair of boots and gives her a pair too. He carries a shovel and they set off, one following the other, into the depths of the forest. The air is cold, their footsteps crackle on the floor of pine needles and fir cones and dead branches dried through the icy winter so that they snap with the slightest pressure.

Again there are no signs of life, no birds, no animals racing away into the safety of the shadows. This is a dead land, she thinks, and we are here to meet the dead.

They reach a clearing. Branches, their leaves turned brown, have been dragged into a kind of collapsed tent. Lykowski photographs and then drags away the branches to reveal turned earth, a large mound blacker than its surroundings because it has no covering of pine needles. He takes another photograph.

'Is this it?' she asks.

He nods in reply but says nothing. He walks across the mound, carrying his shovel. Then he attacks the earth in a frenzy, throwing it anywhere, digging frantically deeper and deeper. She cannot watch. It is too awful.

'Look,' he cries suddenly. 'Come here.'

'No.'

'You must see for yourself.'

He is coming towards her, eyes blazing, anger visible in his stance. She relents. He takes her roughly by the arm and drags her back to where he has been digging.

'Look there.'

She looks down and is sick at once. There, blackened and rotting, are three human heads – three women, their eyes already empty sockets, scarves still in place around their heads, their open mouths like tears in a sheet of old canvas.

'There are more,' he says, angrily. 'If I were to dig here. Or here. Or here.'

He drives at the earth with his shovel as if the force will split it open and reveal the corpses beneath. There is a terrible smell, a poisonous miasma and she vomits again and again, as she runs away into the trees. She puts her arms around the trunk of a fir tree and sobs. How can he do this to her? She believed him, she did not need proof. Why has he brought her here?

He is shouting at her, his voice hoarse with tears. 'They did not die in a fire, there are no burns on their bodies or their nightclothes. They died because they were shot in the back. Where we are standing is a killing ground.'

She turns round. He is refilling the hole he has made, covering up the dead once more. He drags back the branches, working with a demented energy as if his life depended upon it.

'What have we been told?' he shouts at her. The words echo among the trees and are lost in the depths of the forest. 'There was an explosion, people died in a fire. That is a lie. Look. Here. They were brought in lorries. Look!'

He points to the tyre marks, evidence frozen until the spring melted the snow but too soon for the rains to wash away the marks, and flowers to push through the earth to conceal the evil of the place.

'Did you notice that the heads were female? Females bodies side by side. I imagine, if I dug over here, I would find male bodies. Before killing these old people, they separated husbands from wives.'

This at last is the evidence she has been searching for. The apartment building was empty when it exploded. Its occupants had already been forcibly removed, brought to this deserted place, shot and buried secretly. It is not the image of the dead and dying that haunts her, it is the presence of the thin, pale figure of the intelligence officer at the crime Pavel has uncovered, the man without whose continued protection she is as good as dead.

He walks back towards her. 'Is this what we have become? Murderers of our own people? These men and women were taken from their beds at gunpoint, our own citizens, innocent of any crime, their only mistake being that they lived in that block. They were driven here like cattle, separated from each other and shot because that was the order that had been given. This is the burial ground of the state's crimes and we have uncovered their dirty secret.'

She wipes her face and her eyes, the nausea only just under control.

'Sixty-eight people lie here,' he says. 'I have not counted the bodies, but I have stolen the list of residents from the block near D4 and I have counted them. I know their names. Their ages. The numbers of their flats. This is their final resting place, a clearing in a forest that, had it not been for the last confession of a young soldier, might have remained undiscovered for years. There is only one question to ask. Why did it happen? Why?'

He shouts the word *why*, and it reverberates among the branches of the trees. Is it her imagination, or do the stilled branches move in reply to his entreaty? Do they bow out of respect for the terrible scene he has revealed?

She cannot answer him. He has told her nothing new. She has known the truth all along. Not the terrible details he has shown her – she has not recreated the appalling suffering of the last minutes of their lives – but the intolerable injustice of killing innocent people in the middle of the night for no other purpose than to make a political argument that much stronger, to reinforce the lie on which someone's power is based.

'Look here,' he says. His hands are full of spent cartridges he has collected. 'What more evidence do we need?'

'Take me away from this place,' she says.

But Lykowski is busy. He has stripped the bark off two branches and now he is tying one piece to another. He has made a cross. With difficulty he plants one end in the frozen earth and supports it with stones. It is something, a marker of where the dead lie. No one will see it and in time, soon, it will collapse. But they will both know that they have done something, however small; that they have paid their respects.

11

MONTY

The downpour which had been threatening since I'd left Strutton Ground broke as I was crossing Horseferry Road, and caught me in full flood. I was dripping wet when I put my head round Miss Pertwee's door.

'Oh, Mr Lybrand,' she said, 'Mr Maitland's so sorry. He's been called away. He said would you mind waiting.'

I was given a cup of tea and offered a digestive biscuit from the famous floral tin. I was either unexpectedly in favour or Miss Pertwee was deeply embarrassed by Colin's absence. Her treasury of digestive biscuits was famed for being as tightly guarded as her virginity.

Two days before, Colin had given us the 'good news' that a small group of senior civil servants had written a confidential policy paper for the Cabinet, arguing that in the light of what we now knew about the present political situation in the Kremlin, and given our own straitened circumstances, it was surely responsible to investigate the possibility of a negotiated nuclear settlement with the Soviets before committing ourselves to building our own bomb.

I was taken aback at the strength of support on our Committee for this course of action. Guy Benton saw it as a vindication of the consistent Foreign Office line that 'we must not allow ourselves to become captive to the easy characterization of *Homo sovieticus* as our natural enemy'. Arthur Gurney viewed it as a reprieve for his growing opinion that 'building the bomb cannot be seen as a suitable activity for a civilized society'. Boys-Allen sucked his pipe and nodded while Adrian Gardner, cynical as ever, whispered that Corless was beating us with the stick of our own importance so that we would continue doggedly down 'the line of investigation Rupert's career is anchored to'.

'You've been very quiet, Monty. Any comments?'

What could I say? I was as responsible as anyone else round the table for the interpretation of Peter's intelligence. We had produced a stream of reports on which the conclusions of this Cabinet paper were based. Who would believe me if I said I now thought its recommendations had their origin in the offices of Moscow intelligence?

'Is the Cabinet likely to endorse this advice?' I asked, avoiding a direct answer to the question.

'Reading between the lines,' Colin said, 'I think we may assume that secret diplomatic contacts with the Soviets are on the cards, if they haven't already happened.'

I had asked for this meeting with Colin because of my conviction that Peter's campaign against Stevens, the explosion in the Moscow laboratory and the reports of the anti-nuclear faction in the Politburo were all scenes in a grand Soviet deception, a more complex drama than any we had come across before, and one that was working its powerful magic on us. How disastrous if the Cabinet were to revise their policy as a result of Soviet manipulation. We were doing the enemy's work for him.

My first thought had been to go straight to Rupert Corless, but my experience of his lack of sympathy over Krasov deterred me. Better to get Colin on my side before approaching Rupert. I expected Colin to be sceptical initially and reject my theories but he was a fair man, and I knew that if I could get him to listen long enough I had a chance of winning him over. Then we could both tackle Rupert. Together, we might win the day.

Thirty minutes later there was still no sign of Maitland. I put my head round the door again. Miss Pertwee was on the telephone. She cupped her hand over the mouthpiece.

'It's Mr Maitland now,' she whispered. 'He sends many apologies. He's so sorry to keep you waiting.'

I was to stay. He was returning, ten minutes at the outside. I sat down again and tried unsuccessfully to finish the crossword Colin had started on his journey into Vauxhall. I heard the tapping of the typewriter and occasionally the dull ring of the telephone. The ever-vigilant Miss Pertwee had left the connecting door open so she could keep an eye on me without moving from her desk. Whatever else might happen, I was not to be allowed to escape before Colin's return.

The core of my case was that Peter had been turned. This was supposition on my part but I was increasingly sure that amid so much good information was a secret seam of deception coming directly from sources within Moscow intelligence. SOVINT had probably been misled for months as the web of the Soviet deception was spun ever more tightly around us.

'Let them think we're trying to cover up a massive failure in our nuclear programme,' I could hear the Soviet planners saying. 'Deceive them into believing we are desperate to negotiate a nuclear standstill. Wait as the divisions in the Western alliance erupt and their bitter arguments slow down their own progress. Then watch their faces as we explode the weapon they thought we could never make and move rapidly on to the superbomb.'

Was I right? Were the events we had so far been unable to explain only understandable as part of a daring Soviet deception? Being right didn't mean I would carry the day. Rupert had to be persuaded to accept the notion that Peter was no longer his friend but his enemy. Was I deluding myself to imagine that that was possible? Rupert owed Peter the late flowering of his career. Nothing is harder to shift than a vested interest. My confidence, which had not been dampened by my soaking in the sudden shower, began to evaporate.

'Rupert's in a flap. I couldn't get away,' Colin said twenty minutes later, pipe clamped firmly between his teeth. 'Sorry.' He seemed unwilling to talk in front of Miss Pertwee. 'No calls, Miss Pertwee, please. Mr Lybrand and I have to put our thinking caps on.'

He ushered me into his room, closed the door, sat down at his desk and said: 'We have a crisis, Monty.' He opened the file he was clutching. He had clearly forgotten why I was there.

Did the name Watson-Jones ring any bells? He didn't know much about the man either, but whether we liked it or not, a degree of intimacy was about to be thrust upon us.

The Minister had received a letter from Watson-Jones in which he claimed he had learned from his American contacts that a Soviet intelligence source had given the British information in January that one of our leading scientists was betraying nuclear secrets to the Russians. 'Watson-Jones's wife's American,' Maitland explained. 'Her father's in manufacturing, he's made millions.' The British authorities had ignored this warning and failed to investigate the suspect. For months vital secrets had been flowing out of the country. Watson-Jones was not surprisingly – 'his words' – shocked at these allegations, and he wanted the Minister's assurance that none of it was true.

'There's a sting in the tail,' Colin said. 'He has a dossier he's offering to share with the Minister. That means this letter's an opening salvo and there's more dirt to come.'

'How the hell does he know about Stevens?' I asked.

'No point in speculating,' Colin said. 'He knows, that's all that matters. The Minister is jumping up and down like a scalded cat because, so he told Rupert this morning, the Foreign Office has had secret talks in Moscow and there are encouraging signs that the Soviets may be prepared to discuss some kind of nuclear arrangement. The stakes are high, Monty, and the Minister doesn't want Watson-Jones rocking the boat. If he's going out soon, he wants to go out in glory.'

This was a reference to Gaydon's expected departure from office. He was neither a popular nor an effective Minister. A former railwayman who was owed a small political debt which it would not take long to repay, he was widely expected to go at the next ministerial reshuffle. That couldn't come soon enough for most of us who had to work for him.

'Do you think the Soviets are serious?' I wanted to see if I could push Colin into declaring where he stood. Over the past months in particular, he had used his role as Rupert's deputy to avoid taking sides. Was this wariness, self-preservation or had he run out of opinions?

'In my experience, Monty, people believe what they want to believe. Sceptics seldom have a following. They're usually lone voices, drowned out in the din.'

'That's an evasion,' I said. 'If you believe all this talk of an opposition to Stalin is nonsense then you should say so as loudly as you can.'

'The emperor's new clothes?' Maitland smiled ruefully. 'The truth is, Monty, I've been in this game too long. I've lost my perspective. I don't know what's true and what's not any more.'

'If in doubt, don't,' I said. 'Isn't that the rule?'

'What if I'm wrong?'

'What if you're not?'

He sucked on his pipe, his face expressionless. I couldn't tell what he was thinking. 'You've not believed in what we're doing for some time, have you?' he said.

'I think we're being manipulated, Colin. It's as simple as that.' I gave him my theory. He listened attentively.

'If we're victims of a Soviet deception, then Watson-Jones is right. That puts us in a spot, doesn't it? How can we subvert our own investigation?'

It wasn't a question I could answer. I wanted to know how strong Maitland's position was.

'Have you had doubts about Peter for long?' I asked.

'Months, yes.'

'Why keep them to yourself?'

'No evidence. Simple as that. Supposition in plenty. The hard evidence is all against us.'

'That's the Soviets being clever,' I said.

'Are you sure?'

'How can I be sure?' I asked, irritably. But at least I was prepared to be honest about my concerns. I didn't bury them because I was afraid of upsetting the apple-cart. That silenced Colin for a while.

'Look at the political dilemma,' he said eventually. 'No bomb, and we can remake the country economically. The blueprints have been ready since 1943. Rebuild our industries. Stake our claim as an economic power. Jettison the ties with the Empire – it's history now. Earn our place at the top table not just through our military power, our nuclear bomb, but through our economic performance. What's the other side of the coin? Divert massive energies and resources we don't possess into building this dangerous weapon. Starve the country of what it needs but take our place in the game with the other nuclear players. What do we do, Monty? What do we do?'

I could tell he hadn't finished by the way he was puffing at his pipe.

'Look down the tunnel into the future. Go left and we emerge into sunlight. Go right and we're stuck in the gloom. Maybe we're being offered an olive branch. Maybe we have to grasp it. It would be irresponsible not to do so. We have to reach for it, even if it turns out to be nothing at all. Politically, we don't have a choice.'

'Watson-Jones wants blood,' I said, 'and we're to do his bidding.'

'We have to protect our Minister's interests.'

'Even though Watson-Jones might be right.'

'Watson-Jones is raising serious questions about Gaydon's competence,' Colin said. 'Those questions have to be stifled at birth. Rupert's certain he wouldn't have bothered to write to the Minister in the first place unless he had Stevens's name up his sleeve.'

'But why? What can he possibly hope to gain by denouncing Stevens as a traitor?'

'His motive remains a mystery,' Colin said. 'Unless it's the traditional self-importance of the ambitious MP.'

A year or two before Rupert had told me, in an unexpected burst of confidence, that as a young man Colin Maitland had wanted to be an MP. Repeated failure to be selected had bred in this moderate man a hearty distaste for the members of the club he had failed to join.

'Suppose he names Stevens. What happens then?'

'There's a procedure to follow. We'd suspend Stevens and there'd be an investigation.'

'The police?'

'Not if we could help it. We'd want our people to conduct the enquiry, but you never know. Scotland Yard could be brought in.'

'What's the effect of suspension on Stevens?' I asked.

'Devastating,' Colin said. 'He'd be removed from anything to do with our nuclear programme. The enquiry would take weeks, possibly longer. Things wouldn't come to a halt, but they'd slow down dramatically.'

'What would be the effect on our programme?'

'Conservatively, I'd say it would put back our bomb by at least a year. Under the scenario we've been discussing, there'd be smiling faces in the Kremlin if that happened.'

'That's what's baffling me,' I said. 'Watson-Jones is rabidly anti-Soviet. You've only got to read that awful tract he finances to see that, and the rumour is he doesn't think the newsletter goes far enough. Yet here he is, apparently playing into Soviet hands. I don't understand it.'

'Unless.' Colin took his pipe out of his mouth and examined the bowl with the perplexed look of the dedicated pipe-smoker. How was it that such a good pipe had suddenly gone out?

'Unless what?'

'Unless he doesn't understand what he's doing.'

'He can't be that stupid, Colin.'

'There's always a danger we're attributing motives where none exist. I said the same to Rupert and he took your view. But suppose this information suddenly fell into his hands and the letter is a knee-jerk reaction? What then?'

'I'd take him behind the bike sheds and let him know what's what,' I said.

'If scaring him into silence has been tried, and I'm not saying it has, the tactic doesn't appear to have worked.'

'Then we've got to try harder,' I said. 'If he won't listen willingly, he'll have to be made to listen. Someone's got to speak to him or one of his people.'

'Your friend works for him, doesn't he?'

'I can't ask any more favours, Colin. Why can't you talk to Charlie Faulkner?'

'Charlie's dying, Monty. He's out of it. No influence any more.'

'How can I ask Danny Stevens to ask his employer not to denounce his father as a spy? It's impossible, Colin, and you know it is.'

Maitland accepted that, nodding silently at me and pulling at his pipe. 'So where does that leave us?'

'Where we came in half an hour ago.'

'No further forward.' He looked gloomy. 'I'll go back to Rupert. He won't like it. Someone will have to take Watson-Jones to one side and tell him to shut up. I'd be surprised if he did. But it's all we can do.'

We never got to speak to Watson-Jones. I got a telephone call from one of our watchers in Cambridge shortly before lunch to say that Stevens had disappeared. One moment, he assured me, he'd been there, the next he'd vanished into thin air. By seven that evening we'd had reports that someone answering Stevens's description had been spotted on a cross-Channel ferry and by midnight we'd caught up with him in Brussels. I thought we would pull him in at once but Rupert was against the idea.

'We can pull him in any time we want,' he said. 'Let's see where he's going and who he's going to meet. You never know, we might learn something.'

12

DANNY

Charlie didn't appear next morning. He'd had a bad night and the doctor wasn't prepared to let him out, or us in to see him.

'Complete rest,' Beryl told us. 'No telephone calls.'

There were two messages on my desk when I got back to my room. Monty had telephoned and someone called Lord Iredale wanted to speak to Charlie, but as Charlie wasn't in he said he'd speak to me. I tried to contact Monty but he was out. I left a message and telephoned Lord Iredale. I was curious to know what he wanted.

'Sorry to hear Charlie Faulkner's laid up. I was wondering if you'd care for a spot of lunch? One o'clock at my club in St James's.'

Iredale was an imposingly tall man, elegantly dressed in a blue pinstripe suit and a tie I know I was meant to recognize but didn't. He must have been in his forties, though it was hard to tell how old he was. He swept me past the bar and into the dining room.

'I'm off the booze at the moment. Doctor's orders. Let's go in and eat. Nursery food, all fairly tasteless, but what isn't these days?'

I drank Bloody Marys while Iredale sipped tomato juice, and we ate a strange mixture of sausages and batter covered in a thin, luke-warm gravy. Iredale hardly touched his.

'You'd have thought they couldn't go wrong with a sausage.'

He pushed his plate away and lit a cigarette. 'I gather you were in Italy in forty-four.' He had done his homework on me. 'Come across my nephews, William and Frank Iredale?'

I had met them once in Naples, a couple of boneheaded officers whose incompetence was legendary. Their reputation was made in bars and brothels, not on the battlefield. I had done my best to avoid them.

'Useless pair. God knows how they got their commissions. I thought we'd better get that over with before we talk.'

I was meant to warm to his frankness but it put me even more on my guard. There was something in Iredale's patrician manner I didn't take to. I asked if he'd been in Italy too.

'No. I mucked about in the desert for a bit, then Yugoslavia.'

'With Tito?'

'Mihailovitch.' He gave me the impression his wartime exploits were not what he had asked me there to talk about.

'Tell me,' he said, looking around the room to see how many of his fellow diners he knew. 'This business with Watson-Jones. What would it take to call the hounds off?'

'What business with Watson-Jones?' I had no idea what he meant.

'What would you want to put a stop to it?' There was a chill in his voice. His attention was now focused wholly on me.

'Shouldn't you ask Watson-Jones that?'

'I'm not sure you heard me, Stevens. I am asking what you want to pull Watson-Jones out of this thing and close it down. Money? New job? Women? What's your price, man? I can't put it plainer than that.'

'What if Watson-Jones wants to go on as he is?'

I thought he would be reluctant to answer but he wasn't. I found his directness intimidating.

'The man's rowing in someone else's pond. The water's rough and he's not used to the conditions. That's dangerous. The people I represent don't want to take their eye off other more important matters in order to rescue him from drowning. We want our friend safely back in the boathouse, tucked up out of harm's way and we think you're the man to do it. That's simple enough, isn't it?'

I recognized the fixer's language. Nothing was ever what it seemed, and I didn't need an interpreter to work out what Iredale was telling me. Watson-Jones was up to something and neither Charlie nor I knew anything about it. In the pursuit of whatever it was he was after, he had upset the people Iredale worked for. They had to be powerful, otherwise why bring in Iredale to offer me bribes? This put Watson-Jones's unnamed action, his 'rowing in someone else's pond', in a more serious light. What could he have done? Why had Iredale fixed on me as the man to get his friends off the hook? Who were the 'people he represented'?

'I've got some questions,' I said.

'I don't promise to answer anything.'

'Why attack Watson-Jones in print?' I was sure Iredale was behind the Naismith article. 'What did you hope to gain?'

'The bloody fool wouldn't listen to warnings.' Iredale's laugh was contemptuous. 'God knows, we dropped enough hints but he still wouldn't clear off our patch.'

'So Naismith's piece is a shot across the bows?'

'We're way past that stage.' He drew heavily on his cigarette. 'Our guns are trained on the waterline. If we shoot, Watson-Jones sinks. Do I make myself clear?'

There was no mistaking the threat in his voice. I still had no idea what was going on, but I wasn't about to reveal my confusion to Iredale.

'If Watson-Jones were with us now, he'd be very surprised to hear he's upset anyone. He's completely unaware of any warnings.'

'Don't be naive, man,' Iredale said. 'He knows damn well what he's doing and what he hopes to gain from it and so do you. For all I know this may have been your idea in the first place.'

'It would be a mistake to overestimate my role,' I said.

'I can tell you this,' Iredale said, stubbing out his cigarette. 'We want your man to pack his tent and bugger off. Either you remove him or we do. Right now I'm giving you a choice. But I'm not known for my patience.' He fixed his cold expression on me once more. 'The only question that remains unresolved is whether or not you're a man of the world, Stevens. My people hope we can do business.'

Slowly Iredale was putting his cold hands around my throat and beginning to squeeze. There was little I could do about it.

'What needs to be kept quiet? You're going to have to give me more ammunition if you want to get Watson-Jones to move.'

I could see the calculation Iredale was making. How far did he have to take me into his trust in order to keep the dialogue going? Before he spoke again he engaged in his curious habit of looking round the room. He spotted a friend by the window and waved to him.

'There are some strange goings-on in the Soviet Union at the moment, events we don't fully understand. Are we witnessing the natural restlessness of a repressive regime or real signs of revolt? Are there positive signs of change we should encourage or do we wait and see? All very delicate. Then up pops Watson-Jones making a hell of a lot of noise while we're listening to hear a pin drop. I'm sure you've got the drift. So I ask my question again. What's your price?'

'When it comes to decisions like that,' I said, 'I'm the monkey, not the organ-grinder.'

'If I thought that were true I wouldn't be wasting my time here.'

For every avenue I closed off, Iredale opened another. He was a formidable opponent.

'I'm not sure I can deliver the answers you want.'

'Good God, man, what's the matter with you?' He was getting impatient. 'We can't afford to let Watson-Jones bugger this thing up. If you don't do something damn quick, we will. In matters like this, my people lack finesse.'

'Who are your people?'

'I am sure you can respect their anonymity.'

I was being warned off questioning him too closely.

'I'll speak to Watson-Jones.'

'That's not the answer I came for.'

'It's the only answer you're going to get,' I said with more aggression than I'd intended.

'I'm disappointed, Stevens. I had hoped for more. I think we've made you a fair offer.'

'Perhaps you haven't got anything I want,' I said. 'Perhaps my price is beyond your reach.'

'Coffee?' He folded his napkin. I took it as a gesture of dismissal. Lunch was over. 'What they laughingly describe as coffee here.'

'No thank you.'

Iredale called for the bill.

'When you rang the office this morning, you asked for Charlie,' I said. 'You knew he wouldn't be there, didn't you?'

'Yes,' he said, smiling for the first time. It was an empty smile, a contraction of the muscles around his mouth that showed his teeth. 'I wanted to speak to you.'

That told me Iredale's people, whoever they were, knew Charlie and probably knew him well.

'Why not Charlie?' I asked. 'He's the boss.'

'Charlie's dying. You've got Watson-Jones's ear. You're the man in the hot seat now.' He signed the bill with a flourish of an unrecognizable signature. 'Think it over, Stevens.' He took a card out of his wallet and gave it to me. 'Call me when you've something to say. My people have got itchy fingers and they're resting on the trigger. We both know where the gun is pointed. I wouldn't take too long about it if I were you.'

★

The resilience that I so much admired in Sylvia Carr appeared to have vanished when I showed up at her flat that evening. She was gloomy and undeniably if not seriously drunk. Her speech was slurred, and she made no attempt to get off the sofa.

'You made me look under a number of stones, Danny,' she said. 'I hated what I found there. If I'd known that was going to happen I'd never have agreed.'

As she talked I began to get some sense of the depth of her feelings. She was drinking to take the edge off them.

'Something's going on. I don't know what it is, no one will tell me, though I do know you were right about Naismith. He doesn't count. What frightens me is David Iredale's involvement. That's bad news.'

'Tell me about Iredale,' I said.

'Friend to the rich and infamous. Surely you've heard of him?'

'I've been babysitting in Berlin,' I said. 'Before that I was away fighting a war.'

'Old Scottish landed family,' Sylvia said. 'Claims kinship with Robert the Bruce, or someone like that. Very well connected. More money than he knows what to do with. Sits on boards and advises people. Runs the estate in his spare time. Had a good war behind the lines in the desert, then did some shady things in Yugoslavia. Numerous wives and lady friends. Fidelity is not one of David's virtues. Generally regarded as not someone to tangle with, which being translated means avoid at all costs. A hateful man.'

'He gave me lunch today,' I said.

'Oh, Danny.' For a moment I thought she was going to burst into tears. She recovered herself quickly. 'Then he must have wanted something pretty badly. He's not known for his generosity.'

'It was an awful lunch.'

'Did he talk about Simon?'

'Yes.'

'What did he say?'

'He tried to bribe me to stop Simon doing whatever he's doing.'

'What is Simon doing?'

'I'd feel a lot happier if I had a clue, but I don't.'

289

'Listen to him, Danny. Do what he says.' There was an unexpected urgency in her voice. Her mind was concentrating now, grappling with the effects of the alcohol. 'Get Simon out of Iredale's clutches and have done with him. Do it as fast as you can.'

'Are you warning me off?'

'Iredale's friends call him in to do their dirty work when they want something fixed. Powerful men make dangerous enemies. If Simon's upset someone badly enough to bring David Iredale in, then he's in real trouble.' She beckoned me over to sit on the sofa beside her. She took my hand.

'Don't underestimate Iredale, Danny. He comes from a world you've never even imagined. I know him, you don't. He's an evil man. The best thing is do what he wants and get out.'

In her attempt to paint for me a picture of Iredale as she knew him, she'd lost herself in her memories. 'I know his second wife, Joan. She came round to my flat very late one night after they'd had a terrible row. She looked fine until I gave her a bath. He's one of those wife-beaters who never touches the face. I won't describe what her body looked like. She didn't cry. In fact, she hardly spoke. She was frozen, terrified by the experience. No one knew about it, of course. She wouldn't let me tell a soul. Iredale sued her for divorce, claimed she'd been sleeping with other men, and got away with it too, the bastard. I shall never forget what the judge said. "Lady Iredale's behaviour suggests she is unsuited to the state of marriage." Never a word against her husband. Who says it's not a man's world.'

'Are you saying he fixed the judge?'

'David told me afterwards he remembered him from school.'

I questioned her as much as I could but I got little more than a repetition of the warning that I should go along with what Iredale wanted. I had a strong sense that she knew more than she was telling me, though what she was holding back and why I had no idea. Was it possible that she'd had a relationship with Iredale at some point? I dismissed the thought because she gave me no evidence to support it. Iredale, she told me, was a man without any moral sense, and once he had his claws in me he'd never let go until he'd got what he wanted. I was an outsider and I should avoid a world whose rules and conventions I neither knew nor would ever understand.

'I'm standing in the way between Iredale and Simon,' I told her. 'My problem is I don't know what Simon's done, which means I can't meet Iredale's demands.'

If it was going to get rough, it was pretty clear who would be hurt.

'Poor you, Danny. Poor Simon. He may deserve it but you don't.'

As I walked home I felt out of my depth. I had been swept up into events over which I had no control, but where I played some kind of central role. A straight fight I could understand. But guerrilla warfare, where the issues were cloudy to say the least, I was untrained for. The trouble was, I couldn't see any way out. My only choice was to put myself through a rapid process of adaptation so that I was ready for whatever happened. I hoped I was up to it.

13

RUTH

Elizabeth Markarova has her handkerchief pressed tightly to her mouth. Gromsky is weeping openly. Alexei Tomasov is stunned, white-faced and immobile. No one speaks. On the table in front of them lie black and white photographs: a country scene in winter, trees and fields, the last ribs of snow wasting slowly away, a collapsed wigwam of broken-off branches in a clearing, an area of recently turned earth, a hole dug in the ground, three eyeless female heads, the rotting skulls of elderly women still with their headscarves neatly in place, a heap of brass cartridges, a makeshift cross. Beside the photographs lies a map and sheet of paper on which has been typed a list of names with numbers against them.

'This is the dossier,' Pavel Lykowski says. 'The evidence of the crime.'

'There can be no doubt?' Gromsky murmurs. Elizabeth Markarova sobs loudly.

'None.'

'I went with Pavel,' Ruth says. 'I saw it all with my own eyes. As much as I could stomach.'

'How many on the list?' Tomasov asks.

'Sixty-eight.'

'That many?'

'Sixty-eight elderly men and women. They did not die in a fire. They were driven from their beds one freezing February night to be shot in the back in a field many miles from Moscow, for no reason other than they lived near the laboratory where we conduct our nuclear research. They were slaughtered in cold blood.'

Ruth has said nothing to Andropov of her discovery of the mass grave. He has no idea she has seen the darkened and disintegrating faces of the dead. Why hasn't she told him? Why hasn't she con-

292

fronted him with the evidence? She is frightened that if she tells him what she knows he will remove his protection from her. And then what? She doesn't dare to imagine the consequences. She feels hollow, emptied by the sense of betrayal that overwhelms her. There is nothing left of her own life now. She is Andropov's creature.

'How did you discover this, Pavel?' Gromsky asks. 'How did you know where to look?'

'Why do you want to know?' Lykowski asks.

'Give me an answer.'

'I seduced a young soldier,' Lykowski says. 'A little kindness in a brutal world and a bottle of vodka. He was there when it happened. He told me everything. Are you satisfied now?'

Gromsky looks away, unsure whether to believe Lykowski. It is not a statement he would have made himself. Ruth knows it is true because Pavel confessed it to her.

'He was a boy,' Pavel told her. 'Seventeen, eighteen, no more. He said it was like killing your grandparents. He wanted to run away, to hide, but there was nowhere to go and they would have shot him anyway. He fired in the air, he told me, over their heads – he couldn't bring himself to kill anyone. Do you know why? He'd never fired a rifle before; he was a cook in a tank regiment, he'd come back to Moscow early to help prepare the barracks for his regiment who were returning from a tour of duty in Berlin.'

They were roused from their sleeping quarters at midnight, marched off to waiting lorries and given orders to round up the old people in the apartment block. It was bad enough driving them through the freezing night to an empty killing ground in the middle of nowhere. The grave had been carefully prepared, he said, a dark trench at the side of a field. Then they had to separate the men and women and shoot them in the back. A few weeks later the boy killed himself.

'We may have the evidence of the crime,' Tomasov says, 'but we're no closer to knowing who was responsible for what happened.'

'A colonel from Military Intelligence was present. I have a description. He watched the event from beginning to end.' Lykowski searches his pockets for a piece of paper, unwraps it and starts to read. 'Medium height, thirty or thereabouts, thin, sandy hair, quite good-looking in a drained sort of way, poor eyesight.'

'How do you know that?' Gromsky asks.

'He has tinted lenses in his spectacles.'

Andropov was there that night. He witnessed the execution. Perhaps he gave the order to shoot them.

'It won't be difficult to find him,' Lykowski says.

'If we bother to look,' Gromsky says.

'Of course we will look.'

'Why?' Gromsky asks. Lykowski has given him the opportunity he has been looking for. He can turn his distress into anger against the younger man.

'We can't let a crime of this nature go unpunished.'

'It's not our job to bring men like that to justice. We're scientists, not policemen.'

'We are involved in their murder . . . in some way we are culpable.' There is silence. Lykowski's sense of guilt is not shared.

'Say we find him, then what?' Elizabeth Markarova asks.

'Then we will try him, find him guilty and execute him.'

Ruth freezes. Whatever she may feel about Andropov now, she cannot possibly let that happen. They must not imitate the behaviour of their oppressors. Somehow she must divert Lykowski.

'This intelligence officer, whoever he may be, is not our enemy,' she says calmly. 'We must not let Pavel's evidence divert us from our cause. These people are dead. We cannot bring them back to life. Our task now is to stop the slaughter of future generations.'

'Do we let murderers go free?' Lykowski asks. 'Is that the morality of this new world we're risking our lives for?'

'One life, sixty lives, a thousand even. These numbers are meaningless compared to the devastation we have discussed. A million lives. Ten million. A hundred million. That is what we have to stop. The death of the planet.'

'Ruth's right,' Gromsky says. 'We have a greater responsibility. In the total scheme of things, these deaths are meaningless.'

'If one life is not important,' Lykowski says angrily, 'how can a million lives have any meaning at all?'

The issue is discussed. Are they to pursue the murderer, the evidence of whose crime Pavel has so cleverly uncovered? The rules of procedure that Ruth and Elizabeth Markarova have drawn up decree that any issue on which opinion is seriously divided must be discussed and an agreement reached. If they cannot agree unanimously, then only a decision with a two-thirds majority may be adopted.

Ruth stares at Lykowski, trying to catch his eye, make him respond to her silent plea. Do nothing. Say nothing. Please do as I ask. To her relief and surprise, he suddenly climbs down and they agree that it is not their duty to avenge the deaths of the old people by tracking down their murderer. They must stick to the agenda they have set themselves.

At first Ruth feels an intense relief, an overwhelming warmth of gratitude to Pavel who has rescued her from her dilemma. The procedure she set up has worked well; the committee remains intact, their aims still holding them together. Then, insidiously, her anxiety returns. She is haunted by the pale, brooding figure of Lykowski, the young man who has discovered so much, who secretly, she knows, cannot stop now. Lykowski will continue his search until he finds Andropov, and then he will confront him with the evidence of the crime. At that moment, it will be left to chance whether Lykowski finds out about her before Andropov tells him.

*

They meet again within forty-eight hours. By now their horror at the crime has given way to anger. If they cannot take justice into their own hands (and that decision holds, there are no second thoughts), then they must do something for the cause they so strongly believe in and for which they are risking so much. In their minds the faces of the dead women and the dying of Hiroshima become one, innocent people who have died unnecessarily. There are countless others ready to be saved.

'Our actions have achieved a brief delay to our nuclear programme,' Elizabeth Markarova says, expressing the feelings of the group. 'A few months, possibly a year – certainly no more. Though we remain unscathed, we must not forget that while our cause has found a convenient expression in our actions, we have won no concessions, we have engaged in no debate either with our own directorate or any political authority. We have stopped nothing. To the world the doors of the Institute remain closed. Our triumph is to have survived this far. But it could all end tomorrow if the authorities choose to move against us. We must use what little power we have before it is removed from us. Somehow we must widen our cause, gain support, to ensure not only that it survives but that it succeeds. We must do all we can to make sure there is no Soviet bomb.'

Andropov could have written those words, Ruth thinks, with

relief. Could Elizabeth be working for Andropov too? Surely not.

'What do you suggest we do?' Lykowski asks. There is a challenge in his voice that alarms Ruth. He is a victim to moods that make him impossible to read.

'We must smuggle your evidence to the West,' Elizabeth Markarova says. 'Let them look at your photographs and understand the true nature of our government.'

Elizabeth Markarova is suggesting a complete change of approach, Ruth says. There are great dangers in moving out of the arena which they know and over which they have control. Protest is one thing. International politics is another.

'I agree that the West should know of our protest and the humanitarian nature of our cause,' Gromsky says. 'But to engage in any political act would be wrong. That would give our government the excuse they may be waiting for to repress us. I oppose your course of action.'

Tomasov shares his view. 'Our protest is about the dangers inherent in the production and political management of nuclear weapons. That is what we must stick to because we know more about this than anything. We are the experts. That is our strength. If we attempt anything else we will weaken our case and confuse the argument.'

There is a sombre mood in the room, brought on by Elizabeth Markarova's proposal. She wants to take them further than they are willing to go.

'Our argument,' Gromsky says, looking for a compromise, 'is with the Central Committee, no one else. The only way we can reach them is through the director of this Institute. We must persuade him to be our ambassador, to put our case to higher authorities.'

Elizabeth Markarova reminds them that the Institute's director is a scientist appointed by political masters. Why should he show similar courage in opposing the nuclear programme from which he derives not only his position but so many other benefits as well?

Pavel Lykowski proposes a revision to Markarova's plan.

'Elizabeth is right when she says we must gather greater support for our cause. Support within the Soviet Union is impossible. We must approach the international scientific community to put pressure on our government on this single issue. Our objective must be to get representatives from the West to negotiate directly with the Supreme Soviet. We have no place in that process. We cannot offer political bargains; we do not have that kind of power. Our power is our knowledge, that is what we must use. We must hope that the news of our dissent will excite sufficient response in the West.'

It is Lykowski's most considered response. Ruth wonders what has prompted the quietening of his tone. She gives her support because she knows that is what Andropov would want her to do. Her task is to maintain the protest and to keep the resistance going.

How will they get their message to the West? Tomasov asks.

'I will be going to the Helsinki conference in May,' Elizabeth Markarova says. 'I would expect to meet many Western scientists there. I will be able to put our case to them.'

'I didn't know a final decision on the Helsinki delegates had been taken yet,' Ruth says, rounding on her. She is horrified by what Elizabeth has said. She has always imagined she would go to Helsinki. For some reason she is certain Stevens will be there. Now it would seem she has lost her chance. 'I understood there was at least a week before we would hear any definite news.'

'The director informed me yesterday. He is deciding on whether to send any others in the next few days.'

Elizabeth Markarova has made a mistake. She has alienated the committee by raising an unnecessary question in everyone's mind. What was she doing speaking to the director?

Ruth knows that Elizabeth has sensed the sudden hostility of the group. What will she do? Any lengthy explanation of her actions will be seen as an admission of guilt. Best to ignore it. Tomasov comes unexpectedly to her aid.

'Elizabeth is as competent as any of us to put our case resolutely to our Western colleagues. She will, I am sure, speak with great conviction.'

A difficult moment passes. She is left battered by Elizabeth's unexpected challenge. There is a lesson in it. She must assume that she is automatically the leader in all aspects of the group. That means she must go in Elizabeth's place. She must speak to Andropov. She must put her case to a murderer.

14

DANNY

We sat at the table in Charlie's office, Watson-Jones, Gelfmann, Charlie and myself. The morning sun poured through the window with dazzling intensity, bringing everything into sharp relief. Gelfmann was sweating and wiping his brow and the top of his head with a handkerchief. Charlie had been allowed back to the office on the understanding that Beryl would see Thomas took him home at lunchtime. He was still exhausted, the doctor said, and he looked far from himself. Watson-Jones sat at the head, his back to the sun. He cast a long shadow down the centre of the table.

The office was stifling even though the window was open. I could see into the rooms on the other side of the street: an old man pouring himself a cup of tea, a woman in a white housecoat making a bed. From below came the sounds of cars and people passing. Dimly, through the closed door, we could hear the clack of Beryl's typewriter. The world outside was going about its business. Ours was trying to discover whether it had a future or not.

The meeting had been called as a council of war but it was rapidly turning into a council of despair. I had described my conversation with Iredale. It had not been received well, Simon furious at the unheralded intervention of a man he disliked and, I suspected, probably feared. Charlie's line was that until we knew why Iredale was in the frame, there was precious little we could do. That wasn't what Watson-Jones had come to hear.

'Where does that leave me, Charlie?' he asked, leaning back in his chair, his eyes closed as if in pain. 'Up a creek without a paddle.'

If this was nothing more than a performance, then it was clear how high the stakes were that Watson-Jones was playing for. I wondered how long he'd get away with it.

'You'll have to sit on your hands until we know what brought Iredale in,' Charlie said. 'We're working on that now.'

'Pulling up at the first fence looks like a loss of nerve, Charlie,' he said. 'I can't afford to do that. This is a test I've got to pass.'

'We don't yet know what we're up against,' Charlie said. 'It's pointless to retaliate till we know who we're fighting and what we're fighting about.'

'I want a plan, Charlie. I won't accept doing nothing without a plan.'

'I haven't got a plan, Simon. That's what I keep telling you. I don't have any plan at all.' This was the first time Charlie had raised his voice with Watson-Jones, an indication of how angry he was.

'That won't do, Charlie. It won't do at all.'

Charlie was hurt by that. I saw the tension in his face as he struggled to keep his temper. I saw the strain sweep through his body like a wave.

'I've said my piece, Simon. You know where I stand. There's nothing more I can add.'

'Damn it, Charlie, you're leaving me to drown! You can't do that.' Watson-Jones hit the table with the flat of his hand. He was shouting. Outside, the sound of the typewriter stopped. 'I'm paying you to manage this crisis and the only proposal you come up with is do nothing. Well, that isn't good enough. You can't abdicate responsibility because it suits you.'

'That's a bit hard, Simon,' Gelfmann said.

'Keep out of this, Bernard.'

'If I knew what kind of trouble you were in, Simon, I'd be ready to help. But I don't. I'm baffled, mystified. Something's gone wrong but I don't know what it is. I've got to know more before I can propose any course of action. Anything else is sheer folly.'

'For God's sake.' Watson-Jones was dismissive. 'This isn't the Charlie Faulkner I know. What's happened to you? Lost your nerve all of a sudden?'

'Simon, please,' Gelfmann said. This time his remark went unnoticed.

'One man, Charlie. That's all it took. That bastard Iredale sticks his oar in and you're cowering in the corner with your hands over your eyes. That's not like you, is it?'

He was softening up on Charlie now, trying to bring him back on his side. I could see it was having no effect.

'Iredale's a dangerous man, Simon. His appearance has changed the game. We're on a different pitch now, playing by different rules. I'd like to find out what those rules are before I'll agree to join in.'

'Perhaps he's acting for himself on this one,' Simon said.

'That's not Iredale's style. He's acting for others. Who are they? What do they want and why? Too many questions needing answers, Simon. That's the difficulty at the moment.'

'Iredale's powerful,' Gelfmann said. 'And dangerous.'

'Iredale beats his wives and sleeps with young girls, minors,' Watson-Jones said crossly. 'Why the hell does that make you all so afraid of him?'

It was the opportunity Charlie had been waiting for, though now it had come he barely had the strength left to take it.

'We can look after ourselves, Simon. It's you we worry about.'

'Me? Why?' Charlie's remark seemed to take him aback.

'You've been set up, Simon. Why and by whom I don't know. But you're in someone's sights and we can assume they're powerful because Iredale's in the frame. You must have done something serious to upset them. My advice is, until we know more, be careful. You don't have to listen to me. You can go to damnation your own sweet way. You're the one at risk, not me. All I can do is tell you what I think.'

We waited in silence while Watson-Jones thought about what Charlie had said.

'I'm sorry, Charlie. I've been hasty. You're right. Tread carefully. Quicksand. Point taken.'

'Quicksand,' Gelfmann said. 'Treacherous.'

Charlie looked relieved. He'd got through to Watson-Jones at last. It had been a struggle and no doubt he would pay the price for it. He was like a damaged cliff before a raging sea. Each day a bit more fell off into the water. For the first time I began to wonder how much longer Charlie would last.

★

Over the next two days I hardly saw Charlie and when I did he was preoccupied. I asked Beryl what was going on.

'Meetings, that's all he says. All these years together and he won't talk to me when there's trouble.'

Beryl took refuge from my questions in the familiar defence of a woman ignored. It was a transparent disguise but an effective one because it was so hard to counter. We both knew that she was fully aware of what was going on, but if Charlie wanted me to know he would tell me in his own time. That was his job, not hers. Charlie had no secrets from Beryl, which gave her great power. But she used her power sparingly, and it was never worth pushing her if she didn't want to reveal what she knew. Her loyalty to Charlie came before everything.

I had grown genuinely fond of her in the time we'd worked together. I enjoyed listening to her stories of the start of the war when she and Charlie came to London from Manchester. Charlie had been one of a number of successful businessmen who were asked to join the war effort by bringing their expertise to Whitehall. He had been seconded to the Ministry of Supply. Politics became a late love affair in his life. He had sold his chain of shops, moved into Belgrave Square and for years had lived and breathed the political atmosphere he had come to love so much. His wife hated London. She remained in Manchester. Charlie never mentioned her.

'I don't think they could understand his accent, dear, it was that broad then,' Beryl told me, describing the early days. 'Of course, it's softened a great deal since. Charlie always was a quick learner,' she added, laughing.

We all knew, though Charlie pretended not to, that Beryl had devoted her life to a man she loved but couldn't marry. She mothered him instead, and he responded to it and in their way they were both happy. It wasn't the relationship Beryl had hoped for but she had decided years before to settle for what she could get and that was a lot more of Charlie than anyone else got, including his wife. In our idle moments, we would speculate on whether or not Charlie and Beryl had slept together. Opinion was divided. It remained an open question.

'When do you expect him back?' I asked.

'He said he'd be here by nine-thirty. Look at the time – after ten. Heaven knows what's keeping him.'

The Rolls appeared ten minutes later but when I rang Beryl, she said that Charlie didn't want to see anyone until after lunch. I had hardly put the telephone down when he rang me himself.

'Come up, Danny, will you?'

I was concerned at his appearance. He had lost weight in the last week or two, and his complexion was greyer than before. Even in his wheelchair he seemed bent, older, more worn. Beryl brought him in a cup of tea and then stood behind Charlie shaking her head at me. I gathered the meeting hadn't gone well and I shouldn't bring up the subject.

'Beryl,' he said, putting down his tea. 'Take this disgusting liquid away, will you? I want a large gin and I'm sure Danny does too. Don't tell me it's too early because it isn't.'

Beryl gave a show of disapproval but Charlie ignored her.

'This conversation is between the two of us,' he said as soon as she had closed the door. 'Beryl knows everything. But nothing to the boys for the moment, agreed?'

'Of course.'

'Something's up,' he said. 'Something serious.'

'I'd guessed that.'

'I had breakfast this morning with Willy Glover, he's Gaydon's permanent under-secretary. It was his invitation. He asked me straight out what game Simon was playing, what he was after. I played innocent and said I had no idea. Glover didn't believe me and said so pointedly because it's my job to know what Simon's doing. He said his Minister was very unhappy and he passed on what he called an unsanctioned request, adviser to adviser, to lower the flame on this one. I've no doubt he was acting under instruction.'

'Lower the flame on what?' I asked.

Charlie looked up at me startled. In his head he had debated the issue with me, we had talked about it, I was fully briefed. Now I was in his presence he had forgotten that he had told me nothing.

'Forgive me. I'm sorry.' He put his head in his hands for a moment. 'Simon's been hunting on his own.'

'Working without us?'

'Or despite us. Suit yourself.'

'What's he done?'

A week or two ago, he said, Simon had written to the Minister, an event Charlie had known nothing about. He claimed he had learned the identity of a British scientist who was betraying nuclear secrets to the Soviets and that the government had known about this for months and done nothing. Gaydon had replied privately, denying the story and hoping that would see the end of the issue.

'In the jargon,' Charlie explained, 'Gaydon was saying stay off my patch.'

Simon either didn't get the message or he ignored it. Whatever, he wrote again, this time increasing the pressure.

'Glover thinks I put him up to it, when in fact Simon's deliberately kept me in the dark because he knows I'd never have agreed to anything like at. It's sheer folly and quite wrong.'

I began to see a picture emerging. Watson-Jones, unhappy with the unexpected coolness of Charlie's anti-Soviet stance, had got hold of damaging information which he'd decided to act on himself. For reasons Charlie didn't understand, Simon must have hit nearer the bone than he'd imagined. He'd been given 'keep off' warnings – enter Naismith – which he'd chosen not to see. Iredale the bully boy had been called in to leave Watson-Jones in no doubt about what would happen if he didn't lay off.

'Simon's swimming out of his depth on this one,' Charlie said. 'Glover made that all too clear.'

'What gave you that impression?'

'Glover said these are delicate times. A lot of difficult decisions have to be made. The options are being narrowed but at this precise moment no one wants Watson-Jones rocking the boat. There's more at stake than he could disclose.'

No doubt Glover had tapped his nose and good old faithful Charlie had believed him because he always believed what people like Glover told him. What a loyal, old-fashioned ally Charlie was, I thought, and how they were exploiting him. A bit of pressure from 'up there' and he could be relied upon to do the right thing. How they must despise him.

'Glover would know about these things,' Charlie added.

'Indeed,' I said, not believing a word that Glover had told him. But I couldn't say that to him, it would break the old man's heart.

Charlie slowly pieced together what he imagined had happened. Watson-Jones had got hold of this traitor story from somewhere – 'his American connections probably' – and he had decided to use this inside knowledge to put his career firmly on the map by exposing it. He'd asked the Minister a string of awkward questions. In Charlie's book that was wrong. Spies were secret, whether ours or theirs. Simon was muscling in on someone else's game. MPs had to recognize there were limits to their powers too.

Charlie had become so politicized by his years in Whitehall that he was automatically on the side of the advisers. Whatever the colour of the government, you didn't question the impartiality of the administrative services, he would say. They ran the place. They got things done. They knew more than the rest of us and quite right too, they were meant to. They were above reproach. That was not a school of thought Simon recognized.

I guessed too that Charlie's nose was out of joint because he had not been consulted. Simon had acted on his own, 'on an impulse', as Charlie said, one of his heavier condemnations. His protégé, the man whose career he had set himself to manage, was seeing Charlie in a different, perhaps dispensable, light. Charlie's political child was learning to stand on his own two feet and develop a mind of his own, and Charlie didn't like that.

'Of course, he's got to make his own mistakes,' he was saying. 'We can't protect him from that. Nor should we. There's no substitute for experience in politics, knowing how far you can go, where to draw the line, all that. But you don't cut your teeth on issues as sensitive as this. That's just plain stupid.'

Charlie was an old stag, weakened by the wounds of time, hanging on to power against the new challenger. I felt sorry for him. But I couldn't see he was going to win on this one.

★

'Supper ready.'

It was Esther calling from the kitchen. I was at the bottom of the stairs when the telephone rang.

'Have you eaten?' Monty asked.

'I'm about to.'

'I'll buy you dinner.'

'I'm eating with the Lemans.'

'I need to see you, Danny. I'll join you.'

'There won't be enough.'

'We can stretch it to four,' Esther called. There was no privacy in this house at all.

'I'll bring something,' Monty said. 'I'll be there in five minutes.'

He arrived breathless and carrying a brown paper bag from which he emptied Cheddar cheese, oranges and a portion of butter. He sat down with us in Esther's kitchen to eat Esther's stew. Whatever he wanted to say to me could clearly wait until he had eaten.

'We all here have something in common,' Manny said. 'You know what?' We shook our heads. 'Cambridge,' he laughed. 'That's what.'

'Their son is at John's,' I explained to Monty. 'Reading Russian.'

Manny shook his head. 'I learn Russian from my father and now

304

our Joe he learn it from professors at Cambridge. Life is strange, no?'

'Only you didn't learn it,' Esther said. 'That's why your father always disappointed in you.'

'I never learn because my father no good teacher. Not like Danny's father. That's why our Joe go to Cambridge. Cambrige is the best, no?' He laughed again.

'Tell us what it was like when you boys were there,' Esther said. 'I like to hear these stories.'

I had had this conversation with her many times before. Cambridge was a mythical city in her imagination. She had never been there and would probably never go.'

'No, that not a place for people like us,' she had said to me once. 'Joe don't want us around. We not good enough for him now. He got his own life there. We leave him be.'

Joe was the joy of their lives, the boy who broke the mould, who had left them to live in another world of which they could only dream. The fact that Monty and I had been brought up there meant we were part of her myth too. Cambridge was where people like us came from. I tried to dissuade her from thinking like this but it didn't work.

'We grew up together,' Monty said. 'We've known each other for more than twenty years. His father's a professor and mine's a shopkeeper.'

'Like me,' Manny grinned. 'I own a shop.'

'Like you, yes.'

'My boy, maybe he end up professor like your dad.' Manny thought that was a huge joke and laughed loudly. 'He don't go to Cambridge to come back here and mend shoes like his dad.'

'Now you work in London, always together,' Esther said. 'Very nice.'

'What you do for a living, Monty?' Manny asked. He could never keep his curiosity down for long. Esther was making noises in the background but he took no notice.

'Me? I keep an eye on the Russians here, make sure they behave, don't break the rules, don't steal our secrets, that sort of thing.' I had never known him to be so open.

'A policeman without the clothes,' Manny said. 'What do you call that in English?'

'Manny,' Esther said disapprovingly.

305

'You chasing dirty Russian spies around the country, eh? That makes me sleep good at nights. We don't want no Soviet bastards here. Where do you go, then? I bet you go to Cambridge. That's where all these professors are, like Danny's dad, all these men who make these bombs. I bet you go there to make sure they safe, yes? No bloody Reds under their beds, eh?'

When supper was over Esther pushed us upstairs out of her way. She always insisted on doing the dishes by herself while Manny read the paper and listened to the news on the wireless.

'Have you seen your father recently?' Monty asked, helping himself to my whisky. I recognized the tone of voice. This was Monty the interrogator, Monty the spycatcher, the Monty who only got in touch when he needed something. The man who had cornered me when he came to Berlin was on duty again tonight.

'No. Why?'

'He's gone to Helsinki to speak at a scientific conference.'

I didn't find that hard to explain, I said. My father spent much of his life speaking at conferences.

'While he's there he's expected to meet a Russian scientist called Ruth Marchenko.' No explanation of how he knew.

'That doesn't surprise me,' I said. 'He knows Marchenko.'

'What do you know about her?' he asked.

'They met years ago, long before the war. Marchenko works in the same field of nuclear physics as my father. If she's going to be at this conference too, I'd be surprised if they didn't bump into each other.'

'There's nothing casual about this. We understand she asked for the meeting.'

'Maybe she saw his name on the list of delegates before he saw hers, and she wants to see him again.'

'Your father submitted his name to the conference organizers at the very last minute. His name isn't on any published list. We think he did that deliberately.'

'How on earth do you know Marchenko wants to meet him?'

'You know I'm not going to tell you that.' The atmosphere between us was suddenly strained. 'You don't seem surprised,' he said.

'Why should I be?'

'British nuclear scientist meets Russian nuclear scientist. That doesn't strike you as odd?'

'If he's going to a conference and there are Russians there, I am sure he will meet them.'

'It's unlikely there's an innocent explanation for this meeting. The Soviets don't work like that. We're worried for your father's safety.'

'Helsinki's neutral territory, unlike Moscow. They can't touch him there.'

'Don't be naive, Danny. The Soviets can do what they like in Finland. They could kidnap your father, blackmail him, murder him, if they so chose.'

'If you're so worried for his safety, get your people to look after him while he's there. Isn't that what you're paid to do? So we can sleep safe in our beds at night?'

The irony was wasted on him. I should have remembered, it's something he's never reacted to.

'I thought you might like to do that.'

'Do what?' I couldn't believe what I was hearing. 'Go to Helsinki?'

'It's lovely at this time of year and you've got reasons for wanting to be there, haven't you?'

How he knew about Tanya was beyond me. There must have been a follow-up to my visit I knew nothing about, or I'd been watched closely while I was there.

'That's got nothing to do with your outfit,' I said furiously.

'Your father's in deep trouble, Danny. I can't say any more than that. I'm trying to help him. I'm asking you to go there and stop him meeting Marchenko. What else you get up to while you're there is entirely your business. I don't want to know about it.'

'If you want to stop him, do it yourself, Monty. I'm not your mercenary.'

'We've done all we can. Your father won't listen to us.'

Outside the light had vanished. The evening had become unnaturally dark, a blanket of blue-black cloud having descended, crushing the heat in. It was very close. Occasionally there was a light rumble of thunder in the background. We were in for a storm.

'It's too hot to argue and this is too serious to fight about,' Monty said. 'We may not be able to prevent your father going to Helsinki, but the meeting with Marchenko mustn't happen. It's too risky. We think he might listen to you.'

'When did he ever do that?'

'Tell him we think the Russians want him.'

'What for?'

'What he knows, presumably.'

'You don't mean they're going to kidnap him, do you?' The whole idea was preposterous.

'Listen to me, damn it! We know he's a target of the Soviet intelligence services. In some way they're out to disable him. I'm begging you, Danny. He's in great danger and he's completely unaware of it. You have to bring him out of there before it's too late.'

★

The account of the fire in Watson-Jones's house in South Street was short and to the point. It had been discovered at two in the morning, the fire brigade had rescued Watson-Jones and his wife Meredith by ladder from their top-floor bedroom. Neither had been injured. There was extensive damage to the ground floor, with a number of family possessions feared destroyed. What had caused the fire remained a mystery.

I was out of the country when it happened and didn't learn about it until long afterwards.

★

I arrived in Helsinki on a beautiful midsummer morning. What surprised me was not the blueness of the sky nor the calmness of the sea but the soft wind, full of warmth, that blew lightly off the water as we approached the harbour. The city I remembered as cold and in darkness was now warm, light. It was an extraordinary transformation.

I walked up the street from the harbour, carrying my jacket, my few belongings in my army haversack. I saw fair-haired, fair-skinned women in summer dresses; I saw tall men with deep-set eyes, some wearing student caps, their arms around the girls, sitting in the cafés and drinking in the bars. The world had come out into the streets, and I sensed a frantic energy, a dedication to absorbing the light which for these people lasted so short a time.

It was not far to Tanya's flat. As I walked up Mannerheimintie, the sunlight and the warmth got to work on me, banishing the doubts that had gathered as I'd watched the islands slip past on my passage up the Baltic. Would she be there? Would she want me? Had she really said she would wait for me? It was too warm a day for disappointment. I climbed the steps and rang her bell. For a moment or two I thought there was no one in. Then I heard someone moving and the door opened and there she was, standing in front of me.

'Danny! Danny!'

She threw her arms around my neck. I had to drop my haversack to prevent myself falling. She kissed me again and again as she dragged me into the apartment. She was wearing a blue dress without sleeves. Her hair was longer than I remembered, her skin darker. But the curves of her body were the same, her eyes just as blue. My memory had not deceived me.

'I cannot believe it. I cannot believe you are here.'

She put her arm through mine and made me sit on the sofa.

'I want to hear everything you have done since I saw you last. Everything.'

'There's nothing to tell.'

'Everything.' She kissed me again, and it was some time before I could speak.

'Did you think I'd come back?' I asked. I wanted to know how sure of me she was.

'I am two people, Danny,' she said. 'For the dreamer in me we have never been apart. But the doctor knows what it is like to be alone. In this country, the winters are very long. You can become very pessimistic in the dark.'

'It's light, the sun is shining and I'm here,' I said.

'This is the best day of my life,' she answered, putting her arms around me again. 'The best. The very best.'

She captured my heart then, in a way she had not done before. What enchanted me was her happiness, her delight in my presence, and I loved her for it because it was something that I alone could give her. On her face I saw the smile that I knew was on my own face, in her arms I felt the excitement in her body that I knew was in my own. I saw in her whole being the reflection of what I had always wanted, and for the first time I believed that it was possible my life could change. It was like the discovery of something you have always known existed but which until now has remained concealed. The moment of discovery is unimaginable. That morning was unimaginable, even though I had dreamed it a thousand times.

She lay against me as we looked out of the window at the blue sky.

'I will not ask why you have come here or how long you can

stay, and for now I do not want to know. It is enough that you came back. For these few days you are mine. I have a boat. Tomorrow we will go to our summer house. This is our secret time and no one will know where we are. We will escape from the world together.'

If you want to escape, there can be no better place than the Finnish lakes, vast expanses of inland waterways peopled with islands, minute havens covered with trees, some uninhabited, some with wooden summer houses set back from narrow beaches. We saw other boats and occasionally other people, but during that time our lives were entirely our own.

Tanya's house itself was built on the banks of a reedy inlet where we moored the boat and was surrounded by birch trees. We carried up the boxes of provisions, unlocked the door and went in. The air inside was dry and warm. We opened the shutters and the windows. Dust particles rose in the shafts of sunlight that poured in. Everything I touched was warm: the cupboards, doors, and, when I took off my shoes, the floors. The wooden building creaked as we moved around, as if it was slowly waking up to our presence.

'When I was younger and I heard these noises,' Tanya said, 'I used to imagine the house was talking to me.' The floor creaked again and she laughed. 'Like an old man stretching after a bad night.'

I stood in the doorway and looked out across the water, clear and still. There was a slight breeze and the branches of the birch trees dipped and brushed their leaves against the side of the house. But I could hear no other sound. We were truly alone. The world was very far away and quite forgotten.

Tanya put her arms around me. 'I used to dream of being here with you,' she said. 'Then I would wake up and fight the dream, in case you never came back. Now, I won't ever have to dream again.'

We spent the morning cleaning the house, scrubbing the floor, wiping the dust of months off the surfaces of everything and washing the windows. When we had finished, Tanya said: 'Time to swim.'

She took off her clothes and ran naked into the water. She swam out to the boat, climbed on board and lay down in the sun.

It never really gets dark at night at that time of year. The light changes at the end of the day, it loses its brightness and the sky becomes a matt blue tinged with yellow. It seems to close in then, in some mysterious way appearing to bring horizons closer, marking each detail, each change of contour coming into sharper relief as the shadows grow. But there is no moment of darkness, no time when the shadows disappear altogether.

We sat on the veranda, watching the light move on the water. We saw wispy plumes of smoke rising from one or two of our neighbouring islands, and we knew that others, like us, were eating outside.

'We used to spend our summers here when we were children,' Tanya said. 'Whole summers, swimming, sailing – can you imagine that? Then the war came and all that ended.'

'Everything was still here, untouched, after the war?'

'Oh yes.' There was no surprise in her voice. 'Nothing had changed. There was more dust, of course, but it was still our house. It had waited patiently for us.'

I wondered whom she had come back with and felt an icy shaft of anxiety. I tried to tell myself that her life before I met her was no concern of mine, but the idea persisted of someone else sitting where I was now, looking out over the same view, with Tanya next to him.

'What was it like, coming back after all that time?'

'Very sad. In the last summer before the war my father had been here with us. Now it was just my brother and myself.' Relief flooded through me. 'Though he has never liked it here.' Doubt again. Perhaps she had not come back with Mika.

'Why not?'

'Mika is restless. He cannot keep still. Here there is nothing to do. He prefers to sail.'

'He left you alone here, did he, sailed off once you'd opened up?'

There was silence between us. A bird rose up from a tree, flapping its wings lazily as it flew off over the lake.

'I wasn't here alone, Danny.' The words I had dreaded. I heard her changing her position in her chair. I felt her hand reach for mine.

'You cannot claim the past,' she said. 'Not the years before I knew you. If I could, I would wish them away. But they are there, a part of me as much as yours are a part of you. I am not sorry for those years. They taught me to know myself and to know what I want. Then I found you. That is all that matters.'

'I'm sorry.'

'Oh,' she said in mock irritation, 'the English sorry again. Are there two of you, Danny, one who says I love you and one who says I'm sorry?'

She laughed at my bewilderment.

'You can ask me what you wish,' she said. 'You can know about me what you want to know. I will always tell you the truth. But why? Why hurt yourself with memories you cannot change? Why look backwards? The past is gone. It is forgotten. Its only value is, it led me here, to you.'

'I know.'

'Then leave it, Danny. Let it go. Let it all swim away into the night.'

For a time I managed to do what she said. I forgot everything and lived in an eternal present with her. We sailed and swam and made love, we talked about each other, what we believed in, what we wanted for our lives. It was a time of discovery for both of us. We never talked about the future and we never mentioned the past. But the world cannot be jettisoned for long. Unknown to us, it had slipped its moorings in the night and every day was drifting slowly but irrevocably towards us.

PART FOUR

1

DANNY

'Professor Stevens? Good morning. Lander. From our embassy here. Welcome to this northern land.'

The voice on the telephone was conspiratorial, as if the relief of discovering our shared nationality in this distant outpost was a comforting secret. We were English, and that set us incontrovertibly apart from the locals. It made us superior, too, but it would be tactless to play on that in front of the poor old Finn.

'We were wondering if you might be free for a drink tonight.'

Monty's instructions had been far from explicit, though he had been clear in his view of the British embassy. 'Avoid them at all costs. Useless lot. We don't want them involved.'

'Very informal,' Lander was saying. 'Just a few Brits and one or two distinguished locals. H. E. would be so pleased. No need to dress.'

'H. E.?'

'His Excellency. The ambassador.'

'That's very kind of you,' I said.

'Shall we say about six then?'

'Thank you.'

'We look forward to it.'

'There's just one thing.'

'Oh yes?'

'My name's Forster, not Stevens.'

William Forster, one of the small British delegation to the Helsinki conference, had fallen ill the week before but his name had been left on the list. Monty had agreed that I could impersonate him in an emergency. 'God knows,' he had said, 'I don't want you anywhere near the Brits. If you have to go into the conference, and I'd rather you didn't, keep your head down and your mouth shut.'

I heard the rustle of paper in the background. Lander was searching for some mention of the name Forster. I was sure it wouldn't feature on the ambassador's list. Forster was Reading, not Oxbridge.

'Here we are,' Lander said, lying through his teeth. 'Forster, William. I'm so sorry. We've got you down for Thursday night.' There was a beguiling smoothness to his resumption of control that I had to admire. 'I'll be in touch again soon. I'll know where to reach you, won't I?'

That was the jolt that set me tumbling headlong into the real world. Monday and ambassadors and distinguished locals for Nobel-prize winning professors, Thursday for the rest – bottles of beer and a second secretary if we were lucky. I was back with the old brigade of hypocrisy, privilege, snobbery and the diamond-edged rules of a game that men like Lander played effortlessly every minute of their waking lives. I had come up against Lander and his kind in the army, and I had never overcome my dislike of them. Monty's view didn't go far enough. Lander wasn't useless. He was pernicious.

The sun streamed into the apartment. I lay back on the sofa, hands behind my head, and closed my eyes. I sought some kind of consolation for my return to civilization by reliving the events of the past few days.

How long had Tanya and I been away? I had no idea, no sense of day or night or the passage of time, only an overwhelming awareness of Tanya, her presence, her body, her laughter, her questions, her uncertainties, her passion and her love as we absorbed each other with an extraordinary desire. We lived in the absoluteness of our involvement with each other, our world bounded by the experience of our selves, what we could touch, what we could feel. All other concerns were ignored and forgotten for those few days because they could neither be touched nor felt by either of us. It was an overwhelming sensation. You cannot live for long in that intensity of feeling, but while you do it is intoxicating.

To others – if there had been any others to see us or care about us – we were one more love affair, one more passionate exchange in thousands of years of passionate exchanges, while the sun rose, blazed overhead, and sank back to hover over the horizon before it rose again in all its glory. There were no days and no nights: I lived by the light in Tanya's eyes, I forgot myself and found myself in one wonderful unending moment. We were obsessed with each other because we had so little time, and in the exercise of that obsession we had no sense of time passing. There is nothing new in the discovery of love except for those who do the discovering. For three whole days we loved each other as if the world was about to end.

Then it was over. The world didn't end. It did what it always does, it reclaimed us.

Tanya had kissed me awake, and we had swum naked in the lake for the last time. We had eaten at the table under the birch tree, closed the shutters and taken down to the boat the boxes that it seemed we had brought ashore only a few hours before. As I watched the house slip from my view, I felt an uncontrollable sadness, tears welling suddenly in my eyes, as I relived all the partings of my life in a single moment.

★

'The Soviet delegation won't arrive until Monday afternoon,' Monty had told me, 'in time for the opening ceremony. We expect March-enko to make contact on Tuesday morning when she'll fix the meeting with your father for Wednesday or Thursday. That gives you forty-eight hours to get your father to pull out of this madcap scheme. If you can't get him to see sense, and I hope to God you can, stick to him like glue. The last two days of the conference are when he'll be at greatest risk.'

My dilemma had been whether or not to tell Tanya what had brought me back to Helsinki.

'Follow your instinct,' Monty had said. 'If you don't want to involve her, say nothing.'

He had been surprisingly unsympathetic to the argument about a relationship built on lies.

'So what? She can't help you if you don't tell her and she can't help you if you do. Let her get on with her doctoring. She doesn't need to know what's going on.'

I wanted to tell Tanya when we went to her island but I didn't know how and I took the coward's way out – I put off the moment, arguing to myself that it would have spoiled everything. She helped me in this, not asking to know why I'd come to Helsinki, simply accepting that I was there. I was a fool to leave it, in more ways than one. It was a betrayal of trust and I should have told her.

I slept after that, and when I awoke it was nearly five and the day had become very hot, the air still and lifeless. I walked down

317

to the harbour. I passed the *Havis Amanada*, the young woman emerging from the sea, the monument to Finland's youth, and looked around the open market where I was offered winter hats and coats in sable and silver fox. How difficult it was at that moment to imagine ever being cold again.

Then on past the harbour, the gulls dazed into silence by the heat, to the Uspensky Cathedral, the Russian Orthodox church. I watched the women, all with scarves on their heads, kneeling on the stone floor, and listened to the sounds of the deep bass voices intoning plainsong behind the coloured wooden panels that separate the congregation from the clergy. Occasionally the panels would open and we would glimpse the gold cloth of the priests' vestments and see the candles glittering on the altar, a rich world of mysteries invitingly displayed. Then the panel would close and the act of worship became invisible once more. I wandered back as the market was packing up for the day, and laughing attempts were made in sign language to get me to buy a fur hat before it was replaced in its box.

I heard raised voices as I let myself into the apartment. The sounds of a quarrel are the same in any language. Mika was there, standing over Tanya. He came unsteadily towards me.

'My English friend. Welcome to our country.' He grinned foolishly at me and held out his hand. 'The last outpost of the civilized world before you experience the barbarism of our neighbours.'

'He's drunk,' Tanya said in anger and embarrassment.

We shook hands and he sat down heavily on the sofa.

'I want to know everything,' he said. 'Are you looking after my sister? What are your intentions? Will you marry her?'

There was a furious exchange in Finnish. Mika grabbed Tanya by the arm and tried to drag her on to the sofa but she resisted.

'She is my little sister,' he said. 'I swore to our father before he died that I would always look after her.'

'I'm sorry,' Tanya said to me. 'Please forgive him.' She looked hurt. I felt powerless.

Tanya spoke to her brother in Finnish again.

'No,' Mika said. 'You must speak in English before our English friend. Do you know what she is saying? She is asking me to leave.' He spoke a few words in Finnish to Tanya. Then he turned to me. 'I will tell you what I am saying. I am saying no, I will not leave. I have things to tell you. Information you will like. Useful information.'

318

'Say what you have to say,' Tanya said in English, 'and then go.'

'I need a piss first.'

Mika lurched towards the bathroom. There were tears of anger and humiliation in Tanya's eyes. 'I am sorry, I am so sorry,' she kept saying. 'He has been drinking all day.'

Mika came back into the room. He put his arm round my shoulder and leaned his weight against me. I could smell brandy on his breath.

'Do you remember your friend Hammerson?' he asked. 'Well, he is recovered. His wound is mended. The Soviets have emptied him of all his secrets and now he is useless to them. So they are sending him back to the West. Probably at this moment he is not far from us, maybe he is locked in a cabin on one of those warships in the harbour. Very soon he will be free. There. That is my information. What do you think of that, my English friend?'

'How do you know all this?'

He laughed loudly at that. 'Do you think I will tell you?'

'How do I know what you're telling me is true?' I said. I should never have said it.

Mika gripped my jacket by the lapels and almost lifted me bodily off my feet. He brought his head very close to mine.

'People I trust tell me soon he will be free. And do you know what will happen then?' He let me go at that, standing back and looking first at Tanya and then at me. 'When I see him, I will kill him.'

He produced a revolver from his jacket pocket and pointed it towards me. Tanya screamed and put her hands to her face. Then she spoke harshly to Mika in Finnish and for the first time she had some effect. He lowered the gun and answered her. Then he turned to me.

'She is trying to tell me that Hammerson has not betrayed my people, but I know that he has.'

'Hammerson is your friend. He would never betray you.'

'The Russians asked questions. Hammerson told them answers. My friends are dead. He is the one who has killed them.'

'Hammerson killed no one,' Tanya said.

'He did not put bullets in their heads. But he betrayed us. He is responsible for their deaths. He deserves to die.' Mika sat down on the sofa, his eyes streaming with tears. He put his head in his hands. 'They were good friends. Now they are gone. They must be avenged.'

'That is not your task,' Tanya said. 'Nothing you can do will bring them back to life again.'

Again they shouted at each other in Finnish. This was a conflict between brother and sister, its roots in the history of their lives together. I was forgotten because I had no part in it.

Tanya went into the bathroom and fetched a flannel. Mika wiped his face with it slowly and deliberately as if his skin was painful to the touch.

'Get her to tell you about Matti Sigrin,' Mika said to me. 'Then you will see whether she is the angel you think she is.'

'Go,' Tanya shouted. She flew at him, her fists flying. 'Leave us alone. You've done enough damage. Go away from here. Get out.'

He stood up. 'I will look for Hammerson,' he said. 'When I find him, I will kill him. Do you hear that? I will put bullets into his heart and head.'

I watched him stumble out of the door of the apartment. He left it ajar and Tanya banged it shut. When she turned to me she was crying. I held her in my arms.

'When he is like that, he is not my brother,' she said. 'I wish you could see him as he is. He is a good man, not a murderer. He cannot understand that the war is over. For him, there must always be a battle, always an enemy. Whatever I say, he will not give up. One by one his friends are dying. Soon it will be his turn to be killed. That is what I am afraid of.'

She cried again, and there was little I could do except let her cry it out of her system. I knew then that somehow I had to tell her what was going on, or as much as I knew, which was less than I needed to know. But this time my excuse for doing nothing was that she was too upset to listen.

★

The damage that Mika wanted to inflict was done. He had fuelled my anxiety. I had a name now, Matti Sigrin, and with a name came an identity, an imagined one that I created in my mind, but effective none the less. He was the creature of my uncertainty: could Tanya really love me? Would she leave Finland if I asked her to? Did I dare ask her? If she said no it would be the end of my dreams. Slowly, Matti Sigrin worked his sinister way into my consciousness until I was completely in his power.

Why did I care about her past? It was over and unalterable, a time on which I could have no possible claim. Sigrin and his presence in Tanya's life, unspoken, unspecified but all the more insidious because it could not be pinned down, haunted me. Had she been his lover? Surely, yes. Did she think of him still, did he appear in her dreams? Was she free of him now? If I could not trust myself, how could I trust her protestations that she was?

I wanted to squeeze Sigrin out of her life by possessing all of it, present, future and past. I wanted to make Tanya wholly and completely mine, to exclude any experience that might threaten us. It was an impossible dream but one I could not relinquish because I needed an escape route in case her love couldn't match the demands I made on it. I had created a monster out of my own lack of confidence which I could blame if our relationship were to fail. I was inflicting on her the weakness I perceived in myself. I was griped by a madness, powerless to deny it.

We'd had dinner in a restaurant near the Opera House and were walking back through a square with a wooden church in it and, to one side, a statue of Zacharias Topelius, one of the founders of modern Finnish literature. I listened as Tanya explained the *Kalevala*, the epic poem of the ancient myths of Finland collected by Topelius and published in 1822, which had created a platform for the nascent Finnish nationalism that had resulted, in 1911, in the departure of the Russians and the establishment of the first Finnish state.

'He was one of the great men of our country. He gave us our language and our past. A mythical past perhaps, but something from which we can take strength. Before that, we had no roots, nothing to link us with a history we could proclaim, only generations of peasants working the land. Not very inspiring. With those stories he told us who we were. It was a moral liberation.'

Her pride in her country and her eagerness to tell me its history reminded me of our night walks around a winter-dark Helsinki, but the sense of elation I had experienced so strongly then was missing now.

'What is it?' Tanya asked. 'Why are you so silent?'

I could restrain myself no longer. 'Tell me about Matti Sigrin.'

I regretted it the moment I said his name but it was too late. I had spoken the words I should have buried for ever.

'He was someone I knew once.' She let go of my arm and walked on beside me. 'An old friend. You have old friends, don't you?'

'Tell me about him.'

'Oh, Danny.'

She threw her head back, drawing her hair tight against her skull with both hands and slowly pulling backwards until her hair was released and it fell over her face again.

I heard the beating of my own heart, I felt the pressure of jealousy and anger about a past which I had no right to ask about. She was giving me a last chance to stop before it was too late, time to change my mind, but I ignored her.

'Tell me,' I said, careless of the damage I was doing.

The expression on her face changed but at that moment I did not understand the reason why. 'Matti Sigrin was once my teacher. Then he was my lover. Then he was neither my teacher nor my lover. That is all I want to tell you, but it will not be enough, will it?'

She had folded her arms and was holding her elbows tightly.

'We met in my first week at university. I was very young, little more than eighteen. I had never met anyone like him before. He was so much more certain about everything than the boys I knew because he was so much older. For a time he obsessed me – I would have done anything for him, married him, lived with him, gone to the ends of the earth for him. But slowly, perhaps with his help, I grew up. I saw myself more clearly, I saw him more clearly too. He was no longer a god I worshipped but a man who was good but not that good, who could disguise his selfishness so cleverly but who was selfish. I knew he had a wife and children but I had never thought about them, only about myself and him. Then one day I saw them together, laughing and happy, eating in a restaurant, and I knew that I was the one deceived, and the truth was that I had deceived myself. It was a very painful moment. I went back to my room and cried. I tried to stop seeing him, but he was persuasive, clever. He told me he loved me. He wanted me to take him back. I hated myself for it but I did.'

There were tears in her eyes now and her face was drawn. I wanted to stop her but I knew that if I tried, she would push me away. I had to wait until she had told me everything.

'When a love affair ends, why do you think you will never fall in love again? I was afraid of being unloved, that is why I took him back and stayed with him until the war broke out, when I left Helsinki to look after the wounded soldiers at the front. That was my chance to leave him and I took it. He wrote to me again and again, he told me how much he needed me, he promised to leave his wife if only I would return to him. I never answered his letters.'

She wiped her eyes but the tears kept falling.

'The years went by. The letters stopped. I had almost forgotten about him. Then last summer I met him again. He had aged. His hair which once had been blond and thick was grey and thinning now. The laughter that I had once loved so much was gone. In the years we had been apart he had lost so much. His wife had left him, one of his sons had been killed in Karelia, the other had gone to live in America. I was all he had left, his memories of our happiness together. We went to the island together. I felt sorry for him. That was all.

'One evening, a week after you had left Helsinki, Matti came round to my apartment to beg me to come back to him. I told him it was impossible. I said I had found the love that I always wanted. I was happy. My life was closed to him now. He wouldn't accept that at first. Then I told him that the marks he had made on me, which once had been so strong, were now barely visible. Soon there would be nothing left at all. That was when he accepted that I was telling the truth.'

She took my hand.

'That was the moment when I wanted you most. I had made a declaration of my love for you, but to another man. Now I wanted to make the same declaration to you. But you were not there. I was very sad. I wondered where you were, what you were doing, whom you were with. I wanted so much to tell you, not everything I have told you now, but enough for you to know that I am yours and no one else's, and I always will be.'

She had told me so much but not the secrets I wanted to know. Had she taken off her clothes and swum naked in the sea? Had he watched her in the half-light, water falling off her soft brown skin like diamonds? Had he reached for her hand in the cold of the night and had she let him into her bed because she felt sorry for him? Whatever Tanya said the questions remained, the ghosts of an imagined past haunting me, destroying the present and my happiness. My obsession was forcing me to make an enemy of the woman I loved.

★

The telephone rang.

'May I speak to Mr Stevens?' It was a woman's voice, hesitant and deeply accented.

'Speaking.'

'I am Ruth Marchenko. You are Goffrey's son?'

'Yes.'

'I have found you. Good.' It sounded as if she was reading from a badly written script. 'I would like to arrange a meeting with you.'

'With my father.'

'No, first I wish to see you, please.'

'When do you suggest?'

'I have not much time. This morning?'

'Very well. Where?'

She gave me an address. 'There is a garden opposite. Please meet me there in half an hour.'

'How will I recognise you?'

She laughed at that. 'I have grey hair,' she said. 'I am small and I am Russian.'

She was right. I recognized her at once. She was a small woman, her long grey hair drawn back from her face in a bun. She wore glasses and a shapeless cotton dress.

'There is a bench,' she said. 'Let us sit and talk for a moment.' She looked nervously around her.

'Were you followed?' I asked.

'I expect so,' she said. 'They will want to make sure I speak to you.'

She tried to make light of it but I could see in her expression that she was afraid.

'You know,' she said, 'I asked myself the question you asked me. How will I know you are Geoffrey's son? But there is no question, is there? You look so like him.'

Her skin was fair and unlined and she had dazzling blue eyes. There was a kind of simplicity in her expression, a lack of guile, that I took to instantly. She was not a beautiful woman. But there was something about her, a vigour that was enchanting. I wondered what my father had thought of her all those years ago, whether he too had felt the power of her attraction.

'Has your father arrived in Helsinki?'

'Yes.'

'We have arranged to meet. Perhaps he has told you that.'

324

'Yes,' I lied. There was no point in telling her that my father didn't even know of my presence in Helsinki.

'This is the address.' She took a piece of paper from her handbag. 'Please ask him to be there tonight.'

That was twenty-four hours sooner than Monty had anticipated. I had very little time in which to change my father's mind and at that moment I had no idea where he was.

'What time?'

'Nine o'clock.' She stood up. 'Thank you.'

'I have some questions,' I said.

'I can say nothing.' Once more I saw the fear in her eyes and the furtive look over my shoulder. 'You must know that.'

'Why do you want to meet my father?'

'Please. I cannot stay.'

She tried to walk away but I held her by the wrist.

'Five minutes,' I said. 'That's all the time I need.'

'I cannot say anything in five minutes.'

'Then answer my question.'

She stared at me. 'If you are here to stop him seeing me, then you must break the promises you have made. Your father will come to no harm. I promise that. But I must see him. I cannot tell you why but we must meet. You must let that happen.'

'Will you be alone tonight?' She had started to walk away. 'Will there be others with you when you meet my father?'

'In our country,' she said quietly, standing close to me, 'we are never alone. But we are used to that. Tell your father not to be afraid. He will come to no harm. I give you my promise. But please, bring him to me tonight. I am sorry. I have no more time now. You look so like Geoffrey. I could never have mistaken you for someone else.'

★

Through binoculars, I watched the main steps leading up to the glass doors of the science labs. For an hour or more there had been no movement, except for a woman carrying a bowl of flowers down to a waiting delivery van. Now there was a flurry of activity as the doors burst open and the delegates emerged from the lecture hall and began to disperse for the day. After twenty minutes I caught sight of my father. He lingered on the top steps for a time, talking and laughing, then linked arms with an elderly white-haired man

325

and together they walked down the steps to the street. I saw him stop, take out a pocketbook, write something in it, nod to his acquaintance, shake hands and set off towards the centre of Helsinki.

I caught up with him within a couple of minutes.

'Father.'

'Good God! What are you doing here?'

'I've been speaking to a friend of yours. Someone from your past who's looking forward to seeing you. Ruth Marchenko.'

'How do you know about her?' He looked shocked.

'Monty Lybrand gave me an introduction.'

'Are you working for Monty now?'

I could have been talking to a stranger. My father had not shaken my hand or greeted me in any way. He looked as if he had been trapped and was frantically searching for a means of escape.

This was a situation beyond his experience and he had no idea how to cope with it. I felt a moment's sympathy for him. I must have been the last person he was expecting to meet in Helsinki.

'We can't stand here in the street,' I said. 'Why don't we find somewhere where we can have a drink.' I looked at my watch. 'Ruth says your meeting's fixed for nine tonight. She's given me the address.'

'Let's get a drink.'

I led my father silently through the crowds to the Esplanadie. We sat at a table in the open air and drank beer. In the bandstand naval musicians from one of the visiting Soviet warships were playing Russian folk songs. A young sailor with a wonderfully deep voice was singing of disappointed love. At the front of the audience two young girls held flowers and gazed up at the singer. It was early evening and the heat of the afternoon had not yet dispersed. My father removed his jacket and loosened his tie. There were beads of sweat on his brow.

'What does Monty know about Marchenko?'

There was an anger in his voice which told me he'd been shaken not just by my presence but by Monty's involvement in all this.

'He said your reason for coming to Helsinki was to meet her.'

'How does he know that?'

'He's paid to know things people don't want him to know. He doesn't tell me where he gets his information from.'

'Has he sent you to spy on me?' he asked bitterly.

'I'm here to help you.'

326

'I don't need help. Yours or anyone else's. God knows what you're doing here but I wish you weren't.'

All his years of enmity towards me, of disappointed hopes, of breakdowns and false starts in our relationship were brought together in that single sentence. He told me what both of us had known for so long but never dared say to each other. I was not the son he wanted, nor he the father I needed; he did not know me nor I him. We were strangers to each other and would most likely remain so. It was a frightening admission of the truth that we had always avoided. The summer air cooled suddenly around me and I shivered.

There was a burst of clapping as the Russian sailor ended his song. He bowed shyly to his audience. The two girls ran forward and gave him their flowers, kissing him as he bent down to take them. The young sailor looked embarrassed and uncertain, the colour in his cheeks rose and he hurried off the dais. There was laughter and more clapping, and calls for him to return to sing again. The sounds of people around us enjoying themselves defused the awful moment.

How our lives are balanced on chance. If the song had not ended when it did, what might we have said or done that we regretted later? We had confronted each other for a moment but we had drawn back from open hostility. We remained trapped, as we always had been, in a long cold war.

'Tell me about Marchenko,' I said.

'Why?'

I chose to ignore the aggression in his voice as he struggled to build his defence.

'Why are you meeting her here?'

'She said she was going to be at this conference and suggested we meet.' Then, as an afterthought: 'We haven't seen each other for years.'

'What's the meeting about?'

'You can tell Monty it's a reunion. A meeting of old friends. Nothing more sinister than that.'

I went to get him another drink. When I returned he said, 'I met Ruth Marchenko years ago, in the Netherlands. We were working in the same field. We corresponded a bit over the years, then the war came and I heard nothing more from her. A few weeks ago, out of the blue, she got in touch again.'

'You can't believe Marchenko made contact out of the goodness of her heart,' I said, trying to keep my temper. 'Nor is she here on her own. You may not be able to see her puppetmasters but they follow her wherever she goes. I don't know of anyone who'd accept this meeting as simply a reunion between old friends.'

Except you, was the implication. I wondered if he could hear what I hadn't said.

'Ruth would never get involved with people like that.'

'How can you be sure? She may have no choice.'

'I know the woman, you don't.' He was trying to reassert himself, to regain his traditional ascendancy over me.

'The Soviets live by different rules, Father.'

'The differences are much exaggerated.'

'Ask her to describe the compromises she has to make to survive,' I said, my anger slipping out of control. 'How much of her life she keeps secret, even from those closest to her. Get her to tell you the price of dissent and whether she has ever paid it. If you live in the Soviet Union, you're part of the Soviet system. That's unavoidable.'

He turned away. I didn't know if I had struck home or if he was irritated with my response and was rejecting my script. Behind us, the band was now playing Russian martial music. The crowd was dispersing, showing its feelings by moving on, an act neither of protest nor of acceptance, but a quiet, dignified assertion of freedom. I admired the subtle, unhurried way they defined their independence against their overbearing neighbour.

'Monty and his people don't want you to meet Marchenko.'

'You're their errand boy, are you?' I was too angry to say anything. 'It's none of their damn business what I do.' He had raised his voice and the people at the next table stopped talking and looked at us.

'That's why they asked me to make it mine.'

'It's none of your business either.' He was hurling his anger at me but it was falling short of its target.

'You could be walking into a trap. You could be in danger.'

'I'm going to see a scientific colleague I haven't spoken to for years. Nothing's going to happen to me.'

'You don't know that.'

'I trust Marchenko.'

'You may be wrong to do so.'

'You've no grounds for saying that.'

'Marchenko works on the Soviet nuclear programme. You work on the British programme. You meet secretly in Helsinki. Can't you see what could be made of that?'

'I'm not interested in what other people think.' There it was again, the unconquerable superiority of the academic, his hubris against my experience, the eternal, unwinnable contest. 'Anyway,' he added slyly. 'No one knows about our meeting.'

I'd lost patience. I couldn't believe in his naivety. If this was his defence, it was best to destroy it at once.

'Everyone knows about it. The British. The Russians. The Finns, probably. You've been under surveillance for weeks, Father. They've read your letters, listened to your telephone calls, they can tell you what you've done every hour of every day better than you can, I expect. There isn't a moment when someone isn't watching you.'

The enormity of what I had said stifled his reply. He sat there gazing at me in incredulous silence.

'Monty and his lot think you're giving nuclear secrets to the Russians and they're looking for evidence to trap you. If you meet Marchenko, they'll have it.'

Silence still. I pressed home my advantage.

'The Soviets are no different. A leading British nuclear scientist, here in Helsinki – home territory for them – takes Marchenko's bait and walks straight into their embrace. What a coup. They won't believe their luck. They'll whisk you out of Finland, parade you in front of the world's press in Moscow and dress up their kidnap as a defection from the West.'

I'd gone on too long. I'd given my father a chance to find a defence.

'Can you find it in your heart to believe that sometimes the worst won't happen, that there is some scrap of decency left in the world? Or has your association with Monty and these appalling people led you to think badly of everyone?'

'I know the Russians, Father. I've lived alongside them for too long not to know what they're capable of. You can't judge them as you'd judge me because they don't recognize the same rules. You may not like that but it's true. I've seen it with my own eyes.'

'Helsinki is not Berlin.'

'Where the Soviets go, Berlin and all its madness follows.'

'I don't accept that.'

'This is a dangerous place, Father, and you're on your own here. You've got no friends and maybe a lot of enemies. Listen to me and get out before it's too late.'

'You make it sound as if war had already been declared.'

'You're caught up in a game with very high stakes. You and I don't matter, we're victims of their paranoia. When you're up against people without scruples, the innocent always suffer. I don't want to see that happen to you.'

He put his head in his hands. I knew that gesture. It was not capitulation, it was a sign of uncertainty. I kept going.

'Don't see Marchenko,' I said. 'Don't go anywhere near her. Leave her alone. Go home now, before it's too late.'

'If she's in trouble, I've got to help her.'

'Who says she's in trouble?'

'She does.'

'How do you know she's telling the truth?'

'Why would she do otherwise?'

'She may be working against you.'

'I won't have it, Danny. She'd never do that.'

'How long since you saw her last? Fifteen years? The world has changed since then. Maybe she has too, maybe she's a different woman now. Maybe she's been trapped by the Soviets. Have you thought of that? Maybe she's doing this against her will.'

'I refuse to believe anything like that of her.' It was not stubbornness I was up against. The reality of Marchenko's life in Soviet Russia lay beyond his imaginative reach. My father defended Marchenko's innocence and good faith because that is how he knew her to be. 'I'm seeing her because I agreed I would. I won't go back on my word.'

I knew then that no argument I could put up would shift him from his position. The meeting would go ahead as planned. I had lost, and so had Monty. I prayed my father wouldn't be a loser too.

'I can't let you go there by yourself.'

'You're not coming with me.' I was surprised by the speed and vehemence of his reply. 'I'm seeing her alone.'

'I'll take you there and I'll wait for you.'

'Ring this number.' He was writing on one of the mats our beer mugs had been standing on. 'Talk to Jamie Laurentzen. He'll remember you. Tell your story to him. See if he believes you.'

It was a glimmer of hope. I took the beer mat from him gratefully.

★

If Laurentzen was surprised at my presence in Helsinki he certainly didn't show it. The car-mad Finn I saw now was little different from the man I remembered: tall, gaunt, eyes set deep in his head, a cropped

330

beard, always with a pipe in his mouth. Only his colouring had changed. The hair cut close to his scalp was now white, his beard more white than grey and his skin a darker brown than I had known it.

'Do you remember my MG, Danny? Now that was a car. I sold it when I left Cambridge. That was the last time I cried.'

I remembered exhilarating afternoons roaring round the byways of the Fens and narrow Cambridge streets, scaring the locals out of their wits. I was too young then to be frightened.

Laurentzen now had a white, pre-war Mercedes convertible and the top was down. He proudly explained its finer points to me, opening the bonnet to show me the polished cylinders and making me listen to the engine.

'Is that not the sound of pleasure, Danny?'

I asked him if he knew that my father was in Helsinki.

'His name was a late addition to the list of delegates to our conference. I was pleased to see it.'

'He hasn't got in touch?'

'He is much in demand. I am sure he will make contact when he has a moment.'

Laurentzen smiled sadly, as if his experience of human nature gave him little to hope for. His disappointment was deep. I told him about my father's planned meeting with Marchenko.

'Do you have the address where they are to meet?' I gave it to him. He shook his head. 'This is the home of a known communist sympathizer. Quite unsuitable. I think we should surprise our Soviet friends with a small change of plan, don't you?'

He roared with laughter at that, stuck a huge pipe in his mouth and drove off with a squeal.

'What acceleration,' he shouted above the roar of the engine. 'Are you impressed?'

★

'Is she with you, Jamie?' my father asked, his voice full of anxiety. These were the first words these two men, once close friends and collaborators, had spoken to each other in ten years.

'She is coming, yes,' Laurentzen said. 'She wishes to brush her hair first.'

'And the Russians?'

'There is no sign of the Russians but that does not mean they are not watching us. It is good to see you again, Geoffrey.'

331

The two men shook hands through the open window of the car. 'And you, Jamie,' my father said, 'and you. I'm grateful.'

After so many years apart was that all these two men had to say to each other? Their partnership had produced one of the most significant scientific discoveries of the last decade, then they had fallen out for reasons that were never fully explained, and there had been no contact between them since. Now they greeted each other as if they met each day of the week.

'Here she is now,' Laurentzen said. 'I told you she would come.'

There had been a transformation since our meeting earlier in the day. Ruth Marchenko had let her hair down, it was set with two combs on either side, and she had changed her dress and her shoes. I was struck at once by a kind of girlish radiance about her.

'Geoffrey.'

It was a cry across the years, the past echoing into the present. It reached my father and touched him.

Marchenko was running towards him. A strand of hair broke loose and she tried to push it back under the comb. She laughed then, she laughed with excitement, with pleasure and delight. I realized, watching her, that she was in love with my father.

She spoke breathlessly. 'Geoffrey? Oh, Geoffrey.'

My father had got out of the car and was holding Marchenko in his arms. She was clinging to him.

'Ruth? Are you all right?'

They kissed each other on the cheeks and my father helped Marchenko into the car. We saw two men run out of the house and race to a car. We presumed they were Russians.

'Get in and hold tight,' Laurentzen said. 'Now the fun begins.'

We were followed for a time, but Laurentzen knew the countryside, which our pursuers did not, and his car was much faster than theirs. I guessed we had doubled back on ourselves a couple of times, and once we had left the city I kept getting glimpses of the sun on the water. We were travelling east, along the coast, but I no idea where we had ended up, except that we were some distance from Helsinki.

'Welcome to my summer home,' Laurentzen said. 'Here you will be safe. Not for ever, but for a few hours. You may speak freely. You will not be overheard. Please. You are welcome here.'

He led us into a painted wooden house on the edge of the sea.

2

RUTH

'Many years ago, in a moment of rashness I bitterly regret, I told my husband what happened in Leiden. If I had not done that he would not have been able to betray me all those years later. You would not be in danger now. I must ask your forgiveness for what I did.'

'Did he force you to tell him?'

She remembers that terrible night, the night she told Ivan in a moment of desperation that she had slept with Stevens. Why did she tell him? What did she hope to gain but his anger, his disdain and rejection of her? How many years later did that pathetic man offer the secret of her infidelity to his inquisitors in exchange for his own life? They accepted his offer, then changed their minds and executed him anyway. In that moment, unknowingly, he drew her into Andropov's power.

'No,' she says quietly. 'No, he never forced me.'

'There is nothing to be forgiven,' he adds quietly. 'How could there be?'

Across the years his hand reaches out to her and she feels his warmth. The gentleness of his words bathes her like a warm breeze. She wants to kiss him and love him. But she doesn't move. His grip tightens on her fingers, closer, closer. She wants him to draw her closer.

'How you have suffered,' he says. 'How wrong it all is.'

They sit there, linked together, in silence. Outside the sun is climbing. She wonders what time it is but dares not ask. They are in their own world again now; time doesn't matter. Nobody will disturb them. She is safe with him. This is where she is meant to be.

★

'This is our task,' he is saying to her, 'our responsibility.'

She is not here on her own account. Gromsky, Tomasov, Lykow-ski, Markarova have placed their trust in her, as has Andropov. Though she is exhausted, she must fulfil her duty to them all. She must hear what he is saying.

'Every day more of us believe that what we are being asked to do is wrong.'

'What can we do, Geoffrey? What power have we got?'

'We have the power of our knowledge. If the scientific com-munity says "no" loudly enough, our voices will carry across national frontiers. If we refuse to work for any political regime, East or West, until our demands for international scientific control are met, then political strategies based on the development of nuclear weapons will be stranded and we will have delivered the world from the possibility of annihilation. We will have banished nuclear arsenals because we, the builders, refuse to build. Instead of being the architects of destruc-tion, we will have started the design of a new world. We will earn the respect of future generations.'

It is a courageous speech, whose sentiments she endorses. She also knows it is wholly impractical. Geoffrey is an innocent dreamer. She knows the world as it truly is because she lives it every day of her life, while he can only imagine. All her disappointments rise again.

She looks out to sea. The morning is bright now. A couple are walking a dog on the beach. She can see a man swimming. The world is waking up to another day.

'I must get you away from here,' he says, his face lighting up as he speaks. 'We will be the symbol of a new world order, a Russian scientist and an English scientist, working together for what we believe in, speaking the same language. We will fight this madness together.'

He smiles at her and squeezes her hand.

'We will begin the campaign in Cambridge. I will find you some-where to live – you can stay in our house until we get you a place of your own.'

'Geoffrey.' She must stop him before it is too late.

'Why not? What other solution can there be? Together we will present an unanswerable argument.'

'Geoffrey. I have a mother and a son.'

'If you leave Moscow they will send them after you.'

'If I leave they will keep them as hostages and force me to return.'

'What possible use can they have for an old woman and a child?'

'That is how they operate.'

She sees his hopes begin to fade.

'Will you go back? When this conference is over?' he asks.

'To Moscow? Of course. I live there.'

'Everything will continue as before?'

'What choice do I have, Geoffrey? It is the world I know.' She puts her finger to his lips. 'Don't make parting harder than it already is. Please say nothing more.'

'You cannot imagine how difficult this is.'

'I know only too well.'

★

He has looked at his watch twice in the last five minutes. She knows it is time for them to leave. She has told him everything but the greatest secret of her life.

'There is something I want you to see.' She reaches into her handbag and produces a wallet of photographs. She chooses one and hands it to Stevens.

'This is my son, Valery.'

Stevens looks at the photographs. His expression registers nothing. Surely he can see what to her is so obvious? She smiles and puts her hand on his shoulder.

'Can't you see it?'

'See what?'

Those grey-blue eyes, staring at her quizzically. How well she knows that look.

'See what?' he asks again.

How can he fail to see that which is so clear to her?

'You are the father he has never seen.'

'Valery is ours?'

'Yes.'

'You never told me.'

'He is a good boy,' she says. 'You would be proud of him.'

'Why did you never tell me?'

'How could I? At first I was not sure. But when I was sure, it became my secret. It kept me close to you; I could look at Valery and I could see you. There was some comfort in that. As he grows older he becomes more like you every day, not only in looks but

335

in manner too. Sometimes it makes me laugh to listen to him. I am hearing you speaking Russian.'

'All these years,' he says. 'All these wasted years.'

She holds his head against her as his body shakes. She tries to calm him but the tears flow out of him as if a dam has broken: all the sorrow, the rage, the hurt of the years is released and he lets it run out. It is some time before he is calm again.

'Can I see him?'

'That is impossible,' she says. 'You mustn't even think it.'

'I must see him. I have to. I am his father.'

'He knows nothing about you.'

'You never told him?'

'How could I? It would be intolerable for him to know the truth. We live on opposite sides of a divided world. He would never be allowed to see you. You cannot ask him to live with the knowledge of something he can never realize.'

'But I know. *I* know.'

'He is young, Geoffrey. Think of him. You're not living in Moscow. You're not Russian. He is all those things. For as long as our two countries see each other as enemies, your son will remain unknown to you. That is the legacy of what we scientists have done to the world. That is what you must fight to destroy. For his sake and those of his age, and younger. You must go on to make his future secure.'

Can telling him the greatest secret of her life provide the motive that will drive him on to overcome whatever obstacles are thrown in his path? Will he go back to his own people, his own leaders, and ask them to speak to the Supreme Soviet?

'I will send you photographs,' she says. 'I will write to tell you what he does with his life. But you cannot see him.'

He looks at her, desperation in his eyes. She knows what he wants to say. If something happens to you, his eyes tell her, how will I know if he is still alive? How will I know?

She wants to say, there is no consolation, that is what we have made of our lives; there are no answers, no reprieves. We are victims of politics. Now our lives must be about making a safer world for our son.

She kisses him. 'We cannot let ourselves think these thoughts. We must remember that once we loved each other and that Valery is the living testimony to that love. We may be apart but we are

336

luckier than some. Perhaps,' she smiles as she says this, 'perhaps he will grow into a famous physicist like his father. Perhaps you will read of his achievements in the scientific journals and be proud.'

He looks at her, a man lost and desolate, and she feels her heart almost break. Why must she always be strong? Why her? Why can't she break down and be comforted by him?

'What am I to do?' he asks.

'Keep the secret,' she says. 'We cannot burden his life with our guilt, our needs, our recriminations for secrets not shared. He must be free to live the life he chooses, in so far as any choice is possible within the Soviet Union. We must do what we have to do to make that possible. That is the greatest gift we can give him.'

She knows that what she says is true, but it is not what she wants. She wants Stevens to sweep her up into his arms, to rescue her and Valery; to take them away from Moscow to a life without fear, where she can dedicate herself to the two men she will never stop loving.

It is morning now. Light, she knows, brings with it truth. She is Russian and she must return to Moscow. He is English and must return to Cambridge. That is their fate. She smiles to herself. Fate is such a Russian concept. She wonders if the English think of their fate. She suspects not.

'It will be very difficult to say goodbye,' he says.

'We have done it before and we must do it again.'

'There will be other conferences. Rome in November. Oxford next year. You must come to Oxford, bring Valery to Oxford. We must meet as often as we can. That is our obligation to each other.'

'No dreams, Geoffrey. Not this time.'

She remembers the red university diary, and the names of towns she has never visited. Milan. Basle. Oslo.

She takes his hand. 'No false promises. No self-delusion. If we meet again, it will be entirely by chance. I have only one regret. For you, I wish I was beautiful.'

'You are beautiful,' he says, and she laughs again, disbelieving but pleased, because she knows he means it even though it is untrue.

'Let me go, Geoffrey.'

He has taken her in his arms. She removes his hands and holds him apart from her. In that moment she understands him as she has never done before. His fate is that he can never have the one thing he wants.

'It is time we returned to our real lives.'

3

DANNY

'Whatever you may think of the Russians,' Laurentzen said as he poured two glasses with care, 'this is their gift to the world. They should have stuck to exporting vodka, not Lenin.'

He was sitting at his desk, beneath the stern gaze of his father portrayed in academic dress. In his time he had been Professor of Physics at Helsinki University and later its Rector. Jamie Laurentzen possessed the same confidence in the processes of science to unravel the mysteries of the world. I envied the certainties of their relationship.

'He built this summer house,' Jamie had told us as we came in, 'in the last year of the last century. Before that there was nothing here, just a headland, a few trees, the beach and the sea. My father said that what attracted him was the peacefulness of this place. He would come here to think and to write.'

He had pointed to a shelf of leather-bound volumes. 'He was a productive and meticulous man. These are his papers, his articles, the original manuscripts – all written in the same black ink. All bound, all numbered. Over there are his books. He taught all his life in Helsinki. I don't think he once thought of moving. He was a true Finn.'

He pushed the vodka across the desk towards me.

'This is the real thing, not some pale Soviet imitation masquerading as Russian. To old friends.'

I experienced the familiar burning, the cold flame coursing through my body, exploding in my stomach and then sweeping up and entering my brain.

Laurentzen refilled our glasses.

'You may go to bed if you wish. Marina has made up the spare room. In our short summer, we Finns need very little sleep.'

Marina was Laurentzen's English wife. They had met and married while he was working at Cambridge. I never knew her well because for some reason my mother didn't like her and, in any case, her sons were older than me at a time when differences in age matter. On his desk were framed photographs of two young men, fair-haired and grinning.

He took a pipe from a rack and started to fill it with tobacco from a leather pouch.

'So what is going on, Danny?' he asked. 'What is Geoffrey doing here? I cannot imagine it is by chance that you are both in Helsinki at the same time.'

There seemed little point in concealing the truth from Laurentzen. After all, he had responded to my appeal for help without questioning me.

'I was sent here to stop the meeting that's taking place next door.'

'It would seem your mission has been unsuccessful,' Jamie said. 'But that does not answer my question.'

'Our people think my father is here to give nuclear secrets to the Russians.'

'So that is what Geoffrey is doing. He is handing over secret information to Marchenko.' He looked at me over the top of his glasses. 'You are a good son. You do not believe that Geoffrey is a traitor?'

'Of course I don't.'

'You sound very sure.'

'I know he'd never do anything like that.'

'Do you say that out of loyalty because you are his son? Or do you have evidence to support your view?'

'You were close to him for years, Jamie. Do you think he could betray his country?'

'I offer no opinion. I ask what makes you so sure he would not.'

I was discouraged by his refusal to take sides. I should have realized the dangers of easy partisanship when, like the Finns, you are trapped in the vice between East and West.

'You make it sound as if sharing secrets with the Russians isn't wrong.'

'Are there no circumstances when the act of giving secrets to another country might be justified?'

'None that I know of.'

'I envy your certainty.'

There was something on his mind. What it was I couldn't guess, and he appeared reluctant to tell me.

'In theoretical physics,' he said, 'there is a test, one among many, which we apply to every new theory. We ask ourselves: is this idea crazy enough? I think we should apply that test to your father's behaviour.' He smiled at me. 'Let us assume that at this minute Geoffrey is indeed passing British nuclear secrets to Marchenko. Is he doing so out of political conviction? He is not a Marxist. For financial gain? He is not interested in money. Perhaps he is being blackmailed and he is doing this against his will. It is possible but unlikely, no? We draw a blank. His motive remains an enigma. But there must be a reason, otherwise why would he be here? Let us examine the problem from another angle. Might there not be a moral basis for his actions?'

'An act of conscience?'

'Is that not possible?'

'It's still a betrayal.'

'The time to condemn the act is when we have established the cause. Our hypothesis suggests Geoffrey could be trying to do something good.'

'Like what?'

'There are many scientists, and your father is among them, whose consciences rebel in the face of the risk of a nuclear explosion destroying the world in a giant chain reaction. They have created these dangers, they see it as their duty to prevent such a disaster occurring. Could Geoffrey not be at this conference of nuclear physicists because he wants to do exactly that? Are not such actions good? Do they not have morality behind them?'

'It's possible,' I said, sounding doubtful. My father as saviour of the world. Was that the role he cast himself in now? I thought back to the articles he had written, to his barely suppressed anger at my working for Watson-Jones, a man who endorsed nuclear arms as a prerequisite for lasting peace. I remembered his use of Ridout's death to promote his own cause, that either we must remove nuclear weapons from political control or attempt to reject war as a political solution. Perhaps in my easy dismissal of his position I had underestimated his determination to act on his own convictions.

'You and I both know where your father stands on this issue. He believes we have given the world a gift too powerful for its own good. He sees our politicians misusing that gift and blowing up the world. I disagree. That was the cause of our quarrel. Perhaps he is not here to give Marchenko secrets. Perhaps, oblivious of personal risk, he is here to convince her of the rightness of his cause. Is that not a courageous, far-sighted, crazy act, for which humanity should be grateful, particularly if it helps to save all our lives?'

His theory had a logic to it, and it was a view I hadn't considered.

'Is Marchenko the right contact? Does she have political influence? Can she help his cause, if indeed he has one?'

'It is possible,' Jamie said, 'that Marchenko is giving the same message to your father.'

Then he told me about the rumour that had been sweeping through the conference since Monday. In a gesture of defiance, a group of leading scientists at the Institute of Nuclear Research in Moscow had deliberately blown up their own laboratory, destroying much valuable research and setting back the development of the Soviet bomb by months if not years. They had done this, Jamie said, because the political authorities had refused to listen to their concerns.

'If that were true,' I said, 'they would all have been shot by now.'

'That is the pragmatist's answer,' Jamie said. 'I accept the rumour may not be true. I prefer to believe that the explosion was an accident. I know that the scientists are still alive, because Marchenko is one of them. If her colleagues had been shot she would either be dead or not here.'

'You don't believe this rumour, do you?'

'It is too early to ask that question. The rumour exists. What one must establish is why does it exist? Why now, in Helsinki? Who has started it? What might their motives be?'

'Are you suggesting it comes from the Russians?'

'That is one possibility, certainly.'

'They're incapable of such subtlety.'

'You see the Soviets as brutal and ruthless, which is undeniable. But they are as capable of great sophistication as they are of brutality, or of making stupid mistakes.

'You'll have to convince me,' I said.

'Maybe the Soviets have their own reasons for ending this race to build the bomb. Maybe they have realized it is something they cannot do, that they do not have the technology or the economic resources to create such a weapon. What better way of avoiding the political disaster of failing at such an important task than to get the international community to take the matter out of your hands? In politics, it is better not to do something because you have given in to international pressure than it is to admit your own weakness.'

He paused to stare at me. 'Marchenko is one of the leaders of this revolt.'

The small, shy woman I had seen clutching my father's arm. It was impossible to imagine her in such a role. Laurentzen had read my thoughts.

'Don't be taken in by her appearance. She is more determined than she looks. I am sure she speaks out of conviction. The question we have to answer is: is it her voice we hear, or is she being manipulated?'

All my experience, particularly my months in Berlin, denied what Jamie was saying. The Russians would never give up building their own bomb, whatever the cost. Too much was at stake. Their foreign policy depended on the strength of their opposition to the democracies of the West. Owning their own atomic bomb was the index of that strength, a necessary symbol of the triumphant path of Marxist-Leninism. I could see nothing stopping them building a nuclear arsenal to equal that held in the West.

If that were the case, why was Marchenko talking to my father? Very slowly, as I listened to Laurentzen, an appalling thought emerged.

What if this was the message that the Soviets *wanted* us to believe? Suppose their own development had come up against obstacles that were taking much more time to resolve. Desperate, they had hit upon the idea of slowing the West's progress. What if the West was being tricked into a false sense of security? What if we believed what they wanted us to believe and reduced our own commitment to nuclear development?

It didn't end there. The British intelligence service believed my father was a traitor, which is what the Russians wanted them to believe. If that was true, this was no innocent meeting with Marchenko. She was as much on their side as the rest of Stalin's gang. She was the siren call my father could not resist. Somehow the Soviets knew that, and they had made use of Marchenko to lure him to Helsinki. He had answered her summons and now, in his innocence, he was about to walk into a trap. It would be impossible to conceal this meeting. The Russians would leak the information to the British, my father would be arrested by Monty's people on his return home.

His secret meeting with a Soviet nuclear scientist would be indisputable evidence of his treachery. Our intelligence services would be doing what the Soviets wanted – removing a senior scientist from our own programme, sowing dissension among our allies, the Americans, keeping both countries apart.

I got to my feet. 'We can't let this go on, can we? He's in real danger. The consequences of this meeting are too awful to think about.'

'It is too late to stop them now,' Laurentzen said. 'They have begun. Your friend Monty was right. Our one chance was to stop them meeting. We are too late for that. We have been deceived into helping them meet. Somehow we must retrieve the situation. God knows how.'

4

RUTH

She watches the white car drive away, one face in the back window turning round to catch a last glimpse of her; no wave, no smile, just those dark eyes she remembers so well looking at her. Then they are gone, and she returns Stevens to the secret treasury of her memory where, except for the last eight hours, he has lived since she met him so many years before. She can hardly believe that she has seen him again. She is dizzy with physical impressions of him: his voice, the touch of his hand, the colour of his eyes, the lines on his face, the texture of his clothes, the weight of his presence beside her. (In her imagination he is always a weightless being whom she can make appear or disappear at will.) She is relieved that she has to make so few adjustments to the image she has preserved of him. Her memories at least are true, and that is some consolation.

She realizes how exhausted she is, how much of a strain the last few hours have been. She wants to throw off her clothes and sleep for as long as she can. She goes upstairs to her room. As she opens the door, the early-morning light is in her eyes and she can make out only the contours of a thin, angular figure silhouetted in the window. She is too tired even to feel frightened.

'Where did you go?' Andropov asks.

She is in no mood for questioning. 'I'm sorry,' she says. 'I am too tired to talk.'

'Where did Professor Laurentzen take you?' he insists.

'I don't know. Somewhere on the coast. Please.' She knows she is pleading with him but she doesn't care. 'I haven't slept for over twenty-four hours.'

'Did you tell Stevens he is the father of your son?'

How could Andropov know that? This is her secret, the secret around which her entire life has been built. No one knows except her and now Stevens because an hour ago she chose to tell him. She has never told anyone else. How can Andropov know? Can he listen to the secrets of her heart? No, this is a trick. He is trying to get her to admit something he suspects may be true but is not sure.

'Why should I tell him something that isn't true?'

'Come now, Comrade Marchenko.'

She has an overwhelming desire to close her eyes and sleep. She sees the sunlight momentarily reflected on the lenses of Andropov's rimless glasses. Two fiery lights burn into her soul. She knows this is no dream; she fights to keep awake, to remain alert.

'Show me the photographs you have of your son,' he says.

Reluctantly she opens her bag and hands them to Andropov. He lays them out across the table as if he were playing solitaire. Where is the man who asked her to question him? Who came close to expressing his need for companionship, for some kind of relationship? Or did she dream that moment? Andropov has opened his briefcase and now he brings out a set of photographs which he places on the table beneath those of Valery Marchenko.

'Do I need to say more?'

She stares at photographs of her forgotten husband Ivan, ancient photographs of him as a young man, taken at the time they first met. She can find no trace of the dark hair and narrow face that she has almost wiped from her memory, imprinted on her son.

'Stevens knows,' she says. 'I told him.'

She can hardly believe she has made this admission, but she only has to look at the expression on Andropov's face to know that he has won and she has lost. At that moment the core of her life breaks within her. She is emptied of will, purpose, identity. This is not the effect of fatigue. Now there is nothing left. Ruth Marchenko, as a woman in possession of her own life, has ceased to exist. She has lost the identity of her son to Andropov, the last emblem of her being.

'Good,' he says. 'I am pleased you told him. Now we must arrange a meeting between father and son.'

'Stevens won't come to Moscow.' She is fighting him with the very last of her strength.

'He doesn't have to. He can meet his son in Helsinki.'

At that moment Andropov comes as close to destroying her as he has ever done. He knows her greatest secret and he has her son in his possession. She has no resistance left because there is nothing left to resist with. Now her secret is gone, where is the basis of her will? What is there to protect? She feels invaded, soiled, unclean. She has become that which she has always fought against, she is 'someone else'. Her private war is over. She has been defeated. Andropov has complete control over her life.

'Why are you doing this to me?' Her question is a last echo of the self that is no more.

'Get some rest now. We will talk later.'

'How can I rest? What are you doing to me? Where is my son?'

Andropov looks at his watch. 'It is six o'clock,' he says. 'Your son is asleep. The young have a great ability to sleep.'

'I want to see him now.'

'That will not be possible. You will be confined to your room until we are ready. Goodnight, Comrade Marchenko. Or should I say, good morning?'

★

She lies on the bed drained of strength but unable to sleep. She has not bothered to take off her clothes. Her mind is racing out of control, taking her into a waking delirium where reality is replaced by a monstrous and threatening confusion. She is alone in her terror, shaking with cold and fear. She wraps the blanket around herself but the shaking continues. She wants to weep but finds that she cannot. Everything has been taken from her. She is a shell, without feeling or purpose.

There is a knock at the door. Slowly the door opens.

'Mother?'

She holds her son in her arms, she feels the warmth of his breath against her neck, the weight of his body against her. He is alive, and that is the only reality she cares about. The future has no promise any more. She lives only for the moment.

'Are you all right?'

'What's happening?'

What can she tell him? What would Stevens want her to say? Perhaps after today she will never see Valery again. Better to tell him the truth, however painful it may be to her.

'Please forgive me,' she says. This time there are tears in her eyes and he sees them.

'What is it?'

She sits up and tells her son the secret she has kept from him all these years. He listens to her. She does not excuse herself for lying to him about his birth. How can he understand what love is, she asks herself? He is too young to know how irresistible a force love can be, turning the world on its head, defying politics and race and law and religion. Whatever else I have failed at, she tells herself, at least I have known love. I have sacrificed my life to it. In its way that sacrifice has brought its own reward. It gave me a purpose, a direction, and allowed me to survive because it gave me my son.

'Tell me about my father,' the boy asks.

How can she describe him in a manner the boy will understand? She cannot tell him of her own feelings towards Stevens. She must try to look at him objectively and scientifically; she must paint a portrait of a man Valery will probably never see but whom he must never forget.

'He is a scientist,' she says. 'A professor at Cambridge.'

Valery knows about Oxford and Cambridge, the light and dark blue, the boat race, the Cavendish Laboratory where Peter Kapitza worked with Rutherford and together they split the atom (Cambridge is always superior to Oxford in her descriptions, she has caught that from her few days with Stevens). Over the years she has told him about Cambridge because it allowed her to bring Valery closer to his father without giving anything away.

'A year before the war he won the Nobel Prize for Physics, for work he did with a Finn called Laurentzen.'

'What kind of work?'

'He is a nuclear physicist.'

'Describe him to me.'

'You look like him,' she says. 'You have some of his gestures.' She laughs at the memory. 'When he talks to you, he holds his head at an angle. You do that too. He is tall, thin, his hair is white, he has deep blue eyes, lines around his mouth. He is quite serious most of the time but when he smiles his face lights up. He is wise.'

'Wise?'

What she means to say is, when he speaks to me he makes me feel wise, as if I know more than I do, and I am better for it. It is a great gift to be able to share your wisdom with others, rather than intimidate them with it.

'He understands everything. When you talk to him, he makes you think you are better than you are.'

'Would he want to talk to me?'

'I think he would want that more than anything else.'

'Did he ask you about me?'

'All the time.'

'What did you say?'

'I said he would be proud of you.'

The boy smiles at that. 'So I have an English professor for a father.' She wonders what he is thinking at that moment, but he gives nothing away.

'I cannot ask you to forgive me,' she says.

'For what?' he asks.

'I never told you what you had a right to know. I should not have kept this secret from you. I was wrong to do what I did.'

'Not telling me was a sacrifice for you too,' he says. 'You had your reasons. Why should I question them?'

How much older he sounds. In these few moments he has grown up, he is changing before her eyes from a boy to a man. She takes his hand and kisses it. She notices at once that his warmth has gone too. They are both afraid.

'What will happen now?'

'I don't know.'

'Will Andropov come back?'

'He is sure to.'

'Will he take me to meet my father?'

'I don't know. I don't know what he will do.'

Lying on the bed, side by side, mother and son under a single blanket, they wait for Andropov to return.

★

He looks bemused and lost, as if he cannot believe what is happening to him. He has been involved in a struggle. His jacket is torn, his tie has gone, his hair is all over the place. Blood is seeping from his nose and collecting on his shirt-front, and there is a swelling under his eye. Andropov comes into the room after him and offers him a chair.

Stevens looks at his watch. 'I am giving a lecture this afternoon,' he says. 'I am due to speak in fifteen minutes.'

'Professor Laurentzen has been alerted. He will give your apologies and tell the conference you are indisposed.'

She watches him as he slowly becomes aware of his surroundings.

349

First he sees her and his face betrays his horror that she too is involved, that he can do nothing to protect her. He gets up from his seat and comes to sit beside her.

'Are you all right?' he asks.

She kisses him on the cheek and takes a handkerchief from her bag. She dips it in the glass of water by her bedside and starts to clean the blood from his face.

'What happened?' she asks.

'I was dragged from my room,' he says. 'Who is this man?'

'I am Colonel Andropov,' he says in cold, clear and surprisingly unaccented English. 'Let me introduce you to your Russian son.'

He has taken even that away from me, she thinks. Even now in moments of distress he must humiliate me. She knows then the depth of Andropov's brutality. He must win. At all costs, he must always win.

The man and the boy look at each other but they say nothing. She realizes that Stevens can speak no Russian and Valery no English. She must act as interpreter between them.

'Valery.'

Andropov says the boy's name. The boy looks at his mother. She says nothing. The room is filled with silence. For a long moment nobody moves. Then Stevens extends his hand. She watches, astonished, as the boy approaches his father and they shake hands.

She says in Russian, 'Kiss him. Embrace him. He is your father.' Her words are an instruction.

Valery looks embarrassed. He is frozen to the spot. He cannot move. Man and boy stare at each other in silence.

'Very English,' Andropov says in English. 'No tears. No emotion, no embrace. That is not the Russian way. Perhaps your son is a true Englishman after all.'

He makes it sound like a crime.

She wants to scream at him, go away, can't you grant us even a few moments alone together?

She looks at Andropov. He is sitting at a table, writing in his notebook, and she knows that the thought would be incomprehensible to him, so she says nothing.

The door opens and tea is brought in by one of Andropov's minders, a brutal-looking man with close-cropped hair and extraordinary, misshapen ears.

'I can assure you,' he says, 'the tea is not poisoned.'

It is the closest he has ever come to showing he has any sense of humour. He asks Marchenko to pour the tea.

'This is a small moment of history,' he says. 'I do not imagine there can be many other days on which a distinguished English professor has met his Russian son for the first time. Is there a protocol for such occasions? Do we offer a toast? Should I send back the tea and order champagne?'

His question is met with silence. Marchenko watches him take a biscuit, break it in two and eat it. He wipes a crumb from his mouth with a cold, precise gesture.

'Professor Stevens,' he says, 'you see before you the son you did not know until a few hours ago was yours. I am sure the news has come as a shock to you. However, time is short, and I am not in a position to allow you to absorb that shock and come to terms with it, much as I might wish to. Let me come to the point. I am empowered to put a proposal to you. We would like you to come to Moscow as our guest. There, for a few weeks, you may see your son, get to know him; you will have the time to establish a relationship with him. Any costs, of course, will be borne by my directorate. Now, what do you say to that?'

'What are the conditions of your offer?'

Andropov smiles his thin, watery smile, the contraction of the facial muscles that she has come to fear so much.

'I hope you will believe me when I say the offer is unconditional. If you accept it, you will be free to come and go as you choose.'

'Why should I believe you?'

'Why not? At this moment, Professor Stevens, you are in my power. I can keep you here, take you to Moscow or return you to the West at my choosing. Well, I have chosen. I have chosen to make you an offer that I trust you will accept.'

The voice inside her is screaming at Stevens: refuse him, don't trust him, get out of here as quickly as you can, these people are more dangerous than you can imagine. But another voice – one she has not heard before – is saying accept, you can live with us, we will be together again as we should always have been, even if it is only for a few weeks. For the first and perhaps the only time in our lives we will be a family.

'I must have time to think it over,' Stevens says.

'Time is the one gift I am not able to give you.'

'If I refuse your offer?'

Andropov shrugs. 'To some extent, Professor Stevens, we are playing poker. You must assess how strong my hand is.'

Then something extraordinary and unexpected happens. She sees her son come over to his father, kneel down by his chair and take his father's hand. The boy looks up into Stevens's eyes.

'I see we have our answer,' Andropov says. 'Good.'

5

DANNY

I had gone straight to bed when Laurentzen dropped me off at Tanya's flat shortly after six. She'd left me a note to say that she was at the hospital, an emergency with one of her mothers-to-be, and she didn't know when she'd be back. I must have slept right through her return because when I awoke in the early afternoon, her clothes were on a chair, the bathroom floor was wet and I could smell her scent, but she was gone again. This time there was no note, so I assumed she was back on duty at the hospital.

How could the closeness of only a few days ago have vanished, so that now we could come and go without making contact with each other? What had happened? Was it all my fault? I tried to examine my obsession with her relationship with Sigrin. Why could I not accept that it was over? My questions had allowed Sigrin to come between us, and as the hours went by his presence became more and more of an obstacle. Some part of me that I was ashamed to recognize refused to accept that he had gone from her life. The thought of Sigrin was eating away at everything Tanya and I had created for ourselves in those few days on the island. I was aware of the damage he was doing and I seemed to have no power to prevent it.

I got up, had a bath, made myself something to eat and rang the Marski to talk to my father. There was no answer from his room. I remembered that he was due to speak at the conference at some point in the afternoon, which explained his absence. For a while I thought I ought to go to listen to him, but in the end I didn't. My excuse was that he and Marchenko should have some time together away from me. I was an intruder in their lives.

Was my father in love with Marchenko? It was hard to tell. They had been so exhausted after their night of talking, that the fact that

353

he had his arm around her when they came out of the room in Laurentzen's summer house meant nothing. They had said little on the journey back. Marchenko had slipped out of the car with no more than a quiet 'goodbye', and my father had said nothing. He had not touched her, kissed her; he seemed not to hear her, though I noticed that he had turned round to get a last glimpse of her before she disappeared. It must have been a traumatic night for them both.

It was so hot I slept again after that, to be woken by the sound of Tanya in the kitchen making supper. She let me kiss her but there was a coolness in her response, and she did not stop what she was doing. I poured myself a drink.

'If you won't believe me,' Tanya said much later, 'then you must meet Matti and hear the truth from him.'

I rejected the proposal half-heartedly. There was something strangely exciting in the idea of meeting face to face the man I saw as my rival.

'It's far too late,' I said. 'I don't want to meet him and I'm sure he doesn't want to meet me.' But she didn't listen.

'I will telephone him,' she said.

She spoke in Finnish. I could not understand a word, but I had the sense that at first Sigrin was unwilling to do what she asked. She persisted, and finally he agreed. She put down the telephone.

'He is coming here now,' she said. 'I'm going to bed. I don't want to hear you talk about me.'

It was after midnight when the bell went and I opened the door to a man in his late fifties, with grey thinning hair.

'You must be Danny,' he said, shaking my hand. 'I am Matti. Tanya has told me much about you.'

He asked for a drink. 'She keeps her whisky in the cupboard.' I was immediately made aware of his familiarity with the apartment.

'These are troubled times,' he said. 'We are faced with threats we do not understand. We Finns try to practise our neutrality but sometimes it is hard, with the Russians sitting on our borders. What we see alarms us, East and West arming themselves with ever more powerful weapons; we hear the same threatening messages coming from both sides, sometimes it is hard to distinguish one from the other.

'If war is to be avoided, then our country must be the meeting ground of East and West. We will play host to the most important dialogue of the century, the dialogue that avoids nuclear war. We must learn to be the world's diplomats. That is the role we seek for ourselves.'

At that moment I didn't care about nuclear war, East or West or the role the Finns wanted to play. I wanted to know whether or not Sigrin had left Tanya for ever. My world had shrunk to the only issue that mattered to me.

Suddenly Sigrin laughed. 'Why don't you ask me the questions that are written on your face? Shall I answer even though you have not asked them? Is that not why I am here? Tanya wishes me to speak to you but she does not tell me what I am to say. When I look in your eyes, I have no more confusion. Now it is easy. If you do not believe what she says to you, then you do not trust her and your relationship with her has no future. There is nothing I can do to help you.'

'Then why did you come?'

'Tanya wanted you to set eyes on me. It is better to know your supposed enemy than to imagine him. Our dreams are usually more dangerous than the realities we face in our waking lives. If you think I am your rival for Tanya, then so be it. If not, then so be it also. It is not in my control.'

He got up and shook my hand.

'I have been in love with her and she has been in love with me. I am sure she has told you that. In some ways I will always be in love with her. She will not have told you that but, man to man, I am sure you will understand.'

He was taunting me, humiliating me as he had every right to do, and I had no response but to smile bravely and say nothing. If it had been Tanya's plan to solve our dilemma by getting me to talk to Sigrin, it had failed.

I didn't like him and I wanted him to go but, unlike so many of his countrymen, he was a talkative Finn, and an arrogant one. He wanted me to know how important he was; how he knew everyone in Finland from the President down, how he had introduced Tanya to his world.

'Her father was a diplomat, he had some knowledge of the world, but it was I who made her intimate with it.'

He gave me a picture of their life together: the parties he had taken her to, the journeys she had shared with him, the clothes he had bought her, the wines they had drunk together. I suppose it was meant to hurt, the creation of this image of a world that was closed to me, where he had moved effortlessly with Tanya beside him.

As I listened, Sigrin as a threat began to shrink. I saw him for what he was, a man clinging to the past, lost in memories of a time when he had counted, when he had loved and been loved in return. I saw that the glamour that was now in shreds around him had understandably beguiled a young girl's eyes and heart.

The Tanya he described was not the woman I knew. In his eyes, she was a child he had led by the hand into a grown-up world, given gifts because of her beauty but allowed to be no more than a decoration for a vain and worldly man. How far that was from the woman I knew, the doctor who had dressed men's wounds and watched them die, who had faced her brother with the truth about his self-destructive will, who had waited through the bleak winter months for the return of a man, of which she could never be sure.

I knew then that Sigrin no longer counted. I had nothing to fear from this man. My shame at my own behaviour grew more acute with every minute that he stayed.

'I know your people too,' he said, smiling at me. 'I am surprised they did not tell you that.'

'My people?'

'Lander. Maitland. Corless, though I have not met him. I am there when they need me. I can be useful to them. They know the value of my connections. Over the years I have done them good service.'

I was no longer listening to what he was saying. All I could hear were the words in my head, what I would say to Tanya when he was gone. I was impatient to see her, to hold her, to beg her forgiveness. I longed for Sigrin to go.

He left soon after two, more than a little drunk by now. He embraced me as he said goodbye. I shrank from his touch.

I was shamed by my experience. How could I done that? I had to find her, to apologize, to try to rewrite the past hours of doubt and despair, to go back to the love we had shared on her island.

'Tanya.'

I went into the bedroom. The light was out. Without thinking I turned it on.

'Tanya.'

The bed was still made. The room was empty. All the while I had assumed that Tanya was there. But she wasn't. She had gone.

6

MONTY

The first sign that there was a crisis in Helsinki came in a telex from David Lander. Stevens, he reported, had failed to give his speech at the conference. Professor Laurentzen's apology for his absence concealed the fact that no one appeared to know where he was or why he hadn't turned up. An hour later a second message told us Stevens had left the Marski hurriedly in the company of an unknown man, thought to be Russian, some time after three o'clock. At half past midnight we had an unconfirmed report that Stevens had been seen entering the Soviet embassy. By one-fifteen we learned that he had left the embassy but no one knew where he'd gone. We drank tea, smoked cigarettes, hardly dared to leave the room.

Shortly before three, we got a call from Moscow on the scrambler. Maitland took it. He said little but listened hard.

'All right. Thanks. Keep in touch. We'll be staying by the telephone.'

He looked at us, his face grey with exhaustion and doubt.

'That was Martineau. Stevens arrived in Moscow an hour ago. He was driven away from the airport with an intelligence officer called Andropov and a senior member of the Fourth Directorate. He doesn't know where they've taken him. It would appear that our leading nuclear scientist is in Moscow as a guest of the Soviets.'

'Christ,' Adrian Gardner said, 'the bastard's gone over.'

'It certainly looks that way,' Maitland said grimly.

'I never believed he'd do it.' Arthur Gurney looked at each of us in turn. 'Not for a single moment.'

'Somewhere along the line, we got it badly wrong,' Gardner said. he echoed all our thoughts. We had made a serious miscalculation. Now the unthinkable had happened.

'Our enemies have built a bonfire around us,' Corless said, visibly shaken, 'and we're sitting on top of it. It's first a question of time before they put a torch to it and we all go up in smoke.'

7

DANNY

'He was seen getting on a plane for Moscow some hours ago,' Laurentzen said. 'There were three other Russians with him. One of them was identified as a woman.'

'Marchenko?'

Laurentzen nodded. 'She had a boy with her. We presume it was her son.'

'What was her son doing in Helsinki?'

'That I cannot tell you.'

'Did my father struggle?'

'No. He walked unaided.'

'You're sure he wasn't forced?'

How I wanted my mental images of an enforced, Krasov-like departure to be real: my father, strapped to a stretcher, drugged into unconsciousness, being carried away against his will.

'I am sure of nothing but I have no evidence to suggest he left Helsinki against his will.'

He'd gone because he had wanted to go. That was what Jamie was saying. Marchenko had invited him to Moscow and he'd accepted. It was unthinkable. Impossible. Yet that was what had happened. My father had changed sides.

Angry and miserable, I rewrote the events of the previous twenty-four hours in a hopeless attempt to scrape some comfort from the disaster that now stared me in the face. What hurt most was that I had broken the habit of all the years of enmity between us: for the few hours of his meeting with Marchenko I had trusted my father. I had not questioned him. I had not burst into the room and demanded to know what was going on, what they were talking about, why they were meeting in secret. I had accepted Jamie Laurentzen's argument that they needed time together. If I had asked those questions, as I should have done, perhaps I might have shaken some sense into my father before it was too late, and his defection might never have taken place.

I had done nothing. I had compounded my error by not making contact with him afterwards. If I had not quarrelled with Tanya, and had gone instead to the Marski to persuade him to leave Helsinki as I had intended, how different events might have been. My inactivity made me an accessory to this whole bloody mess. There was no comfort to be had. I was horrified by my own complicity.

8

**Extract of a leading article from
the *Daily* ———**

There has been no more sickening sight recently than that of a Nobel prizewinning British professor sitting at the same table in Moscow as his Soviet 'hosts' echoing parrot-like their words about the threat to the world of building a nuclear arsenal.

Don't talk to us about the need for nuclear responsibility, Professor. We don't need telling. Try explaining that idea to the men whose company you're keeping. See if they listen. See if they will cut their so-called defence budget by a single rouble.

How could one of our best brains let himself be taken in so easily? How can this misguided man not see that by becoming the pawn of the Soviets, he has betrayed himself, his country and the democracy for which so many young lives were lost? Where were you, Professor, when the sacrifice of our young people gave us the promise of a future?

Don't waste your time talking to the deaf. They can't hear you. Go back to your ivory tower in Cambridge where you belong. Stick to what you know. Leave the real world to the rest of us. It's not your place.

9

RUTH

She stands by the window, the curtain drawn against the glare of the sun, the raging heat of the late afternoon trapped with her in the airless room. Her thin dress sticks to her like glue. She wants a glass of cold water but her fridge has broken, and however long she runs the tap the water is never quite cold. The fan on her desk whirrs irritably and disturbs her papers, bringing her back to the present and drawing her towards the letter she knows she must write.

For the moment that can wait. She stares sightlessly down at the street below and sees again only the images in her mind.

Her mother is asleep next door, a pale figure visibly shrinking with each day that passes. How much longer will she last? Once it was months – now it is weeks, possibly days. There is nothing to do but make her comfortable and watch her slowly die. Valery has gone swimming with his friends. At the moment she wants him out of the house as much as possible. He is devoted to his grandmother, and she is afraid of what her death will do to him in his present state. He has achieved a certain notoriety in the apartment block because of his newly discovered English father. There have been some difficult moments at school (one of his teachers refused to have him in her classroom for a few days) but such incidents appear to have subsided for the present. What causes her anxiety is that she cannot know if the revelation of Stevens as his father has damaged him.

Her own life, like that of her colleagues at the Institute, remains suspended. They exist in a cushioned limbo. No work is done at the Institute but no action is taken against them. None of their privileges has been rescinded. They have not been questioned or harassed. They are not followed in the street by the secret police (or if they are, they remain unaware of it). On the surface, life goes on as normal. They turn up at the Institute each day: Gromsky, Tomasov, Lykowski, Elizabeth Markarova and the others. They drink tea (Gromsky drinks vodka, no longer secretly), and they talk, openly now – what is the point of concealment when their lack of activity reveals their position? There is a growing sense of unreality about their lives because their position causes no reaction. They are left to their own devices. They are isolated, ignored and powerless. She fears the group will lose its coherence and do the authorities' task for them and destroy itself. Perhaps that is their plan.

Stevens's arrival in Moscow appears to have deflected Lykowski from his search for the murderer of the pensioners in the block near D4. She hopes this is permanent. His attention is now focused on a meeting with Stevens, the reasons for which she is not sure of but she is afraid to arrange this without Andropov's approval, and he refuses to answer her requests for a meeting.

Then there is Stevens and his unexpected presence in her life. How extraordinary that, after all these years, he is here, in Moscow. At times she finds it hard to convince herself she is not still living in the world of her mind.

'He has been here, in my apartment. He has eaten at this table, sat in this chair. He has met my mother who didn't understand why he couldn't speak Russian. He has spent as many hours as he could with his son.'

Not as many as he had wanted. (Why can he spare so little time with her? Why won't he tell her what he does all day in Moscow?) To her surprise she is relieved at this. She is pleased at how well they have communicated through the common language of science. But the science Stevens talks is heretical in a country where Lysenko's aberrations are accepted orthodoxies. She cannot allow him to make Valery forget the importance of the double life. Stevens may insist on telling him the truth but if the boy is to survive, he must conceal his knowledge. That is not something Stevens truly understands, even now.

But he is here. She sees him often. Her dream has come true.

★

Some days after his arrival in Moscow he knocks on her door clutching a bunch of flowers he has bought in the market. She kisses him in greeting, puts the flowers in a vase and offers him vodka.

'I would introduce you to my mother,' she says, 'but she is not well. She spends most of her days asleep now. Perhaps later, if she wakes up.'

He looks around the small, shabby apartment which, to her eyes, looks smaller and shabbier than ever before.

'I have often tried to imagine where you lived.'

'It is very small,' she says. 'Apartments are hard to come by in Moscow. It was difficult after my father died. Our official Party flat was taken away from us.'

'Are these your father's?' He points to the shelves of volumes of political theory – Marx, Lenin, Stalin – that over the years her father religiously accepted from the state publishing house but, she knows, never read.

'Yes,' she says. She has always hated what he cynically referred to as his 'badges of office'.

'Learn a few phrases and quote them publicly,' he explained to her once. 'Don't bother to read these books, no one does – they're far too heavy to read. See them as your credentials. Medals of loyalty to the Party. Display your knowledge of them to protect yourself from the doubts of others. People are wary of opposing anyone who can quote the orthodoxies.'

'These are mine,' she says.

The Cyrillic script on the spines defeats him so she reads out the titles. Tolstoy and Chekhov he knows ('*Anna Karenina* very depressing, *Uncle Vanya* marvellous') but not Dostoevsky ('too much altogether, those brothers. Too deep for me.')

He wanders around the room, picking up objects to examine them, taking books from the shelves even though he can't read them. He peers at photographs: her as a child, a smiling five-year-old in sepia, hands gripping the skirt of her dress; her parents smiling fixedly on their wedding day; her grandparents stiffly upright in front of a statue of Lenin; stilted groups at their summer dacha when they entertained her father's friends, politicians and Party officials (how she hated those occasions); a portrait of her father, heavily retouched, a middle-aged man with the face of a thirty-year-old.

She wants to believe he is taking it all in but she detects a restlessness in his actions. There is some distraction, some anxiety on his mind, that he won't tell her about. At first she puts it down to his unfamiliarity with Moscow. Only later does she sense the strain he is under. She wishes she had the courage to ask him, but she doesn't because she is afraid to hear the truth. This evening with her, and subsequent evenings, are, she suspects, no more than an interval in some other unrevealed drama.

'And Valery?' he asks self-consciously. 'Is he here?'

'It was too hot to stay in,' she says. 'He went to the swimming baths with his friends. He will be back later.'

'Does he have his school books here?' he asks. 'May I look at them?'

She fetches Valery's exercise books from his room and Stevens settles down in a chair while she prepares supper.

'You must be pleased,' he says as they sit down to eat. 'He's very good.'

She has never before shared her son with anyone. He is her possession, hers to guard and protect. She finds it strange to answer questions about his education, which university he will go to, what branch of science he will make his own. She is surprised at the resentment she feels. She does her best to conceal her emotions. She does not believe that Stevens notices her unease.

10

Letter to *The Times* from Professor Edgar Lodz and others of Cambridge University

Is it an act of supreme folly or supreme courage to go to the enemy's camp, sit at his table and warn him of the dangers we face if the development of nuclear weapons is not brought under control?

We believe that Professor Stevens deserves the heartfelt thanks of the citizens of Great Britain, the Soviet Union, indeed every country on the planet for daring to speak the truth. To many of us involved in the teaching of science to younger generations, the prospect of the destruction of all life as we know it is too terrible to imagine. That is why Professor Stevens's act is one of great moral courage. He has dared to imagine the unimaginable; he has reminded us of the uncomfortable truth of our responsibilities, that each generation holds the planet in trust for the next.

Yet our political leaders ignore trusteeship. They argue that their duty is the defence of the realm, and they advance the failures of the 'thirties to attend to this very duty as one of the contributory reasons for the war just ended. The greater the destructive nature of the weapon, they argue, the greater the possibility of peace.

We stand shoulder to shoulder beside Professor Stevens in the belief that the level of potential destruction of a nuclear arsenal invalidates this argument. We are no longer talking about the defence of realms, but the survival of *Homo sapiens*. National barriers will offer no resistance to the deadly hurricane of a nuclear chain reaction. There can be no winners or losers now, no victors and vanquished. There is life on earth, or there is nothing, a void, a poisoned emptiness.

Professor Stevens is right to speak out. We join our voices to his. We hope the growing chorus of sanity from peoples of all nations will drown the folly of our national leaders for the benefit of this and all succeeding generations.

11

RUTH

He comes to see her again (she has lost count how many times now), bringing flowers. He spends time with Valery, asks after her sleeping mother, paces around the apartment, leaves at midnight. He makes no demands of any kind on her.

Tonight he is with her again. Her mother is asleep. (In the rare moments when she is awake she says nothing, eats nothing – soon she will be a presence without substance. How she wishes her mother would die. Her life seems so pointless.) Valery comes home at eight, and she translates the conversation between father and son. When they are together, it seems she has no independent existence: she is merely the means of communication between the two of them. They have supper together. She wonders if he notices the poor quality of the meat and vegetables. They talk. Valery goes to bed. It is midnight and still very hot.

'I must go,' Stevens says, without moving.

Does she want him to stay? Is that what he is asking? How should she respond?

'Stay a little longer,' she says, refilling his glass. 'It's too hot to move.'

Is that the sign he wanted? Has she said the right thing?

He asks about her life. He tries to get her to comment on Soviet society but she is circumspect. How does she know someone has not placed a microphone somewhere in her apartment while she was away in Helsinki? She reveals little, makes a few comments. It is a life, much as any other. They manage. He listens but doesn't question her.

'I must go,' he says later, and this time he stands up. Then she is in his arms again, she doesn't know how this happens, and he is kissing her. This time she is the led, he the leader. As she feels the

367

strength of his arms around her, her mind travels back to that summer night in Leiden. How cool it was then, how perfect, how gentle the heat. Now it is stifling, the air squalid and damp with humidity. They are eight floors up in a cramped apartment, near them are a dying woman and a teenage boy.

He murmurs to her, words she can hardly catch let alone understand. She accepts his kisses, she holds his head in her hands (wasn't it like this all those years ago?). She feels his hands across her back. There is a desperation in his gestures as if she will evaporate under his grasp. (She is so hot she might do just that if he doesn't let go of her. She can hardly breathe.) She is aware of the sudden urgency in his touch.

She has not slept with a man since Miskin and that was many months ago. Somehow with Miskin it was never satisfactory (her memories are of fumbling fingers, buttons refusing to undo, clasps sticking, obstacles undermining their lovemaking). She remembers Leiden, and the feeling that in giving herself to him she had brought a sense of perfection into her life. Will she risk losing that memory if she sleeps with him now?

She leads him to the bedroom and the narrow bed with the hard mattress. The walls are paper-thin. Valery must be asleep, surely. Whatever they do they must do it quietly. She does not turn on the light. The room is illuminated by the street lights below. (Wasn't it moonlight in Leiden, not this awful neon?)

'Wait,' she says. She goes into the bathroom (why can she never get rid of the smell of human waste, no matter how hard she tries?) and takes off her dress. She stares at her reflection in the mirror. She assesses the damage of the years, dark shadows under her eyes, pallid skin, grey hair (damp over her forehead), furrows on her cheeks, stippled lines around her lips as if a string were being pulled tight around her mouth. How dry her skin is. (For years she kept in her drawer the empty bottle of skin cream she had bought in Leiden until in frustration she threw it away. Why is there never face cream in the Soviet Union?) The redness of her neck. How heavy her bosom is – she has inherited that from her mother. She is old and dry and ugly. How she hates herself. She wants to cry.

Look at me, she says to the mirror. 'How can he possibly want me now?

Dressed only in her slip she goes back into the bedroom. He is sitting on the edge of the bed, his cuffs unbuttoned, his tie off, the top button of his shirt undone. He holds out his arms towards her and takes her hands in his. She stands in front of him. Their knees touch. He smiles reassuringly up at her.

'We must be very quiet,' she whispers. 'The walls are so thin here.'

'Do you remember Leiden?' he asks.

'I will never forget it,' she says.

'Nor will I,' he says.

'Was it love or passion?' she asks.

'Do you separate love from passion in Russia? Is that a Politburo diktat too?'

'I fell in love for the first time that night,' she says. 'You knew that, didn't you?'

'Of course. It was all very unexpected.'

'No more than that?'

'Wonderful, too,' he says shyly. 'Wonderful and exciting.'

'I heard your voice and immediately I was in the grip of something, a force I had never experienced.' Now they have begun to talk of that time she cannot stop herself. 'It raged inside me, dictating my every action. I was no longer in control of myself. I fell in love with you the moment you first spoke to me. I have never forgotten how that felt.'

At last she is telling him what every day for too many years she has longed to tell him. That part of her dream, too, has come true.

'I remember the first time I saw you,' he says. (Did he love her? Will he tell her that?) 'I was sitting on the platform, bored rigid, wondering what on earth I was doing in that place, when I saw you. You were staring at the speaker, your face was shining and beautiful.'

'Beautiful, no,' she laughs with pleasure. 'Shining, well I expect that was the heat.'

He has let go of her hands and she is sitting beside him on the bed, one leg drawn up under her. She can feel the heat of his body next to hers.

'Beautiful,' he says, 'So beautiful I couldn't stop looking at you.' He touches her face with his fingers. She takes his hand and kisses it.

'In the coffee interval I had to speak to you. I remember pushing rudely past friends and colleagues who wanted to talk to me, saying "Later, later". I thought that if I didn't reach you quickly you would vanish and I would never see you again. Nothing could have stopped me, I could have walked through a concrete wall.'

She wants him to go on and on, to talk to her for ever about those days. She wants to float in her memories of Leiden, with him beside her.

'And later?' she asks. 'What did you think of me then?'

'How brave you were, how I would do everything in my power to spend the rest of my life with you.'

I have spent the rest of my life with you, she wants to say. But she remains silent. Has he ever thought of her? Has he preserved her in his mind as she has preserved him? Of course not, that would be impossible. He is not sentimental. He has no secret life like her. What man does?

'I was in a dream,' she says, 'for weeks afterwards. I wanted to shout to the world, I know what love is! It is a wonderful thing. Then I discovered I was carrying your child. I was happy, ecstatic with my secret.'

'Why did you never tell me?'

'If we had met again, I would have told you.'

'Couldn't you have written?' he asks thoughtlessly.

'If someone had read that letter, I would have been exposed as little more than a prostitute for sleeping with a Western scientist. Who knows what would have happened then?'

She knows, only she dare not tell him.

'I'm so sorry. I should not have said that.'

'Please. There can be no regrets. We have lived our lives apart because that is how it was meant to be. We must count ourselves lucky to have our memories and our son.'

'You were always more practical than me,' he says, laughing.

'Will you stay?' she asks eventually.

'Do you want me to?' he asks.

'Yes,' she says, with a conviction she doesn't feel.

They lie naked on her narrow bed with just a sheet to cover them. Suddenly he sits up and looks down at her.

'I must tell you the truth,' he says. Is this the moment she has waited for all these years? 'I loved you. It was not just passion. Passion alone doesn't possess your soul, doesn't wrench your heart, turn your world upside down, make you see everything differently. For weeks afterwards I could do little, hardly any research work, little teaching. My memories were the only reality I knew. I thought

I would go mad with wanting you. But you can't sustain a life at that level of intensity. Cambridge alone was not Leiden with you.'

I could die now, she says to herself, secure in the knowledge that I have loved and been loved.

'Gradually; I found a sense of proportion. I forced myself to accept what was possible and what was impossible.'

'It would be impossible to see me again?'

'I have regretted that decision ever since.'

She is crying silent tears. He wipes the tears away from her cheeks but still she cries.

'Please don't cry,' he says. 'I can't bear it. I have failed you. I failed to rescue you from this terrible city where you live. I never gave you the life you deserved.'

'You could not have rescued me,' she says. 'That was impossible. Not to have recognized that would have been madness.'

That is why I found a secret place where I could keep our love safe and undiscovered.

She reaches up and touches his face. 'We may be older,' she says, 'but passion needn't desert us yet, need it?'

She puts her arms around him and kisses him, his neck, his shoulders, his arms, his chest, all of him, tasting him on her lips, drawing his spirit and his strength into her body, until she cannot tell what is him and what is her. All she knows is that what she experiences is love, the sharp, sweet tongues of love whispering songs she has not heard for a long time.

★

Sometime in the night, she wakes and asks, 'Why do you stay here? What do you want from us? We have nothing to give you. Surely you know that.'

He sleeps the sleep of the innocent. If he hears her he says nothing.

'Please be careful,' she whispers.

12

DANNY

I sat alone in the apartment with the blinds drawn. It seemed safer that way. When the telephone rang I ignored it. I wanted to be alone, out of sight, left to myself.

Twenty-four hours ago Matti Sigrin had sat in the chair opposite me. Tanya had been right. Her gamble brought me to my senses. But it had been too late. Soon after I had lost the woman I loved to my own madness and my father to the Russians. I was full of self-contempt for the way I had behaved towards Tanya. I loathed myself. There was no one else I could blame for what had happened. I reached for the whisky and poured myself another glass.

An hour later – perhaps it was more, I had no idea of the time – the doorbell rang. I awoke with a start and stayed put, hardly daring to breathe. It rang again, a longer blast this time, then the letter box was rattled. Then silence again, leaving me to my misery.

I had failed in everything I had tried to do. I had been unable to control my anxieties about Tanya, I had not persuaded my father to leave Helsinki, nor had I protected him while he was there. Was there nothing I could do properly? Helsinki was the city of my humiliation and I wanted to get away from it as fast as I could.

Where to? Home? To do that I would have to go past the mocking stares of the embassy officials, run the gauntlet of the suspicions of the Finnish police – I must know more than I had let on, why else would I have been in Helsinki at the same time as my father? Then back to what? The sneering hostility of the British press, grave-robbers of my father's reputation. It was an appalling prospect.

I must have dozed again because the next thing I was aware of was the door opening and a shadowy figure creeping into the apartment.

'Danny?' A whisper. Fingers lightly touching my hand. 'Are you all right?' The voice I thought I'd never hear again.

'Yes.'

'I heard the news. I'm so sorry.'

Was that why she'd come back? She'd heard about my father and had felt sorry for me. I bit my tongue and stopped myself saying the first thing that came into my mind.

How long did we stand there like that? A second? A minute? An hour? I wanted her in my arms, I wanted to hold her and to feel in her touch that the past was erased, that I was forgiven for my unforgivable behaviour.

'I went because I was not sure of you any more,' she said. 'I did not know what you might do or say. I stayed away because I was afraid you would not be here when I returned.'

'I'm here,' I said. 'I'm never going away again. Never.'

'Never without me,' she said, her fingers tightening around mine. 'Never without me.'

She was in my arms, kissing me, giving herself to me. I knew then that what she had told me was true. The past is nothing because it's dead. What matters is the present and the future. Her present and her future were mine, and mine hers.

13

Extract from a letter from Geoffrey Stevens
to Danny Stevens

I will not ask you to understand what I have done. I can explain my motives. What judgement you make is up to you.

I believed that I could do some good. Saving Ruth's life became a metaphor for saving the world from nuclear disaster by arguing the case with the scientists here. What is science if not the only true international language? We have the power to destroy our civilization, I told them. I thought I could face them with the dire consequences of our mutual folly and get them to change their minds. I thought I would speak to men and women of like mind, members of the same community. I thought individual opinion might become a chorus.

How wrong I was. There are no grounds for argument here because argument is forbidden. There is only one truth, and that truth is dependent upon the Central Committee whose decisions cannot be questioned because they are the logical deductions of the principles of Marxist-Leninism. The process of debate has been dismantled. Scientific enquiry does not exist. The answers to everything are to be found in Marxist theory.

Scientists who honour truth have been dismissed from their posts, some denied their academic degrees; they have vanished or are in prison camps or work at menial jobs. All opposition has been crushed. Reason is dead. Time-servers rule. I am surrounded by men and women who owe their positions to the fervour of their Marxism, their belief in socialist reconstruction, not to any inherent ability nor any objective truth. They are dangerous evangelists of a corrupt dogma and such is the depth of the corruption that surrounds me here, their gospel cannot be challenged because its political origins are considered to be without blemish. Their truth is the new faith. These men and women are the ruling elite here.

Surrounding them are the sullen masses who close their ears to every noise in the night, who avert their eyes from the realities of life around them because they are frightened. I have never before seen a society built on fear. I have never understood how fear of your wife, your husband, your son, your daughter, your neighbour, your teacher, your employer can shrink your humanity to nothing, annihilate your responsibilities to others, erode your sense of self until all that is left is the will to survive, a pure animal instinct and nothing more.

We have been betrayed in the West by so many who came here in the years before the war and saw what they wanted to see, heard what they wanted to hear and proclaimed the new socialist dawn. But in reality it is the blackest endless night imaginable.

As for my own circumstances, I am a mixture of prisoner and celebrity. I have my own apartment, I am looked after, my clothes are washed, my food is cooked for me, I can see Ruth and Valery whenever I choose, I have been allowed to speak to scientists at the Institute of Nuclear Research. I have been paraded in front of the press, much against my will. Statements have been issued in my name which I have no knowledge of, praising the Soviet system. I have been betrayed at every turn, used by Andropov and his people as a pawn in a propaganda war. Whatever you may read about me, it is not true.

Is it worth it? Might some shred of goodness come out of all this mess that can save me from my own humiliation? The safety of Ruth and her son is, if not secure (is anything secure here?), at least possible but I cannot guarantee it. I have seen how Ruth has become another person here. When we are together my presence reminds her of what she was. She can only survive in this city of darkness by eradicating that woman and becoming another. These two selves are incompatible. I am a permanent reminder of what she has lost, and if I stay much longer I will drive her to despair. I cannot do that to her. Somehow I must get out of here before I do more damage.

Today I went for a walk. I am followed everywhere I go, there is no attempt at disguise. I looked out at the Moscow River and wished it were the Cam. A man came and stood beside me. At first I didn't notice him. Then he spoke to me in English.

'Professor Stevens?'

'Yes.'

'My name's Williams. I'm a journalist here.'

'Oh yes?'

'I wanted you to know how much we despise you for what you've done.'

He looked at me with contempt and walked away.

Help me, Daniel. Help me. I thought I could do good and I was wrong. I have made a terrible mistake. I have gained nothing and lost everything. Help me. Please.

14

RUTH

One night he wakes her and whispers that he is a prisoner in her city, that he cannot do anything without Andropov's approval, that when he is not conforming to Andropov's timetable he has to stay in his small apartment, reading, smoking, listening to the radio, for hours on end. Andropov's guard sits all day and all night by the lift at the top of the stairs.

'He smokes disgusting cigarettes.'

'Red Stars,' she says. 'They always smoke Red Stars, the filthiest cigarettes in the world.'

He has been interviewed by officers of the intelligence service in a large yellow building in the centre of Moscow. She recognizes his description of the Lubyanka and wonders if their interviews have taken place in the same room. He has told them nothing. To his surprise they have accepted his right to keep silent and have not questioned him further.

'Why didn't you tell me before?' She asks, at last understanding his strange restlessness.

'I didn't want to disappoint you,' he says. 'I didn't want to add to your burdens. I have almost told you many times.'

Then, in the dark, holding her hand tightly, he pours out his misery and frustration to her. She has to remind him to whisper.

'I am shown continuously round laboratories, scientific engineering works, model factories, apartment blocks under construction. I meet factory workers, builders, architects, I see plans for vast new workers' cities, I am given instruction on the richness of resources in the Soviet Union by economists from government institutions. I am told of limitless budgets for scientific enquiry. It would seem I am on a conducted tour of the Soviet wonder-state.'

'Do you believe what you see?' she asks.

He hesitates before answering. 'What no one will tell me is the price that is paid for it all. How can I believe anything until I know that?'

For an instant she wonders herself. How is this possible? Where do these resources come from? Her mind toys momentarily with the idea that within the state she knows there is another state, a mirror image, inverted, where freedom is slavery, day is night. This city is hidden somewhere in the endless Soviet deserts, cruelly dedicated to the ambitions of the men in the Kremlin; a hateful, cancerous secret in this kingdom of secrets, one that is too awful even to be whispered. She dismisses the thought.

His requests to speak to Soviet scientists (his old friend, Peter Kapitza) or to lecture to scientific students have all been refused.

'If it weren't for you and the boy . . .' he says, and stops.

They lie in the dark, prisoners behind invisible bars, looking up at the pattern of light reflected on the ceiling of the bedroom. His sudden silence tells her he is learning to live in this strange country.

★

They are washing up when he surprises her with his question. 'I have a day free. I would like to meet your colleagues. Can that be arranged?'

(When he asks, Andropov told her after she had finally pinned him down to a brief meeting, you must agree.)

'Of course,' she replies. 'You must come to the Institute.'

That is why they are gathered now in one of the meeting rooms, Tomasov, Gromsky, Markarova, Lykowski. The sun pours in through the opened windows and it is very hot. Elizabeth Markarova has asked for a fan to be brought (the fan that usually serves the meeting rooms has disappeared while being serviced), but there are no spare fans in the building.

'Would it be cooler,' Tomasov suggests, 'to pick up our chairs and sit outside under the cedar tree?'

Outside is a dying wilderness. The long grass is uncut and burned brown in the drought, no one has bothered to clear away the dead flowers. Ruth wants to hide all this from Stevens (would he notice?) because she knows that in Cambridge the grass in the colleges is always green and well kept and the flowers are neatly arranged in narrow beds. (She remembers him telling her this all those years ago.) She is embarrassed by this example of Soviet neglect.

'Couldn't we pull down the blinds?' she asks, adding defensively. 'To keep out the glare.'

Tomasov, who is chain-smoking, gets up, cigarette between his lips, and draws the blinds. The room is cast into gloom. The heat is as intense as ever.

'Now we can't see a thing,' Gromsky says.

Lykowski opens a bottle of mineral water using a penknife (there is no bottle-opener on the table, there never has been for as long as anyone can remember. Bottles of mineral water are seldom opened). He pours himself a glass.

'Does your professor speak Russian?' Elizabeth Markarova asks. She is smoking nervously. 'If not, how will he know what we have to say?'

'I will translate,' Ruth says.

'You've concealed your ability to speak English very well, Ruth,' Markarova says, stubbing out her cigarette angrily. 'What a clever moment to reveal it.'

She has felt Elizabeth Markarova's hostility since this meeting was arranged. She suspects it is jealousy. Markarova was one of the group that went to Leiden. She remembers her disapproval then. Ruth is sure Markarova never imagined that Stevens would reappear in her life in this way. She is frustrated that there is no advantage she can gain from it.

'When did you say he was coming?' Pavel is strung up, more so than usual. 'It's half past now. If he's going to be late—'

'He is always punctual,' she says trustingly.

The tension is worse than she imagined and she doesn't understand why. They are restless, irritable with nerves, on edge, too ready to find fault with each other or with her. She is alarmed by their state of mind. What are they expecting from Stevens? Is there something going on she knows nothing about? Or has she miscalculated? Should she have warned Stevens? She is suddenly terrified that the meeting will slip out of her control.

There is the sound of voices in the corridor. The door opens and Stevens is shown in.

'I hope I haven't kept you waiting,' he says. Ruth introduces him to each member of the group.

'Professor Stevens of Cambridge University. This is a great honour for all of us.'

Did she ever imagine in all her dreaming that one day she would see her English professor shaking hands with her colleagues in the main meeting room of the Institute?

'May I sit here?' He takes a seat at the end of the table. 'Thank you for your invitation. It is a great pleasure to be asked to come here. I am sure you have questions for me. Why don't you begin?'

He looks round at each of them while she translates his question into Russian. Gromsky and Tomasov nod self-consciously to signify that they have understood.

'We have only one question and it does not matter which of us asks it,' Lykowski says, spitting out the words in the urgency of his request. 'Please tell us what we are all anxious to know. What has our protest achieved? Has it been successful?'

Ruth can see that this is not the question Stevens had expected. He has come prepared for a scientific discussion. Her stomach turns as she realizes that she has completely misread the mood of the group. She knows that around this table the questions will be largely political.

'I am sitting here now among you,' Stevens says. 'My presence in Moscow is proof of your success.'

His remark does not receive the response he is expecting. There is bafflement and uncertainty around the table as they listen intently to Ruth's translation.

'I do not think Professor Stevens understands,' Lykowski insists. 'What we want to know is whether our actions have changed anything.'

'It is too soon to say,' Stevens replies. 'But I can assure you the bravery of your stand is widely known outside the Soviet Union. The idea of renouncing nuclear weapons is now actively debated in the West. It is an idea with many supporters, some of them powerful men. There is a growing body of public opinion in favour of inter-national, non-political control of nuclear development. Without your courage, perhaps this debate might never have started.'

Lykowski is shaking his head. 'Please,' he says, 'you misunderstand my question. It is not the West I am referring to. It is our own Soviet leadership. Have we convinced them by our actions? That is the question you must answer for us.'

'How can I answer that?' Stevens asks Ruth. 'I don't know what your government thinks.'

'You must tell them the truth,' she says, feeling sick.

Stevens surveys the questioning faces in front of him. 'I know nothing about your government's reaction,' he says. 'I cannot answer your question.'

There is silence in the room. The gloom deepens.

'You have no idea?'

'How could I have?'

'Have you not spoken to members of the Central Committee since your arrival in Moscow?'

'No.'

'Have you not met members of the Politburo?'

'I have met no senior political officials. Nor have I been presented with the opportunity to do so.'

'Do you not want to meet our leaders?' Tomasov asks.

'What could I say to them?'

'Are you not here as an emissary from the West to persuade our government to change its policy on the manufacture of nuclear weapons?'

'No.'

'Then why have you come?'

It is worse than she has imagined it could be.

'I'm here on my own account,' Stevens replies. 'My presence has nothing to do with the Central Committee or any political body, Soviet or Western.'

'However important you may be in your country, what can you achieve here on your own?'

'I come with messages of encouragement from the West. You are strongly supported by your fellow scientists in other countries. Many of us are solidly behind you. I represent that support. You have the protection of our voices. Now you can sleep easier at night.'

Gromsky turns away, shaking his head. 'That is nothing,' he says. 'Nothing at all.'

'I did not expect to find that people in the West worry about whether I sleep at night.' Lykowski laughs contemptuously. He spits his remarks at Ruth. She is losing him now.

'You must help me,' Stevens says to Ruth. He is bewildered. 'Your colleagues want me to deliver something that is impossible.'

Before Ruth can say anything, Elizabeth Markarova interrupts.

'This is not the message we thought you would bring us, Professor Stevens,' she says. 'We understood you had been sent by your government to talk to ours. We expected you to report on the success or failure of your meeting. We see that we were misinformed. You can understand our disappointment.'

'He does not understand the truth about our socialist republic, does he?' Tomasov says. 'A man alone can achieve nothing.'

'Tell him we are grateful for what he has done,' Elizabeth Markarova says. 'Don't tell him the truth, that if his presence here has nothing to do with his government, then there is nothing he can do for us. Let him return home believing he has accomplished some good.'

Is that what they believed? That they could change their own government's policy? Are they so insular that they care nothing about international opinion?

'We have been defeated,' Lykowski says. 'Defeated, deceived and humiliated.'

'What are they saying?' Stevens asks.

'Dr Markarova is grateful for your efforts,' Ruth lies. 'It is good to know that we have international support. We are sure this will influence the policy-makers on the Politburo.'

Elizabeth Markarova's insistent nodding underlines the lie as Stevens smiles at her.

★

The boy's expression is solemn. He stares at his father and says in Russian: 'You cannot stay.'

She translates. Stevens asks, 'Why not?'

'Our lives are built on lies. Surely you know that by now.'

'Valery, no.' She wants to stop him before it is too late.

'Please, mother. Translate for me.'

'Why must you tell him this?'

'I want him to understand. I want him to know that I understand.'

She translates and Stevens listens. 'We live double lives here,' the boy says. 'We hide our true selves from discovery by the state or by our neighbours. Many of us have buried our hearts and consciences. We have forgotten who we are. That is why we behave like slaves, why we accept, succumb. We are a lost people, without morality, without courage, waiting for a day that may never come. Our lives are being stolen from us by stealth. One day the illusion will break and we will wake up. We will see the enormity of the crime in which we are passive conspirators. It will be too late then;

382

you cannot turn the clock back and relive your life by different rules.'

'What are you telling me?' Stevens asks.

'You do not belong here,' the boy says. 'You must go home.'

★

An insistent rhythm penetrates her dreams, invading the floating world of her mind, forcing her to rise from its depths and wake up. She hears it again, edgy and sharp, alarming her. She gets out of bed and puts on her nightdress. She hears it again. A hand drumming urgently on the door of her apartment.

Nearly two o'clock. Surely it is too late for a visit, even though it is a hot night. (People are out in the streets, all evening she has heard the sounds of their voices through the open windows.) She unlocks the door, her heart pounding, and as she opens it, Andropov bursts in.

'Is Stevens here?' he asks, pushing past her.

'It's two in the morning.'

'I want to see him.'

'I was asleep.' It isn't what she means to say, but in her confusion and fright these are the only words she can say.

'Get the English Professor out of bed.'

She looks at him blankly, her mind in turmoil. What is happening? Why is Andropov in her apartment at this time of night? Why is he shouting at her? She has never heard him speak like this before. His raised voice strikes fear into her heart.

'Bring him to me.'

He takes her by the arm and shakes her. Horrified, she shrinks from him.

'What's going on?'

Stevens is standing at the door, an absurd figure, his hair uncombed, his body eccentrically wrapped in the sheet from the bed, like a toga. He is fumbling with his spectacle case.

'We have a visitor,' she says feebly.

'This is surely too late for a social call, Colonel Andropov, even in Russia,' Stevens says. 'What do you want?'

'Sit down,' Andropov says. He pulls out a chair. 'I presume it is me you have come to see.' Stevens sits down and puts his hand through his hair, brushing it into some kind of shape.

'That is correct.'

'What is this about?'

'Do you wish to speak in front of Dr Marchenko?'

Stevens nods, uncertain.

Andropov leans against the window ledge and looks down at Stevens. He takes out a cigarette and lights it.

'We made a bargain and you have broken it,' Andropov says.

'What bargain? I made no bargain,' Stevens says. (Is he expressing outrage or confusion?)

'We agreed that you would retain your freedom so long as you left the boy alone.' Andropov's tinted lenses appear menacingly dark in the half-light of the room.

'I agreed nothing of the kind.'

'You were to leave the boy alone.'

Her instinct tells her that Andropov is not talking to Stevens, he is giving a message to her.

'Did you expect me not to talk to my own son?'

'You know exactly what I mean,' Andropov says bluntly.

'Geoffrey?' She is frightened now. Threats to her own life, Geoffrey's, even her mother's, are all things she can cope with. But her son is the most precious thing in the world to her. 'What did you promise?'

She sees Stevens turn towards her, horror in his eyes. How can she say that? How can she ask such a question of the man she loves? Has she sunk so low now that she doubts the father of her son?

'You were not to speak to the boy,' Andropov says coldly. 'You were to teach him nothing.'

'I made no bargain and I have broken no bargain.'

'His teachers say differently.' Their reports give accounts of V. Marchenko subverting his fellow students by persistent attacks on Academician Lysenko's theories. That is anti-communist propaganda.'

'That's not true,' Ruth says, the desperation in her heart making her voice hoarse with emotion. 'My son would never do such a thing. Never.' She has trained him too well for that.

Andropov ignores her. It is as if she was not in the room. There is a contest going on between these two men whose meaning she does not understand and in which she has no part. But she knows that is what Andropov came for.

'There is only one possible source that allows him to promote such opinions.'

'There are many sources for those views,' Stevens says. She is proud of the vigour of his rejection. 'His own common sense, his scientific instinct, the doubts of his fellow pupils, the opinions of other scientists. Anyone with any knowledge of the laws of physics. Lysenko's theories are dangerous nonsense and should not be taught.'

'They may not be taught in the West.'

'They're bloody nonsense, of course no one teaches such absurd ideas in the West.'

'They are endorsed officially here.'

'If you knew any science you would have nothing to do with Lysenko. What's happened to the great tradition of Soviet scientific enquiry? How can you allow yourselves to be beguiled by such idiocy?'

Stevens is shouting at him. She still does not understand what is happening. Andropov cannot have come to her apartment at two in the morning to argue about scientific theory.

'If Valery is denouncing Lysenko's mad ideas, then he is right to do so. But he isn't, is he? He isn't denouncing anything because he hasn't opened his mouth. You and your people have invented this whole ludicrous story. God knows what you hope to gain by it.'

Andropov pulls an envelope out of his pocket.

'Here are the reports of his teachers, his classmates. That is all the evidence I need.'

'Evidence for what?' Ruth's heart is beating so fast she can hardly speak.

'To order his arrest.'

There are the first words he has addressed to her.

'My son is not a dissident,' she says quietly. 'He has done nothing. I will not allow you to touch him.'

'The boy's sixteen. Little more than a child,' Stevens says. 'He poses no threat to you or anyone. Why can't you leave him alone?'

'We cannot tolerate the son of a Soviet scientist who proclaims unorthodox views,' Andropov says.

'A boy of sixteen cannot undermine this or any other state,' Stevens says defiantly. 'You can do better than that.'

'Your son will be charged with offences against the state.'

'No!' Ruth screams. 'No! You won't touch him! He is my son. He belongs here with me. You cannot touch him. He has done nothing.'

She rushes at Andropov but Stevens holds her back. She tries to break from his grasp.

'He's not here to arrest anyone,' Stevens says, taking charge. 'That's not why he came, is it?' He turns to Andropov. 'He's threatening Valery in order to frighten me. He wants something else. All right, I'll listen to what you have to say. But the boy must be left out of it.'

Andropov stares blankly at him and doesn't move. Ruth waits. Once more she has the sense that this confrontation has another agenda, another script, the purpose of which she has no idea.

Stevens pulls the sheet tighter around him. 'Tell me what you want.'

The sight of these two men in her small sitting room, facing each other like gladiators, is a moment of illumination for Ruth. Suddenly she sees the truth with awful clarity. She knows that she can have either her son or her lover but for reasons she doesn't understand she can never have both.

'What are we playing for?' Stevens asks. It is a game they are playing now, where the bets are human lives.

'The boy,' Andropov says.

'No,' Stevens says. 'The evidence against him is false. A few typed sheets. Anyone could do that. We play for the truth or we don't play.'

Andropov smiles. 'If I have created it once, could I not create it twice?'

'The question you must decide is, will it be worth it?'

'That we will see,' Andropov says. 'It depends what you can offer me.'

They are not fighting over her, these two men (did she believe for a moment that they might be?), she is forgotten. They are fighting another battle which will decide whether or not Stevens survives intact. She knows without a word being spoken that Stevens must leave Moscow, that her greater loyalty is to her son. That is not the point at issue. It is the method of Stevens's leaving that counts. Will he be allowed to return to Cambridge whole enough to be able to continue as before?

'What must I do?'

'We want you to go home.'

'Just that?'

'Just that.'

'Why?'

Andropov lights a cigarette. 'Our assessment was wrong. We imagined you might help us. We were mistaken. You cannot or you will not give us the information we need. We could use force against you to persuade you to talk, but strange as it may seem, we can see no purpose in that. It is better that you leave the Soviet Union and return home.'

She knows then that he cannot go home undefeated. The battle that Andropov is fighting is already over. Whatever is agreed now, Andropov has won. Stevens will return to Cambridge disabled by his weeks in Moscow and she, Ruth Marchenko, will have been the instrument of his defeat. Why did she let Andropov use her to bring Stevens to Moscow? She should never have told Stevens that Valery was their son. She should have resisted the opportunity to meet him again after so many years. She should have had the courage to go on living alone in her dreams where she and Valery were safe. Imagining that she could have Stevens to herself again, even for a few days, was her mistake.

In any case, in the years they have been apart he has forged another life, just as she has done. She has tried to steal that other life by rekindling the love that she once felt for him, and in doing so she has put her son in jeopardy and caused her lover's downfall. Stevens does not understand that now but one day soon, when his life lies in tatters around him, he will come face to face with the truth of what has happened. Then he will condemn her. How she hates herself for her weakness.

★

It is dawn. She is alone. She sits at her desk and writes the letter to Stevens she has been wanting to write for days.

Are some dreams more precious than the reality of life itself?
Do we need the safety of escape to a world we can control
for the sake of our own sanity? In the imagined universe
where I have protected our memories, we have loved and
lived together all these years, we have shared delights and
sorrows. I have had the faithful companionship of a wise
friend from whom I could seek advice, whose voice has
always come to my rescue in the moments of my greatest
loneliness. In that secret world you have always been mine
and I yours.

387

Part of me does not regret seeing you again. The man I met was the man I remembered, the only difference being that I could touch you, see you, experience your presence beside me. They were wonderful hours. But they made me weak. They made me want more of you. I hated to think that you might leave me a second time. Selfishly, I agreed to get you to come here, to Moscow. I was deceived and I deceived you. What greater crime is there than to deceive the man you love?

My love for you has been used against you. You were brought here to the son you didn't know you had. Whatever you may have gained by coming to Moscow, you will pay for on your return home. No one will ever understand your motives for being here, you will not be forgiven. Your career will be ruined because you were true to your feelings. Is the gain worth the cost? For all our sakes, I can only hope so. If I did not believe that, my life would not be worth living.

You must leave Moscow before its evil damages your life any further. Already you have suffered appallingly. Please go while there is still time to salvage something. There is nothing to stay for here. I have you in my son, and we will survive because that is what we have learned to do. But this is not your world.

Ask your other son, Daniel. See in him the goodness that I see in you. Listen to him. He knows the world in a way you never will.

You have given me my son. My gift to you is to return to you your other son. Now leave this awful place and go to him. I have my memories of you, and they will be with me always.

I have brought you so much trouble. Can you find it in your heart to forgive me?

Remember us and our love for you, always.

15

MONTY

The room on the second floor of the house off Park Road in Wimbledon is dark. Someone has pulled down the blinds, even though it is daylight outside. The bulbs in the overhead light and the lamp on the table are weak and give out a watery glow, adding to the hallucinatory atmosphere of the proceedings. The interrogation team works in shifts. The questioning continues relentlessly.

★

His first impression is not how crowded the room is, nor how many people are there (certainly many more than he had expected), nor how noisy it is (everyone is talking at once), but how full of smoke, as if someone had lit a bonfire, the acrid smell of Soviet cigarettes. Bloody Red Stars. His eyes burn, he can hardly see to the back of the room where the film cameras are. He is just able to read *Pathé News* on the side of one of them. The talking dies away as he takes his seat, and the smoke gradually clears. Andropov draws up a chair beside him and pours a glass of water for them both. A battery of microphones faces him, strange metal fish waiting to capture what he says and swim away with it to an invisible world.

Is this the world's press? he thinks as he surveys the room. What a grand phrase for such a dismal collection.

'Professor Stevens would like to read a statement.'

Andropov nods at him. He takes the paper from the inside pocket of his jacket and unfolds it. The action revives memories of the day-long battle he and Andropov have waged over what he should say. For a moment he wonders, shall I tear up the text? Shall I say what I want to say? But he decides not to. Yesterday's compromises were hard won.

'I would first like to express my gratitude to Colonel Andropov and his colleagues for their hospitality towards me since my arrival in Moscow. I have wanted for nothing.'

He hears his own voice and it is as if someone else were speaking. He is astonished that he could be praising the Soviets in this way, when at every turn they have put obstacles in his path, they have lied continuously, they have deliberately misled him. He told Andropov yesterday that no one would believe him if he were to thank his Russian hosts in this way. But Andropov insisted that this appalling, hollow introduction remain in the script.

'What is a British nuclear scientist doing in Moscow? That is what you want to know. I came here because I believed that if I appeared in the Soviet camp, there was an even chance I might be listened to.

'The importance of what I have to say lies beyond ideology, nation states, the ambitions of world leaders. It concerns us all, every man, woman and child, every living organism on this planet.'

★

There is a knock at the door. They stop talking at once. Someone brings in a tray of mugs of tea. They each take the mug offered in silence. He sees that milk has already been added. There is a bowl of sugar and one spoon to be shared for stirring. He declines the sugar.

'Why did you go to Moscow after Helsinki?'

'I wanted to see my son.'

'You and Marchenko had been planning this for some time.'

'On the contrary, it was a shock to learn from Dr Marchenko that I was the father of her child. A great shock.'

'We know you met your son in Helsinki. Why was it necessary to go to Moscow?'

'He and his mother were under guard in Helsinki. It was impossible to talk to him in such circumstances. I wanted to be alone with him. I wanted to see him without Colonel Andropov listening to every word I said.'

'The circumstances would be more favourable in Moscow?'

'That is what I believed, yes.'

'That was the idea Colonel Andropov sold you.'

'I see that now.'

'You trusted Andropov?'

'I believed what he told me at the time, yes.'

'Were you justified in your belief?'

'No. That is why I behaved as I did.'

★

It is going well, he thinks to himself. They are listening to me. Andropov sits beside him, very still, occasionally drinking from his glass. He can hear the whirr of the film cameras at the back of the room, he sees the bowed heads of his audience as they write in their pads, some with earphones on are listening to the female translator's voice. ('Don't speak too fast,' she had asked him in faultless English when he had been introduced to her shortly before the press conference began.)

He feels his confidence growing. His own identity is submerged by the words he is using. He and his message have become one. He feels a surge of power. This is the world's press and they are listening to him. Through them the world will listen to what he has to say.

This is his chance, he thinks, this is his opportunity. To hell with Andropov and the promises he's made to him. He must go through with it whatever the consequences. He must take the opportunity that is offered to him because it will never occur again. He has to do it. His mind is made up.

Now.

★

'Let me take you forward in time again. You are now in Moscow. Are you living with Marchenko?'

'No. I was given my own apartment.'

'Did you spend much time with Marchenko and her son?'

'Not as much as I wanted to.'

'Did that surprise you?'

'Yes.'

'You were prevented from doing so?'

'Yes.'

'What did you do about that?'

'I complained to Andropov.'

'And what did Colonel Andropov say?'

'He asked me to fulfil certain official functions, as he put it, and then I would be free to spend as long as I wanted with Marchenko.'

'A bargain, in other words.'

'No, a proposal. A change of plan.'

'Did you accept his change of plan?'

'No, I refused to go along with it.'

'For what reason?'

'I hadn't come to Moscow on that basis. I had agreed to come to see Marchenko and her son. That was it. Nothing more. Certainly no conditions.'

'After your arrival Andropov imposed conditions?'

'Continuously.'

'When he first put to you the idea of going to Moscow, did you think that you might achieve something more than just getting to know your son?'

'My objectives were to see my son and to protect Ruth Marchenko if I could. I had no other motives.'

'What happened when you turned down Andropov's offer?'

'He insisted we meet to discuss my response.'

'Can you describe that meeting to us, please?'

'There's not much to describe. I said I wouldn't accept what Andropov was proposing for the reasons I have given you. He said news of my arrival had slipped out to the international press corps and the circumstances were now changed. He asked me if I would speak to the press. Reluctantly I agreed.'

'Why did you agree?'

'Andropov made me a series of promises which he subsequently dishonoured. I agreed to see the press on the understanding that then I would be free to see Marchenko and my son. In the event, I always had one more obligation to fulfil before I was able to do properly what I had come for.'

★

He pushes aside his text. He is seeing everything with an astonishing clarity: who he is, what he is, what he wants to say, what must be said, all fitting so perfectly that there is no blurring at the edges, no lack of focus. Everything is precise and correct and sharp. One complete, perfect circle of truth.

'I would like to add this one point,' he says. This is it. This is his moment of greatest power and influence. Andropov looks at him nervously.

'Scientific knowledge is used for political purposes when there is an imbalance in knowledge, when one side knows more than the other. That is the case now. The West has exploded the atomic bomb. The Soviet Union has yet to do so. The West is striving to maintain its advantage, the Soviet Union to reduce its disadvantage. How much safer the world would be if this race was not being run, if nuclear secrets did not exist. How much safer our lives would be if we shared everything between us, if we put this extraordinary knowledge at the disposal of humanity, not ideology.'

This is what they came for, he can see that in the greedy looks on the faces of his audience. This is the news they wanted, the real story of the British scientist in Moscow.

'I appeal to the scientists of the world to forget their national origins, to take their rightful place as citizens of the world and to serve mankind. I appeal to my colleagues in the West and my friends in the Soviet Union to pull down the towers of secrecy. Let us ignore the politicians, and together put all our energies into the task of using science for the benefit of all mankind. A world without secrets would be a far safer place.

'My prime purpose in asking you to meet me here today was to state publicly the offer I now make to the Soviet government. In order to reduce the growing tensions in the world, I am prepared to remain in Moscow and work with my Soviet colleagues on the peaceful uses of nuclear energy, providing they will send a senior scientist to take my place in a similar programme in the United Kingdom. That way, we will ensure that there is no longer any knowledge that can be exploited against us.'

He sits back. He has done it. He is pleased with himself. He has said what he wanted to say and the world's press has listened. Andropov can do what he likes now, it is too late.

★

'Let us come now to your press conference. Remind us, please, of what you said.'

'I repeated the views I have expressed on numerous occasions, that the control of nuclear weapons must pass from the hands of politicians into those of the international scientific community.'

'I have here a transcript made by the Reuter's man in Moscow who was present. He agrees that is how you began.'

'It was an appeal for sanity above the emotional draw of nation or ideology.'

'That's one way of putting it. Our reading is that you urged scientists everywhere to reject the whole concept of secrecy by opening their files and giving away to their enemies the information those files contained.'

'That is what I said because that is what I believe.'

'Why did you choose to make this statement in Moscow? Why not in London or Washington?'

'I have spoken to Ministers, to senior politicians in Government and in the Opposition, and I have got nowhere. I have made similar appeals in the British press for some months now and in all that time I have received no more than a dozen letters, the majority of which do not support my views. I have corresponded with my American counterparts but my views have not met with any positive response there.'

'You felt upset that you were being ignored, so you went to Moscow to get more attention.'

'I repeat what I have said before. I went to Moscow to see my son. While I was there, I was presented with an opportunity to give my message to the world and I took it. I have no regrets about what I said.'

'I suggest you said what your Moscow host Andropov wanted you to say.'

'If that were true, why had I been putting forward the same message for so long before I went to Moscow?'

'You have answered my question. You have been saying for some time what the Soviets have wanted you to say.'

There is uproar. He cannot make out the questions over the babble of voices. Everyone is shouting at once, some are waving their pads to attract his attention. One or two are standing up. The cameras whirr furiously.

Andropov leans towards him. 'That was misguided,' he says. 'Very foolish. Outside our agreement.' His tone is threatening but Stevens hardly hears it above the roar of his audience. He knows now that he has achieved what he set out to do.

'Let us look at some of your unscripted remarks, Professor. "The antidote to an arms build-up is to share information about nuclear development." "There should be no national or political barriers to the freedom of movement of research in nuclear energy." Did you really say that?'

'Yes. I continue to hold to every word.'

'You advocate the giving away of nuclear secrets to our enemies?'

'Perhaps they would no longer be our enemies if neither side had secrets to defend.'

'That is a dangerous philosophy, Professor.'

'How do you know? Have you ever tried it? The purpose of scientific enquiry is to find solutions to problems. The same is true of politics, except our politicians do not practise this method. They stick to their narrow ways, which is why they so often make a mess of things.'

Somehow order has been restored. The hubbub dies down. The first questioner raises his hand. Andropov nods at him.

'Professor Stevens, have you already followed your own advice since you have been in Moscow, and given British nuclear secrets to your opposite numbers here?'

'Did you follow your own advice while in Moscow? Did you share your knowledge of our nuclear secrets with the Soviets?'

'No.'

'Why not?'

'It was not appropriate to do so.'

'Is appropriate the right word?'

'You know exactly what I mean by it.'

'You gave them no secrets, yet you spent time in the company of members of the Institute of Nuclear Research in Moscow.'

'These people are academic colleagues, we work in the same field. We deal in similar problems. Some of us have known each other for years.'

'I would remind you, Professor, that these people are in the pay of a state whose ideology is committed to the elimination of capitalism from the world, which is another way of saying they want to conquer the free world, submit it to the barbarities of Marxist-Leninism and eradicate the unbelievers. If you ask me, at best they have an advocate in you, at worst a fellow-traveller.'

'They are scientists, not politicians. They have no interest in ideology. Their commitment is to scientific truth.'

'You are asking us to believe, Professor, that in your meetings with them, you betrayed no secrets to the Soviets.'

'I had one meeting with them. They thought I was an emissary from the West come to treat with their government on their behalf.

395

When they discovered I had no such role, they ignored me. They never asked me one single scientific question. They weren't interested in me as a scientist. It was a major disappointment.'

'We must cut this short,' Andropov says. 'It is getting out of hand.'

He gets to his feet and grips Stevens firmly by the arm. There are shouts of complaint at his action from the audience. Stevens remains unmoved. The sense of complete power has not left him. He wants to make this moment last.

'Sit down,' he says to Andropov under his breath. 'You asked them here to listen to me. Let them have their chance.'

Andropov sits down. There is some laughter at this from those in the front rows, who have caught at least some of the whispered conversation between the two men. They do not often see an officer from Military Intelligence bettered by an English academic.

'We have time for two more questions,' Andropov says grimly. There is a renewed appeal at this but Andropov is adamant.

'Professor Stevens, will you be going back to Britain in the near future?'

'I expect to do so, yes.'

'How do you think you will be received? As a hero, or a villain?'

★

'During your time in Moscow, Professor, you saw yourself on a one-man mission to save the world. What made you think you could succeed where others had failed?'

'I failed.'

'You set out in the expectation that you would succeed.'

'At the press conference I thought it might be possible, yes. Worth a try.'

'I suggest you had no such thought in your head. You went to Moscow for selfish, personal motives, to save your former mistress and to see the son you didn't know you had. All this concern about the safety of the world is posturing, ad hoc justification and very unconvincing. While you were there, you betrayed nuclear secrets to the Soviets and you allowed yourself to be used by Andropov and his cronies for the benefit of the Soviet Union. You became a pawn in their game. You even went so far as to say you were prepared to stay on in Moscow. They used you successfully to promote themselves as responsible and the West as irresponsible. I would

396

say that, as a result of your visit, you have advanced the Soviet cause in a number of important ways. Not least, you will have helped to bring forward the day when they explode their own nuclear device. No doubt you'll soon be getting your Order of Lenin through the post to add to your other awards.'

'I was wrong to go to Moscow, I realize that now. I was used by the Soviets, I see that too. But I betrayed nothing.'

'That's not the information we have.'

'Then the information you have is false.'

'Our intelligence is from a hitherto impeccable source, one we have no reason to doubt. He informs us that, as a result of your visit, it is now possible to foresee a Soviet nuclear device being exploded within a year at the most.'

'That is untrue. I did not give away any information.'

'Our source maintains you did.'

'There is no chance the Soviets will detonate anything for three or four years at least.'

'That is your opinion.'

'I am far from alone on that point.'

'So you are asking us to believe that our information is wrong. What is your explanation then?'

'How can I have an explanation? I have theories, nothing more.'

'What is your theory, then?'

'It is very simple. False statements are being attributed to me for reasons of propaganda. For as long as you believe them and disbelieve me, you are in the pay of the Soviets. You are the traitors, not me. My conscience is clear. I may have acted foolishly, I accept that. But I have not criminally. I am no traitor.'

★

'Last question,' Andropov says coldly. Some sense of his authority has reached the audience and for the last few minutes the press conference has been more orderly. He looks around the audience for a raised hand.

A blonde woman, in her late thirties, sitting in the front row looks up. She has not said a word so far. She puts up her hand.

'Yes.'

Andropov points at her. For a second or two she is unsure if she has been selected. She looks round to make sure. Holding her pad tightly in her hand, she looks up at Stevens.

'We have heard your proposal, Professor Stevens. What intrigues me is your motive in putting this idea to the great powers. Is it true, Professor, that you have a son in Russia?'

★

During the three days of questioning Stevens did not leave the house in Wimbledon. He was not under arrest but nor was he free. There were guards in the building and a watch was kept at night as much on his bedroom window as at his door. He ate all his meals alone. Corless and Maitland conducted the interrogation in relays, two or three hours at a time. They were joined for one or two sessions by Adrian Gardner, who went over ground that had been fully covered the day before. I supposed the point was to spot the discrepancies and try to trick Stevens into changing his story, but he didn't. I'm not even sure that he was aware of the technique we were using. The rest of us listened through concealed microphones. A transcript was made.

I felt sorry for Stevens. He was bemused and exhausted by the process he was engaged in, utterly lost dealing in a world of which he had no experience at all. It was clear to me an hour or two into the first day that the man was a fool, naive, arrogant, that his mood alternated between moments of humiliation and superiority. But during those three days he never cracked, nor even showed signs of cracking; he never deviated from his story, he never fell over himself, and that convinced me that what we were seeing was not a performance but the expression of truth from a complicated and difficult man.

Whatever else Stevens may have been, I was sure he was no traitor. We were going to have to let him go.

16

RUTH

She does not see the car racing up alongside them, nor the sudden nervous glance from the driver. The car drops back out of sight only to reappear a moment later. This time the movement catches her eye. She sees the driver come level with them, then spin the steering wheel and drive into the limousine. They rock violently from the impact. There is a tearing sound as metal engages metal and body-work is shorn away. Tyres scream on the tarmac as the car swerves to the right. Their driver desperately fights to regain control of his vehicle.

She is thrown off her seat and on to the floor, a movement that saves her from serious injury. Andropov is projected forward against the glass partition that separates the passengers from the driver, and she sees his forehead split open as his head hits the glass. Blood spurts from the wound. On her knees on the floor, her hands protecting her head, she feels the jarring impact as the Zil is rammed a second and a third time and a tyre bursts.

They are out of control now, slewed across the highway, unable to change direction, unable to stop. Their car mounts the kerb, narrowly misses a street light and crashes against the wall of an office building until it comes to a halt, steam hissing from the broken radiator, the bonnet buckled and dented, the headlights smashed and empty. The cracks in the windscreen fan out like a spider's web. Their driver lies unconscious against the wheel. The acrid stench of spilled petrol and burning rubber permeates the night air.

The other car, itself a wreck, pulls up a few yards ahead. The passenger door is forced open and the driver gets out. He limps towards the Zil. His face is concealed by a balaclava.

'Colonel Andropov.' It is a voice she knows so well. He has found his prey. She wonders how he did it, while she cowers on the floor, holding her hands against her face, hoping her presence will not be noticed.

'What the hell are you doing?' Andropov holds a blood-soaked handkerchief against his head. 'You could have killed us.'

'Get out of the car.' The barrel of a revolver reflects the light from the street lamp above them. 'Do as I tell you. Now.'

Andropov steps over her and gets out. Dazed and bleeding, he leans against the battered body of the Zil.

'And you.' He pulls her roughly to her feet. She stares into the horrified face of Pavel Lykowski.

'Ruth.' The expression on his face registers the shock of betrayal. 'You, here, with him?' He recoils from her as if she were contaminated. 'You were in it together? No. It's not possible. No, no.'

'Pavel.' I can explain everything, she wants to say, but he is not in a mood to listen.

'Keep away,' he cried. 'Don't come near me.'

He is beyond her reach now. She knows she cannot alter what will happen. Will she die now amid the broken glass and twisted metal of a state Zil? Is this her fate? She is surprised at the sense of reconciliation she experiences. Is this what remains for her, an ignominious death at the hands of Lykowski? Why doesn't something inside her protest? Why can't she believe in the possibility of her own death in a few seconds' time?

'What are you *doing* with this man? He's a murderer. He ordered the deaths of seventy people.'

She wants to defend her association with Andropov, to deny Pavel's accusations, to tell him that but for her association with Andropov, he would probably be dead by now. But she knows he won't listen to her. The time for explaining is long past in his young life. He is trapped in the grip of obsession, deafened by the pounding in his ears. He can only deal with what he sees, and he has found her in the same car as his prey. She is condemned by association as a traitor to the cause, and she knows there is nothing she can do about it.

Pavel is shouting at her, tears streaming down his cheeks.

'I knew there was someone, Ruth. There had to be someone. Otherwise we would never have survived. I never believed for one moment it would be you. How could you betray us like that? How could you bring yourself to do that?'

The first shot misses her. She hears it ricochet off a wall somewhere behind her and spin off harmlessly into the darkness. She hears the second shot too, but less distinctly, because in the split-second interval between the two shots Andropov has thrown himself across her. He takes the full force of the bullet in his chest. She feels the jarring impact as he is thrown back into her arms, a movement so strong she has difficulty keeping on her feet. For an instant she holds him in her arms, a parody of affection, then Andropov's body goes weak as the life flows out of him. She hears him gurgle something as he slides out of her grasp.

There is no third shot. Lykowski is running away, his feet echoing in the empty street, as she kneels beside Andropov and closes his eyes. She pulls his jacket straight, puts a hand through his hair, honouring in death the vanity she knew was part of his life.

In that instant she asks herself no questions. Her mind is empty, blank with horror and shock. Andropov has saved her life. Is she aware of that? Was his action instinctive? An act of self-sacrifice? Or an act of redemption by a executioner who knows he must die for the people he has killed? As the blood seeps across his uniform, she knows those questions will never be answered.

Behind her the Zil explodes, a burst of red flame and then a column of black smoke floating upwards like a funeral pyre. Then she screams, her cries echoing against the soot-grained walls of the buildings and vanishing into the desolate silence of the night.

17

DANNY

Charlie Faulkner was asleep when I arrived at his bedside, a pale diminished figure, the illness slowly stealing from him what little life remained. Beryl, on duty to the last, sat with her hands tightly clasped, staring at him as if the slightest movement was a signal of the end. As I came into the room she looked up, exhausted from her long vigil, and managed a brief smile.

'He sleeps most of the time,' she explained. 'When he wakes he talks about getting back to work, but the doctors say he hasn't got long now. I want it to be over, for his sake. He'd hate to see himself in this condition. Poor man. Life can be so cruel sometimes, can't it?'

Charlie stirred in his sleep, muttered something incomprehensible and sighed deeply. His eyelids flickered and Beryl got to her feet. She put a wet sponge to his lips and adjusted his pillow.

'They give him morphine, so he's not in any pain. That's something to be thankful for, isn't it?'

It had all happened so unexpectedly, she told me, about a week after I had left for Finland. She'd taken dictation after lunch and Charlie had seemed tired but there was nothing unusual in that. Then about four, just when she was in the kitchen making his afternoon tea, she heard a noise in his room. She rushed in to find him out of his wheelchair and lying on the floor. She called an ambulance and he was rushed to hospital in a coma. He'd regained consciousness a few hours later and had shown brief signs of recovery. Then he'd suffered a relapse and the final process had set in.

Was Eccleston Street closed because Charlie was taken ill? I asked.

'That was Mr Watson-Jones's decision,' she said, nervously checking that the sleeping figure on the bed wasn't listening in on our conversation. 'Charlie knows nothing about it. He mustn't know. It would break his heart.'

Three weeks before, when I left so hurriedly for Helsinki, the organization had been flourishing. Now it was gone and Charlie was dying. I was taken aback by the speed of the close-down. There had to be more to it than Beryl's selective account.

'What happened?' I asked, guessing she had edited her version of Charlie's collapse. There was something to add, but I couldn't persuade her to be as forthcoming as I wanted.

'Charlie found out what Mr Watson-Jones had done and confronted him. There was a terrible row and Mr Watson-Jones stormed out. Charlie was very upset. I tried to get him to go home at lunchtime, but he said he didn't want to eat, he wanted to work. So I came in with my pad and we did a lot of letters. At four o'clock, he said: "I could do with a cuppa, Beryl."' She brushed away a tear. 'That was the last time he called me Beryl.'

I waited for her to recover her composure. Then I asked what Charlie had found out.

'Mr Watson-Jones had been working behind his back. I knew Charlie suspected that, but there's a big difference between suspicion and proof, isn't there?'

I waited for her to tell me what Simon had done, or what proof Charlie had found.

'He meddled where he shouldn't have done, he upset a lot of powerful people. If Charlie had known about it, he would have stopped it at once. That's why Mr Watson-Jones did it behind his back. He knew, Charlie would disapprove but he still went ahead.'

It was as much as Beryl would tell me without Charlie's sanction, and she was never going to get that now. She talked on about Charlie for half an hour or so, recreating in her mind the man she remembered that would outlast the image of the shrunken figure in the bed. I felt sorry for her and the long, painful farewell she was bidding to the man who had occupied so much of her life. I promised I'd return the following day. But early the next morning Beryl rang me to say that Charlie had died soon after six, peacefully and in his sleep.

'He'd been very restless around midnight,' she said, 'and I joined his sons at his bedside. Then he turned over, mumbled something and seemed to settle into a peaceful sleep. He never moved again. Quite suddenly the life in him just stopped, no fuss, just like that, and Charlie was gone. I was glad it was light when he died, I don't think he would have been happy dying in the dark.'

I was surprised at how upset I was. We'd met only seven months before, yet in that short time he had become an important part of my life. How I wished I'd known him longer. How much more I might have learned.

★

The funeral was private, for Charlie's family and close friends. Beryl insisted I accompany her.

'He always had a soft spot for you,' she said on the telephone. 'He'd be pleased if he knew you'd seen him off.'

I went up to Manchester by train and stayed the night with Beryl's mother. Beryl came by after supper and we sat in the small garden as the sun went down and she talked about Charlie.

'After the row the strength seemed to go out of him,' she said. 'It was a sad moment, seeing him buckling under the weight of it all. Nothing like that had ever happened before. I knew it was all over then.'

'Did he make it up with Simon before he died?'

Beryl smiled. 'You don't make up with Mr Watson-Jones. You win or you lose. This time, we lost.'

'You never liked Watson-Jones, did you?'

'He exploited Charlie's good nature and I could never forgive him for that. Charlie was an innocent, a man who wore his heart on his sleeve. There was no subtlety to him, he had no guile, but he was fearless too, he always said what he thought. He never deceived anyone in his life, he never sold anyone short, he was the same to everyone he met, it didn't matter who you were. When Watson-Jones came along, I begged him to say no, he'd done enough. It was time to call it a day. But he wouldn't. He saw some purpose to it that I didn't understand and he couldn't resist the temptation.

'"This is the last one, Beryl, I promise," he said. "Then we'll shut up shop."'

'He was right about that. It was the last one. There'll be no more causes now.'

On a beautifully warm and clear July afternoon I helped to carry Charlie's mortal remains to their last resting place in a churchyard in the village where he was born. As we lowered him into his grave

404

in the shadow of an ancient stone wall, I heard doves cooing in the trees above. Then the birds, disturbed by our presence, clattered their way into the sky. Charlie had truly gone.

★

Unfinished business can be very unsettling. I needed to get to the bottom of what had happened in Eccleston Street before I could concentrate on rebuilding my life. With Charlie gone, Beryl silent and Watson-Jones unreachable (he was in America), my only available sources were Sylvia, Meredith Watson-Jones and Monty. Each knew something. I hoped that by piecing together their stories I would reach some understanding of the truth.

I discovered that Simon had got hold of damaging evidence against my father. Probably his American contacts had told him that a secret intelligence source in Moscow had named my father as a traitor. It was an opportunity too good for Watson-Jones to pass up, but one he knew Charlie would never sanction (Charlie the great upholder of the status quo). Simon had written to the Minister, asking what actions had been taken by the British authorities to investigate the accusations against my father, secure in the knowledge that nothing had been done. No explanation was forthcoming, just the usual platitudes ministerial departments are trained to deliver.

Simon's reaction had been one of fury. He took this reply as a sign that the socialists were soft on the Soviets, in his book a major crime. If he had harboured any doubts about the wisdom of what he was doing, the ministerial response would have banished them. I could see him, full of righteous anger, blind and deaf to any warnings of caution, threatening the Minister that he would reveal what he knew if he did not receive a satisfactory answer this time.

Gaydon and his advisers, Glover and Corless (their names reminded me of a partnership of shady solicitors), were thrown into panic. Not only was there accumulated evidence of a growing opposition to the manufacture of the Soviet nuclear bomb by the scientists at the Moscow Institute of Nuclear Research, but there were also signs (mostly unconfirmed) that this position was supported by an anti-nuclear group within the military led by a senior Russian general. At worst, this might be the start of a serious opposition to Stalin, at best the basis of a coup.

Politically, this unexpected development in the Soviet Union was seen as a gift from heaven, an escape route for a government at a loss to know how to build a nuclear bomb without the resources. A secret policy was agreed. Because the stakes were so high, the movement inside the Soviet Union had to be given time to grow. Nothing was to be allowed to upset this possibility until we knew whether or not the opposition forces were successful. All decisions on nuclear matters were to be shelved while the West, holding its collective breath, watched anxiously for signs of change inside the Soviet Union.

Watson-Jones knew nothing of this. It didn't take much to imagine the furore that his intervention caused when everyone else was treading on eggshells. Corless was instructed by Glover to get Watson-Jones off the case as fast as possible. There was too much at stake to leave him alone. Corless had to agree. He had no choice. When he was out of the room, Glover telephoned Iredale.

In the end, it wasn't Corless or Iredale who stopped Watson-Jones, it was Charlie. His dogged detection got him copies of Simon's letters to the Ministry. Faced with this damning evidence, Corless told him as much as he could about the delicacy of the political situation, and Charlie saw what he was meant to see. Surely it was better for Charlie to stop him than Iredale?

Charlie confronted Watson-Jones after his interview with Corless. I never discovered what Charlie said to make Simon change his mind, nor what kind of a hold he had over him. (Beryl knew but I was sure, however hard I tried, she wouldn't tell me, and she never did.) I imagined Charlie had found some weakness in the Watson-Jones armour, he had used his knowledge and he had won. The threat must have been formidable because within hours Simon had withdrawn his letter from the Minister and agreed to keep his mouth shut. But the effort killed Charlie.

Within days of my father's return from Moscow, I heard that the Soviet anti-nuclear faction had collapsed and any whispers of a possible coup against Stalin dried up, never to be heard of again. Ironically, in the months that followed the international anti-nuclear outcry in the West, created by my father's appearance in Moscow, was to make my father into a kind of folk hero, the 'scientist who repented', as one of the popular papers put it.

*

'There are some mysteries,' Monty said philosophically, filling my glass with claret, 'which never get resolved.'

We were dining at his suggestion 'downstairs', in the restaurant in his block of flats. It was the first time I had been back there since my meeting with Krasov, months before.

'What kind of mysteries?' I asked.

'Who wins, who loses. Where the truth lies. In our business you resign yourself to the probability that you will often know far less than you want to.'

'It's pretty clear in this case,' I replied. 'We lost and the Soviets won.'

'We may have lost the battle,' Monty said, 'but the war's not over yet. In fact, it's only just begun. We're in for a long haul.'

It was all too oblique for me and I said so. Surely, I argued, the Soviets had successfully slowed down our nuclear weapons programme and bought themselves much needed time, created a platform of doubt about the need for nuclear power that wouldn't go away and ruined one man's reputation so that he would never contribute to the our bomb. If that wasn't a victory, what was?

'The real winner in this affair is Watson-Jones.'

'How do you work that out?' I asked incredulously.

'His vision has won the day. The Soviets have played into his hands, declared themselves as unscrupulous villains, never to be trusted on anything. Watson-Jones and that awful newsletter you worked on, what was it called? *Front Line*. They're vindicated. That's got the Soviet threat to the top of the agenda now. That may be where Watson-Jones wanted them to be but it's bad news for the rest of us.'

I asked him why. Our lives are now pledged to a cold war, he said. For a time, perhaps, we had had a chance to push Watson-Jones to one side, take the signs of a softening of line in the Soviet Union (and perhaps it was more than that, who will ever know?) to push the creation of nuclear weapons down the agenda. Whatever the immediate gains to the Soviets, the events of the past few months had proved Watson-Jones right. We were on our guard now. What kind of country would we build now, if the post-war world was to be dedicated to an undeclared war with the Soviet Union?

'The end of the war gave us a chance to remake our society,' he said. 'That's why we worked so hard on the possibility that maybe there was a revolt in the Soviet Union. That's why we tried to discredit Watson-Jones. We wanted to keep that chance alive. Now we have had to jettison that idea. It'll be a struggle from now

407

on, years of trying to get up steam and never quite succeeding. If only . . .'

'If only what?' I asked.

If only, was all he would say, keeping the mystery intact.

★

News report from *The Times* dated 3 August 1947
The Soviet news agency Tass reported, today that an Ilyushin military aircraft crashed soon after take-off in Tashkent. There were no survivors. Among the casualties were General A. Kosintzev and members of his staff.

★

Watson-Jones wasn't at Charlie's funeral ('In the circumstances, Charlie wouldn't have wanted him there, dear,' Beryl told me). But four weeks later he gave the address at Charlie's memorial service in a crowded St Clement Dane's. His voice echoed around the church as he recreated for us his image of the man he had done so much to destroy.

'Charlie Faulkner was one of those rare creatures who grace our lives from time to time, a man without pride, powerful in his goodness. From his early beginnings in Manchester to the triumph of the war years in Whitehall, his life was about service to others. His reward was to see those he had helped succeed. Perhaps the greatest tribute we can pay to Charlie's life is to ask how many of us would be here today, sitting in this beautiful chapel, were it not for Charlie's influence, Charlie's benevolence and above all, Charlie's friendship. I count myself lucky to be among that select band.'

I felt an uncontrollable anger sweep through me. Here was public hypocrisy on a scale I hadn't met before, brazen posturing that lifted Watson-Jones out of the common ruck into a *select band* that Charlie had chosen. For a while I wasn't sure I'd be able to sit through what he had to say. I calmed myself by thinking of what Charlie would have done. He'd have looked puzzled, agitated, he'd have fidgeted in his wheelchair, but he'd have said nothing and when it was over, he'd have gone on as if nothing had been said, the only sign of his discomfort a demand for Beryl to bring him a large gin and tonic.

My attention wandered as I tried to close my mind to what he was saying. I looked at the rows of men in dark suits, as they listened to Watson-Jones. Pale faces, pale men. Did they too share my anger?

Or would they shake his hand after the service, congratulate him on his address and walk away echoing sentiments that Charlie had chosen well, Simon was a man to watch?

There, in the pew opposite, grinning at me, was a face I knew, paler than before ('where'd do you think I've been all these months, Danny?'), thinner too ('what do you expect, on a diet of cabbage soup? You don't get hamburgers where I've been') but still recognizably the same. I smiled a genuine and delighted response.

'The old lion is gone. Hubris, bombast, pomposity, Charlie's lifelong enemies, may breathe a little easier today. But not for long. We will keep faith with the old warrior. We will subdue these ancient opponents just as he subdued them. We will match his vigilance and carry on the fight just as he did all the days of his life. This post-war world, with its problems and confusions, needs men of clear insight and goodness of heart like Charlie. We must do our best to live up to the ideals he represented. God bless you, Charlie, for the good you did. May your soul rest in the peace you worked so hard for and which you have so richly deserved.'

As I emerged from St Clement Dane's and walked out into the strong morning sunlight, I heard my name called and the next moment my hand was being vigorously shaken.

'Well, if it isn't my old skiing partner.'

'I didn't expect to see you here, Glenn,' I said. 'Aren't you supposed to be languishing in a Soviet prison?'

Hammerson was in US military uniform, a shadow of the man I'd last seen in January, but alive and seemingly no worse for his experience.

'The Reds got tired of me,' he said, 'so they let me go.'

'It's good to see you again.'

'It's good to be back,' he said, lighting a cigarette. 'I was sorry about old Charlie. I never knew him that well, but he had a fine reputation. I came to the service because I thought you might be here.'

'When did you get out?'

'Some weeks ago. Didn't you hear what happened?'

'No. Tell me.'

'The Soviets agreed a swap. Me for Krasov. Our old friend decided he didn't like America after all and asked to go back. Just as well: by then our people were sure he wasn't kosher. So somebody worked out an exchange. Neat, huh?'

'Very neat.' Krasov was back in the Soviet Union, one more

operation to confuse the West over and done with. What now? I wondered. Where would he surface next?

'I went through a debriefing,' Hammerson was saying. 'They thought I might have changed sides but I managed to convince them the old prejudices were alive and well. I hate the Reds even more now I've lived with them awhile.'

'Let's go and find a drink somewhere,' I said. I was pleased to see him, I wanted to hear about his months in captivity, what it was like to have the door locked shut and your freedom removed.

'You get used to prison,' he replied, reading my thoughts. 'If you don't adapt, you go mad. The trick is to narrow your world, accept the boundaries imposed upon you, forget outside, the freedom you've lost. Concentrate on what you can see and hear and do, the freedom you can control. Redefine your life. It's a world in itself, prison, with its own language, its own ethics, its own systems of communication, its own perverse morality, its own justice. The world turned inside out.'

'What was your worst fear when you were there?'

'That I might be forgotten. Left to rot on my own, far from home. I never knew if our people had any bargaining counters up their sleeve.'

'Then Krasov came to your aid?'

'I guess I've got a lot to thank him for. Just a pity it all took so long. I wonder if he knew he was saving my life.'

I asked whether the fact that he was American caused difficulties with his fellow prisoners.

'When I got there I imagined the other prisoners wouldn't accept me. I was wrong. We were all prisoners of a regime we had fallen foul of, we were all facing the same enemy. Nationality has little meaning in prison. We were all on the same side. They got to know I was American very quickly, don't ask me how. One or two of the other prisoners spoke passable English. They would whisper to me in the exercise yard, or when we washed. What was my name? My cell number? They told me to wait, to listen out, they would have news for me. All this under the eye of the guards who never knew these communications were taking place.'

He lifted his arm above his head. 'Look, most of the movement's back. Not bad, eh?'

He'd spent some months in a prison hospital while they repaired his badly broken shoulder, broken ribs and torn cartilage.

'Not a good time, that,' he said. 'The doctors are OK, the conditions are terrible.'

It was there, in the prison hospital, that he got his first message.

'The word had got out that I was American. I was told by one of the guys there, a Ukrainian who'd lost a leg, to listen out for a message. It was passed to me later that day. The writer was a scientist, he said, a theoretical physicist who had held a high position in one of the institutes, God knows which. He was being held in the psychiatric ward attached to the hospital. When you are freed, he said, tell your people that the Soviets know who Peter is. That was all. The Soviets know who Peter the Great is. Now what kind of a message is that?'

★

We'd agreed to meet in the restaurant at the Great Eastern Hotel in Liverpool Street station. My father had telephoned to say he was on his way back to Cambridge and could we meet before he left. He was already there when I arrived, sitting at a corner table, reading the paper.

'I'm sorry if I've kept you waiting.'

'I was early. Do you want a cup of tea?'

A cup was already waiting for me, and the teapot was large enough for two. My father poured.

'Now you're here,' he said, 'I don't know what to say to you.'

'Tell me how you are,' I asked. 'That's as good a place to start as any.'

'Tired, disoriented, shaken. But alive. I suppose I should be thankful. Does that leave me in credit or not?'

'That depends,' I said. 'Is the official business over?'

I had decided that was the best way to refer to the days of questioning I knew my father had undergone, and he responded to the euphemism.

'Thank God, yes. I'm free of all that.'

I could guess what he would have been subjected to since his return from Moscow, though neither then nor later would he ever say anything on that subject.

'Nothing further can happen?'

'They're not going to put me on trial or imprison me, if that's what you mean. I'm sure they'd like to, but they can't. They haven't got any evidence because there isn't any.'

The old arrogance wasn't completely dead. Looking at him across the breakfast table, I saw a man who was exhausted and distressed by his recent experiences, but the hard edges of a few certainties still remained.

'What happens now?' I asked.

'Life is meant to return to normal but I know nothing will be the same again. The suspicion that I gave secrets to the Soviets won't go away. It will hang over me for years, a cloud of doubt that I must have used the opportunity to tell them what I knew. My life will be different, but how different we will have to see.'

'Nothing ever changes that much,' I said more in hope than expectation.

'I think this time the changes will be very profound,' my father said. 'Did you get my letter?'

'Yes.'

'It was by way of an apology.'

'I don't want an apology,' I said. 'There's no need.'

'There are many things to apologize for. I see now how wrong I've been.'

'Perhaps I was wrong too.'

'Do you condemn me too?' he asked. 'For what I did?'

'No,' I said. 'I admired your stand. It took courage to do what you did in Moscow, only a fool would deny that. I still think you went about it the wrong way, but we're never going to agree on that and it doesn't matter anyway.'

'I'm not guilty of any crime,' he said. 'But I'm being made to pay heavily for what a man called Rupert Corless describes as my indiscretion, my foolishness, my lack of judgement. The government won't have anything to do with me now. They've sacked me from my committees. I'm no longer advising Lord Portal. I've lost my newspaper column. I am contaminated by my weeks in Moscow. So any influence I may have had on our future nuclear policy has been completely removed. I shall miss that.'

'You'll continue to teach, won't you?'

'Dons are given tenure for life. Ironic, isn't it? The college would love to see the back of me, but there's nothing they can do to get rid of me. Yes, I shall continue to teach. There's not much else I'm fit for.'

'Generations of young scientists will come to your lectures. If you teach them, you'll influence them. Isn't that the greater power? The rest is temporary. Committees here, advisory groups there. It's the minds of the young you want to be after. As long as they don't take those away from you.'

'How much wiser you are than me,' he said. 'That's what Ruth told me. He knows the world, she said. Listen to him. Listen to him for your own good.'

'How is Ruth?'

'She survives, I think. I'm not sure what else I can say.'

And her son? I wanted to ask. My brother. What about him?

There was a garbled announcement over the tannoy system. I caught something about the train for Cambridge and King's Lynn. The moment for asking questions was snatched away from me. Or did I simply let it slide out of reach? My father stood up and looked at his watch.

'Thanks for coming,' he said. 'I'm sure you've got better things to do with your time. What are you up to now?'

I told him that the experiment in Eccleston Street had come to a sudden end. He wasn't surprised.

'I could never see what you were doing there anyway. Awful propaganda stuff. You're well out of it. What are you going to do now?'

'I look for a job,' I said.

'Anything lined up?'

'Nothing so far.'

'What about that girl in Helsinki?'

'Tanya?'

'What's happening to her?'

'She's here with me.'

'She's a doctor, isn't she?'

'Yes.'

'Plenty of jobs for doctors here, especially in the light of all these changes the government's brought in.'

There were more strangled words from the tannoy.

'I'd better make a move.' He stood up. 'You'll come and see us, won't you? Celia and the children would like that. So would I. Bring Tanya. Who knows? With her help I might even persuade you to finish your degree.'

He smiled at that.

'I'll carry your case,' I said. 'I'll see you into your seat.'

It wasn't an intimate exchange. Yet something in our relationship

413

had altered, some small but important balance had shifted. As I followed my father out of the restaurant, I knew that this was not the last conversation we would have, but the first of many. There were other things to talk about. It might take some time to get there, but for the first time in my life I was reasonably sure we would.

Together we walked down the platform joining the crowds for the Cambridge train.